BEST NEW AMERICAN VOICES 2010

GUEST EDITORS OF
Best New American Voices

Tobias Wolff

Charles Baxter

Joyce Carol Oates

John Casey

Francine Prose

Jane Smiley

Sue Miller

Richard Bausch

Mary Gaitskill

Dani Shapiro

BEST NEW AMERICAN VOICES 2010

GUEST EDITOR

Dani Shapiro

SERIES EDITORS

John Kulka and Natalie Danford

A MARINER ORIGINAL • MARINER BOOKS

HOUGHTON MIFFLIN HARCOURT

BOSTON • NEW YORK

2009

"Lizard Man" appeared in different form in *Playboy* and *New Stories from the South 2008*.
"Up High in the Air" appeared in different form in *Boston Review*.
"The Changing Station" appeared in different form in *Colorado Review*.
"The Critic" appeared in different form in *Emprise Review*.
"Save the I-Hotel" appeared in different form in *MANOA*.
"Plato" appeared in different form in *Colorado Review*.
"The Burning of Lawrence" appeared in different form in *Zoetrope*.
"Intermodal" appeared in different form in *Tin House*.

For information about permission to reproduce selections from this book,
write to Permissions, Houghton Mifflin Harcourt Publishing Company,
215 Park Avenue South, New York, New York 10003.

www.hmhbooks.com

ISSN 1536-7908
ISBN 978-0-15-603425-8

Printed in the United States of America
DOC 10 9 8 7 6 5 4 3 2 1

CONTENTS

PREFACE

With the publication of *Best New American Voices 2010,* the Best New American Voices series is now a decade old. In that time, the way we buy and read books has changed and so, too, have our reading habits (more and more of our reading is decidedly *not* book reading). Interest in the short story, anyway, has not lessened. Perhaps it's even possible, as some observers have supposed, that the short story has been the happy beneficiary of changes in our reading habits brought about by the increasing demands on our time. At any rate, the Best New American Voices series continues to dedicate itself to discovering short fiction by new and emerging writers.

The series has become recognized as a rite of passage for American fiction writers and an important stepping stone in their careers. Joshua Ferris (*Then We Came to the End*), Rebecca Barry (*Later, at the Bar*), William Gay (*Provinces of Night* and *I Hate to See That Evening Sun Go Down*), Julie Orringer (*How to Breathe Underwater*), Ana Menéndez (*In Cuba I Was a German Shepherd*), Frances Hwang (*Transparency*), Adam Johnson (*Emporium*), David Benioff (*The 25th Hour*), Eric Puchner (*Music Through the Floor*), Kaui Hart Hemmings (*House of Thieves*), John Murray (*A Few Short Notes on Tropical Butterflies*), Maile Meloy (*Half in Love* and *Liars and Saints*), Jennifer Vanderbes (*Easter Island*), the late Amanda Davis (*Circling the Drain* and *Wonder When You'll Miss Me*), and Rattawut Lapcharoensap (*Sightseeing*) are just some of the acclaimed authors whose early work has appeared in Best New American Voices since its launch in 2000. And this is far from a complete list.

How does the Best New American Voices competition work? Each year we invite workshop directors and instructors to nominate stories for consideration. We ask them to send on what, in their judgment, were the best stories workshopped during the past year. Participants include MA and MFA programs (such as Brown and Iowa), fellowship programs (such as Stegner and the Wisconsin Institute for Creative Writing), and summer writing conferences (such as the Wesleyan Writers Conference, Sewanee, and Bread Loaf). A directory at the back of the anthology lists all of the U.S. and Canadian institutions that participated in this year's competition. After we receive all of the nominations, we read them at least once, grade them, and debate their merits. From a much larger group we pass on a few dozen finalists to our guest editor, who then makes the selections for the book.

Guest editor Dani Shapiro has chosen sixteen stories for inclusion in *Best New American Voices 2010*. If the authors of these stories are not as familiar as those mentioned earlier, strong evidence suggests that will soon change. Of course, the raison d'être of the anthology is that they *are* unknown. Here, then, is an opportunity for the reader to discover a promising group of writers, perhaps at the same time they are first encountered by agents, editors, and publishers. Some of the contributors have previously published fiction in magazines and/or literary journals. Others make their publishing debuts here. They are, generally speaking, young or young*ish,* though age is not a criterion for eligibility. They seem to have little in common other than their relative youth and the fact that they were recently enrolled in a writing workshop. The stories speak for themselves.

We thank Dani Shapiro for her editorial suggestions, for her perspicacity and professionalism, and for her general support of the Best New American Voices series. We extend thanks, too, to all of the teachers, administrators, and workshop directors who nominated stories for this volume. Without their continuing support, this anthology would not be possible. We must thank and congratulate all of the contributors, whose book this really is. We also thank Andrea Schulz at Houghton Mifflin Harcourt for her ongoing support; our editor, Adrienne Brodeur; Lisa Lucas in the Harcourt contracts department; Sara Branch for her careful copyediting; and our families and friends for their love and support.

—*John Kulka and Natalie Danford*

INTRODUCTION

Dani Shapiro

As I write this — on the final fumes of a rough year — the doomsayers are once again out there beating their drums, announcing the End of Literature. Granted, the news is grim: Esteemed literary editors have lost their jobs; publishers have merged, then downsized; departments have been shuttered. Each week, it seems, another independent bookseller closes its doors; the chains report their worst sales figures ever. We — the American public — are not reading, or so it would seem. Or if we are reading, we're doing it on electronic devices, one little manageable driblet at a time. Our gray matter has shriveled, our attention span neurologically altered through decades — generations now — of La-Z-Boy television viewers flicking through the channels, plastic bowls of nachos resting on their soft bellies.

Morale on all sides of the publishing industry does seem to have hit a low point. But what about writers — particularly young writers? Are they closing their computers, retiring their pens, listening to their parents, and going into a more practical profession? Say, law? Or accounting? A friend of mine — an out-of-work newspaper journalist — called me recently with the usual lament and then asked, *Why do you bother to teach creative writing? I mean, what use can it possibly have?* I told her that enrollment in graduate writing programs is at an all-time high; that applications to the writing conference I started in Italy just a few years ago have tripled since we began. Young people want to write and are willing to do whatever it takes to expose themselves to the art and craft of fiction. *Well, God bless them,* she said, somewhat condescendingly. *I mean, they might as well be learning how to blow glass.*

There are many things that becoming a writer is not: It is not practical, nor is it easy; it is not cathartic (my favorite!); it doesn't make for a comfortable or comforting life. It doesn't promise fame or fortune; it won't make you friends. You will suffer indignities. People will be suspicious: *You can't use that,* they'll say after telling a particularly juicy story, as if you might just steal that story right out from under them. As if writers are carnivores, starved and sniffing around for the best meat. Or better yet, they'll be condescending; the mother of a childhood friend once turned to me at a holiday dinner and said: *Dani, I'm going to tell you the story for your next book. If you write this story, it'll be a bestseller.* As if my job, as a writer, were simply to transcribe.

Despite all of this, I don't think the End of Literature is nigh. I don't think there will ever be an end to literature, not at the hand of electronic devices, nor the Internet, nor postmodernism, poststructuralism, deconstructionism, neoironic minimalism (I made that one up), all of which have brought out the doomsayers in their current full force. When I was in graduate school, I heard Allan Gurganus remark that writers are people to whom stories happen. At the time, I wondered if by that he meant that writers are special people, singled out by fate. As the years have gone by, I've mulled this over, and I don't think that's what he meant at all. I think he meant that stories happen to everyone, that all of our lives are made up of stories. But to be a writer is to be a particular kind of creature who has an all-consuming need to take what happened and twist and turn it every which way like a Rubik's Cube, until it no longer bears more than a passing resemblance to real-life events, but rather has become an organized and balanced piece of music. Something that makes order out of randomness. Something that makes chaos sing.

More than ever — in this world of ours in which we communicate on palm-sized screens and in sentence fragments, often not even using real words — these particular creatures, these writers, have the need to make chaos sing. But they don't do so in a vacuum. Sure, the reader is exhausted, overstimulated, and suffering from ennui. But that human longing for stories is basic to us all. *Show me,* the reader seems to be saying these days. *Show me why I should care.*

You hold in your hands a small, powerful beacon of hope: a passionate and eclectic, highly refined response to the question of why you — why anyone — should care. John Gregory Dunne once called writer's block "a failure of nerve." The sixteen writers collected together here have exhibited quite the opposite of a failure of nerve. Here you will find daring acts of both head and heart — the intellectual high wire of craft combined with that elusive thing: the capacity to make the reader *feel something.* In choosing these stories, I was looking to be moved. Cynicism is easy. Ironic detachment feels like a cop-out. My personal bias, both as a writer and a reader, pulls me toward stories that illuminate something about how we live. I want to be reminded — even instructed — about what it means to be alive on this earth, to grapple with the complexities of family, love, fear, impending loss, grief — the "whole catastrophe," as Zorba the Greek put it.

Sentimentality has gotten a bad literary rap in recent years. Find any derivative of the word in a review and likely it isn't meant as a compliment — whereas *unsentimental* has become praise of the highest order. For a while, I think young writers have been afraid to attempt anything emotionally tender, for risk of being slapped down. But, as my graduate school mentor, the late Jerome Badanes, used to say, good writers know how to ride that line of emotional intensity for all it's worth without falling over the edge into a bog of purple prose. There's nothing purple here. Not even a light shade of lavender. But trust me: You will find yourself choking back a lump in your throat more than once. And that's no bad thing at all.

Here we have a group of writers who have taken risks. In the ambitious "The Burning of Lawrence," a piece of history— Quantrill's raid on Lawrence, Kansas — is illuminated through the notes of a Kansas University graduate student, whose obsession with history colors her romantic relationships. "Horusville" retells the story of Horus, the Ancient Egyptian god, as a strange and beautiful parable about art and surveillance. A middle-aged cemetery director has his life turned upside down by a young woman in the process of deciding whether to become a nun in "Plato." A different sort of middle-aged man contemplates his own decline in "Portrait of a Backup." "The Critic" is a young woman's laserlike take on an older, well-known art critic — a withering look at small-town academic life. The devastating "Save the I-Hotel" hauntingly captures the lifelong friendship of two aging Filipino immigrants in San Francisco.

Many of these stories are about family — the lack of it, the loss of it, the longing for it. Taken together as a mosaic, they warn us of the perils of love. In the gorgeous and unlikely love story "The Changing Station," two grown-ups, already beaten up by life, take a chance on each other. "Up High in the Air" artfully exposes the layers of silence in an unhappy marriage. Two young girls are made anxious by the discovery of an older half sibling in "Half Sister." "Bethlehem Is Full" centers on a young man who has been deeply affected by his girlfriend's abortion. A terminally ill mother takes her estranged daughter on a diving trip in "Cape Town." Another life reaches its end in "Flight," as a sad and lonely widower contemplates and then commits suicide.

A surprising number of father-son stories found their way into this volume, each of them unique and powerful. "Some Things I've

Been Meaning to Ask You" is in the form of a son's letter to his dead father. "Intermodal" is about a teenager's confused and confusing loyalty to his father, who lives in a portable freight unit after separating from the boy's mother. In "Hero" a young man longs to escape from his father and the Indian reservation where they live, but can't transcend his own emotional paralysis. And "Lizard Man," a richly atmospheric story set in the swampland of Florida, explores the legacy of one father's mistakes, and the improbable beauty of his attempts to make things right.

Bravo to David James Poissant, Andrew Malan Milward, Claire O'Connor, Timothy Scott, Christian Moody, Andrew Brininstool, Laura van den Berg, David Lombardi, Boomer Pinches, Greg Changnon, Ted Thompson, Leslie Barnard, Baird Harper, Edward Porter, Lysley Tenorio, and Emily Freeman. They're some of the courageous ones, coming out swinging hard against the End of Literature, and it appears to me that they're winning.

BEST NEW AMERICAN VOICES 2010

BOOMER PINCHES

University of Massachusetts, Amherst

BETHLEHEM IS FULL

The abortion went well and there was no need to postpone their trip to Australia. A few hours after leaving the clinic she had fainted while waiting on line to buy a pint of ice cream, and he sometimes woke to the sound of her sobbing in the middle of the night — he went on pretending he was asleep — but these were minor incidents, and two weeks after the procedure they were high over the false stillness of the Pacific.

The beach in Cairns was a mudflat shaded by palm trees. Birds hopped and poked in the mud, scattering when packs of stray dogs came trotting down the beach. Keith and Amy sat on the verandas of the main strip, drinking beers and looking out at the gauzy horizon. They rented a car and drove with sandwiches and bottles of wine to isolated sand beaches where nothing sounded but wind and waves. On one of these beaches, with the moon rising over the sea, they made love for the first time in weeks. Afterward they lay side by side with the wind cooling their sweat and riffling the silvered water. They were both laughing with the ambivalence of liberation, though he knew it was not really liberation he felt. The sex itself had been labored and remote, like a high school chemistry experiment one carries out without understanding the atomic details that catalyze the flame, the violet smoke.

In the hotel room that night, Amy said, "I'm feeling better. Aren't you?"

He nodded. He was not. They had been together almost two years. She had just finished school and had a marketing job lined up in New York, where he was already working as an IT consultant. They were one of those couples whose placid happiness seemed effortless, and their friends often cornered them to ask, "How do you guys *do* it?" When they found out about the pregnancy, he had felt an immediate distance between them. On his end, that was; she was all smiles and shining eyes. He knew this would fade into a more reasonable attitude within a few days, and it did. When she asked, "What do you want to do?" he told her, "Whatever you want to do. It's your decision." He had felt such a stance was at once correct, cowardly, and convenient, as he knew she would not keep the baby and saw no reason to make himself complicit in the decision. Secretly, he blamed her. Now it was done and he could only blame her so much.

The next day they went scuba diving out along the Great Barrier Reef. His first few seconds underwater elicited a panic he knew to be irrational. He held his breath longer than necessary, the mouthpiece clenched in his teeth, and looked at the vibrant crests and ruffles of the coral and the puffy flowers growing everywhere. All around him, the water glowed a dusky aquamarine. He was suspended at this depth, treading water, and knew he would have to breathe soon. His first breath was loud in his ears and sent bubbles up from the mouthpiece. It felt like a surrender. But in a little while he got used to the feeling, and breathing underwater seemed no stranger than breathing up in the sunlight.

He looked around and saw Amy ten meters distant, swimming away.

He swam close to the surface at first. Passing over a high coral ridge, he came suddenly upon a deep valley of color and movement: Pink anemones swaying as though in a breeze, patrolled by yellow-and-white clown fish; blue starfish sprawled over what looked like giant heads of cauliflower; cartoonishly huge clams with their corrugated maws, some of them open to reveal interiors of purple velvet; vast schools of small blue fish shaped like teardrops that changed direction frequently in mutual confusion; a pair of enormous sea turtles, soft shelled and wise eyed and surprisingly swift, passing almost close enough to touch.

On his way back to the boat, he saw a black-tipped shark the length of his own body, swimming alone. It seemed an error of creation, a thing of nightmare that had wandered into a postcard. Its sleek menace and casual disdain for the thousands of potential meals around it gave it a charged beauty none of the other sights could match.

He tried to explain it to Amy on the boat ride back to land.

"Weren't you scared?"

"I don't know if that's the right word," he said. "Not scared in a bad way."

"Thank God *I* didn't see it," she said.

The scuba guide overheard them and laughed.

"Sharks are nothing. We have saltwater crocs thirty feet long who swim out here to *eat* the sharks."

"Thirty *feet*?" Amy said. "What do you do against something like that?"

"Saw one myself. Nearly crapped my pants. Cruelest animals in the world. They'll kill you just because. Even if they're not hungry. They drag you down underwater and thrash you around until you drown."

He grinned as he described it.

They took a train down the coast to Melbourne and spent three nights going to pubs and jazz clubs and a small gallery opening for a plaster-cast balloon art installation. During the day, they walked through the botanical gardens, where Amy marveled aloud at the strange trees and shrubs, the man-made creeks and fountains. They splurged on dinner the last night, and she laughed at his imitation of a drunk Australian they'd met in a club the night before who went around to everyone barefoot and near tears, asking had they seen the little dwarf who'd stolen his shoes.

They drove west through wine country, stopping once to visit a national park. They hiked up a path through the woods that let out onto a hillside where they were suddenly confronted by hundreds of kangaroos standing upright and alert, all of them staring as though the young couple had just intruded upon an important and highly private meeting. They seemed to blanket the entire hill.

Amy took Keith's hand. "Let's go back," she said.

But he walked on without a word and she followed, because the only other option would have been to let go of his hand.

The kangaroos made no sound as they passed. Some of them shuffled out of their way on all fours, while others simply watched them pass with blank eyes that implied some barely suppressed and bewildered judgment. They were larger than Keith had thought they'd be. They had long claws and bared their yellow teeth with twitchy sneers.

"I never thought I'd be scared of kangaroos," she said when they were walking along a path near the river. "Did you see how they looked at us?"

"Kangaroos aren't going to kill you."

"They do. They kill dozens of people every year."

"But look how harmless we are," he said, smiling.

"Everything in this country kills people."

From Adelaide they drove north up the King's Highway, past Port Chester into the outback. The traffic evaporated; the foliage grew smaller and sparser. A sign indicated that the next settlement was four hundred kilometers away. The sunbaked earth ran cracked and dry to the barren mountains looming on the horizon. Sometimes it seemed the land was not solid at all but composed of gradient shades of brown, tan, yellow, and orange that blurred into one another in striated bands, broken at intervals by the white haze of a great salt flat. Green and tawny scrub lay unstirred by wind, shadowed at times by termite mounds several meters high. Amy thought she saw a dingo. She pointed but Keith saw nothing but desert.

He did most of the driving while Amy played a rotation of mix CDs they were both already sick of. There was no speed limit and rarely did they see other cars. They pulled over not because they were tired but because they needed to do something besides shuttle through the desolate plains at 140 kilometers an hour. The car doors made a flat sound when slammed and then the silence swallowed them completely, unbroken by wind or sifting dust or even the blood in their ears. Out in the desert, nothing moved. There was not a bird in the sky. Even the flies that swarmed and bit them seemed silent.

"How far do you think we are?" she asked.

"I don't know."

Their voices sounded intrusive and they did not speak again. The color of the sky and the colors of the earth were not disparate entities but different aspects of a fused whole. It was not the passive kind of landscape you looked at, but rather one you stood within, at its mercy. *Beautiful* was not the right word for it, but there was no better one.

He started walking through the brush toward a dry riverbed.

"There might be snakes," she called.

"There might," he said, walking on.

The river had not seen water in who knew how long and was only a trench of parched and fractured earth. The plants along the bank had all withered to dust and the few trees were leafless. He turned back to look at her, shielding his eyes from the sun. She waved, a speck of shadow against the sky.

The gas gauge was in the red on the evening they pulled into Coober Pedy. There had been no gas stations for over a hundred kilometers. They set up their tent among several others at a campsite and, sleepless, listened to a neighboring couple make love with desperate cries and whispers.

In the morning they went into what passed for downtown and had breakfast at a little café that served only eggs and bacon. They sat outside looking at the expanse of pale hills. It was already so hot that they were both sweating. Amy fanned herself with a brochure from the campsite.

She was the first to see the dog, its black fur spotty with mange and sheathing an emaciated frame. It was small enough to have still been a pup. It walked weakly toward them, head hung low and brown eyes plaintive beneath stripes of tan fur that looked like eyebrows.

She made a kissy sound and held out a strip of bacon to the dog.

"Be careful," he said.

The dog approached hesitantly and licked the bacon once before taking it into its mouth. It turned away to eat, as though afraid the bacon might be snatched away.

"Poor thing," she said.

"You shouldn't get so close," he said.

She looked at him. "It's a dog," she said.

It was a mining town. Dynamiters blasted holes beneath the earth in search of opals, and over the decades settlers had moved into the man-made caves and set up homes there, so that nearly the entire population lived underground, out of the sun. They took a tour of one of the homes, surprised at how modern it was. There were light fixtures embedded in the rock, and a full kitchen with an oven and a dishwasher. There was a water bed in the master bedroom and a swimming pool in the living room. The house had everything but windows. It was perfectly domestic and it was hard to imagine the explosions that had created it.

They bought some opals at a gift shop and were halfway back to the campsite when she stopped and said, "Look."

He glanced over his shoulder and saw the dog following them with its pathetic gait. It stopped when it saw they had stopped. When they did not move, it looked around nonchalantly and sat down. They went on walking, and when he looked back it was following them again.

"It likes us," she said.

"It likes food," he said.

The dog sat at the edge of the campsite and watched them fold up the tent. Keith was careful not to look in its direction. Every now and then Amy made kissy sounds at it.

"Is it a boy or a girl?" she asked.

"Where did you put the bag for the tent spikes?" he said.

When everything was packed into the trunk, she knelt by the dog, scratching its head. The dog winced but did not move away.

"Look how sweet it is," she said. "Who would just leave a dog like this?"

"We've seen stray dogs in every town we've been to."

"Look how gentle."

"It's almost noon."

She looked at him and he knew she would not leave without doing something for the dog. They went back into town, walking slowly so as not to outpace the dog. When they asked the boy behind the counter of the café about an animal shelter, he laughed.

"But there must be somewhere you bring stray dogs," she said.

The boy aimed an imaginary rifle at the dog and said, "Boom."

They asked at the gift shops and tourist homes but everyone shook their heads. Finally, one woman said, "There's probably a pound up in Alice Springs. But they'll just put her down."

They walked back to the café and got the dog some water.

"It's almost a thousand kilometers to Alice Springs," Keith said.

"We can't just leave it here."

"You heard what the woman said."

Amy looked away. Shadows of clouds moved slowly across the hills.

"We can see," she said. "We can at least bring her there and see."

They gave the dog a bath in the basin at the campsite. It did not even whimper when Keith lifted it into the water. It weighed next to nothing, and he held the shivering, spindly body still as Amy shampooed it. Black mites rinsed off into the suds.

At the town's one supermarket, they bought a bag of disposable diapers to keep the dog from pissing all over the car. At the last minute Amy ran and got a red rubber ball and bought that, too. He didn't even know what to say about that.

The diaper had to be put on lopsided because of the tail, and it hung so loosely on the dog's frame that Keith doubted it would do any good at all.

"It's a girl," Amy said. It lay curled up at her feet as they drove. She scratched its head and cooed at it. The dog looked at her with wary optimism. It stank of something like rot that the shampoo did not quite mask.

"We'll have to call her something," Amy said.

"For two days?"

"We can't just call her Dog."

"How about Rheumy?"

He was talking about the goop in the dog's eyes, but Amy smiled and said, "Like the poet."

That night they camped some twenty meters off the side of the road. The stars closed in above them, low enough to touch in the vaulted dark. They left the dog in the car and lay in the tent, trying to sleep, but the dog would not stop barking. It had a high, piercing bark.

"I'll let it out," he said.

"What if she runs away?"

"Then it runs away."

"What about the snakes?" she said.

In the dark he could not quite make out her face. Two minutes later they lay in the tent with the dog curled up quietly at their feet.

"She was just scared," Amy said. "Look how good she is now."

Keith turned away from her and tried to sleep.

He woke to the dog's tongue on his cheek. When he shoved the muzzle away, the dog whined and took a step toward the tent flap, and he realized it had to go out.

He unzipped the tent and watched in the blue dawn as the dog sniffed out a spot. Inside, Amy snored softly. When the dog was done, Keith knelt to examine the steaming shit and saw white worms writhing in it.

The dog was sitting near the tent, watching him. Keith stood with his hand on his hip a long moment. He went to the car and got out the bag of dry dog food and the jug of water and the two metal bowls. He filled the bowls and set them down and watched the dog hurry over to eat. Every now and then she looked up at him as she chewed and wagged her tail.

The sun had crested the horizon, and every small thing in the desert cast a shadow many times its size. The dog sat next to the empty bowls, looking at him.

"What?" he said. The dog cocked her head. She did look healthier. He got the rubber ball out of the car and held it in front of her. She kept her eyes fixed on it.

"Anyone ever throw a ball for you before?"

The dog glanced at him and went back to staring at the ball. Keith threw it out into the desert, not too hard. The dog took off after it — she ran much faster than Keith would have thought possible — and snatched up the ball before it had stopped bouncing in the dust. She brought the ball back to him, walking with a proud little prance, and dropped it at his feet. When Keith picked up the ball, the dog watched it avidly and again gave him a glance that offered something like gratitude. The thing to keep in mind, he told himself, was that it was only a trick of evolution that made the dog seem so human. God or nature had conspired with time to create this very creature, with its unwitting humanity and opportunist affections.

He threw the ball until the dog got tired and lay down. When he turned, he saw Amy sitting just outside the tent, watching.

The pound was outside Alice Springs, just a sign on the side of the road. They drove up to where the buildings were. On their left was a massive kennel with dogs in rows of cages stacked three high. All of them were barking and howling when Keith and Amy got out.

The dog shrank behind Amy's legs.

A woman in a beige uniform came out of one of the buildings and waved. She had a broad sun-browned face and sandy hair and everything about her seemed the same tawny color.

A three-legged Labrador followed her and trotted up to Amy with that panting smile some dogs have. Amy offered her palm to be licked.

"That's Walter," the woman said. "We found him living behind a restaurant."

"Hi, Walter," Amy said.

"We have a dog for you," Keith said.

"She looks mangy," the woman said.

"We found her in Coober Pedy."

Amy surveyed the kennel, where the dogs were still barking. "There are so many."

"You brought her all the way from Coober Pedy?" the woman said. She looked perplexed.

"She would have died there," Amy said. "Look at her."

The woman smiled uncertainly. Another woman came out of a different building with a bucket and mop and walked over.

"They brought this dog all the way from Coober Pedy," the first woman said.

"Is it sick?"

"Probably."

"Do you find homes for most of the dogs?" Amy asked.

The women looked at her, and when they saw she was not being sarcastic, the first one said, "Sure we do."

The second woman looked at the first woman and said nothing.

"How long do you wait before you put them down?" Amy asked.

"Two or three days," the second woman said.

"That's not very long."

"We get about twenty new dogs every day. A lot of them are dingo mixes. We can't let them run around."

"Let's take your dog inside and check her out," the first woman said. She led them toward one of the buildings.

"*Wal*-ter," the second woman said in a singsong voice when the Labrador tried to follow. "Come here, Walter."

The same parasites responsible for the dog's patchy fur were also in her blood. It was a disease usually found in sheep, and there was no treatment completely safe for dogs.

"You could find a vet who works with sheep," the woman said. "It would cost you some money, but he might be able to fix her up."

"We're not really looking to keep her," Keith said. "We just didn't want to leave her there."

The woman wiped her forehead and made a short breathy sound that was not quite a sigh.

"If you like that dog, you should keep her," she said. "She won't last more than three days here."

"We can't take her," Keith said. "We're from America."

The woman shrugged. Amy was looking at Keith, but he did not turn.

"You never know," Keith said casually. "She might get lucky."

"She might," the woman said.

The woman carried the dog out to the kennel and lifted her up into one of the cages.

"Maybe you could put her in there," Amy said, pointing to a small pen on the ground. "She'd have more room."

"We rotate them," the woman said. "Each of them gets a few hours in there before they go."

The dog whined in her cage. Amy stroked the dog through the bars.

"We might be back," she said to the woman. "Three days, right?"

"Come on," Keith said. "We still have some driving to do."

Getting in the car, they saw the other woman come out of one of the buildings carrying Walter's limp body in her arms, his tongue lolling out the side of his mouth.

They drove up to Kakadu. The desert grew greener until they were driving through a rain forest. Giant ferns bowed over the dirt road, and they caught glimpses of dingoes and giant lizards scurrying through the foliage. A towering waterfall stormed down into a green lake.

At the campsite, they made a fire and sat silently in the flickering light. Amy had been quiet for most of the drive, and Keith watched her now.

"Don't kid yourself," he said. "It wouldn't have changed anything."

She had her hands pulled up inside the sleeves of her sweatshirt, and rested her chin on them now.

"It's a dog," he said. "You saw how many dogs there were. Why her and not that three-legged Lab?"

"You're absolutely right," she said. "We did all we could. We did the absolute right thing."

"What were you going to do with it? Bring it home?"

"You're right. It would be so inconvenient. Just think of how incredibly inconvenient it would be for us."

"I'm being honest," he said. "You should at least be honest about it."

She stared at the fire awhile.

"I would like to do one brave and selfless thing," she said, "before I die."

They got up before sunrise and took a boat tour of the river. Mist hung over the black water and diffused the morning light so that the air glowed first white and then pink. There was the boat's motor and the quiet lapping of water on the hull and the wild cries of morning birds. Black-necked storks stood along the bank looking this way and that. Crocodiles lay snaggletoothed in the mud, their snouts nearly touching the water. Every now and then one slid into the water with a lazy scrabble of its legs. They were dumb animals, Keith knew, but as they watched the boat their eyes burned with a cruel intelligence.

"The crocs will often look like logs in the water," the tour guide said. "Except for the eyes and teeth."

A few people on the boat chuckled. Sitting next to Keith and Amy was a handsome Japanese man who kept nudging Keith and offering him his binoculars. Looking through them, Keith saw the green trees and brush crystallize into conglomerations of individual leaves and fronds of river grass. He saw a long green snake looped around the branches of a tree. He saw a stork standing on its spindly legs at the water's edge, picking at mites in its feathers with its long beak, its feathers ruffled and soft like fur. The bird dipped its head toward the water. A black blur erupted from the river, and instead of a bird there was now a crocodile with half a bird sticking out of its mouth. The crocodile stayed absolutely still like that, its head out of the water and the white bird between its jaws. The bird struggled, trying to open its pinned wings, craning its head all the way left and all the way right, back and forth like it was locked in some kind of pattern. Its beak opened soundlessly. The crocodile thrashed the bird from side to side and the bird now looked about helplessly, its free leg kicking in futile reflex.

Everyone on the boat gasped and laughed and pointed. The Japanese man took back his binoculars. Keith relinquished them but could not look away from the crocodile until it had dragged the bird down into the water. It must have been close to eighteen feet long.

"It's horrible," Amy said.

She was looking out at the river, and only at the last moment did she see what he was doing.

He was not a good diver and tumbled awkwardly into the water. The turbulence of broken water eclipsed Amy's cry, and the permeating underwater chill was like an awakening. For one brief moment, the enormity of what he had done — the insanity of it — struck him in a white flash of panic. He opened his eyes but saw only bubbles and motes in the pale green water. He swam, holding his breath, and when his lungs couldn't take it anymore he swam up toward the light and broke the surface, shivering and gasping.

He turned around until he spotted the boat, and was impressed by how far he'd come from it. The small figures there were shouting in alarmed voices, and he saw Amy at the front with her hands over her mouth. He liked to think that something passed between them in that moment, that she recognized in his eyes something he himself was still trying to figure out.

He waved.

"Stay there," the guide shouted. "We're turning around."

Keith turned and swam downstream with steady strokes, away from the boat. His feet were heavy with the weight of his waterlogged socks and sneakers, and his arms had to do most of the work. Along the shore the crocodiles basked in the new sun, watching him with their strange expressions that were not really smiles but only accidents of nature. He dove again and came up, closer to the bank now, and treaded water there a moment, watching the crocodiles watch him. Only open water separated him from them, and for all he knew there were other crocodiles swimming beneath his kicking feet in the unseen depths.

One of the crocodiles heaved itself into the water with what sounded like a sigh of resignation. It vanished with a soft splash. When it appeared again, its eyes and back just breaking the surface, it was only a few meters away from Keith and drifting effortlessly toward him. It watched him with bright yellow eyes, the pupils like black teeth.

He took a moment to note his shuddering heart. How it felt full of something more vital and mercurial than blood. The crocodile gleamed in the sun. He waited for the lightning moment when the jaws would spring open and snap shut on him. It was inevitable. He was not afraid, only curious, and grateful that he should be so fully aware of what was happening.

But the crocodile had made some subtle shift in trajectory. It was not swimming at him anymore, but past him. Keith blinked, not quite believing it. There was relief, but also a sense of betrayal. With-out thinking he reached out to touch the crocodile's back. The black hide was like wet stone beneath his pruned fingertips. The squared pattern was not as symmetrical as it had appeared from a distance and bore long scars and odd bumps. Never before and never again would he have the feeling he had in that instant, a moment of recog-nition that seared his heart, scarred it, and was not without a certain unforgivable mercy.

The crocodile seemed not to notice. Keith watched it go. He was laughing, shivering, choking on water. He looked around for some-one to share the moment, but there was only the blinding sun.

The boat pulled up beside him. A hand reached down for him and he took it. They pulled him up onto the deck, where he lay wet and shivering. He could not stop laughing. It got to the point where he was hyperventilating. Amy was shouting and slapping at him and someone had to hold her back.

"Breathe," a man said close to his ear. "You're okay. Breathe."

Huddled in a towel, he explained to the guide that he had fallen in by accident. The guide was furious. Keith didn't listen to a word he said. Spilled out across the river were thousands of silver flecks, flashing in the fading mist.

They went back to the campsite. Amy drove. Only when he had changed into new clothes and they were sitting around the ashes of last night's fire did she say, "I'm going home."

"We don't fly out for another week," he said.

"I'm going home."

"What about your dog?" he said. "Remember your dog?"

She started packing. He watched her go in and out of the tent, stuffing things into her bag. They had each brought their own bag, and only now did he realize how careful they'd been to keep their things separate.

"You're not packing," she said.

"You were right," he said. "We have a responsibility."

"Keith."

"A brave and selfless thing, you said."

He was peeling soft green bark off a stick with his thumbnail.

"Please come home," she said.

"I'm on vacation."

"It was hard for me, too. But it wasn't the end of the world."

"It was the end for somebody."

"I love you," she said. "I love you and I want you to come with me. Do you understand?"

"No," he said.

She got a ride to Darwin with a young couple from Munich. He packed up the tent once she was gone, rolling it very tight and tossing it into the back of the rental car. He stood alone, listening to the birds in the canopy overhead. Low on the trunk of a tree clung a tiny black frog with orange spots. Its eyes seemed too big for its body, its fingers too long and slender. Its fragile body expanded and contracted with air, three breaths for each one of Keith's.

He drove south out of the rain forest. He drove all afternoon and all night into the desert blackness. Enormous insects materialized out of the dark and exploded on the windshield, on the hood, their long alien appendages whipping about.

Just before dawn, he stopped at a roadhouse for gas and coffee. He drank the coffee outside, leaning against the bug-spattered hood of the car. Soft bands of red striated the eastern horizon. That day in the clinic he had held her hand while she lay on the table staring at the ceiling with her teeth clenched in a tight smile, breathing measured breaths, her spread knees covered by a sheet. The doctor sat at the other end of the table, focusing on what was happening between

Amy's legs. They had dilated her cervix and inserted a tube. The only sound was the loud drone of the vacuum pump. Keith squeezed Amy's hand and smiled at her wanly and only once made the mistake of looking past her knees, past the doctor, at the clear plastic tube that went a messy red as it sucked from her a smattering of blood and tissue that had not quite been his child.

He didn't reach the pound until late afternoon. He walked the length of the kennel and did not see the dog until his second pass because she was no longer in the cage. She was standing in one of the little pens, staring at him with her tail wagging.

He went over and let her lick his hand. He tossed the rubber ball the length of the pen and watched her chase it down and prance back with it.

The blond woman was walking toward him from the building.

"You came back," she said, smiling. Her delight sounded genuine.

"How is she?"

"She's okay. She's got a lot more energy than when you left her." She looked at the dog. "She remembers you."

She was a black dog with tan eyebrows and tan paws and a white throat and belly and soft brown eyes.

He reached in and lifted her out of the pen. He could feel her breathing. She was not as bony anymore but still very light, and he cradled her in his arms, letting her lick his face.

"Lucky girl," the woman said. "We were going to get around to her today."

Keith nodded. He kissed the dog once, on the forehead, and looked at the woman.

"I would like to do the procedure myself," he said.

DAVID JAMES POISSANT

University of Cincinnati

LIZARD MAN

I rattle into the driveway around sunup and Cam's on my front stoop
with his boy, Bobby. Cam stands. He's a huge man, thick and muscled from a decade of work in construction. Sleeves of green dragons
run armpit to wrist. He claims there's a pair of naked ladies tattooed
into all those scales if you look close enough.

When Crystal left him, Cam got the boy, which tells you what
kind of a mother Crystal was. Cam's my last friend. He's a saint when
he's sober, and he hasn't touched liquor in ten years.

He puts a hand on the boy's shoulder, but Bobby spins from his
grip and charges. He meets me at the truck, grabs my leg, and hugs
it with his whole body. I head toward Cam. Bobby bounces and
laughs with every step.

We shake hands, but Cam's expression is no-nonsense.

"Graveyard again?" he says. My apron, rolled into a tan tube,
hangs from my front pocket, and I reek of kitchen grease.

"Yeah," I say. I haven't told Cam how I lost my temper and yelled at a customer, how apparently some people don't know what *over easy* means, how my agreement to work the ten-to-six shift is the only thing keeping my electricity on and the water running.

"Bobby," Cam says, "go play for a minute, okay?" Bobby releases my leg and stares at his father skeptically. "Don't make me tell you twice," Cam says. The boy runs to my mailbox, drops to the lawn, cross-legged, and scowls. "Keep going," Cam says. Slowly, deliberately, Bobby stands and sulks toward their house.

"What is it?" I say. "What's wrong?"

Cam shakes his head. "Red's dead," he says.

Red is Cam's dad. "Bastard used to beat the fuck out of me," Cam said one night back when we both drank too much and swapped sad stories. When he turned eighteen, Cam enlisted and left for the first Gulf War. The last time he saw his father, the man was staggering, drunk, across the lawn. "Go then!" he screamed. "Go die for your fucking country!" Bobby never knew he had a grandfather.

I don't know whether Cam is upset or relieved, and I don't know what to say. Cam must see this, because he says, "It's okay. I'm okay."

"How'd it happen?" I ask.

"He was drinking," Cam says. "Bartender said one minute Red was laughing, the next his forehead was on the bar. When they went to shake him awake, he was dead."

"Wow." It's a stupid thing to say, but I've been up all night. My hand still grips an invisible steel spatula. I can feel lard under my nails.

"I need a favor," Cam says.

"Anything," I say. When I was in jail, it was Cam who bailed me out. When my wife and son moved to Baton Rouge, it was Cam who knocked down my door, kicked my ass, threw the contents of my liquor cabinet onto the front lawn, set it on fire, and got me a job at his friend's diner.

"I need a ride to Red's house," Cam says.

"Okay," I say. Cam hasn't had a car for years. Half the people on our block can't afford storm shutters, let alone cars, but it's St. Petersburg, a pedestrian city, and downtown's only a five-minute walk.

"Well, don't say okay yet," Cam says. "It's in Lee."

"Lee, Florida?"

Cam nods. Lee is four hours north, the last city you pass on I-75 before you hit Georgia.

"No problem," I say, "as long as I'm back before ten tonight."

"Another graveyard?" Cam asks. I nod. "Okay," he says, "let's go."

Last year, I threw my son through the family-room window. I don't remember how it happened, not exactly. I remember stepping into the room. I remember seeing Jack, his mouth pressed to the mouth of the other boy, his hands moving fast in the boy's lap. Then I stood over him in the garden. Lynn ran from the house, screaming. She saw Jack and hit me in the face. She battered my shoulders and my chest. Above us, through the window frame, the other boy stood, staring, shaking, hugging himself with his thin arms. Jack lay on the ground. He did not move except for the rise and fall of his chest. The window had broken cleanly and there was no blood, just shards of glass scattered over the flowers, but one of Jack's arms was bent behind his head, as though he had gone to sleep that way, an elbow for a pillow.

"Call 911!" Lynn yelled to the boy above.

"No," I said. Whatever else I didn't know in that time and place, I knew we could never afford an ambulance ride. "I'll take him," I said.

"No!" Lynn cried. "You'll kill him!"

"I'm not going to kill him," I said. "Come here." I gestured to the boy. He shook his head and stepped back. "Please," I said.

Tentatively, the boy stepped over the jagged edge of the sill. He planted his feet on the brick ledge of the front wall, then dropped the few feet to the ground. Glass crunched beneath his sneakers.

"Grab his ankles," I said. I hooked my hands under Jack's armpits and we lifted him. One arm trailed the ground as we walked him to the car. Lynn opened the hatchback. We laid Jack in the back and covered him with a blanket. It seemed like the right thing to do, what you see on TV.

A few neighbors had come outside to watch. We ignored them.

"I'll need you with me," I said to the boy. "When we're done, I'll take you home." The boy was wringing the hem of his shirt in both hands. His eyes brimmed with tears. "I won't hurt you, if that's what you think."

We set off for the hospital, Lynn following in my pickup. The boy sat beside me in the passenger seat, his body pressed to the door, face against the window, the seat belt strap clenched in one hand at his waist. With each bump in the road, he turned to look at Jack.

"What's your name?" I asked.

"Alan," he said.

"How old are you, Alan?"

"Seventeen."

"Seventeen. Seventeen. And have you ever been with a woman, Alan?"

Alan looked at me. His face drained of color. His hand tightened on the seat belt.

"It's a simple question, Alan. I'm asking you: Have you been with a woman?"

"No," Alan said. "No, sir."

"Then how do you know you're gay?"

In back, Jack began to stir. He moaned, then grew silent. Alan watched him.

"Look at me, Alan," I said. "I asked you a question. If you've never been with a woman, then how do you know you're gay?"

"I don't know," Alan said.

"You mean, you don't know that you're gay, or you don't know how you know?"

"I don't know how I know," Alan said. "I just do."

We passed the bakery, the Laundromat, and the supermarket and entered the city limits. In the distance, the silhouette of the helicopter on the hospital's roof. Behind us, the steady pursuit of the pickup truck.

"And your parents, do they know about this?" I asked.

"Yes," Alan said.

"And do they approve?"

"Not really."

"No. I bet they don't, Alan. I'll bet they do not."

I glanced in the rearview mirror. Jack had not opened his eyes, but he had a hand to his temple. The other hand, the one attached to the broken arm, lay at his side. The fingers moved, but without purpose, the hand spasming from fist to open palm.

"I just have one more question for you, Alan," I said.

Alan looked like he might be sick. He watched the road unfurl before us. He was afraid of me, afraid to look at Jack.

"What right do you have teaching my son to be gay?"

"I didn't!" Alan said. "I'm not!"

"You're not? Then what do you call that? Back there? That business on the couch?"

"Mr. Lawson," Alan said, and here the tone of his voice changed, and I felt as though I were speaking to another man. "With all due respect, sir, Jack came on to me."

"Jack is not gay."

"He is. I know it. Jack knows it. Your *wife* knows it. I don't know how you couldn't know it. I don't see how you've missed the signals."

I tried to imagine what signals, but I couldn't. I couldn't recall a thing that would have signaled that I'd wind up here, delivering my son to the hospital with a concussion and a broken arm. What signal might have foretold that, following this day, after two months spent in a motel and two months in prison, my wife of twenty years would divorce me because, as she put it, I was *full of hate*?

I pulled up to the emergency room's entryway, and Alan helped me pull Jack from the car. A nurse with a wheelchair ran out to meet us. We settled Jack into the chair, and she wheeled him away.

I pulled the car into a parking spot and walked back to the entrance. Alan stood on the curb where I had left him.

"Where's Lynn?" I asked.

"Inside," Alan said. "Jack's awake."

"All right, I'm going in. I suggest you get out of here."

"But you said you'd drive me home."

"Sorry," I said. "I changed my mind."

Alan stared at me, dumbfounded. His hands groped the air.

"Hey," I said, "I got a signal for you." I gave him a hitchhiker's upturned thumb and cast it over my shoulder as I entered the hospital.

I wake and Cam's making his way down back roads, their surfaces cratered with potholes.

"Rise and shine," he says, "and welcome to Lee."

It's nearly noon. The sun is bright and the cab is hot. I wipe gunk from my eyes and drool from the corner of my mouth. Cam watches the road with one eye and studies directions he's scrawled in black ink across the back of a cereal box. He's never seen the house where his father spent the last twenty years.

We turn onto a dirt road. The truck lurches into and then out of an enormous waterlogged hole. Pines line the road. Their needles shiver as we go by. We pass turn after turn, but only half of the roads are marked. Every few miles we pass a driveway, the house deep in the trees and out of sight. It's a haunted place, and I'm already ready to leave.

Cam says, "I don't know where the fuck we are."

We drive some more. I think about Bobby home alone, how Cam gave him six VHS tapes. "By the time you watch all of these," he said, "I'll be back." Then he put in the first movie, something Disney, and we left. "He'll be fine," Cam said. "He'll never even know we're gone."

"We could bring him with us," I said, but Cam refused.

"There's no telling what we'll find there," he said.

Ahead, a child stands beside the road. Cam slows the truck to a halt and rolls down the window. The girl steps forward. She looks over her shoulder, then back at us. She is barefoot and her face is smeared with dirt. She wears a brown dress and a green bow in her hair. A string is looped around her wrist, and from the end of the string floats a blue balloon.

"Hi, there," Cam says. He leans out the window, his hand extended, but the child does not take it. Instead, she stares at his arms, the coiled dragons. She takes a step back.

"You're scaring her," I say.

Cam glares at me, but he returns his head to the cab and his hand to the wheel and gives the girl his warmest smile. "Do you know where we could find Cherry Road?" he asks.

"Sure," the girl says. She pumps her arm and the balloon bobs in response. "It's that way." She points in the direction from which we've come.

"About how far?" Cam asks.

"Not the next road but the next. But it's a dead end. There's only one house." She flails her wrist and the balloon thunks against her fist.

Cam glances at the cereal box. "That's the one," he says.

"Oh," the girl says, and for a moment she is silent. "You're going to visit the Lizard Man. I seen him. I seen him once."

Cam looks at me. I shrug. We look at the girl.

"Well, thank you," Cam says. The girl gives the balloon a good shake. Cam turns the truck around and the girl waves good-bye.

"Cute kid," I say. We turn onto Cherry.

"Creepy little fucker," Cam says.

The house is hidden in pines and the yard is overgrown with knee-high weeds. Tire tracks mark where the driveway used to be. Plastic flamingos dot the yard, their curved beaks peeking out of the weeds, wire legs rusted, bodies bleached a light pink.

The roof of the house is littered with pine needles and piles of shingles where someone abandoned a roofing project. The porch has buckled and the siding is rotten, the planks loose. I press a fingernail to the soft wood and it slides in.

Our mission is unclear. There's no body to ID or papers to sign. Nothing to inherit, and there will be no funeral. But I know why we're here. This is how Cam will say good-bye.

The front door is locked. "Right here," Cam says. He taps the wood a foot above the lock before slamming the heel of his boot through the door.

Inside, the house waits for its owner's return. The hallway light is on. The AC unit shakes in the window over the kitchen sink. Tan wallpaper curls away from the cabinets like birch bark, exposing thin ribbons of yellow glue on the walls.

We hear voices. Cam puts a hand to my chest and a finger to his lips. He brings a hand to his waist and feels for a gun that is not there. Neither of us moves for a full minute, then Cam laughs.

"Fuck!" he says. "It's the TV." He hoots. He runs a hand through his hair. "About scared the shit out of me."

We move to the main room. It, too, is in disarray, the lampshades thick with dust, a coffee table awash in a sea of newspapers and unopened mail. There is an old and scary-looking couch, its arms held to its sides with duct tape. A pair of springs pokes through the cushion, ripe with tetanus.

The exception is the television. It is beautiful. It is six feet of widescreen glory. "Look at that picture," I say, and Cam and I step back to take it in. The TV's tuned to the Military Channel, some cable extravagance. B-2 bombers streak the sky in black and white, propellers the size of my head. On top of the set sits a bottle of Windex and a filthy washcloth, along with several many-buttoned remote controls. Cam grabs one, fondles it, and holds down a button. The sound swells. The drone of plane engines and a burst of gunfire tear across the room from one speaker to another. I jump. Cam grins.

"We're taking it," he says. "We are so taking this shit."

He pushes another button and the picture blips to a single point of white at the center of the screen. The point fades and dies.

"No!" Cam says. "No!"

"What did you do?" I say.

"I don't know. I don't know!"

Cam shakes the remote, picks up another, punches more buttons, picks up a third, presses its buttons. The television hums and the picture shimmers back to life.

"Ahhh," Cam says. We sit, careful to avoid the springs. While we watch, the beaches at Normandy are stormed, two bombs are dropped, and the war is won. We're halfway into Vietnam when Cam says, "I'm going to check out his room." It is not an invitation.

Cam's gone for half an hour. When he returns, he looks terrible. The color is gone from his face, and his eyes are red-rimmed. He carries a shoebox under one arm. I don't ask and he doesn't offer.

"Let's load up the set and get out of here," Cam says. "I'll pull the truck around."

I hear a glass door slide open then shut behind me. I hear something like a scream. Then the door slides open again. I turn around to see Cam. If he looked bad before, now he looks downright awful.

"What is it?" I say.

"Big," Cam says. "In the backyard."

"What? What's big in the backyard?"

"Big. Fucking. Alligator."

It *is* a big fucking alligator. I've seen alligators before — in movies, at zoos — but never this big and never so close. We stare at him. We don't know it's a him, but we decide it's a him. He is big. It's insane.

It's also the saddest fucking thing I have ever seen. In the backyard is a makeshift cage, an oval of chain-link fence with a chicken-wire roof. Inside, the alligator straddles an old kiddie pool. The pool's cracked plastic lip strains with the alligator's weight. His middle fills the pool, his belly submerged in a few inches of syrupy brown water, legs hanging out. His tail, the span of a man, curls against a length of chain link.

When he sees us, the alligator hisses and paddles his front feet in the air. He opens his jaws, baring yellow teeth and white, fleshy gums. Everywhere there are flies and gnats. They fly into his open mouth and land on his teeth. Others swarm open wounds along his back.

"What is he doing here?" Cam asks.

"Red was the Lizard Man," I say. "Apparently."

We stare at the alligator. He stares back. I consider the cage and wonder whether the alligator can turn around.

"He looks bored," Cam says. And it's true. He looks bored, and sick. He shuts his mouth, and his open eyes are the only thing reminding me he's alive.

"We can't leave him here," Cam says.

"We should call someone," I say. But who would we call? The authorities? Animal control?

"We can't," Cam says. "They'll kill him."

Cam is right. I've seen it before, on the news. Some jackass raises a gator. The gator gets loose. It's been hand-fed and knows no fear of man. The segments always end the same way: *Sadly, the alligator had to be destroyed.*

"I don't see that we have a choice," I say.

"We have the pickup," Cam says.

My mouth says no, but my eyes must say yes, because before I know what's happening, we're in the front yard examining the bed of the truck, Cam measuring the length with his open arms.

"This won't work," I say. Cam ignores me. He pulls a blue tarp from the backseat and unrolls it on the ground beside the truck.

"He'll never fit," I say.

"He'll fit. It'll be close, but he'll fit."

"Cam," I say. "Wait. Stop." Cam leans against the truck. He looks right at me. "Say we get the alligator out of the cage and into the truck. Say we manage to do this and keep all of our fingers. Where do we take him? I mean, what the hell, Cam? What the hell do you do with twelve feet of living, breathing alligator? And what about the TV? I thought you wanted to take the TV."

"Shit. I forgot about the TV."

We stare at the truck. I look up. The sky has turned from bright to light blue and the sun has disappeared behind a scatter of clouds. On the ground one corner of the tarp flaps in the breeze, winking its gold eyelet.

Cam bows his head, as if in mourning. "Maybe if we stand the set up on its end."

"Cam," I say. "We can take the alligator or we can take the television, but we can't take both."

Taping the snout shut, Cam decides, will be the hard part.

"All of it's the hard part," I say, but Cam's not listening.

Cam finds a T-bone in Red's refrigerator. It's spoiled, but the alligator doesn't seem to mind. Cam sets the steak near the cage, and the alligator waddles out of the pool. He presses his nostrils to the fence. The thick musk of alligator and the reek of rotten meat turn my stomach and I retch.

"You puke on me and I'll kick your ass," Cam says.

We've raided Red's garage for supplies. Lying scattered at our feet are bolt cutters, a roll of electric tape, a spool of twine, bungee cords, a dozen two-by-fours, my tarp, and, for no reason I'm immediately able to ascertain, a chain saw.

"Protection," Cam says, nudging the old Sears model with his toe. The chain is rusted and hangs loose from the blade. I imagine Cam starting the chain saw, the chain snapping, flying, landing far away in the tall grass. I try to picture the struggle between man and beast, Cam pinned beneath five hundred pounds of alligator, Cam's head in the gator's mouth, Cam dragged in circles around the yard, a tangle of limbs and screams. In each scenario the chain saw offers little assistance.

Cam's hands are sheathed in oven mitts, a compromise he accepted begrudgingly when the boxing gloves he found, while offering superior protection, failed to provide him the ability to grip, pick up, or hold.

"This is stupid," I say. "Are we really doing this?"

"We're doing this," Cam says. He swats a fly from his face with one pot-holdered hand.

There is a clatter of chain link. We turn to see the alligator nudging the fence with his snout. He snorts, eyes the T-bone, opens and shuts his mouth. He really is surprisingly large.

Cam's parked the pickup in the backyard. He pulls off his oven mitts and lowers the gate, exposing the wide, bare bed of the truck, and we set to work angling the two-by-fours from gate to grass. We press the planks together, and Cam cinches them tight with the bungee cords. The boards are long, ten or twelve feet, so physics is on our side. We should be able to drag him up the incline.

We return our attention to the alligator, who is throwing himself against the fence, except that he can only back up a few feet and therefore builds very little momentum. Above his head, at knee level, is a hand-sized wire mesh door held shut by a combination lock. With each lunge, the lock jumps, then clatters against the door. With each charge, I jump, too.

"He can't break out," Cam says. He picks up the bolt cutters.

"You don't know that," I say.

"If he could, don't you think he'd have done it by now?" Cam positions the bolt cutters on the loop of lock, bows his legs, and squats. He squeezes and his face reddens. He grunts, there's a snap, and the lock falls away, followed by a flash of movement. Cam howls and falls. The alligator's open jaws stretch halfway through the hole. All I see is teeth.

"Motherfucker!" Cam yells.

"You okay?" I say.

Cam holds up his hands, wiggles ten fingers.

"Okay," Cam says. "Okay." He picks up the T-bone and throws it at the alligator. The steak lands on his nose, hangs there, then slides off.

"It's not a dog," I say. "This isn't catch."

Cam puts on the oven mitts and slowly reaches for the meat resting in the grass just a few feet beneath all those teeth. Suddenly, the pen looks less sturdy, less like a thing the alligator could never escape.

The cage shakes, but this time it's the wind, which has really picked up. I wonder whether it's storming in St. Petersburg. Cam should be at home with Bobby, and I almost say as much. But Cam's eyes are wild. He's dead set on doing this.

Cam says, "I'm going to put the steak into his mouth, and when I do, I want you to tape the jaws shut."

"No way," I say. "No way am I putting my hand in range of that thing." And then this happens: My son walks out of my memory and into my thoughts, his arm hanging loose at the elbow. The nurse asks what happened, and he looks up, ready to lie for me. There is something beautiful in the pause between this question and the one to come. Then there's the officer's hand on my shoulder. "Would you mind stepping out with me, please?" Oh, I've heard it a hundred times. It never leaves me. It is a whisper. It is a prison sentence.

I want to put the elbow back into the socket myself. I want to turn back time. I want Jack at five or ten. I want him curled in my lap like a dog. I want him writing on the walls with an orange crayon and blaming the angels that live in the attic. I want him before his voice plummeted two octaves, before he learned to stand with a hand on one hip, before he grew confused. I want my boy back.

"Come on!" Cam shouts. "Don't puss out on me now. As soon as he bites down, just wrap the tape around it."

"Give me your oven mitts," I say.

"No!"

"Give me the mitts and I'll do it."

"But you won't be able to handle the tape."

"Trust me," I say, "I'll find a way."

We do it. Cam waves the cut of meat at the snout until it smacks teeth. The jaws grab. There's an unnatural crunch as the *T* in the T-bone becomes two *I*s and then a pile of periods. I drape a length of tape over the nose, fasten the ends beneath the jaws, then run my gloved hands up both strands of tape, sealing them. Then I start wrapping like crazy. I wind the roll of tape around and around the jaws. The tape unspools from the roll and coils in a flat, black worm around the snout.

When I step back, the alligator's jaws are shut tight and my hands are shaking.

"I can't believe it," Cam says. "I can't believe you actually did that shit."

The alligator's one heavy son of a bitch. We hold him in a kind of headlock, arms cradling his neck and front legs, fingers gripping his scaly hide. It's a good twenty feet from cage to truck. We sidestep toward the pickup, the alligator's back end and tail tracing a path through the grass. Every few feet, we stop to rest.

As we drag the alligator, his back feet scramble and claw at the ground, but he doesn't writhe or thrash. He is not a healthy alligator. I stop.

"C'mon," Cam says. "Almost there."

"What are we doing?" I say.

"We're putting an alligator into your truck," Cam says. "C'mon."

"But look at him," I say. Cam looks down, examines the alligator's wide, green head, his wet, Ping-Pong ball eyes. He looks up.

"No," I say. "Really look."

"What?" Cam's impatient. He shifts his weight, gets a better grip on the gator. "I don't know what you want me to see."

"He's not even fighting us. He's too sick. Even if we set him free, how do we know he'll make it?"

"We don't."

"No, we don't. We don't know where he came from. We don't know where to take him. And what if Red raised him? How will he survive in the wild? How will he learn to hunt and catch fish and stuff?"

Cam shrugs, shakes his head.

"So, why?" I ask. "Why are we doing this?"

Cam locks eyes with me. After a minute, I look away. My arms are weak with the weight of the alligator. My legs quiver. We shuffle forward.

I didn't give Jack the chance to lie. I admitted guilt to second-degree battery and kept everyone out of court. I got four months and served two, plus fines, plus community service. Had that been the end of it, I'd have gotten off easy. Instead, I lost my family.

The last time I saw Jack, he stood beside his mother's car showing Alan his new driver's license. They reclined like girls against the hood but laughed like men at something on the license: a typo. *Weight: 1500.* I watched them from the doorway.

Alan had helped me load the furniture. With each piece, I thought of Jack's body. How it hung between us that afternoon, how it swayed, as if in roughhousing where you and a friend grab another boy by his ankles and wrists and throw him off a dock and into a lake.

Everything Jack and Lynn owned we'd packed into a U-Haul truck. I was not meant to know where they were going. I was not meant to see them again, but I'd found maps and directions in a pile of Lynn's things and had written down the address of their new place in Baton Rouge. I could forgive Lynn for not wanting to see me, but taking my son away was a thing I could not abide.

I decided I would go there one day, a day that seems more distant with each passing afternoon. And what would Jack do when he opened the door? In my dreams it was always Jack who opened the door. I would hold out my arms in invitation. I would say what I had not said.

But that afternoon, it was Alan who sent Jack to me. Lynn waited in the U-Haul, ready to drive away. Alan gestured in my direction. He and Jack argued in hushed voices. And finally, remarkably, Jack moved toward me. I did not leave the doorway, and Jack stopped just short of the stoop.

What can I tell you about my son? He had been a beautiful boy, and, standing before me, I saw that he had become something different: a man I did not understand. His T-shirt was too tight for him, and the hem rode just above his navel. A trail of light brown hair led from there and disappeared behind a silver belt buckle. His fingernails were painted black. The cast had come off, and his right arm was a nest of curly, dark hairs.

I wanted to say "I want to understand you."

I wanted to say "I will do whatever it takes to earn your trust."

I wanted to say "I love you," but I had never said it, not to Jack — yes, I am one of those men — and I could not bear the thought of speaking these words to my son for the first time and not hearing them spoken in return.

Instead, I said nothing.

Jack held out his hand and we shook like strangers.

I still feel it, the infinity of Jack's handshake: the nod of pressed palms, flesh of my flesh.

––––––––

The rain arrives in sheets and the windshield wipers can hardly keep up. I drive. Cam sits beside me. He's placed the shoebox on the seat between us. His arm rests protectively against the lid. The alligator slides around with the two-by-fours in the back. We fastened the tarp over the bed of the truck to conceal our cargo, but we didn't pull it taut. The tarp sags with water, threatening to smother the animal underneath.

Cam flips on the radio and we catch snippets of the weather before the speakers turn to static.

"... upgraded to a tropical storm ... usually signals the formation of a hurricane ... storm will pick up speed as it makes its way across the Gulf ... expected to come ashore as far north as the panhandle ... far south as St. Petersburg ..."

Cam turns the radio off. We watch rain pelt the windshield, the black flash of wipers pushing water.

I don't ask whether Bobby is afraid of storms. When I was a boy I was frightened of them, but Jack never was. During storms, Jack stood at the window and watched as branches skittered down the street and power lines unraveled onto the sidewalks. He smiled and stared until Lynn pulled him away from the glass and we moved to the bathroom with our blankets and flashlights. It was only then, huddled in the dark, that Jack sometimes cried.

"We should go back," I say. "The power could be out."

"Bobby's a tough kid," Cam says. "He'll be fine."

"Cam," I say.

"In case you've forgotten, there's a fucking alligator in the back of your truck."

I say nothing. Whatever happens is Cam's responsibility. *This,* I tell myself, *is not your fault.*

Thunder shakes the truck. Not far ahead, a cell tower ignites with lightning. A shower of sparks waterfalls onto the highway. Cars and trucks are dusted with fire. Everyone drives on.

I don't know where we're headed, but Cam says we're close.

Cam, I think, *after this, I owe you nothing. Once this is over, we're even.*

"If it's work you're worried about," Cam says, "I'll talk to Mickey. I'll tell him about Red. He'll understand if you're late."

"It's not Mickey I'm worried about," I say. I don't say, *Mickey can kiss my ass.* I don't say, *You and Mickey can go to hell.*

"Look," Cam says, "I know why you're pulling the graveyard shift. Mickey told me what you did. But this is different. This he'll understand."

I recognize the ache at the back of my throat immediately. The second I'm alone, it will take a miracle to keep a bottle out of my hand.

"Take this exit," Cam says. "At the bottom, turn right."

I guide the truck down the ramp toward Grove Street. The water in back sloshes forward and unfloods the tarp. Alligator feet scratch for purchase on the truck bed's corrugated plastic lining.

"Where are you taking us?" I ask.

"Havenbrook," he says. I wait for Cam to say he's kidding. But Cam isn't kidding.

The largest of the lakes cradles the seventeenth green. Cam's seen gators there before, big bastards who come ashore to sun themselves and scare off golfers. I've never golfed in my life, and neither has he, but Cam led the team that patched the clubhouse roof following last year's hurricane season. He remembers the five-digit code, and it still works. The security gate slides open, and we head down the paved drive reserved for maintenance.

No one's on the course. Fallen limbs litter the greens. An abandoned white cart lies turned on its side where the golf-cart path rounds the fifteenth hole.

Lightning streaks the sky. The rain has turned the windshield to water, and sudden gusts of wind jostle the truck from every direction. I fight the steering wheel to stay on the asphalt. Even Cam is wide eyed, his fingers buried in the seat cushions. The shoebox bounces between us.

We reach the lake, but the shore is half a football field away. The green is soggy, thick with water, and already the lake is flooding its banks. The first tire that leaves the road, I know, will sink into the mud, and we'll never get the truck out.

"I can't drive out there," I tell Cam. I have to yell over the wind and rain, the deafening thunder. It's like the world is pulling apart. "This is the closest I can get us."

Cam says something I can't hear and then he's out of the truck, the door slamming behind him. I jump out and the wet cold slaps me. Within seconds I'm drenched, my clothes heavy. All I hear is the wind. I move as if underwater.

As soon as Cam gets the tarp off, the storm catches it and it billows into the sky like a flaming blue parachute, up into the trees overhead. It tangles itself into the branches and then there is only the *smack, smack* of the tarp's uncaught corners pummeled by gusts.

Cam screams at me. His teeth flash in bursts of lightning, but his words are choked by wind. I tap my ear and he nods. He motions toward the alligator. We approach it slowly. I expect the animal to charge, but he lies motionless. I check the jaws. They're still wrapped tight. This, I realize, will be our last challenge. If he gets away from us before we remove the tape, he's doomed.

I'm wondering which of us will climb into the bed of the truck when the gator starts scuttling forward. We leap out of the way as hundreds of pounds of reptile spill from the truck and onto the green. The gate cracks under the weight and swings loose like a trap-door in midair, the hinges busted. Then the alligator is free on the grass. We don't move and neither does he.

Cam approaches me. He makes a megaphone of his cupped hands and mouth and leans in close to my ear. His hot breath on my face is startling and sudden and wonderful in all that fierce cold and rain.

"I think he's stunned," Cam yells. "We've got to get the tape off, now."

I nod. I am exhausted and anxious and I know there's no way we'll be able to lug the alligator to the water's edge. I wonder whether he'll make it, if he'll find his way to the water, or if this fall from the truck was the final blow, if tomorrow the groundskeepers will find an alligator carcass fifty yards from the lake. It would make the front page of the *St. Petersburg Times*: GIANT ALLIGATOR KILLED IN HURRICANE. Officials would be baffled.

"I want you to straddle its neck," Cam yells. "Keep its head pressed to the ground. I'll try to get the tape off."

"No," I say. I point to my chest. I circle my hand through the air, pantomiming the unraveling. Cam looks surprised, but he nods.

Cam brings his hands to my face again and yells his hot words into my ear. "On my signal," he screams, but I push him away.

I don't wait for a signal. Before I know it I'm on the ground, my side hugging mud, and I'm digging my nails into the tape. My eye is inches from the alligator's eye. He blinks without blinking, a thin, clear membrane sliding over his eyeball, then up and under his eyelid. It is a thing to see. It is a knowing wink. I see this and I feel safe.

The tape is harder to unwrap than it was to wrap. The rain has made it soft, the glue gooey. Every few turns, I lose my grip. Finally, I let the tape coil around my hand like a snake. It unwinds, and soon my fist is a ball of dark, sticky fruit. The last of the tape pulls cleanly from the snout and I roll away from the alligator. I stand and Cam pulls me back. He holds me up. The alligator flexes his jaws. His mouth opens wide, then slams shut. And then he's off, zigzagging toward the water.

He is swift and strong, and I'm glad it is cold and raining so Cam can't see the tears streaking my cheeks and won't know that my shivering is from sobbing. Cam lets go of me and I think I will fall, but instead I am running. Running! And I'm laughing and hollering and leaping. I'm pumping my fist into the air. I'm screaming, "Go! Go!" And, just before the alligator reaches the water, I lunge and my fingertips trace the last ridges and scales of tail whipping their way ahead of me. The sky is alive with lightning and I see the hulking body, so awkward and graceless on land, slide into the water as it was meant to do. That great body cuts the water, fast and sleek, and the alligator dives out of sight, at home in the world where he belongs, safe in the warm quiet of mud and fish and unseen things that thrive in deep, green darkness.

Cam and I don't say much on the ride home. The rain has slowed to an even, steady downpour. The truck's cab has grown cold. Cam holds his hands close to the vents to catch whatever weak streams of heat trickle out. We have done a good thing, Cam says, and I agree, but I worry at what cost. We listen to the radio, but the storm has headed north. The reporters have moved on to new cities: Clearwater, Crystal Springs, Ocala.

"There was this one time," Cam says at last. "About five years back. I spoke to Red."

This is news to me. This, I know, is no small revelation.

"I called him," Cam says. "I called him up, and I said, 'Dad? I just want you to know that you have a grandson and that his name is

Robert and that I think he should know his grandfather.' And you know what that prick did? He hung up. The only thing Red said to me in twenty years was 'Hello' when he picked up the phone."

"I'm sorry," I say.

"If he'd even once told me he was sorry, I'd have forgiven him anything. I'd have forgiven my own murder. He was my father. I would have forgiven everything.

"Do you know why I got all these fucking tattoos? To hide the fucking scars from the night Red cut me with a fillet knife. And I'd have forgiven that if he'd just said something, anything, when he answered the phone."

Cam doesn't shake or sob or bang a fist on the dashboard, but when I look away I catch his reflection in the window, a knuckle in each eye socket, and I'm suddenly sorry for my impatience, the grudge I've carried all afternoon.

"But you tried," I say. "At least you won't spend your life wondering."

We sit in silence for a while. The rain on the roof beats a cadence into the cab and it soothes me.

"You know, I served with gay guys in the Gulf," Cam says, and I almost drive the truck off the road. A tire slips over the lip of asphalt and my side mirror nearly catches a guardrail before I bring the truck back to the center of the lane.

"Jesus!" Cam says. "I'm just saying, they were okay guys, and if Jack's gay it's not the end of the world."

"Jack's confused," I say. "He isn't gay."

"Well, either he is or he isn't, and what you think or want or say won't change it."

"Cam," I say, "all due respect. This doesn't concern you."

"I know," Cam says. He sits up straighter in his seat, grips the door handle as we pull onto our block. "I'm just saying, it isn't too late."

We pull into the driveway. Cam jumps out of the truck before it's in park. The yard is a mess of fallen limbs and garbage. Two shutters have been torn from the front of the house. The mailbox is on its side. Otherwise, everything looks all right. I glance down the street and see that my house is still standing.

When I turn back to Cam's house, what I see breaks my heart in ten places. I see Cam running across the lawn. I see Bobby, his hands pressed to the big bay window. His face is puffy and red. Cam disappears into the house, and then he is there with the boy, he is there on his knees, and he pulls Bobby to him. He mouths the words *I'm sorry, I'm sorry* over and over again, and Bobby collapses into him, buries his head in Cam's chest, and my friend wraps his son in dragons.

I watch them. They stay like that for a while, framed by window and house and the darkening sky. I watch, and then I open the shoebox and look inside.

I don't know what I was expecting, but it wasn't this. What I find are letters, over a hundred of them. About a letter a month for roughly ten years, all of them unopened. Each has been dated and stamped RETURN TO SENDER, the last one sent back just a week ago. Each is marked by the same shaky handwriting. Each is addressed to a single recipient, Mr. Cameron Starnes, from a single sender: Red.

And I know then that there was no phone call, no forgiveness on Cam's part, that Cam never came close until after the monster was safely out of reach.

I stare at the letters and I know who it is Cam wants to keep me from becoming.

I pull out of Cam's driveway. I stop to right Cam's mailbox, then I tuck the shoebox safely inside. I follow the street to the end of the block. At the stop sign, I pause. I don't know whether to turn right or left. Finally, I head for the interstate. There's a spare uniform at the diner, clean and dry, and if I hurry I won't be late for work.

But I'm not going to work.

It's a ten-hour drive to Baton Rouge, but I will make it in eight. I will make it before morning. I will drive north, following the storm. I will drive through the wind and the rain. I will drive all night.

CLAIRE O'CONNOR

University of Idaho

CAPE TOWN

The wetsuit is supposed to be tight, a second skin. Every knob and bulge on my body is defined, but nobody seems to notice. Most of the other people getting their scuba certification are young professionals, closer to my daughter Sherry's age, twenty-seven. They wag their arms and flex their legs, a rubbery chorus line. They notice each other and share embarrassed glances. I am already a sideways glance, an afterthought.

The instructor's tanned face fills with creases when he smiles. He is not embarrassed in his wetsuit with ALBANY UNDERWATER DISCOVERY TOURS in bright purple stitching. He walks barefoot, with grace, up and down the length of the pool, his wet goatee drying, uncurling. In the locker room, Sherry complained of claustrophobia, but now she gets in line and shuffles forward with the rest. The oxygen tank feels like a loaded cannon on my back. The instructor helps the others into the pool. Then my daughter. Then me.

I sink into the pool, and the mask sucks against my face. The light slices through the water, falling on the walls at odd angles, disregarding lanes. Those who have gone before me have already sunk to the bottom. Colorful fins sprout from their feet, useless wings. What is this, a colony of insects, swarming together to form a new hive? They rest on their knees and hold their hands as if in prayer. My impulse is to struggle, to get back to the surface. The mask sucks against my face. I am learning how to breathe. I let myself fall.

At the airport in Cape Town, South Africa, my daughter is efficient, bargaining for a taxi. In her loose-fitting khakis and hiking sandals, she is a creature unknown to me. She has always been a bookworm; I have rarely seen her in action. With ease she navigates the terminal and collects our luggage, shooing away unwanted porters, leading me through a maze of escalators and moving stairways. The airport is big and modern, an echoing womb. Now Sherry shakes her head at the price the taxi driver quotes, requesting that he turn on the meter, as the municipality requires. He frowns but follows her command.

From inside the taxi we watch the suburbs grow into a city. Stone-crusted mountains run behind the city to the sea. Oak trees give way to asphalt. Cracked white churches with columns and cupolas mingle with modern-day concrete shopping centers. It doesn't look like Africa. If I squint, it could be San Francisco. I roll down the window. It smells like car exhaust and salt water.

"What do you want to do while we're here?" I ask.

"Whatever you want to do."

I take the brochure out of my purse. The pictures are fading — I've fingered them too much. In one frame a great white shark hangs in midair, half its body above the water, half below, surrounded by a magnificent spray, its open mouth locked in a grimace I cannot decipher. I turn the page. Underwater, a great white shark grins at me, the top half of its gray hide dappled with light from above. The bottom half gleams white, untouched. The brochure does not show a picture of the square mesh galvanized steel cage, 1.5 meters in diameter and 2.1 meters high. I hold out my arms as far as they can go, maneuvering around the headrests, trying to imagine how much room we'll have. Sherry shrinks against her seat. I drop my arms and trade my shark brochure for a series of others in my purse.

"We could go to the wineries. We could go to Table Mountain. We could do a historical tour. We could go on a safari..."

I poke Sherry's side, as if to tickle her. Her body stiffens under my hand. "I'm *not* going on a safari."

"We don't have to go on a safari."

"We could go to the prison where they kept Nelson Mandela."

"We could."

"He was in prison for twenty-seven years."

"Would you like to do that?" My daughter looks out the window. Outside, a group of schoolchildren crosses the street. Hand in hand, they move together like a school of fish in their matching white shirts and bright blue ties, the boys in blue trousers, the girls in knee-length pleated skirts.

My daughter frowns. "Would you?"

I sigh. "I'm asking you."

"It's your vacation."

Our appointment to swim with the sharks isn't for a few days. "It's your vacation, too."

Sherry smiles. It is a forced smile. "Thank you for coming," I say, resting my hand on her knee. Her eyes track the movements of the children in the rear of the group as they race to get across the street before the light changes. "So, what do you want to do?"

"It doesn't matter what I want," she says.

She might have a point. Sometimes things happen to us, regardless of our desires. When the doctor first told me I had a brain tumor, I laughed. I said, *Really?* I said, *You're joking.* I said, *You can't be serious. You can't.*

He said, *I'm sorry.*

I said, *You should be.*

The tongue depressors huddled all together in a jar. The clock on the wall ticked.

I apologized. He said it was natural. I said, *What, dying?* He said, *Your reaction.* I said, *Stop. You've done enough.*

Next to the clock hung a map of the human central nervous system that reduced a human being to a brain and a spinal cord — a strange jellyfish, with its bloated head and slender tentacles. I wondered why each time a neuron fired, it didn't sting.

I said, *I haven't.* He said, *What?* I said, *Done enough.*

My daughter sits on the hotel veranda, nursing a glass of tonic water. She is wearing a wrinkled mint-green blouse — the color of pastel candy, the kind she used to beg for as a child when I made her eat fruit leather instead. The hotel room has an iron, but she would never use it. I packed only wrinkle-free clothes.

I sit on the end of the bed, bouncing lightly. I've unpacked everything, even the underwater camera my ex-husband, Sherry's father, gave me. Through the open sliding-glass door I watch my daughter. She is facing the ocean. Glass to lips, glass down, licking lips. Glass to lips, glass down, licking lips. Her face is flushed.

"Sherry. Sherry baby."

My daughter turns her head, searching for my face in the gloom of the hotel room. I ask her if she wants sunscreen.

"I'm fine," she says. Glass to lips, glass down.

I stand and join her. I sip my gin and tonic. The cold hurts my teeth, but I don't mind. It feels decadent, cocktails in the daytime.

Across the expanse of sea, the sun strikes each crest of water, a thousand new flashes every second. "We are in Africa, after all. It wouldn't hurt to put on some sunscreen."

"We're nowhere near the equator." Sherry drops the sunglasses perched on her head over her eyes. They are made of cheap black plastic. I long to buy her designer sunglasses, the kind that make anyone look like a movie star. "Cape Town is actually the farthest we can get from the equator and still be on the continent."

She knows so much. What do I know? I know that sharks can detect one drop of blood in a million drops of seawater. I know that the females are generally larger than the males. I know that great white shark pups are born fully formed. As soon as they are born, they fend for themselves — they get no help from their mother. The remaining ice clinks in my glass. Either I am trembling, or there is a breeze. The leaves of the eucalyptus trees whisper along the railing of the veranda.

I sip my lukewarm drink. "I have to say, it's not what I expected."

"What did you expect?"

"Oh, I don't know. Africa." My hands gesture, suddenly savage things, working of their own accord. "Lions and rhinoceroses. Women in bright fabrics, with baskets on their heads. Watering holes. Men in loincloths, holding spears."

"You're such a romantic."

I take a longer sip. I have a flat nose and high cheekbones. If I believed in past lives, I might fancy myself a former African queen.

Sherry tips her sunglasses and squints at me. "You're idealizing the Other. In some places that more closely resemble the Africa you described, as many as ninety percent of women are ritually circumcised at puberty. Well, that's the polite term for it. Genital mutilation is more like it."

My daughter is a feminist. She insists that I am, too, that a feminist is simply someone who thinks men and women are equal. I do not contradict her, but in my heart I disagree. I think women are better at some things, and men are better at others. Men are better at leaving, at moving on. Women are better at staying, at clinging. I am finding it very difficult to leave this earth. Who will look after her when I'm gone? Her father will welcome her when she comes to visit. He will not hunt her like I do. Who will tell her that she can and should do as she pleases? Who will remind her that she is worthy of love?

We stand in a hall full of hanging whales. Their calls, disembodied, circle the room. The crackle of static is softly audible — the recording must have gone wide to pick up sound. The South African Museum of Natural History claims the hall is four stories tall. The skeletons hover like spaceships, waiting to take us out of here.

"Are they moving?" my daughter asks.

"No." The calcified remains of a blue whale, the largest animal in the world, dangle over our heads, each and every bone suspended by wire. These are creatures that have fallen apart, and someone has painstakingly put them back together. "I don't think so."

My daughter chews her hair, something she hasn't done since childhood. Hidden speakers continue to emit the moans and chirps of the whales' living relatives.

"What do you think they're saying?" I ask.

My daughter keeps her eyes trained above. She walks in circles, strange orbits. "It looks like they're moving. Just slightly. Rotating. Like giant Christmas-tree ornaments."

"You're moving. It's relative."

She stops. The damp ends of her hair lick her shoulders. A shaft of light inches forward, illuminating her silhouette. She has her father's chin, an unfamiliar nose. I see no sign of me in her face.

"Why don't you want to go swimming with whales?"

"Too easy," I say. I've lived a decent but unremarkable life. I spent twenty years as an administrative assistant at a Realtor's office, not to mention my long career as a patient but apparently disappointing wife. And a mother, of course, whatever that's worth. "Whales are gentle. No challenge."

Sherry resumes her pacing. "Why does everything have to be a challenge?"

I can't believe my daughter, of all people, is asking this. She's been studying esoteric texts for years, writing essays that it seems only a smattering of people across the country care to understand. "Why are you getting your Ph.D.?"

My daughter sighs. "Because I don't know what else to do." She cocks her head. The speakers emit a series of grunts followed by a long whistle. "The whales sound lonely."

The whales hang and do not move. The light moves. We move around them.

I wake to darkness. I am on top of the hotel bed's thin bedspread. The adjacent bed is empty.

"Sherry?" I ask, but the word hangs in the room.

I go to the bathroom and run a bath. It's two A.M. Jet lag — I must have fallen asleep in the afternoon. I make sure the water is hot, nearly scalding. I undress and admire my fifty-year-old body. It's a damn good body. I still don't know why my husband left. Maybe he knew. Thirty years and then, *poof!* Six months before the diagnosis, he's gone. Got out in the nick of time, before anyone could accuse him of leaving his dying wife. I know my body itself is not fifty. Every seven years all our cells entirely regenerate. We are constantly replacing ourselves.

The hotel bathtub is deep. I submerge my whole body. Underwater, sound is heightened. The hotel pipes murmur their secrets. The calls of the whales seem to be following me. They are enormous and gentle, amorphous blobs, but soon, in my dreamy state, the whales transform into sharks. Sleek and seductive. Silently, they knife the water around me. Small currents caress my naked body. Closer and closer. The currents get bigger and stronger. A shark approaches, jaws open, three messy rows of arrowhead-sized teeth protruding from the pink flesh of its wide gums. In my vision its teeth are retractable, like a cat's claws. Closer and closer. It comes for me. Its eyes roll back—

The corridor door's lock releases with a click. Sherry enters and closes the door gently. She stumbles through the dark room. Then all is quiet. I drain the bath and dry myself with a fluffy hotel towel. What a pleasure, to dry oneself with a fluffy towel. The mirror is fogged. I breathe a circle of clarity into the mirror. I look. I am still here.

By the time I get back into bed, Sherry is under her covers, breathing evenly.

"Sherry?" I whisper. She stirs. For a moment her head thrashes as she struggles against the clutches of some dream. Like a fish caught in a net, the more she struggles, the deeper she entangles herself. I touch her shoulder. Her body stiffens, then falls still. I ask her if she's okay, but she doesn't answer. Her body seems formless under the covers, and I long to pull them back, to study her shape, memorize the contours. Instead, I listen to her breathe for a long, long time.

Tree branches and rocky outcrops emerge beneath us for an instant before vanishing back into the fog. On our way to the top of Table Mountain in a cable car, we plunge into the mist.

Sherry slumps against the wall, her nose flattened against the Plexiglas. "We won't be able to see the view at all." I shrug. I am happy to be hidden from the world for a while. The window next to me is open a crack, and tiny bullets of moisture needle my cheek.

Somewhere overhead, seagulls are mewing, but I can't see them. It's strange, how the world is reduced to sound. The cable car rocks and squeaks, reminding us that we are held aloft by a steel thread. As we creak to a halt, Sherry wipes her eyes.

We drink coffee in the little touristy café and wait for the fog to lift. The place is nearly deserted. An elderly couple flips through a carousel of postcards. The girl behind the cash register sucks on sugar cubes and reads from a fat paperback, silently mouthing the words. My daughter and I sip weak coffee and eat stale croissants. I ask her where she went last night. She says she went for a walk.

"It's dangerous to walk around Cape Town alone at night."

"How do you know?"

"The guidebook says so."

She is peeling all the layers off the stump of her croissant. "How do you know I was alone?"

I don't. I don't know at all. It terrifies me. I can't picture her with a stranger. But suddenly I can't *not* picture her with a stranger — in a cheap motel room, in a dirty alley. Bare arms and legs flop against each other like dead fish. The image fills my head for the space of a second before a blank screen graciously steps in.

Sherry shakes the slivers of croissant into a trash bin. "I was alone," she confesses. "I'm always alone." I don't know what to say. The fog does not lift. We wander the grounds, trying feebly to identify the different species of flora until we are shivering. At the souvenir shop I buy a postcard of the rare *Disa uniflora,* a spectacular red orchid we failed to see.

We ride down in silence except for the groaning of the cable. We pick our way across the parking lot, weaving around ghostly cars and buses. When we get to our rental car, Sherry sits with her hands on the wheel. I offer to drive. She grips the wheel. I ask if she's okay. She lowers her head, almost to her knees. I try to massage her back, but the fabric of her shirt keeps getting stuck in my fingers. A minute later, she lifts her head and starts the car. "Stomach cramp," she says.

"I'm the only one who's allowed to be sick," I joke. My daughter doesn't laugh. I tell her I'm sorry she doesn't feel well and offer to go back to the hotel. She says no, it's okay. She reminds me that the planetarium has a telescope with the largest aperture in the world.

"An aperture," I say. "Like a hole?"

"Yeah. An opening. It's what lets in the light, so you can see what's out there."

"I don't need any more holes in my life."

My daughter frowns. It was just a private little brain tumor joke. I know the tumor is technically making a ball of cells in my head, but whenever I picture it, I see a hole. Nothing slippery, nothing as tangible as flesh. Just an emptiness. Or something like the hole that Alice tumbles through, and just like that — Wonderland! Once upon a time that was Sherry's favorite book. She would sit in my lap, tracing her fingers along the words, pretending she could read. She always got to the bottom of the page before I did.

Now my grown daughter's face is flushed.

"You want to swim with the sharks," she says.

"Yes."

"And you think that will fulfill you?"

"Yes. Maybe. Yes."

When a great white shark bites into its prey, it shakes its head from side to side. Great whites exert such force with their jaws that when eating they often break off their own teeth and swallow them along with their meal. These stray teeth can tear through a shark's digestive tract. Great white sharks have no natural predators besides the rare killer whale or human hunting for a trophy. What kills them is captivity. Researchers don't know why, but no great white has lasted longer than sixteen days in an aquarium. They starve to death, and until that moment they circle their enclosure, continually bumping into the walls.

My daughter lets the car idle. She gets this faraway look on her face, the kind of face I imagine she makes when she's studying her books, working on her dissertation. Her Ph.D. is in a new field, not postmodernism. Posthumanism. As if we could leave ourselves behind. Air whines in and out of my daughter's nose.

The last time there was a ball of cells growing inside me, it was Sherry.

And somehow that tiny ball of cells became a pink screaming baby who became an adorable little girl who became an anguished teenager who became the mysterious grown woman sitting here in the driver's seat of a rented car in Cape Town, South Africa, asking me, "Are you scared?"

I explain that the company we're using claims they've never had an injury. That the cage is made of galvanized steel. "I don't actually know what *galvanized* means, but it sounds —"

"I don't mean the sharks."

My daughter is looking at me. Her eyes are big. Begging.

I don't know what to tell her. I don't know what she wants to hear. "Of course I'm scared." I look down at my hands, at the age spots I used to fret over. I think of the lotions I used to apply, the annual visits to the dermatologist. What a relief it was to throw away those creams.

I can feel her eyes on me. Greedy.

How do I tell her I'm scared I will wake up one morning vomiting, and then every morning thereafter? How do I tell her I don't want to lose my sense of smell? I'm scared of clumsiness, paralysis, losing my sight, losing my memory, losing my mind. I don't want to tell my daughter I'm scared that one of these days I'll piss my pants without even knowing it.

And how can I tell her I'm scared of death — of nothingness? How do I tell her I hate her father? That I suspect I could have done more with my life? That I'm afraid of being forgotten? During my first stint in the hospital, I got mounds of flowers — from the office, from the neighbors, from the members of my book club. During the second stint, I got a card from my brother and a cheap teddy bear from my former boss. The bear was wearing a sash with the sloppily stitched message GET WELL SOON!

Only Sherry brought me things I actually wanted: chocolate-covered macadamia nuts, oversized furry socks, and a bottle of French perfume that made the nurses frown because someone might have an allergy. "Fuck the book club," Sherry had said, handing me a P. D. James mystery and a stack of trashy magazines. She adjusted my hospital bed and watched bad TV with me, criticizing the banality of American news and cheering on my favorite *The Price Is Right* contestant in between rants about consumerism.

Now Sherry grips the steering wheel and stares at me, waiting for an answer.

"Are you okay driving, or do you want me to drive?" I ask.

She jams the shift into reverse. "I'm okay," she says. We peel out of the parking lot, the squeal of tires cutting through the mist.

"Which bracelet do you like better?"

My daughter shrugs. We are at an outdoor market, where aisles are lined with pseudoethnic crafts imported from other African countries. I don't mind if they're not authentic. I love the gaudiness, I love the abundance. I put down the plastic beaded bracelets and move on to some place mats woven from dried palm leaves.

My daughter is examining a mask. It is not one of the mass-produced, cheap replicas. It is made of some kind of marvelous wood, polished and smooth as steel, hard as bone. It sports a pair of carved spiral horns that extend over a foot in length.

I ask her if she likes it.

"It's beautiful," she says.

I offer to buy it for her.

"It's got the horns of a hartebeest," she says.

At first I hear *heartbeats*.

She repeats what the vendor told her. The San people, the Bushmen, have a rich history of stories about shape-shifters. A favorite character is the Praying Mantis. Once, he turned himself into a dead hartebeest. A group of children, overjoyed at their find, labored to skin the animal and cut it up into pieces. But the pieces put themselves back together again, and the living hartebeest chased the confused children into their huts.

"It's too expensive," she says.

"What do I need with money now?" I say, handing the mask to the vendor. The vendor bows his head and proceeds to wrap the mask in newspaper. His fingers move quickly, and he blinks long, lovely eyelashes as he works the mask into a tidy package.

"You didn't have to do that," Sherry says to me. She nods shyly at the vendor and tells him, "It *is* beautiful."

"So are you," he says, handing her the package. "You are just visiting?" She nods, curtly now. "For how long are you in town? Maybe I could take you out to dinner? I know the best place for kebabs, not for tourists."

She shakes her head, not bothering to disguise the sneer on her face. I race to catch up with her as she walks off in a huff.

"What's wrong with you?" She refuses to slow down. "He was cute."

"I'm not in the mood."

"Why not? You only live once. What, are you a lesbian?" I'm only half joking. She's never been one to wear dresses. She's never introduced me to any boyfriends. Anything is possible.

"What?" She stops. "Jesus. No."

"It's okay if you are." I hold out my hands, reaching for her. "I just want to know the kind of people you love."

She takes a step back and hugs her package. "I came on this trip." Her mouth twists, dragging the rest of her face down. "Isn't that enough?"

Somewhere, someone is playing a drum. The African rhythms cut time into sharp beats, but around us people continue to flow like currents of water, fluid and unstoppable. The drumming accelerates to an impossible tempo. My head hurts. My daughter stands still, clutching her package. The newspaper has already left a smear of ink on her blouse.

My heels keep almost getting stuck on the cobblestone hill. Even though she's in her hiking sandals, Sherry manages to lag behind. It is nighttime, and we are searching for a bar. I inquired discreetly at the front desk, and they recommended this place. They gave me directions that sounded simple. But now we march past rows and rows of houses. The hill is steeper than I expected, and the quiet lawns stare at us. My belly is full of zebra, kudu, ostrich, crocodile — the sampler platter from the safari-themed restaurant was a carnivore's wildest dream. Despite the huge meal, I feel sleek in the night air, like a lioness. It feels good to work my muscles, to get from one place to another. By the time music finally becomes audible, I am gasping for air. The residential area opens into a cluster of commercial buildings. At this hour all the shops are closed — only the bar is open. A muscled, shirtless young man stands at the door. As we approach, he winks and waves us over. Above him, rainbow-colored neon lights glare.

"Mom," Sherry hisses. "It's a gay bar."

The bouncer is oiled. His skin reflects the colored lights. A silver ring hangs from each nipple.

I shrug. "They serve drinks, right? My feet are killing me."

Inside, we squeeze past throngs of sweaty men and women to get to the bar. I order a gin and tonic. Over my shoulder my daughter orders a Diet Coke. I tell her to loosen up, to live a little. We take our drinks and find a seat at a table in the back. Onstage, someone with short, spiky hair and maroon leather pants screeches a Bon Jovi tune for karaoke. I can't tell if it's a man or a woman. There are so many earrings on the outer rim of his or her ear, it's like there's a second layer of ears. The performer wails out the lyrics, successfully hitting all the high notes.

"She's a woman, right?"

"Yes." My daughter sips her drink and sulks. "Did you take your pills tonight?"

"Yes," I lie. I don't want to take my blood thinner with alcohol.

People are in various stages of undress, but it doesn't seem dirty. It's more like they're celebrating their bodies. One man is in leather head-to-toe. One man is in a sequined mini dress. One woman is wearing only a Band-Aid over each nipple, but a patchwork of floral tattoos reaches from her torso to each wrist and provides a remarkable sense of decorum. Everyone is primped. Everyone is preened. My daughter, with no makeup on and her hair unbrushed, looks like a mushroom — earthy, sprung out of nowhere.

The whole crowd joins in the song, overpowering the singer, "WHOA, WE'RE HALFWAY THERE..." I sing, too. We are all part of a chorus. There are no sad drunks. No vacant-eyed hoochiedup girls. Everyone is happy. I have never been to a bar where everyone looks so happy.

I kick my daughter under the table, harder than I intended. "We should do a duet." She cringes.

But as the last strains of Bon Jovi shudder to a halt, the karaoke host decides it's time to take a break. The spiky-haired young singer takes a deep bow and bounds off the stage, where she embraces a girl who seems to be wearing an elaborate web of electrical tape. Disco music takes over the room, and strobe lights pulse. The flashes catch and freeze the dancers one frame at a time, giving the illusion that they are hardly moving at all.

My red polyester-blend dress doesn't wrinkle, but it also doesn't breathe. I'm trying to air out my armpits when a classy woman in her late thirties approaches me. She is beautiful. Her eyes are like emeralds. She doesn't look like most of the clientele. She's wearing a graceful black dress, knee length, with short fluted sleeves. Her mouth opens and moves, but I can't hear her over the loud music. She is wearing perfume, a clean, sharp scent — expensive perfume. Her lips are the color of wine, of blood, of a rare orchid I long to see. She leans in close. Her mouth opens and moves again. She is asking me to dance.

My daughter's eyes grow wide. I'm terrified, but I shrug and offer this woman my hand. I have no idea how we're going to do this. The music is so loud that I mistake the pulsing bass for the pulsing of my heart. This woman leads me to the dance floor. People move around us. They don't notice me. They don't bat an eyelash. Only she keeps her emerald eyes trained on me. And it's easy. So easy. I wonder why I've never done this before.

She leans in closer, carving the air with the sleek curve of her chin, the stained streak of her mouth. Her lips are soft, too soft at first —

I'm afraid I will swallow them. Then I get the hang of it, and a series of explosions radiate through my body, following the long lines of nerves all the way to my toes and fingers. My body is made of jelly. I don't know how I manage to stay upright. The other dancers bounce around us, knocking their elbows against our elbows, hips against our hips, but our pleasure is ours alone, impenetrable.

I wonder, *What else have I missed?*

I wonder, *If I had a whole life to live, what else could I do?*

The next morning the sun glimmers at the edge of the hotel curtains, and for a moment I wonder if the previous night was a dream. But my dress is draped over the chair, and in the mirror, my face is still smudged with makeup I didn't wash off properly last night. When I fling the curtains open, the ocean is still there, flat and submissive beneath a gray sky.

I shower and get dressed. I want to visit the Houses of Parliament, but Sherry groans and pulls the covers over her head. I tell her to stay and rest and I'll be back in time for lunch. I study the map before I go — it's only a dozen blocks or so — and I have the route memorized when I walk out of the lobby. I could take a cab, but I want to walk. The morning air has a different energy than the air last night. Tall glass buildings reflect other tall glass buildings, as though they're trying to turn the street into a mirage. Men and women in suits power-walk down the sidewalks, tackling whole city blocks in the time it takes me to go ten steps. The only people who aren't charging ahead are a couple of tourists, a man and a woman wearing fanny packs. They meander, pausing to take a photo in front of a poster advertising a safari. The man pretends to cower beneath the image of a tusked elephant. His wife laughs, and her fanny pack bounces against her hip. I picture my ex-husband being gored by an elephant. The elephant penetrates him; my husband screams. He sprouts two fountains of blood where the tusks have pierced his torso. That's the way death should come — messy and all at once.

And then the couple is gone. The street is nearly deserted. It looks different than before. The buildings are shorter, the facades worn, haggard. I'm tired. And thirsty. Terribly thirsty. I wander onto a side street to buy a drink from a corner market, but the market is closed, boarded up. I sit down on the steps.

"Excuse me?"

In front of me stands a dark-skinned man wearing a shirt covered with pieces of glass. He has a marvelous Afro and a bushy necklace made of all different kinds of feathers, some white and fluffy, some short and speckled, some long and black and iridescent. Here is Africa.

"Are you okay?" he asks. His voice is resonant, musical.

"Yes," I lie. The world is turning.

"Where are you going?" His voice is a foghorn, only prettier.

I try to tell him I was going to the Houses of Parliament, but now I want to go back to my hotel, but I think I mix up some of the words. He asks if he can call someone. I am not crazy. I do not want my daughter to pick me up. I shake my head.

"You are not well," he says.

"I'm thirsty," I manage to say. He smiles. His teeth are brown and shriveled.

"You're suffering," he says. "Here," he pats the top of his head. His hair compresses, bounces back. His necklace shimmers. "And here." He rests his palm over his heart.

I ask him how he knows such things.

"It is my . . . job. My calling."

"Are you a medicine man?"

"A healer."

Out of a leather pouch tied around his waist he takes a small wooden pipe. Out of another pouch tied around his ankle he takes a little sachet. He pinches a few loose herbs from the sachet and packs the pipe.

"I don't know how I got lost," I say.

He takes out a modern green plastic lighter, lights the pipe, and takes a drag. "Maybe your ancestors were leading you to me." He smiles and hands me the pipe. "This will clear your head."

None of the highly specialized doctors back home have ever looked at me the way he does, as though I am a real person, not just a disease. I accept the pipe. It is smooth to the touch and intricately carved with feathers and ropy vines and what could be waves, or a female torso. I bring the pipe close to my lips. "How do I . . . ?"

"Just breathe," he says.

I feel like I'm in a movie. I inhale through the tapered end. It tastes awful.

"Deeper," he says. His eyes are kind.

I inhale again. This time I can feel something going up the back of my nose, and it seems to go straight to my brain. Some knot in my forehead unravels; all the tension in my shoulders and neck comes undone. I can't quite feel the ground. It's as though I'm hovering just a fraction of an inch above myself.

Then the healer invites me back to his house, which he says is not far. He says he will give me something to drink, to quench my thirst. He helps me to my feet, and I follow the pieces of myself reflected in the shards of glass on his shirt.

When I get back to the hotel, it is already dark. Sherry is furious. "I was worried sick about you!" She looks sick. She is wearing a hotel bathrobe, and she is wan, anemic-looking, with dark circles under her eyes.

I feel worlds better. I giggle.

"What's so goddamn funny?" she asks, seizing my hands, staring in horror at the little red cuts — now welts — that line my arms.

I can't stop giggling. I tell her I found a medicine man. Or rather, he found me. I announce, "I saw God."

Sherry frowns. "Those cuts could be infected."

"I saw the past," I say. "I saw the future. I saw everything."

Sherry stands close, her shoulders almost brushing mine. She hasn't been this close to me the whole trip. For a moment it feels intimate. Then she steps back and says, "You got high."

I hold up my arms. I explain that the cuts are just surface level, so he could put the powder directly inside me.

"The powder?" She raises her eyebrows.

"Medicine. Herbs."

Sherry shakes her head. "How much did you pay him?"

Now it's my turn to frown. "I practically had to throw money at him."

My daughter swivels and raises her arms. "I called the Houses of Parliament, and they said they don't give tours on Mondays. I had no way to find you. What if something had happened to you? What if you had..."

She marches over to the open sliding-glass door. She tries to slam it shut, but it drags and closes with a dull sucking noise. "I would have had no way of knowing..."

I drop my purse on the floor and flop on the bed. "I wish you could have seen him in action. He threw bones on the floor."

"Bones. Wonderful. And then he cut you up. That butcher!"

The hotel bedspread feels softer than before. I caress the bed.

"He could read the bones like you read a book. He knew what was wrong with me."

"You already know what's wrong with you!"

I explain that I'm not talking about my physical disease. The medicine man knew all about my emotional problems.

My daughter snorts. "Oh. So the witch doctor is your new therapist."

I rub my face against the bedspread. The fabric seems to be stroking my cheeks. "And spiritual questions. He helped me recognize my place in the continuum."

"The continuum?" She says it like she's a schoolteacher and I have gotten an answer wrong. "The continuum? I thought we were going to Cape Town, not the set of *Star Trek: The Next Fucking Generation*!" I turn away from her onto my side. The other bed squeaks as she sits down. Then her bed squeaks again, and she is hovering over me. "Let me at least clean up those cuts with some alcohol." She tries to take my arm again.

"Don't touch me."

"I'm sorry." Out of the corner of my eye I can see her reaching for me again.

"Don't," I say.

I close my eyes. Her bed squeaks. I fall asleep.

Above the purpling hills the sun hovers, fat and orange, a languid eye. It casts a faint glow on the rows and rows of grapevines that spread as far as I can see. I'm not quite sure how we got here, to this orderly paradise. We perch on the patio of some winery or another, the fourth or fifth on our makeshift tour. A handful of other visitors buzz like insects behind us: a German couple, and a mother and daughter from Israel, here for some convention on Peace and Children and a Better Future. I envy them all, the way Mother and Daughter finish each other's sentences, the way the Germans study the vineyard — with purpose. They intend to become vintners themselves. They've already been to France and Italy, and after they leave South Africa, they will head to Australia, then Chile.

My daughter is trying to read, but a breeze keeps sweeping her hair in front of her face, and she is constantly tucking it back behind her ear. Despite the wind, I am warm. I slip my feet out of my shoes. The concrete floor is cold on my bare feet. It feels good, the cold. I press my feet against the pavement, grateful to feel them, to know their shape, their outline, where they begin and end.

"I really like the sauving-long bonk," I say. I'm definitely tipsy. The list indicates that this varietal has strong notes of pear and honeysuckle, with a hint of grapefruit. I think they're making it up. It tastes like nothing I've tasted before. It tastes like liquid heaven.

From the neighboring table the Israeli daughter glances at me, her doe eyes round with concern for a moment before her face relaxes into a polite smile. She tugs on the sleeve of her mother's tunic and whispers something. Together they chuckle, and then they raise their glasses in some kind of toast; the chime of glass against glass is sweet in the fading light, sweeter than I thought possible. My daughter doesn't move her eyes from her book, something by her favorite author, Michel Foucault. I envy him. He's already dead, and he gets her attention more than I do. I want her to look at me. "Which wine was your favorite?" I ask.

"I don't know." She frowns and flips a page in a long, drawn-out motion, as though it requires a tremendous effort.

"Well, what were your top three?" I swirl the wine in my tall glass.

"I didn't really taste a difference." All she did was taste, though — at each winery she actually swished each sample around in her mouth and then spit it out. Here, at last, she has ordered a glass, but she's hardly touched it.

I take another sip. My body hums.

I wink at the elongated reflection in my glass, and it returns the gesture. "I'm really enjoying the white wine for a change," I say. "I used to drink only red. Fewer calories, you know. Supposed to be good for your heart." Something is bubbling inside of me. Every time I open my mouth, it threatens to erupt like a shaken bottle of champagne. "A lot of good that did me. Looks like it came down to mind" — I point at my head, at the stubborn tumor — "over matter."

Sherry looks at me. Her mouth is slanted, her eyes askew — she is a modern painting, where even the prettiest of things is rendered grotesque.

"What?" I say. "It's funny."

My daughter closes her eyes. "I'm tired."

I don't know why she's so tired. She has her whole life ahead of her.

"Do you want to go back to the hotel and lie down?" I ask.

Her eyes are squeezed shut. Pinched little clamshells.

"I'm tired of your jokes."

The concrete sends a cold shock through my legs to the base of my spine. The chairs behind us scrape the patio. The Germans pause from their note taking, and they sit, their pencils frozen in their hands like daggers.

"If you can't laugh," I say. Below us, the grapevines whisper, *What can you do?*

She stares at me, teeth bared. "You could cry." The wind whips her hair, and the strands are alive, crawling all over her face. "You could yell."

I grip the edges of my chair, to keep from falling over. I'm practically yelling. "That wouldn't do any good." My voice burns in my throat.

Sherry raises her voice to trump mine. "Nothing does any good!"

Her cheeks are flushed. Suddenly, I fear she might have a fever. I reach for her forehead, and she flinches, staring at my hand in horror.

"Are you feeling okay?" I ask.

"I feel awful."

"What's wrong?" She doesn't answer me. "What's wrong?" The smell of the vineyard — earthy, loamy, fertile — suddenly overwhelms me. "Talk to me. I can't read your mind!" She shuts her book. I lower my voice. "It's not my fault I'm dying."

She scowls. She sighs like a horse, exhaling through her lips. "It's not always about you."

I don't know what to say. Her greasy hair, her chapped lips in full pout — they are imprinted in my mind, in my genes, for Christ's sake. Now she won't stop looking at me.

Sherry picks up her nearly full glass of Shiraz and drains it. She wipes the red beads on her mouth with the back of her arm. "I wish it were me instead of you."

I can feel the glass slipping out of my hand, but I am helpless to stop it. It shatters, sending a thousand flashes across the floor.

"Don't move," says Sherry. "Some glass probably got in your shoes."

She stands and disappears. There is more shuffling of chair legs against the patio, and then concerned voices. The German couple still wields their yellow pencils, as if I were a wild animal. The Israeli mother and daughter have stupid mournful expressions on their faces, as though this incident were a threat to world peace.

Sherry reappears with an empty ice bin. A winery employee tells her to sit down, not to worry, but Sherry reaches into my purse and pulls out a soft hairbrush. She proceeds to brush the shards of glass into the bin.

"What do you mean?" I ask.

Sherry is on her hands and knees, methodically sweeping.

"What do you mean, you wish it were you instead of me?"

She is holding up her hand. It looks like she is holding a single red petal.

"You're hurt," I say.

She studies the drop of blood on her palm. It's a myth that sharks can smell a drop of blood from miles away. A quarter of a mile maybe, a third of a mile tops. But they have electroreceptors that can detect electrical currents from miles away. That's why sometimes they attack boats. Great whites aren't monsters, attacking everything in their path. They just get confused.

Sherry whispers, "I wish *I* were dying, instead of you. I wish I were already dead."

The sun hits the first mountain and sends red tendrils across the sky. Below us, the valley is dark, the grapevines invisible, murmuring. The ruddy light catches my daughter. My heart beats in my throat. My daughter's shadow cradles her. She continues to study her palm.

"We should clean that," I say. I dig in my purse until I find a pair of tweezers and some wet wipes. I kneel next to her and examine the piece of glass. I don't want to cause more harm than good. Slowly, I pinch the glass and tug. It comes out easily. I dab her hand with the sterile wipe.

She tenses. It must sting. I breathe on her wound, like I used to when she was a little girl. She does not pull away.

"I'm pregnant."

And so I am a grandmother. One more thing I wanted before I died, though I would never have dared express it. "Oh," I say. The wind whips her rumpled blouse against her body.

Sherry smiles. A bitter smile. "I don't think I want it."

I don't believe her. Not yet. I want to ask her about the father. I want to ask her if she loved him. If she loves him still. "How long have you known?"

"Five, six weeks." She can read my thoughts. "The father is out of the picture."

"Oh," I say. "Oh, honey." She is crying. Shaking. I tell her that whatever she wants to do, I'll support her. She cries harder. She is choking. "How will you support me?" she asks.

I stroke her hair.

"You'll be gone!"

But she doesn't resist as I take her into my arms. She shakes against me. Her tears sprinkle my face. I cradle her.

A stiff wind rocks the boat. Dark clouds hunch above us, and the surface of the sea reflects the gloomy sky. I can't see underneath. For all I know the sea could be empty. For all I know it could be teeming with sharks. The air is foul — the odors of rotting meat and motor oil compete for the air we breathe. The boat sputters to a halt, and an employee attaches a large metal chain to a buoy. The employee tosses a bucket of chum into the water. Blood blooms all around us. A lure.

I ask the guy where the offal came from, and he winks. "Yesterday's tour group." He must have told the same bad joke a hundred times before. Then his voice gets all serious and teacherly, and he explains that very few humans get attacked by great whites, and those that do are usually able to survive. Great whites attack their prey by surprising them from below. They administer one massive, disabling bite, then they back off and wait for their victim to grow weak and expire. It's at this stage that most people are able to escape.

"Not that anyone's going to get attacked on our watch," he says. The employees unite to drop the cage into the sea. It doesn't look like a cage so much as an escape pod. Only two people can fit in the cage at one time, they explain. If a shark is sighted, we will take turns going down. Of course, they've already told us that seeing a shark is not guaranteed. We had to sign release forms before we left the shore.

My daughter stares at the water. In her wetsuit and loose ponytail, she doesn't look bookish at all. She's not a movie star, perhaps, but she looks like a woman who can take care of herself. Even though I can't see it, I know that inside she's changing, too.

I ask her if we're looking at the Indian Ocean or the Atlantic.

"I don't know," she says. She continues to stare at the sea, as though she fears that if she looks away, it will cease to exist. "This is where they come together." My hand is on the rail. She puts her hand on top of mine, squeezes. The cuts on my arm are already healing. "We forgot the camera," she says.

I shrug. Sometimes when people are too busy trying to preserve memories, they forget to enjoy the ride. "You know," I say, returning her squeeze, "I think you're really brave."

"Me?" she says. The boat pitches, and she clutches the railing. She looks at me, wide eyed. "You're the brave one."

I shake my head. But before I can say anything there is a commotion behind us. "We've got a visitor!" an employee announces as he steps out of the cabin, grinning. "It's a beauty. Big, too — sixteen footer. Who's ready?"

An overeager member of the tour jumps forward. Chest hair sprouts from the unzipped top of his wetsuit. He pumps his arms and makes a fist above his head. The other ten or twelve tour members cheer.

Sherry leans in close to me. "Do you think it's safe?"

"Of course," I say. "I've told you before — I wouldn't ask you to do this if I didn't think it was safe."

She whispers, "Not for me. For the baby."

I try not to grin, but I can't help it. We'll only be submerged a few feet. I nod my head.

"We need one more," says the employee. The first volunteer shrugs, taunting the crowd.

Sherry grabs my arm. "Here! Right here!"

"You should go," I say. I want her to see the shark before it leaves.

"But it's what you wanted to do. It's your last wish."

I want to tell her that my last wish is for her to be happy. I want to tell her that she'll have her whole life to remember this.

"I'm scared," I lie.

My daughter smiles. Despite the cloud cover, her eyes are bright. Luminous. She puts on her mask. I barely recognize her with all her gear on. The other volunteer leads the way, and she follows. She pauses at the edge of the boat and waves at me before she descends.

She is down for what seems like a long time, swimming with the sharks. The boat rolls. The sea issues forth little surges of foam. Tiny waves appear and moments later are reabsorbed. Human beings are 70 percent water. I'm astonished that we don't dissolve on contact.

The red patch of sea where the guts were dumped begins to shudder. The shark is feeding. I squint. I expect to glimpse a sliver of fin, the gleam of a tooth. The blood just churns and churns. The other passengers *ooh* and *aah*. I wonder what my daughter sees, what mysteries have been revealed to her.

CHRISTIAN MOODY

University of Cincinnati

HORUSVILLE

Stephen went to the woods instead of math class. His algebra book was still under the backseat of the school bus, or under his bed, or maybe even somewhere in the woods, swollen and muddy from last week's rain. Losing the textbook had meant weeks of calling out answers with squared *Y*s to problems that had no *Y*s, which equaled weeks of the math teacher yanking him into the hallway and yelling at him. It had been easier when his fellow ninth graders had laughed and made fun, but now, baffled and full of pity, they avoided eye contact. The obvious solution to math class, the answer he arrived at on an average of three days per week, was to take the latest issue of *She-Hulk* from his locker and walk out of the school doors into the dim, shadowy woods, where the sponge-thick and gently bioluminescent moss felt refreshingly cool on his bare feet. He would go to his favorite tree, solemnly turn the carefully dog-eared pages of *She-Hulk,* and jerk off to her muscular green thighs, her bulging green ass. On his way to fulfill this plan, just a short way from his favorite tree, he saw his art teacher, his big brother's fiancée, naked.

What was immediately attractive about Miss Baskin's nakedness was how She-Hulkishly green it was. The wood's thick canopy of leaves filtered light into a muted jade gloom, and the glimmering moss radiated a faintly emerald glow. It was possible that Miss Baskin's thighs were somewhat muscular, too, and her ass possibly bulging, although from a hundred or so yards away and the view partially obscured by trees, it was difficult to say. It looked like she was slow-dancing by herself. She ran her fingers through her long, deep red hair — a little too red, she'd explained to Stephen's wide-eyed art class the morning after she'd dyed it, because she'd used a five-dollar do-it-yourself kit from the clearance aisle. Stephen snuck closer, moving from trunk to trunk.

As he got nearer he could see that Miss Baskin was dancing for the tree eyes. She swayed her hips back and forth while the eyes — the whites especially bright from the recent rain that had also turned the irises blue — swung to and fro, like pendulums. The tree eyes, he knew, were why people went to the woods. Prior to Miss Baskin, Stephen had spied on other people. The former town mayor, shortly before he died, would come to deliver grandiose speeches in acceptance of high offices. The high school janitor had a velvet cape he wore while he failed over and over at sleight of hand, littering the moss with dropped coins and cards. Stephen once saw an old lady confess on her knees to acts of sadism so imaginative and outlandish that, still, on some nights, he wasn't able to sleep until he convinced himself that she'd been lying.

Why people spoke to the trees — which only had eyes, after all, not ears — Stephen couldn't figure out. He was glad they didn't have ears; it was bad enough that they were forced to see whatever anyone showed them. If it were up to him, they'd have mouths and arms so that they could keep people away by screaming obscenities and throwing their own apples, like the tree in *The Wizard of Oz*. But these trees didn't have obscenities or apples, just creepily intense eyes that tracked every movement with the precision of high-tech security cameras. Some eyes were small as shirt buttons, others big as dinner plates. Wet and gleaming, with shining irises that varied in color by tree type and weather, the eyes dappled trunks and limbs and dangled from twig ends like blinking fruit. There was a game he played in which he sat still for a very long time until the eyes forgot him. It wasn't the most exciting game, but when the eyes forgot him they opened and closed their nutshell lids with mesmerizing out-of-sync slowness that made him imagine migratory moths, alighted in the woods to rest. Inevitably, he'd get tired and scratch his nose or balls and — *snap!* — every eye would be on him again.

To get closer to Miss Baskin, to really see in detail what he was anxious to see, Stephen had to hop over the tiny double stream that trickled such a sinuous path through the woods that it often ran right alongside itself in opposite directions. He hopped once, twice, then slipped and planted his face in the moss. The tick-tocking eyes rolled around in their sockets to stare at him. When he got back up, she was running. She had an armful of clothes. Her bare shoulder blades jutted. Her bright foot bottoms flashed. Her ass cheeks switched from dimpled to full while she ran. He saw the bumpy line of her spine. Hip bones. The small of her back.

He picked up a sock, a bra, a boot. The sock was brightly striped in yellow, blue, and white, but the bottom was threadbare, just shy of a big hole. Her bra was white but dingy on the straps and edges. He stuck his nose and mouth in each cup and inhaled. When he saw her bloodred boot shining on the moss, he was afraid to touch it. Miss Baskin's daily stumble through the streets to the high school halls was a favorite local spectacle — Stephen had seen the old people shuffle onto their porches before dawn to wait, watch, and whisper. Each tottering step in those boots threatened to send her tumbling into a front yard, where (hopefully) she'd fall onto the grass, her long limbs splayed. Stephen could see it in people's eyes (he imagined his own eyes must look the same): All of Horusville was ready for the chance to rush forward and help her to her feet, or (even better) to just lie down on the grass beside her. It was obvious from the way no one could look at each other after she passed: There was something embarrassing about the bloodred boots; they made the whole town painfully aware of one another, a community of watchers, so many hearts so alike and so easily stirred. You couldn't blame Miss Baskin for pretending not to notice; it was too much longing for any one person to care about. Her boots were like a talisman that accepted looks on her behalf and reflected them back for what they were: the acute red pang of loneliness, a whole town's worth. Stephen knew he had to give the boot back.

In the graveyard between the woods and town, Stephen watched Miss Baskin button her blouse. He crouched behind the monument of Anne Lynne Brown, memorialized in the act of presenting her famous green-bean casserole. Miss Baskin almost fell down while trying to put on her panties. She caught herself by placing a hand on the big stone belly of a butcher who had a great steak of black marble in one hand, a giant knife in the other. The grave markers were all life-size statues of dead people posing at occupations or hobbies. Stephen noticed that Anne Lynne Brown's statue had a bronze plaque detailing the casserole recipe. The story of the statues, as Stephen had heard it in his fourth-grade local history unit, was that Horusville's founders, anxious about what sort of attention the tree eyes might bring, created the elaborate graveyard as a barrier to waylay wanderers. This solution was, however, too successful, since each year ever greater numbers of visitors came in search of the eccentric monuments.

Miss Baskin hopped a few times to zip up her jeans. She must have sensed someone watching, because she darted up and down the rows of statues. Stephen had to dive, roll, and crawl. The sun was setting, and he hid himself in the long shadow cast by a disheveled mechanic with wild hair. Stephen could see the chipped polish on Miss Baskin's toenails; he could hear each breath.

"Ass wipe!" she screamed in anger, which sounded so ridiculous that Stephen had to bite hard on the heel of his hand to keep from laughing.

The statues of dead men looked a little too tall and muscular. They posed with oversize objects. A nearly seven-foot farmer stood, like Atlas, with what would have been the world's biggest pumpkin on his shoulders. Almost all of the dead women offered food. There was a waitress who poured coffee from a pot that was also a working fountain. She smiled and smiled in an endless attempt to fill a bottomless cup. The liquid poured straight through the mug into a pool at her feet.

"Masturbator!" Miss Baskin screamed again before walking off braless, with only one boot, one sock. This time the insult hurt, the accuracy of it. Either she was a good guesser or she'd seen him in the woods before, doing what he did at his favorite tree. It had almond-shaped eyes, his tree. They were hazel. They aided his imagination. They made the job less lonely by looking on with what he was sure must have been interest and sympathy. The almond-eyed tree was so consoling that he now loathed masturbating anywhere else, which was partly why he skipped school so often, even before he'd lost his math book.

When Miss Baskin left the graveyard, Stephen visited his parents. In the afterlife, Mr. Blue squinted at a test tube and wore a lab coat.

He had frizzled hair, as if electrified. He had been the school's best and dorkiest science teacher. Stephen's mother presented a meat loaf. For weeks after his parents were buried, visitors came to Mrs. Blue's monument, placed tracing paper over the engraved recipe, and copied it down by rubbing over it with pencil. It still startled him to walk down a street in the evening and smell his mother's cooking. For reasons Stephen didn't understand, his parents' monuments were embarrassing to Ed, his much older brother. He suspected Ed's reasons for disapproval were the same reasons he, Stephen, loved them so well.

There was a piece of limestone paper taped to his dad's back, reading KICK ME in an adolescent scrawl. No one would call Mr. Blue a funny man, but students had found his efforts endearing. He'd only had an inch or two added in death, making him one of the shorter men in the cemetery. Next to Stephen's dad was Uncle McCarty, decked out in thespian tights, neck ruffle, floppy hat, and pointed beard. He had been amusing, as far as English teachers go, but for some reason Stephen's dad was the only teacher who liked him, maybe out of a brother-in-law's obligation. A car crash had killed all three of them the night Ed beat Stephen seven times in a row at Monopoly.

Stephen stretched out on the grass between his parents, as he often did, and looked up at the sky. He tried to clear his mind and forget that his favorite teacher had apparently seen him jerk off to a comic book and a tree. Slowly, the afterglow faded and the first stars appeared. He remembered how his father and Uncle McCarty would get drunk and reenact Monty Python skits on the front porch. For a moment he thought he heard their voices, their fake accents. But it was only the squawk of geese flying in a V overhead.

That evening, Stephen sat right across from Miss Baskin at the round dinner table. Miss Baskin had accepted Ed's marriage proposal, attempt number two, a week earlier. The family had never said grace when Mr. and Mrs. Blue were alive, but Ed insisted grace was just good manners, like elbows off the table. During prayers, especially long prayers like Ed's, which always included his big plans for constructing housing developments, Stephen liked to examine people's faces. Lately he'd been looking at Miss Baskin's face. Miss Baskin never noticed, because she was always examining Ed's face while he prayed about development. Miss Baskin watched closely, with such pained, focused intensity that you'd think Ed's praying face held some crucial clue to Miss Baskin's own life, which Stephen supposed it probably did. For Miss Baskin, he could tell, seeing was important work.

But this evening, when Stephen looked up to examine Miss Baskin's face, Miss Baskin locked eyes with him. Her eyes were hazel and unhappy. For the first time ever he bowed his head and tried to follow his big brother's prayer. Ed, who was also the town's unusually young mayor — not a real mayor, but the kind of mayor who officiated the monthly town meeting in the high school cafeteria — prayed that he would get the contract to expand the Horusville Library, which served both the town and the school. He was courting the favor of Miss Mahogany, the shriveled librarian, whose expertise had great sway in the matter, even though everyone knew she had an entire wall full of rare dirty books. Patrons had been known to attempt to steal the rare dirty books. Miss Mahogany, small as she was — and old, too, with wrinkled skin the same burnished red brown of her name — would beat such would-be book thieves so mercilessly with her yardstick that the pyrotechnic scarves holding her braids together would fly off, and then her hair would whip about so fiercely, all snakelike and crazy, that you could imagine the poor recipient of her wrath mistaking her yardstick's crack for the snap of poisoned fangs. Those days, Stephen always felt, were the best days in the library — the only good thing about a research project. However, whenever anyone came from afar to examine one of the few existing copies of some dirty book, Miss Mahogany was attentive and kind and didn't give a damn about whether or not the guest had a library card.

"... and I'm sorry, Lord, that I purchased those rare issues of *The Pearl* and other Victorian erotica and donated them to the library," Ed prayed, and his voice indicated that his prayer was winding down. "Accept my apology also for purchasing and donating the rare set of *My Secret Life*. I didn't read either donation. Not in their entirety. Only a few pages, which I am trying to forget. But some of it rhymes, Lord, and this makes forgetting difficult. I hope they do not end up in the hands of the children, although they probably will, but this concern would really be Miss Mahogany's responsibility. For she is the librarian. Amen."

Rather than raise his head, Ed took advantage of his mouth's proximity to his plate and stuffed it with chicken. "Where are your boots?" he asked his fiancée, his mouth still full of chicken.

Miss Baskin was wearing flip-flops. She paused long enough that Stephen could tell she didn't have an answer.

"I'm painting them," Stephen decided out loud. "I'm doing a painting *of* them."

"Why would you do that?" asked Ed in the slightly annoyed, businesslike tone he used for all questions.

"For your engagement present."

He was sure he could feel Miss Baskin's hazel eyes boring into him, but when he looked she was just watching her fork move through her bowl of greens.

"Let's see it."

"The boot or the drawing?"

"Both."

"I only just started. It's a sketch."

Ed shrugged. "Go get it."

Stephen went upstairs to his room, drew on his pad, and brought it down to the table with the boot.

"It's preliminary."

Ed held the drawing at arm's length and rotated it this way and that. While Ed examined it, Stephen realized that it looked a lot like a paramecium. Ed continued to flip and rotate, comparing it to the boot Stephen had placed in the middle of the table. It still looked like a paramecium. He could see it on Ed's face: fear for his little brother and his dim prospects in life. Drawing was Stephen's only known talent, and here he couldn't make a boot look like a boot. Ed's eyes watered.

"It's really good," Ed lied.

For Stephen, this was a perfect moment: his brother's love and pity, out in the open. Ed, with his good business sense, couldn't help but place himself in the role of villain. Whenever Ed acted like an asshole, Stephen thought back to when he was eight and Ed had caught him experimenting with their mother's lipstick. Instead of mocking him, Ed had carefully instructed Stephen in the intricacies of heavy metal makeup. With a red lightning bolt across his face and Ed painted up into a kind of Rabid Cat Man, they played shirtless air guitar to metal anthems and practiced their scowls in the mirror.

"He's actually quite good," said Miss Baskin. Ed was still looking in pain at the paramecium.

"I can tell," he lied again.

"No — I mean, he's much better than this sketch would indicate."

"It shows great promise."

She looked at Stephen now. "I know it will be good after you put more time into it."

When they made eye contact, Stephen didn't see any anger or shame — just his art teacher.

"Keep the boot as long as you need it," she said.

"Really?" said Ed. "Stephen, how long will that take?"

"Twenty-four hours of hard work," Stephen replied, making the number up on the spot.

Ed nodded thoughtfully; he only accepted firm answers, preferably numerical ones.

During lunch, the cafeteria lady with the beehive and biceps let Stephen smoke cigarettes out back by the Dumpsters near the loading dock. He didn't like cigarettes very much, but he liked the lunchroom less. The humiliation of algebra class had whittled down his seating options. Today, he was sure, he would remember to look for his math book. He spotted Miss Baskin on the far side of the parking lot, walking away from the school. She glanced his way, took a few more steps, then stopped and squinted, shielding her eyes from the sun. He waved, forgetting he had a cigarette dangling from his mouth. She waved back and walked away.

During third period, he redrew the sinking of the *Lusitania* by U-boat in pencil on his desk — an intricate drawing that someone, probably the janitor, was always erasing, and so it had to be redone every day. All those little people floating in the water. When the drawing was finished, he filled in the first bubble of his history exam, which glared bright white beneath the fluorescent lights overhead. Then he closed his eyes and dreamed of the wood's jade gloom. Next period, in the crumbling cement cave of the boys' locker room, he dressed in the required red shorts and white shirt. On the wooden basketball court, he performed a series of squat thrusts, push-ups, and sit-ups. He ran the bases during the chaos of indoor kickball and did not stop, bursting out of the metal door and into the school parking lot, past the courthouse square, through the neighborhood of front porches, and into the graveyard, where he took off his shoes and socks to step barefoot onto the glowing moss, into shadow.

The tree eyes, even while they tracked him, blinked out thick, salty tears that made transparent dots on his thin white shirt. It was the weeping time of year, when the trees cry before the leaves crinkle and fall. The chimelike tinkle of drips dropping, leaf to leaf, and plopping onto the moss or the tops of his bare feet was like rain, except slower and possessed of a pleasant sadness that made the crying almost contagious. Miss Baskin saw Stephen first. She sat naked on the moss in a small clearing, legs pulled tight to her chest. The clearing was all but dry, just a few eyes blinking and dripping from overhanging branches.

"Here's a quick lesson," she said. Her voice was shocking, less sweet than the voice she used in class. "The next time you stand and stare at a naked woman, you might think about saying something. Or doing something. Or at least look her in the eyes. If you just stand there, you come across as a creepy weirdo."

"Sorry." He could feel his face flush. He couldn't think of anything to say. He felt like a creepy weirdo.

"You stole my bra."

"I know."

"It was my only comfortable bra."

He nodded. He tried to keep eye contact, but he wanted to look at her skin — any part of it. It was very fair, and he imagined that if he touched it, it would go flush and then quickly fade to white again. He could almost see her cleavage, but not her nipples — her knees hid them. He could see, just a little, the hair between her legs. Then she pulled her feet and legs in closer, so that he couldn't see between them anymore.

"Well, Stephen, you should give my bra back."

"I tossed it. I didn't want Ed to find it."

"Goddamn," she said, shaking her head. "Well, it's going to be kind of embarrassing for you to buy me a new one, isn't it? Or do you like shopping?"

Stephen thought for a moment.

"Maybe I could just pay you the money and you could order one out of a catalog."

"I guess so. But that wouldn't teach you a lesson, would it? Take off your shirt," she said.

"My shirt?"

"You're the only one who's wearing one."

"Why do you want me to take off my shirt?"

"Because I'm sitting here naked and you're not. And your shirt is already soaked through. I can see your nipples. And why are you dressed like that — are those your pajamas?"

"I ran away from gym class."

She laughed.

"Take off your shirt and sit down," she said, patting the moss beside her. "You came to spy on me. Might as well get a close look and make things even at the same time."

He lifted the wet shirt over his head, but he didn't sit down.

"Take off your shorts, too," she said.

She sounded mean. He couldn't tell if she was serious or mocking him. The thing was, he halfway did want to take off his shorts. Right then, a cold breeze caused a shower of tears to shimmer from the leaves overhead. He imagined himself a grown man in a movie, taking off his pants (they would be pants, of course, and not too-tight gym shorts). He felt cold and numb. His dick felt small. He felt like a child.

"I'm not going to do that," he said.

"Then go away and stop looking at me."

"It's not the same."

She stood and came close to him. She balanced one hand on his shoulder and lifted her leg to show him her thigh. He shivered.

"Describe it," she said.

He couldn't stop shivering. "It's great," he said.

"What do you see?"

There were veins on her leg that looked erupted, spilled over, and painful.

"Just say what you're thinking."

He had a weird impulse to put his mouth on her thigh.

"Say something, goddamnit."

"Purple fireworks," he blurted.

She laughed. "Okay. Like a little celebration happening down there? That's lovely. Before long I'll be a walking bruise. Are you going to come spy on me then?"

Next, she made him describe the white striations on her hips and across her lower back, above her ass. They looked like healed cuts from an X-Acto blade. Like rivers on a map.

"They started in my midtwenties. Soon I'll be one big scar: a walking scar and bruise. Beautiful?"

"Yes," he said, and then felt sorry for saying it. He was often late detecting sarcasm. But as far as he knew, he'd meant it: If he were in a movie, and if he were a man wearing pants, he would trace her scars with his tongue.

"Show me something," she said.

"I have a pimple starting on my neck, right here," he said, cocking his head to one side.

"You don't have anything permanent, do you?"

A cold drop struck the crown of his head. It seemed to fall through his body and exit from the soles of his feet. He began to feel so cold he couldn't think about anything but his own skin. The woods were quiet. He couldn't put his wet shirt back on, so he crossed his arms and continued to shiver.

"I like your goose bumps," she said.

"Okay." He shivered.

"You don't have anywhere to go, do you?"

He shook his head.

"You can't stay here. You owe me a painting of a boot."

Her teapot whistled on the stove. She poured steaming water over a bag and the kitchen filled with the scent of spiced apple. Her rented cottage had a bench swing on the front porch and a garden plot in the backyard. Potted herbs grew in the windows of her art studio, a converted second bedroom. She set him up with an easel and supplies. She put her left bloodred boot on a sheet-covered stool.

"Have at it," she said.

Stephen heard the shower turn on. He started to sketch. It took him over two hours to accomplish a shitty underdrawing. He hadn't heard the shower turn off, but now he noticed that it was no longer on. From the hallway, he could see Miss Baskin sleeping on her bed. He made some more tea. He removed the pot before it whistled. He added four spoons of sugar to his mug. It was so good. He was surprised; he'd never had tea before.

Sitting on a chair in Miss Baskin's room, he sipped his tea and watched her sleep. He brought in the easel and did a few quick paintings. He wasn't meticulous, like he'd been with the boot. He made thirteen. Miss Baskin tossed and turned, tangled up in the sheets. He painted her scars and veins, and then he left them there and got home too late for dinner. Ed was asleep with the TV on. Stephen fixed himself a plate and went up to his room to paint the other bloodred boot, the right one, late into the night.

Stephen carried an easel into the clearing and Miss Baskin carried two red umbrellas. She lay on her side, against the green moss, beneath one umbrella. Stephen tied the other umbrella to his easel, to protect his work from the tree eyes, which still trickled and splattered and would continue to weep for another month. Within a week, both umbrellas were lightly speckled with green. He knew there was an unspoken agreement: Things would have to be even; he would paint her first, and then they would switch. They met on late afternoons and on weekends. They undressed in the graveyard and hid their clothes. They skipped school.

The first time he undressed in front of her, he had to close his eyes and face away from her while she painted him. The second time, two things happened. One, he got a boner. Two, he got embarrassed and cried just a little. She painted him anyway, as if nothing had happened. They both painted the whole figure first, and then they painted each other's individual parts in a progression. They made paintings of tear ducts, the backs of ears, napes, the undersides of breasts, nipples, elbows, navels, wrists, hip bones, assholes, the patch beneath his scrotum, her labia, his inner thigh, kneecaps and behind the knee, foot bottoms and tops. By the time they began working on toe tips and between the toes, the trees had run out of tears. The air in the wood turned bitter. Branches were skeletal and bare. The moss, which had grown to dangle from the red umbrellas in heavy cords, turned dark and stiff. On the day the first snow fell, he was not surprised that she did not meet him in the graveyard. He didn't feel regret, but relief. The tree eyes began to close their lids for winter, but for some reason a few failed to shut, and those eyeballs hardened like marbles and grew crystals like old ice cream forgotten in the freezer.

Miss Baskin did not speak to Stephen beyond her brief, official interactions as teacher. He spent long hours in his bedroom, completing increasingly polished, more complicated versions of the paintings he'd started in the woods. Miss Baskin came over most evenings to eat salad at the round table. During grace one night, Ed described the glass windows of the new library, a project the town council had just awarded him. As before, Stephen examined Miss Baskin's face while Miss Baskin examined the intensely praying face of Ed, who told God about the electronic book stacks his company would install. They would open and close like accordions. Ed abruptly said amen, and then he asked Stephen about his very delinquent engagement present, as if it had occurred to him suddenly during his prayer.

Stephen fetched it from his room, where it had sat finished for over a month. Ed placed it on the mantel after dinner and all three of them gathered on the couch and looked.

Stephen met eyes with Miss Baskin, and in the silent language of looks that he knew from the woods, she signaled her approval without a smile, without moving her face at all.

"Terrific," said Ed. He clapped his hands together. He leaned over on the couch and awkwardly hugged his little brother. He asked Miss Baskin, "Where will we hang it?"

"I'll take it home," she said.

"No no no, it has to go someplace where people will see it. Like here," he said, holding it just above the fireplace mantel, where currently there hung a wreath of holly. "Or maybe...," he said, his voice turning soft, reverent. "In the library."

Stephen had wanted to impress Ed, but unveiling the painting felt weird, naked weird, like he'd felt sometimes posing for Miss Baskin. Later he went, in the dark, to visit his parents in the graveyard. He couldn't help but feel sorry for them, couldn't help imagining how it must feel to stand still all night in the frozen air. It made death seem too long, too still. He had felt this for some time, which was why he kept a broom and a long-handled windshield scraper in the graveyard.

He used to clean the ice and snow from his parents — and Uncle Mc-Carty, too. He had an urge to wrap them in blankets or dress them in parkas. He had a compulsion to sweep and scrape clean the whole field of statues, to light fires between them, and to build them a roof. Thoughts like these, he knew, were why people like Ed were mayors and constructors of buildings, and he, Stephen, was not. While he scraped his father free of ice, he saw a distant light in the woods.

Snow and darkness obscured the frozen, labyrinthine creek, on which he kept slipping and falling. The light came from a small, strange campfire: Flames flicked out their tongues, and above them hovered colors and shapes that did not belong to fire. They looked like warped, watery movie projections.

Miss Mahogany crouched next to the fire and operated the library's newest, most expensive video camera. She waved him closer, and he crouched beside her. The flames came from a brazier of red-hot embers, onto which she tossed twigs, branches, and other small pieces of tree, bit by bit. Each piece burst into flame and released an image, recorded by the camera.

The first image was of one of Stephen's classmates, a girl named Charlie, who sat down on the moss and sliced red lines into her armpits with a razor blade. The stick burned up and the image faded. Some sticks did not yield a clear image. Some images consisted of a slow pan across empty woods, following something invisible. Other times, you could see one of Horusville's legions of masturbating children or hordes of adulterous adults, and plenty of wrinkled exhibitionist old folks from the retirement home. The more branches she burned, the more the woods felt like a covert city parallel to the town in which he slept. He saw himself masturbating to *She-Hulk,* masturbating while gazing into the eyes of a tree, his math book beside him. He saw his own face up close, and it looked strangely sad and pained — which must be how the almond eyes saw him. He wished he hadn't seen it. It was the last thing he wanted anyone — even the almond eyes — to see. He felt like he was about to cry, but Miss Mahogany placed her hand on his shoulder and startled him. Then he saw himself with Miss Baskin, posing naked on the moss.

When Miss Mahogany's pile of sticks ran down, she doused the coals with snow and made Stephen lug her equipment back to the library, where she taught him to label and organize the recordings. Over the next several days, during study hall and after school, he helped her assign numbers, enter the new materials into the database, and store them in the chilly, humidity-controlled media room. He searched through years of database records in search of his parents' names, but when he located the files the recordings were gone. He didn't ask her, but he suspected Miss Mahogany had predicted he'd look for them and had hidden them away. Once, he played footage of a man — someone he knew — having sex with his dog, whom he also knew. Both were much older now than in the recording. Miss Mahogany sprinted across the room on her short stick legs and turned off the monitor.

"Hear me now, Sonny Jim!" she told him. "I've watched these all, and trust me when I tell you I'm battier now than I would've been. It's good information. But it's put me halfway to someplace else. You want to know how I do it? Do you?"

He shook his head no. She continued anyway.

"A mental tablet. A three-subject notebook of the mind. Every word goes on it before I speak it. Otherwise, all these images are coming out."

She tapped her finger on her forehead when she said this.

"That nasty man with his dog. Someone digging in the moss to bury God knows what. Huffers. Injectors. A full appendix to the *Kama Sutra*. It's not like I don't get a kick out of it, you know, but all of that in there..."

She pointed now to the media cabinets. She cradled her forehead in her hands and rocked it.

For the rest of the winter, Stephen recorded burning sticks in the woods and archived them in the library with Miss Mahogany. He sat in art class each day, too aware that he knew the skin beneath Miss Baskin's breasts. He stayed up late in his bedroom to paint what he knew of her. When they made eye contact, he was startled to recall in rapid succession the concentric designs of her iris, thumbprint, anus, navel, and heels. Sometimes she drew caricatures of students on their birthdays, but Stephen's passed with a blank chalkboard. It hurt. But he thought he understood why she couldn't make a cartoon of him. It had to do with her breath on his leg when she came in close to paint him. There was nothing left to say, or draw. Winter filled the woods with ice and snow, and Stephen felt thankful for his work in the archives; otherwise, he'd have had nowhere to go.

Then the weather changed, and the freezer-burned eyes shed their crystals. Sockets crackled and quivered, and lids unstuck with a faint snap. Ice dripped from branches, and the forest floor shifted from white to green. The eyes darted wildly about, learning how to see again. When the moss finally softened into a deep sponge, and the air smelled like earth, and the eyes resumed their creepy scanning, Stephen saw Miss Baskin naked in the woods again. Ed was naked, too. They had a bottle of champagne, and they danced naked and drank from the bottle. They had a picnic basket. Miss Baskin started a painting of Ed, and Stephen thought he knew just how she'd progress, how she would paint him piece by piece. But five minutes into the painting, before she'd finished even one piece, Ed got impatient, tackled her onto the moss, and they fucked. Stephen wanted to look away, but he didn't. The worst was their faces, the way they didn't look sad at all.

He remembered how ridiculous he'd looked in the recorded image, masturbating to the almond-eyed tree, and how pathetic he'd looked, letting Miss Baskin come in close to paint every part of him. It was painful to think of Miss Baskin and Ed in this place — in the woods that he'd always thought of as his — fucking every day while the trees recorded it all. He felt strange enough, sad enough, to go home in search of a hatchet. He didn't even know if they had a hatchet at home, so instead he fetched the long-handled windshield scraper from the graveyard.

Ed and Miss Baskin lay on the moss together until sunset, and Stephen watched them until they left. Then he stared for a long time into the glade's largest eye, embedded in a trunk and big as a hubcap. He studied his own reflection in its wet surface. He stuck it once in the middle with the scraper, catching the lid half open. He hacked at it, all around it. Bark chipped away, chunking off the tree's white meat. The slick of pupil oozed down the trunk. He chopped the glade blind. Inside each eye was a rope of snot followed by a gob of red. It stained the bark and his skin. He plucked the eyes that dangled off limbs. They quivered in his hands. He lined up the trembling eyes on the moss.

He stabbed the first plucked eye and couldn't stop stabbing until he dug through the moss with the scraper, digging deep, more than a foot, until he finally reached dirt. There were still more eyes he'd not blinded — eyes too high on trunks and branches, eyes throughout the forest, and he'd never blind them all. They'd remember and record what he'd just done, which was worse than the masturbating, worse than his brother's fucking, maybe even worse than the man who'd fucked his dog. Whatever his parents had done, whatever their hidden tapes revealed, he knew the file in the archive with his name would now be worse. He cried, and the eye blood swirled with his own tears and snot. He was glad his parents were dead and couldn't see him. Unless they could. No one, he felt, deserved to be seen like this.

He tossed the still-quivering eyes into the creek, now rushing with snowmelt. Every kid in Horusville who'd ever plucked an eye was aware that the eyes could look around in a mason jar of water for at least a week before wilting and going black. He watched them bob and twist away, and he wondered if the trees would chronicle these travels.

The recordings, Stephen felt strongly now, belonged to the recorded, who deserved to know that their secrets were not secret. Maybe some of them even deserved to see who they really were. After dark, he pushed wheelbarrow loads of media material through the streets of Horusville, following the same route he'd bicycled every morning for years when he was a paperboy. He set the recordings in stacks on each porch. Just after midnight, he crawled into bed and, shortly thereafter, someone set the woods on fire.

Stephen found Miss Mahogany at the head of the crowd with her video camera, filming the images that flickered into the sky. The volunteer fire squad worked to keep the blaze from skipping onto rooftops, and the populace of Horusville set up lawn chairs as if it were a Fourth of July display. Soon enough, mothers covered their children's eyes while the children squirmed and cried. Some people went home and retched, unable to stomach the projected collage, the small-scale history of Horusville that hovered above the woods, against the screen of night sky. Most watched. Stephen gently pulled the camera from Miss Mahogany's hands, and she let him. He tossed the camera into the fire, where the contents of the media cabinets already sizzled and hissed. Last of all, the trees shot up the image of everyone there, in real time, eyes and mouths dumbly open.

LAURA VAN DEN BERG

The Bread Loaf Writers' Conference

Up High in the Air

Just after the Fourth of July, my mother called to tell me she thought her hair was on fire. She lived in Nebraska, alone since my father had drowned in the Platte River two years earlier. I hadn't seen her since Thanksgiving and, for the last month, hadn't returned her calls.

"What do you mean you *think* your hair is on fire?" The apartment my husband and I shared was near the L, and the floor shuddered beneath me as a train passed.

"I can smell the smoke," she said.

"Do you see flames?"

"I can smell the smoke," she said again.

"Maybe you should call the fire department."

"I think I'll go outside for a while," she said, and hung up.

I walked down the hall and sat in the linen closet.

I didn't tell my husband about this latest call. A week earlier my mother had phoned to say my father had come home for breakfast, that his clothes were just a little wet and it looked like everything was going to be all right. But I did tell Dean, one of my summer school students. Since June, he'd been visiting my office every Thursday evening. He was a senior in college, an art history major; my etymology class was an elective he needed to graduate early. I'd been an assistant professor at the university for three years and always reminded Dean to ride the elevator to the eleventh floor, then take the back stairs down to my office on the seventh. *I'll be up for tenure in a few years,* I'd told him.

"Have you ever smelled burning hair?" I asked.

He shook his head. I was naked and sitting on my office floor, the blue-gray carpet rough against my legs.

"It's terrible," I said. "It smells like disease."

Dean was standing on the other side of the room, leaning against my desk, wearing only a pair of white tube socks. He had a swimmer's body, lean and broad shouldered, though he tended to slump. Sometimes I pressed my palm against the small of his back to correct his posture. After I told him about my mother's call, he dropped his chin against his chest and sighed.

"It sounds like you should go back to Nebraska for a while," he said.

Since the drowning, I dreaded going home. In the nights before my last visit, I was kept awake by memories of traveling to Nebraska for my father's funeral, of looking out the plane window during the final approach for landing and seeing the Platte cutting across the state like a huge scar. My husband had come along, but spent the whole trip nagging me about visiting the Cretaceous fossil exhibit at a nearby university museum.

"My mother's neighbors have been bringing her dinner every Sunday night for the last year, and she has a cousin nearby, too," I said to Dean. "They'd tell me if something was really wrong."

"She doesn't scare you when she talks like that?"

"Of course," I said. "Of course she does."

It was then he walked across the room and held me, without desire, comforting me the way I imagined he might comfort his own mother. His skin was soft. He smelled like summer, like grass and sweat and white bar soap.

"It's time for you to go home," I said.

I found my husband lying on the living room floor, holding a photograph above his head. The sofa and glass-top coffee table were cluttered with newspaper pages — editorial cartoons from the *Chicago Tribune,* the science and technology sections from the *New York Times.* I asked if he'd remembered to buy more coffee filters and pick up my dry cleaning, and when he didn't answer, I nudged him with the toe of my pump.

"What are you doing?"

"Looking at a picture." He flipped the photo toward me. It was black and white. From where I stood I could make out small peaked waves.

"Is that a picture of Lake Michigan?"

"No," he said. "It's a picture of something *in* Lake Michigan." He sat up and pointed at a dark speck in the center of the photograph. "Right there. The monster is what I'm looking at."

My husband's career was going nowhere. In the spring he'd left his job at the Lake Michigan Federation, where he'd been the assistant director of habitat management. After he'd been passed over for a promotion for the second time and dozens of academic presses rejected his book on the life cycle of chinook salmon, he started spending weekends in his bathrobe and waking me in the middle of the night to discuss the injustices of academic publishing. He sent anonymous hate mail to the Federation and burned an issue of *American Scientist* in the kitchen sink after reading an article about a Ph.D. dropout who had recently discovered, quite by accident, a new species of anemone.

Then one morning he got a call from the director of the Mishegenabeg Discovery Group, who wanted to offer him a position as expeditions manager, since he had extensive knowledge of Lake Michigan. Initially, he was skeptical of the group's practices, but came home from his first meeting impressed by their equipment and organization. And then, only a few weeks after joining the Discovery Group, he told me the Mishegenabeg had come to him in a dream.

"I was underwater," he said, "stuck there, but not exactly drowning, and I saw these huge eyes staring back at me. When I woke up, I thought about the sightings and disappearances that were reported to the Federation and how we always ignored them. I realized how wrong I've been."

"What kind of disappearances?" I asked, still thinking about the dream he had described, of being trapped underwater but not drowning.

"How about the fishing tug that vanished near Port Washington a few years ago?" he replied. "No distress call, no debris. Just gone."

"There are dozens of wrecked boats at the bottom of Lake Michigan," I said. "It probably just sank."

"Don't forget the scales the size of dinner plates that ichthyologist found floating in the lake last summer," he said. "They were never identified."

"Don't forget the size of some of the sturgeon and carp living in Michigan," I said. "You of all people should know."

"Laugh if you want, Diane, but I finally know what I'm looking for."

I had tried to tell him the word *mishegenabeg* translated into "water snake," that whatever people had seen in the lake was probably just a big fucking snake, but he wouldn't listen.

From the floor my husband reached for my hand. He had a bad back. I held his wrist and placed my other hand on his elbow. He pulled hard against me as he stood, his dark hair flattened to reveal the bald spot on the crown of his head. After the mishegenabeg dream, he had thrown out his bathrobe and started dressing well again, in pressed slacks and polo shirts. In exchange for his work with the Discovery Group, he was getting a small monthly stipend; he'd told me salaries and benefits were just things that kept us trapped in soul-killing jobs.

He tucked the photograph into a manila folder and placed it on the mantel, next to pictures of our wedding and a long-ago vacation to Mount St. Helens. He started in again on the sightings he'd heard about at the Federation, how most of them occurred late at night, how some said the creature was at least fifty feet long and the color of moss, how others described it as looking, from a distance, like an overturned boat floating in the water. He told me the Discovery Group had scheduled their first official expedition for September. They were trying to get a reporter from the *Tribune* to cover it.

"But you haven't been diving since college," I said. He'd gone to school in Maine and had been a member of the college scuba-diving team; during our courtship, I heard countless stories about traveling to the Gulf of Maine with the team on weekends to plunge into freezing waters.

"I was pretty good back then," he said. "Plus, Ada and Stephen have raised enough money to buy the group new regulators and air tanks."

"Who are Ada and Stephen?"

"Members of the Discovery Group," he said. "There are ten of us, which you would know if you took more of an interest. We already have three motorboats, and we're pooling money for new underwater cameras."

"So you're just planning to remain unemployed?" I pinched the bridge of my nose. At the Foundation, his salary had been comparable to mine, and our rent had gone up a hundred dollars the previous year. "Perhaps it's time you started looking for a real job."

"Your hair seems different." My husband reached toward my head, then pulled his hand away, as though I might shock him. I realized I'd forgotten to brush my hair and sweep it back into the customary ponytail after leaving Dean.

"Don't change the subject," I said. "And don't think you're going to dip into our savings, either."

"What are we really saving that money for?"

"We could buy a house one day," I said. "We could travel more. We could spend next summer in the Yucatán."

"I'm going outside." Our little balcony had an iron railing, across which we'd strung white Christmas lights in December. After the holidays I kept bugging him to take the lights down, finally giving up in March. He had left the door open, and gnats streamed into the living room. I was about to ask him to close the door when he shouted my name from the balcony.

"I forgot to tell you that your mother called," he said. "I took down a message."

In the kitchen I found a note scrawled on the back of a grocery receipt: *Not a fire, just smoke.*

All summer, I'd been trying to write a paper on the etymology of misunderstandings. I hadn't published much since my first two years at the university, when I placed three well-received papers with *Etymology Today.* Whenever the chair emphasized the importance of contributing to our fields at meetings, I felt her gaze falling on me. My background was in systematic comparisons, the study of which words had originated from their common ancestor language and which had been borrowed from other languages. What happened, I wanted to know, during the process of foreign words being adopted by another language — surely there must have been misunderstandings. At the start of the summer, I went to the chair with my idea.

"Sounds more like theoretical linguistics to me," she said. "What happened to your paper on the etymology of corporate language?"

"It's going to take more time than I'd realized," I said. I had lost interest in the project months before.

"Too bad," she said, pushing a mess of brown ringlets from her forehead. "It's a timely subject."

That same afternoon, I went to see a professor in the history department and asked him to tell me about a significant misunderstanding between historical figures, thinking I could start by researching a story. *I'm not interested in facts and hard data right now,* I said, *just talk to me.* He looked up from a huge leather book with yellowing pages, told me a brief and unhelpful story about Napoleon, and then went back to reading.

One night in August, Dean told me he wanted to watch the meteor shower he'd heard about on the radio. It was supposed to be the best one in years. He sat in the armchair behind my desk, naked save for the tube socks. He had once told me he wanted to be an architect, like Carlo Scarpa or Kevin Roche, and that he was already preparing applications for graduate school. I had taken this to mean he'd be moving away after graduating in December. In Dean's presence I saw myself as I was in my twenties; the perfect, pale softness of my skin. But more than anything, I had come to appreciate how transparent he was, how easily understood: his excitement, his fear, his attraction, all put forth without reservation. I felt a jolt of relief whenever he talked about graduate school; he would leave on his own, I imagined, sparing me from having to become an instructor in suffering.

"When's it happening?" I was sitting in the chair across from him, still naked, my skirt suit a dark mound on the carpet.

"Tonight." He checked his watch. "In just a little while. We really should go see it." He stretched his arms over his head. "Have you heard any more from your mother?"

I told him that I'd given her neighbors a call and they'd said everything was fine.

"Still," he said. "You must be worried."

"*Meteor* comes from the Greek word *meteoros*," I said. "Do you know what that means?"

"Will this be on the next test?"

"It means 'high in the air.'" It had rained that afternoon, though the sky cleared at dusk. I picked up my red raincoat and wrapped it around me, tying the belt snugly at my waist. Dean rose and pulled on his shorts.

"So let's go up high in the air." I opened my window and pointed to the fire escape. Damp heat gusted into my office.

"Wouldn't that be dangerous?"

When Dean finished buttoning his shirt, I noticed he'd done it crooked. I walked over to him and redid the buttons, looking into his face, taking my time. "It's the only way to reach the roof," I said. "We have to get above some of the lights if we're going to see anything."

We climbed the side of the building like thieves. It was risky; security guards patrolled the campus at night, and there was a chance we'd be spotted, but right then I didn't care. When we reached the top of the building, the winds were strong and my raincoat kept blowing open. My thighs hardened with goose bumps. I saw parking lots and a soccer field, the open wound of a construction site, a bright yellow pipe jutting from the hole like a robot's finger. In the far distance, Lake Michigan was black as a pit of tar.

"There's still too much light," I said. "We can barely see the stars." It dawned on me then that I should have been terrified. The fire escape was narrow and slick; I had no idea whether we'd be able to get down safely, and there was a chance I'd be caught with a student, at night, wearing nothing but a raincoat. I told myself that Dean would be moving on soon, that the end of summer was in sight, but none of those things explained the calm I felt on the roof, or why I was living as if these were the last months that would belong to me.

Dean glanced at his watch, the hands glowing neon green in the darkness. "It's almost time."

Seconds later, streaks of light moved behind the clouds, pale and swift as fish in a river. I tried to count them, but they were passing too quickly, and I lost track after a few seconds. Something about all that light passing over my head, so far from my grasp, made my entire body throb. The four walls of my office felt very far away.

The next time my mother called, she asked if I'd seen my father. It was a few days after the meteor shower, and my hands still ached from gripping the wet bars of the fire escape.

"Not in a long time." I had been the one to identify his body at the morgue after he was pulled from the river. I remembered the green bruise on his cheekbone, the bluish color of his skin, the way the veins in his face and hands resembled the intricate lines of a map. He'd looked like a Hollywood corpse, a dummy, a joke.

"He was here for breakfast and I haven't seen him since. Do you think I should start calling the neighbors?"

Her voice was calm. I pictured her standing on the linoleum floor of her kitchen, in a lavender housedress and slippers, bobby pins holding back her graying bangs.

"Dove sei," she said, Italian for "where are you?" The child of Italian immigrants, she had, in the last year, started speaking the language she'd abandoned as a girl. The L passed, and I waited for the shaking to stop before I answered.

"Mom," I said. "Why don't I come to Nebraska next weekend, just to see how things are?"

"Oh, Diane," she said. "We don't live there anymore."

In bed that night, I didn't resist when my husband slid his hands underneath my nightgown. I didn't resist when he began moving over me in a halting rhythm. We hadn't made love in so long that his body had become unfamiliar to me. The broad hands, the dark circle of hair around his belly button. The lights were off. He could have been a stranger. He went soft before either of us could finish and lay on top of me for a minute, a big heap of man resting between my thighs.

After he rolled away, we were quiet. His breathing was deep and ragged, as if he were trying to recover from a sprint. I stayed on my back, blinking at the darkness.

"Diane," he finally said, and when I didn't reply, he started telling me about his practice dives with the Discovery Group at Winthrop Harbor. He talked about how strange it felt to be sealed inside the rubbery wetsuit, how it took him a few tries to suck oxygen through the mouthpiece properly. When he first opened his eyes, it was the deepest dark he'd ever seen, darker than the waters of Maine, and he recalled a calming exercise he'd learned when he was on the scuba-diving team, which was to visualize an empty white room.

"Do you realize how hard that is?" he asked. "To make yourself see only in white?"

"Haven't tried it lately." It was hot, and through the open window I heard traffic below, voices on the sidewalks. That afternoon, I'd left the university and gone to a nearby park, where I had intended to think about my paper on misunderstandings, but instead I read a newspaper article on people who changed their identities. A new social security number, driver's license, birth certificate, passport, name. It could all be bought. One person, quoted anonymously in the article, said he changed his identity every five years, so he never had to be the same person for too long. I watched teenagers kick around a soccer ball and wondered what I would choose for a new name: Betty, Raquel, Lucinda. I had planned to stay in the park for an hour and then return to school, but in the end I didn't go back at all, even though I had student conferences. I called the department secretary and asked her to post a sign — OUT SICK — on my office door.

"When I got to that place, to the white room, it felt like my head opened and my brain floated right out of my body," my husband said. "I was completely calm. I could have swum for hours."

I rested a hand on his stomach. His skin was damp with sweat. That evening, I'd found another message he had taken down for me on a paper napkin, this one from my mother's cousin, asking me to call.

"So let me get this straight," I said. "Your plan is to survey all twenty-five thousand square miles of Lake Michigan with this group until someone sees the mishegenabeg?"

"We have to track it first," he said. "Pay attention to wave patterns and water levels. I am a trained scientist, in case you've forgotten."

"That's not the same as being some kind of explorer."

His stomach tightened underneath my hand. "People can change. What we want can change."

"I don't think that's true," I said. "I don't think we change very much at all."

"I've figured out what I want," he said. "Maybe you should do the same."

"I'm working on it." I pulled my hand away and shifted in the
dark.

My husband turned on the bedside lamp and picked up *Mishe-*
genabeg: The Myth of Lake Michigan from the bedside table. "I'm
learning the most fascinating things from this book," he said. The
earliest sighting of the Mishegenabeg had occurred in the 1800s,
when the giant head of a snake emerged from the lake, dousing a
boating crew with water. One crew member even claimed the monster had spoken to him in Latin.

"That's insane," I said. In the low light of the bedroom, my husband looked different; the stubble collecting on his cheeks and chin
made his eyes appear darker, more remote. *What's happened to you?* I
wanted to ask, but wondered whether he would turn that question
back onto me.

"Go to sleep, Diane," he said, opening the book, "and dream your
dark dreams."

A different summer, five years earlier. My husband and I drove outside the city to see a botanical garden in Glencoe. We visited the bulb
garden, where red and orange tulips were clustered around small
stone statues of foxes, then the Japanese garden, which had raked
gravel and gingko trees and water lilies. At the lakeside garden, we
watched Canada geese lumber from a pond, their bodies large and
awkward on land, and looked for the birds listed in our guidebook—cardinals, egrets, warblers, wrens. We wandered the path
that circled the perimeter of the property, passing a statue of Lin-
naeus and a little bronze bear and picnic tables stacked with flyers advertising a horticultural therapy program. We didn't follow the route
suggested in the guidebook, but walked without direction, my husband occasionally reaching out and squeezing my fingers.

I could not say for sure that I was happier then, though when I look back on that afternoon, the bird watching and the flowers, the day seemed to mark a turn in the path — as in, from there, everything got worse. There was so much we didn't know in Glencoe: that my husband would be twice denied the promotion he'd been counting on, and the book he spent his evenings and weekends researching would never find a publisher; that my father would have a heart attack while trout fishing and capsize his boat; and that I would drop my dry-erase marker after seeing Dean for the first time in the back of my classroom. The truth was, in Glencoe my husband got impatient with me when I took too long exploring the bulb garden, and for a week after our visit complained about the sunburn he'd gotten on his neck. The truth was, we got into a fight on the way back to the city, over an errant comment I'd made in the Japanese garden, about how it depressed me to see so much beauty all at once, as though everything good in the world — or at least in Illinois — were contained right there. The truth was, that same week, during my office hours, I'd come close to taking a flirtatious student up on his offer to go out for a drink. The truth was, I'd always had recklessness in me. The truth was, things were already getting worse. But, in later years, I would not be able to resist rewriting that day in memory; I needed the altered version, I came to realize, in order to keep hoping for something better.

The last place we went was the waterfall garden, where a fifty-foot waterfall roared down a hillside and into landscaped pools. I was looking at a cluster of weeping conifers and rubbing the rough green leaves, even though the guidebook told us to refrain from touching the plants, when I heard my husband, who was standing near the base of the waterfall, cry for help. I dropped the conifer leaf and rushed down the bank.

"What's wrong?" I asked.

"Nothing's wrong," he said.

"I thought you were calling for help."

"No," he said. "I was saying *heron, heron*. A black-crowned one just flew over the falls." He opened the guidebook and flipped through the pages. "It was really beautiful," he said. "I wanted you to see it."

On the hottest night in August, I had drinks with a friend who'd come to Chicago for the weekend. A former colleague, she had married two years earlier and moved to Aurora. At the bar, she ordered white wine. I ordered a whiskey, no ice. Right away, she asked about my husband. Her eyes were such a pale blue that I felt something inside me go cold if I looked at her for too long.

"How's he been since he left the Federation? Has he found something else yet?"

"In a way," I said. "He's still very interested in the lake." I wanted badly to tell her about Dean, about what we did in my office and about going to the roof, about how it frightened me that I wasn't more frightened — for myself, for him. But I knew she would only lecture me on marriage and job security and good judgment. The life she was leading now would demand that of her. When she asked about my work, I told her I was making good progress on a new paper and expected to have a draft finished by the end of the summer.

My friend started telling me about something that had happened to her and her husband, Rick, earlier in the summer. "We went to Montrose Beach for the day," she said. "And this young man, he couldn't have been more than seventeen, swam out too far and got sucked into a strong current. Or so we thought."

The waiter came by and we ordered another round. My friend said the young man had been spotted by a lifeguard, but he was actually saved by someone who was already in the water — a woman who just happened to be a champion swimmer. My friend and her husband had watched the whole thing from the shore. They were there when the lifeguard blew his whistle, when the swimmer cut across the water, hooked her arm around the young man, and dragged him to dry land. My friend said it would have been a wonderful story — inspirational, even — if it weren't for the way the young man struggled against the champion swimmer, and when she finally yelled, "I'm saving you, I'm saving you," he cried back, "I'd rather you didn't, I'd rather you didn't."

"He said it just like that," she told me. "'I'd rather you didn't, I'd rather you didn't.' Can you imagine?"

"Imagine working up the nerve to swim that far out, only to have your plans botched by some do-gooder Olympian," I said.

"I haven't been able to stop thinking about that day all summer," she said. "I couldn't tell you why. I know it affected Rick, too. He refuses to talk about it."

My second whiskey was gone. I traced the edge of the glass with my fingertip.

"The boy was taken away by ambulance," she continued. "He could be locked up in a hospital. Or he could have gone home and shot himself in the head." She stared into her empty wineglass, as though she might find something she'd misplaced there. "I wanted to find him and tell him I saw everything and that I hoped things got better for him, but Rick was against it."

"Maybe he made it," I said. "There's a chance he pulled through."

"I know this probably wasn't a story you wanted to hear, Diane." She wrapped her hands around the stem of her glass and leaned in close. "But it was just so troubling. I had to tell somebody."

"All bodies of water look the same to me now," I said. "Places to get lost in."

When the waiter came to see how we were, I asked for the check.

———

I knew my next meeting with Dean would be the last when he announced his plans to stay in Chicago after graduation. He sat on top
of my desk, cross-legged, picking at the hem of his white tube socks.
His pale shoulders gleamed. The young man my friend had told me
about was still on my mind, and I wondered what it was — drugs? a
love affair? — that had made him swim out into the lake and try to
leave himself there.

"But the whole reason you wanted to graduate early was so you
could go somewhere else," I said, getting dressed.

"I'd been thinking Columbia or Princeton, but DePaul or Loyola
would be pretty good, too," he said. "And then we could keep seeing
each other."

"Dean," I said. "Where did the word *marriage* come from?"

"Latin. *Maritare.*"

"And *nightmare?*"

"Old English. *Maere.*"

"And *story?*"

"Latin. *Historia.*"

"And *trial by fire?*"

"Old English, your favorite again. Comes from *ordal,* meaning a
trial in which a person's guilt is determined by a hazardous physical
test."

"Good," I said. "You're ready for the final exam."

"The final isn't for another week."

"Summer's almost gone," I said. "Time for the next thing."

"Why does there always have to be a next thing?"

"I blame the impermanence of existence."

"You think I'm so young," he said.

"You are so young."

"You think I don't have opinions of my own, but I do." He stood
and stepped toward me, his arms outstretched. "I have lots of them."

"Dean," I said. "Put your clothes on."

"No," he said. "I won't do it."

His clothes were piled in a chair. I scooped them into my arms. I was tired of the games I'd been playing with him, of the games I'd been playing with everyone. I wanted to make sure he understood me. I told him it was fine if he wanted to be stubborn, that he could just spend the night in my office, then I left. On my way home, I dumped his clothes into a trash can. When I looked down, his jeans and boxers had disappeared underneath silver shopping bags from the Atrium Mall, but his black T-shirt was still visible, splayed across a red gasoline can. It would be a mistake, I knew, to keep looking at his shirt. To touch it. To smell it. I reached down and pinched the sleeve. For the first time, I noticed the collar was faded and pocked with tiny holes. I smelled gasoline, felt grease on my fingertips. I was tempted to take his shirt with me, a keepsake from the summer when I took my life apart, piece by piece, like someone unsolving a puzzle. But instead, I just kept walking.

The next time I heard from my mother, her voice was a whisper on the other end of the line. Dean and I had been broken up for a week. He kept calling, first my office and then my apartment, and approached me in our last class, after I'd administered the final exam. He accused me of humiliating him; he said that if he hadn't dug through my office closet and found a commencement gown — which he wore home and didn't plan on returning — he didn't know what he would have done. He made a scene. The other students stared. When my mother called, it was the first time I'd answered the phone in days.

"Diane," my mother said. "I think your father is going to kill me."

"I don't think that's possible."

"He's been banging around in the basement all morning, making his plans," she said. "Last night, he kept shouting at me about the lawn mower. I really have no idea what's going on."

"That makes two of us." I walked down the hall and wedged myself into the cool dark space of the closet.

"I keep telling him that he should disappear," she said. "But he doesn't listen."

"You don't want to say that." I found my husband's baseball cap on the floor beside me and rubbed the brim, wondering how it had ended up in the closet, how *I* had ended up in the closet. "Mom," I said. "I don't know how much longer I'll be able to stay in Chicago."

"You could come here," she said. "You could help me with your father and the lawn mower and the doorbell."

"What's wrong with the doorbell?"

"It's broken."

"So where are you now?" I pushed the cap into the corner, underneath a stack of clean sheets. "If you're not in Nebraska."

"*Da nessuna parte,*" she said.

The phrase she'd used this time translated into "from no place." When I started to ask my mother what she meant exactly — how it was possible not to be in any place at all — she hung up. I stayed in the closet, holding the phone in my hands, feeling on the cusp of some kind of shattering.

Later that evening, I downed a shot of scotch in the kitchen. My husband had started keeping his diving equipment in the guest bedroom, and, even with the door closed, an earthy, raw smell had overtaken the apartment. I had another shot, then went to look at plane tickets online. I wondered what I would say to my mother when I got to Nebraska — if I would learn to comprehend the language she was now speaking, if I would know how to answer her back. I ended up studying the Web sites mentioned in the newspaper article on people who had changed identities: Metamorphosis, the New Life Institute, Disappearing Acts. They all looked like scams, all asked for money up front, and yet I couldn't help imagining myself as Betty or Raquel or Lucinda, couldn't help dreaming up a new life: I would go to some remote part of the West, near the Mojave Desert, say, and let my hair grow long. I would live in a trailer, so I could always pick up and go. I would write a futuristic account of a misunderstanding that led to a war that raged on for a thousand years, a war that could have been avoided entirely if someone had just said one thing differently. Finally, I turned off the computer and stared at the dark screen. I wondered about the one thing I should have said differently, the one thing that set me on this irrevocable course.

That night I dreamed there was a heat wave so intense that the mayor ordered all the city's residents to take refuge in Lake Michigan. Soon the lake was packed with bodies. The water was hot. We bobbed there for weeks, all of us, even after our skin wrinkled and peeled. Then one day I looked across the lake, and everyone was gone except for a single, distant person — so far away that the face was a gray smudge. I felt something like relief, like recognition, and started to swim. Each time I thought I'd reached him, it was only a dark spot on the water.

I came home one evening to find the balcony door open and a strange noise coming from outside. Dean was still calling, and my husband had been politely ignoring the phone calls I insisted go unanswered late at night. The department head had phoned earlier that day to schedule a private meeting with me. Her tone was somber and clipped, and after we set a time, she hung up without saying good-bye. I was in all kinds of trouble, and I knew it.

My husband was standing on the balcony, a tape recorder

clenched in his hand. He'd turned on the Christmas lights; I noticed one of the bulbs had gone dead. I went outside and stood beside him. He clicked off the recorder.

"School's out," he said. "Any exceptional students this time around?"

I looked at him, startled, but he was already staring at his hands, not expecting an answer. I wondered if Dean or someone from the university had contacted him, or if he'd somehow known all along. I pressed myself against the railing, weak with terror and relief.

"I can apologize to you in fifteen different languages," I said. "Where should I start?"

"I'm not interested in the languages you speak anymore."

"Fair enough." I looked at my husband. The bones in his face seemed to be weighing down his skin. I asked what he had been listening to.

"An audio of the mishegenabeg," he said. "I got it at diving practice. A cryptozoologist in Wisconsin recorded it."

"Play it for me," I said.

A low, hollow noise surrounded us, like an echo bouncing around a cave. Or like whales conversing. Or a primordial groan. He played it again and again. Of course, the recording couldn't have been real. It was something anyone with a little imagination could have made, but I didn't tell him that. I gazed at the lit windows staring back at us like eyes, at the glowing orbs of the streetlamps. This was the language he was conversing in now, and I would have to adapt — or not.

"What's going on with your mother?" he asked when the noise finally died.

"I don't know," I said. "I'm going to have to do something soon."

"And what is it you'll do?"

"I don't know that, either." I had so many ideas of what to do, ideas that felt at once intensely possible and as intangible as fog moving across Lake Michigan at sunrise. I could go to Nebraska and care for my mother. I could stay in Chicago and try to figure out how I had gotten to this point, surrounded by people I couldn't understand. I could finish my paper. I could write something new. I could help my husband search for the mishegenabeg. Or I could just disappear.

I looked out into the city, at the shadows between buildings, the peaks of skyscrapers. A row of people bicycling on the sidewalk below. A sombrero on a Dumpster. The smog that sank against the tops of buildings like hair resting on a woman's shoulders.

"Look at that," my husband said, using the tape recorder to point out a distant building and the pair of lighted elevators rising and falling, so bright against the black of the structure.

"I want to be buried in a city," I said. "There's no such thing as night here."

"Lake Michigan's deepest point is nearly a thousand feet." He rested his arms on top of the railing and leaned against the iron bars. "It's so dark down there, nothing grows. It's called the hypolimnion layer."

I didn't say anything more. I watched the elevators rise and fall and thought about the people inside, imagining a group of four or six — couples, perhaps — gathered in one of the compartments, the slight rush of dizziness they would feel as the elevator ascended to the top of the building. Maybe they were laughing, or maybe they were completely silent. Maybe, just before the doors opened, they looked outside and glimpsed the white lights strung across our balcony, or maybe they didn't see anything at all.

EDWARD PORTER

Wisconsin Institute for Creative Writing

THE CHANGING STATION

The walls of the New College Diner are decorated with heroes. Over the cash register hangs a framed clipping of Fiorello La Guardia cutting a ribbon. To the left of Fiorello, Derek Jeter's luminous face glows against a black velvet background, and next to Derek is a gilt icon of Jesus being handed down from the cross into the arms of his dispirited teammates. The New College is a prosperous Greek place with crisp green Formica tables and upmarket coffee on the Silex. At this early hour it's filled with Brooklyn's firemen and ironworkers, who have come in from the penetrating February wind for omelets and pancakes. The mommies with strollers will show up later to order fruit and oatmeal while their infants wail.

Teddy Figliolia downs another therapeutic strip of bacon and ponders what the Little Flower, Captain Clutch, and Our Savior all have in common, besides good nicknames. Maybe it's a quiet tolerance for pain: a sick wife, the grind of the season, the nails and thorns.

Across the table Shayn says, "Priorities change. Times change. This denial shit gets you nowhere." He sucks runny egg out of his Fu Manchu. "It hurts me, positively hurts me to see you with your dignity all fucked up like this. This is friendship talking." Teddy and Shayn go back to grammar school. "You cannot compete with a baby. That shit is Darwinian." Shayn's finger stabs, and his tall Afro trembles. The Fu, the 'Fro, and the long brown leather coat are his homage to seventies movies. The effect is only partly undercut by Shayn's bowling-ball figure and Coke-bottle glasses. As kids, they made an O and I profile together.

"Let me break it down for you," Shayn goes on. "Basically, what you have to offer is manhood, which is good, because whatever's going on in the prefrontal lobe, the temporal lobe is thinking *baby,* I don't care if she's eighty years old. But once there's an actual baby, none of that applies. It makes you totally a posteriori. You know what that means, right?"

"I'm Italian. We invented that shit."

Shayn digs it with a nod. "Anyway, now you're just some sad-ass horse running after the cart while the barn burns."

"I don't know what that means."

"Yes, you do."

Teddy's good thing with Maria has been in the toilet for the last six months, a month for each year they've been seeing each other. At first they worried about her husband, Hector. "That *pendejo* would put my head through the TV," Maria told Teddy, conjuring awkward scenes in Teddy's head about what he would have to do in response, should that come to pass. But then Hector shacked up in Fort Lauderdale with his own girlfriend, who was, in Maria's words, some ninety-pound Vietnamese bitch. With Hector gone, Maria and Teddy relaxed into being normal middle-aged boyfriend and girlfriend. After a while they even had a kind of family life with Maria's daughter, Nina, and later Nina's girlfriend, Peru. A screwed-up, half-assed family, but one that worked as well as or better than others Teddy had known.

Nina's baby changed all that. If she knew who the father was, she wasn't saying. Teddy suspected a boy who worked at a video store, but it could have as easily been someone she'd met at a club, or the janitor. Now Nina was trying to finish high school and Maria was a full-time mommy again, with no time or interest for the kind of games she and Teddy used to play.

Gia comes by and refills their coffee cups. Gia is the New College's secret weapon. Twenty-two, olive skin, long dark hair, she shows plenty of midriff and a jeweled navel. Shayn is her special project. "Hey, Shayn," she says, "you think my butt's too small?" She turns, showing them the packed rear of her Lucky jeans and the blue-green tattoo of the Acropolis across her lower back. "I think maybe I should get steroids in my butt like Barry Bonds." Shayn shifts in his seat, and Teddy finds it impossible not to reflect on what *Greek* means in sexual terminology.

"Everyone gets a big ass eventually in life," Teddy says, trying to get Shayn off the hook. His own is a case in point. "There's no need to rush it."

She takes the Acropolis behind the counter while her father, Stavros, glares at them from the cash register.

"That is some unfair shit," Shayn mutters into his coffee.

"How're things at home?"

"The same." Shayn has moved back in with his mother to take care of her. Her feet, her bowels, and her mind are all failing at the same time. "Let's get out of here. Let's go to work and make some money. Like men."

On the street, Teddy squints against the slanting early light and turns his collar against the wind. A high mackerel sky is lined with pink in the east and oncoming heavy gray in the west. Dust blows straight down Fourth Avenue all the way from the tallest building in Brooklyn, the Williamsburgh Savings Bank, with its high tower and striated cap. The bank has been bought out — likewise the company that bought it. Now the building is being converted into luxury condominiums by, of all people, Magic Johnson. Oz has nothing on Brooklyn. Shayn works there, hanging electrical boxes and running BX cable.

Shayn lights a cigarette despite the wind, cupping his hands over his Zippo like Steve McQueen. "Anyway, you ask me, it's time for you to move on. Ask out Miss Athens."

"The fuck I'm going to do with a twenty-year-old girlfriend?" Teddy says. "Here, honey, listen to this. It's by a band called the Rolling Stones." As if Gia would go out with him.

"Come on, you still a handsome motherfucker."

"I'm bald."

"You could make that a positive. Shave that Friar Tuck shit and get a Captain Picard thing going on."

Teddy bumps fists with Shayn and heads down Union Street. The chilly air burns doubly in his throat — with cold, and with lingering trails of acrid truck exhaust.

The truth is, he's stuck on Maria. He misses her modeling the dresses she makes, standing on the ottoman, arms up over her head, merengue-shuffling her hips and driving him wild. He misses her bed. Maria favors blue and green sheets. Making it in her bed is like falling into the ocean. He misses the contrast of their bodies, his thick squared-off frame thudding like a wedge into her slender curves. He misses lying together afterward, rubbing feet, while she tells him stories about her childhood in Mexico, stories filled with uncles, aunts, great-grandmothers, and donkeys.

Waiting for Teddy on his bench at the casket shop are long runs of mahogany: fifty-odd ten-foot lengths. He milled them yesterday from rough stock, ripping them on the table saw, running them smooth through the jointer and the planer, carefully stacking them up with pieces of three-quarter-inch scrap between each length so that they'd lose moisture evenly and not bow. Today he'll put them through the shaper and turn them into coffin-lid moldings.

The shop's shaper is a brutal thing, a heavy squat green monster from the thirties, still going strong. With the machine unplugged, Teddy spins the height-adjustment wheel and taps the fence, testing the cutter head profile against a scrap of molding. When he's satisfied, he plugs the beast in and settles into the long routine of easing each length into the auto-feeder on one end and lifting it out at the other. Teddy never feels truly comfortable around the shaper. He keeps checking his sleeves, making sure they're tightly rolled. Anything that gets pulled into the rollers of the auto-feeder goes into the cutter head. Anything that meets the cutter head turns into vaporized shit.

The mahogany is ravishing: rich, buttery, light red, open grained, its symmetrical flames flecked with chocolate. A dry, musty floral smell like burned roses fills his nostrils. The cutter head is heating up against the wood. Wood like this makes him want to rub his face against it, brush his lips against it, kiss the center of each flame pattern like a nipple on a breast.

On his lunch break, Teddy pulls his side project out of the spray booth. The mahogany table has a soft insert on top made of cotton batting under a purple silk coverlet. A heavy egg-and-dart molding runs around the top, the beveled legs taper elegantly, and there are two shelves underneath for diapers, Vaseline, and talcum powder. The general idea came from a baby magazine lying around at Maria's house, but what he's built is ten times sturdier, a hundred times classier than the white wire piece of crap in the advertisement. He works over the hardened lacquer finish with ultrafine steel wool.

Maria has been changing the baby wherever she can: on the sofa, on the kitchen table, even on the radiator cover. A few weeks ago, Teddy was at her house and every available surface was covered with dressmaking things. Maria put Caitlin down on her back on the wooden floor, and the baby began to cry. He thought the floor was too hard for her and said so, but Maria told him he knew nothing about babies, and if he didn't have a better solution he should keep his mouth shut.

Teddy blows the stand clean with compressed air and sets it under the skylight to admire the luster. Definitely a better solution.

After work, Teddy carries his project on his shoulder toward his apartment a few blocks away. Time to shower and put on decent clothes before he goes to Maria's. He walks over the Gowanus Canal and past the same school yard where Shayn long ago handed him his first puff of weed. The sky has gone oyster colored, the wind has died down, and a light snowfall is sifting down onto the streets, melting into the chemical-green ripples of the canal.

He and Maria got really tight after 9/11. She came over to his apartment the next day. No one he knew had died. Considering how many of his classmates had become firemen or cops, that was close to a miracle. Maria's cousin had been delivering someone's breakfast in the north tower, or at least that was the family's best guess.

She clung to his sleeves, sobbing against his chest until she'd wet the front of his shirt with tears, saliva, and mucus. She beat her fists hard against his breastbone and shook him. He said nothing, merely receiving her fury until she grew quiet. Then she unbuttoned his shirt, unzipped his pants. She took him in her mouth and looked up into his eyes. Her frankness shocked and excited him. They did that, and many other things. When they could do no more, they lay in the brilliant late summer light that fell between his white sheet curtains, staring at the perfectly blue, perfectly silent sky. The fire escape was covered with ash.

"In Chiapas, when I was a girl, after a funeral my parents always disappeared into the bedroom, and my sisters and I had to play outside. Today, we did the same. You know why we did that, Teo."

"I sure don't."

She grabbed a handful of his graying chest hair and tightened her fist until he took in a sharp breath from the pain.

"Feel that?" she asked.

Maria wants to scream. Her days lately build to this same high point of tension and disappointment at opening the mailbox. The mail comes between four and five, and for the last two weeks now she has been waiting for an envelope addressed to Nina from CCNY, or Brooklyn College, or Hunter. A thin one will mean bad news, and a fat one will mean that Maria's life will continue like this, unbearable, for years to come. But there's nothing in the box today, unless an invitation to buy condominiums in Arizona counts as something.

Once she is back inside her third-floor apartment, it sweeps over her again. She wants to scream now at the clutter. Jammed into the small living room along with the orange sofa, the armchair, the ottoman, and the TV are two sewing dummies, a thirty-year-old Singer electric, her sewing desk, tackle boxes filled with notions, yard rolls of brightly colored cotton, bolts of linen and silk leaning vertically in the corner, and a silver rolling rack on which four summer dresses hang.

Caitlin is asleep on the sofa. Maria smells her to check on her diaper situation: just a whiff of soap and, faintly, milk. For the moment her tiny face is as peaceful as a blank round of cookie dough, and Maria is grateful. Caitlin wakes and complains more and more often every week. Maria can work with the baby on the floor, or in a sling on her chest, jogging the child even as she sews, but it is exhausting and slows her down badly.

She sits at her desk, the baby on the sofa next to her, and pulls out a handful of eye hooks. The eye hooks, the hem, and then this one will be done. She is finishing a cotton summer dress in aqua, beige, and orange, with a wide tie at the waist. Summer dresses are just coming into the stores, and her best client — Margery, the one with the boutique on Smith Street — has asked for six pieces by tomorrow for the weekend shoppers. The dresses sell for $150 each, of which Maria will get half, and then she must subtract for material, although not for taxes — everything happens in cash. The margins are slim, but this way she can work at home; this way everything works out, almost. She is lucky. Things would be different if Margery and a few other shop owners were not so in love with her designs, which they call naive, charming, original. "It's like they come from some Mayan Riviera," Margery gushes. In fact, her designs are shrewdly simple, driven by the need to make many pieces quickly and cheaply.

There is time today to make one more dress, if the baby isn't fussy, if Nina doesn't have a meltdown. It has been forever since Maria has worn anything but a housecoat, forever since she has put on makeup, eaten a meal in a restaurant, or taken a walk. For the moment the house is at peace. As she works, Maria indulges her secret gringo vice: show tunes on her small boom box, the volume turned down low so as not to wake the baby.

She picks *Brigadoon,* hoping it will take her on a familiar trip. She'd like to disappear into the mists herself for a hundred-year vacation. She'd like to go roaming through the heather on the hill, though she's never seen heather, let alone Scotland. But who would she go roaming with? That kind of dream used to be easy for her — someone beautiful would always come to mind. Hector had been like that in the beginning, with almond eyes and black curls. When was the last time she'd been with someone beautiful? She can't even remember. Of course, there is Teddy. She could go with him and watch his big feet trample all the heather in Scotland. It's incredible how much space he takes up — like having a horse in the living room. Teddy Figliolia is anything but beautiful. That had been the wisdom at first: A plain man wouldn't leave or betray, or if he did, he couldn't hurt her so much. She'd wanted a lover without the grief and worry of falling in love. But these days he is just more clutter — in the house and in her head. Maybe it's Teddy now that's getting between her and the music. On the tape, Gene Kelly hits his sweetest notes, about how "the clouds are holdin' still." She reaches for her old fantasy of romance, but it's no good. All she can feel is how she misses feeling, and she wonders if she's arrived at a point in life where those emotions dry up and there's no more Brigadoon, only Brooklyn.

She is cutting out the next dress when Nina and Peru, covered in snow, come stamping through the door in a rush of cold air, singing — or rather, yelling — what passes for popular music these days. Instantly, the baby wakes and screams.

Nina dumps her coat on the floor and rushes past Maria.

"Here I am, baby. Mommy's here." She lifts Caitlin from the sofa and jiggles her, snuffles her face, kisses her, while shooting Maria dirty looks. "Yo, Mom, you changed her and shit, right?"

Nina pulls up her Queen Latifah T-shirt and unsnaps her bra. Just as Nina's milk flows at the sight of Caitlin, something deep flows in Maria at the sight of her daughter, something that both makes her despair at how fast her child is turning into a stranger and gives her the strength to endure it.

With arms folded like the proud poppa, Peru leans against the wall as Nina tries to get Caitlin to take her nipple. Caitlin flails at the breast, wailing. Nina makes owl eyes at Peru and says, "Damn, she's like beating on me again." The girls giggle.

Peru is a lanky thing with spiky blond hair, a skinny ass, and a zipperlike line of silver rings across one eyebrow and down one ear. Until she reached eighteen, Peru was called Maureen. Nina chose her second month of pregnancy as the moment to hook up with another girl. Maybe she'd had it with men, a decision Maria could understand. Or maybe she felt she could sneak this latest bit of experimentation under the wire before giving birth. Naming the baby Caitlin was Peru's idea.

Peru turns to Maria as if she's just noticed her, beams, and says, *"Buenas noches Señora Centelles. ¿Cómo el trabajo fue hoy? ¿Era Caitlin una buena muchacha?"* Maria winces inwardly, but it is more sensible to help Peru with her high school Spanish than to throw her out. Peru is always happy to set the table and do the dishes. Maria would never say it out loud, but the girl has been a good influence on her daughter. As long as she's around, Nina can rebel without leaving the apartment. At least Peru won't get Nina pregnant again.

She should have been much stricter. She should have locked Nina in her room. Instead, look at the example she set, bringing her own lover into the house. Ultimately, she knows Nina's problems are her fault.

Nina breaks in. "Mom, you have to give Peru a ride over to Top-Kat tonight."

Maria's eyebrows knit and her voice is full of casual menace. "You said she quit dancing at that place." She couldn't exactly forbid Peru's career as a stripper, but she'd made her feelings clear.

Nina says, "So now you think I'm a liar?" There is no point in Maria's answering that. "She has to get her paycheck. They still owe her for like a month."

"Just a week, actually," Peru says. "If it's not too much trouble. It's three hours by bus, but I can do it. Only, Nina and I have this big science thing we're supposed to be working on tonight? We're on the same science team?" Peru has her age's annoying habit of making questions out of statements.

"When, exactly, am I supposed to do this?" Maria says, holding up her shears. "Who's making dinner tonight?" She can see how the evening will unfold: She will wait for God knows how long parked in front of a strip club, and they'll end up having pizza for dinner. Then the girls will close the door of Nina's bedroom and make out — or worse. She will have to invent excuses to bother them every half hour to make sure they get some work done. Meanwhile, Caitlin will shriek all through her bath and shit her diaper the moment she has been cleaned and wrapped up. Maria will have to make Peru go home at eleven and endure Nina calling her an uptight bitch, and she will not finish the dress until the middle of the night, assuming she can stay awake. All of which would be endurable if Nina was grateful, or merely civil to her.

Even now, as she jiggles Caitlin on her shoulder, Nina sniffs the air and wrinkles her nose. "Yo, what is that? Something really stinks. I think it's coming from over there." Gene's voice swells from the boom box: The guy could swear he was falling in love. Maria snaps him off, embarrassed to be caught listening to such corny stuff, hurt that Nina will not leave her this one pleasure.

Another male voice, husky and rough, startles her. "Hey, it's the ladies' club. Mirror, mirror, on the wall, who's the fairest of them all? Tough call, but I'm going to say the one with the big scissors."

For a second Maria is afraid it's Hector come back — as he swore he would — to break her neck for registering him as a deadbeat dad and for letting their daughter turn into a Godless dyke. But it's just Teddy standing there like an ox, holding some kind of oversized plant stand in his hands, his face an ugly red from the cold. The girls say his name as if cheering. In a way, Teddy is more embarrassing to Maria than her weakness for musicals: damning evidence that she is no better than Nina.

"What are you doing here?"

Teddy blinks. "We said. Last week. How I'd come around Thursday, check on you."

"We did?" She notices that Nina's shirt is still pulled up. "Cover yourself, young lady."

"Hey," says Teddy. "I'm mature."

Nina puts Caitlin on the couch, arches her back, and redoes her bra. "B-F-D. He's seen tits before, hasn't he?"

"You don't have to wave them around. Have some manners before company."

"What do you think?" Teddy sets his wooden contraption down carefully in front of her. It isn't a plant stand. But what is it? The top of it is an open box with a lining of purple silk.

"I'll show you," Teddy says. "Okay if I pick her up?" He lifts Caitlin and lays her in the pocket. "For when you do her diaper. It's all spline-joined, not a single screw. It should last through Caitlin's granddaughter."

The stand is heavy, dark, and polished. The box on top should contain anything but a baby. It looks like a coffin. This coffin-making idiot from the coffin factory has given her a baby coffin.

She lifts Caitlin off and holds her close. "Get this thing out of my house."

He takes a step toward her. "Look, baby —"

That word in his mouth does it. She slaps him.

Teddy and Peru are in Teddy's car, heading up the BQE toward Queens. "You really ought to learn to drive," he tells her. "What if you had to live in America or something?" Snow is pouring down fast, the road is slippery, and Teddy cranes his head right and left, keeping tabs on the trucks. Every time he checks his rearview mirror he sees the top of the changing station in the backseat.

"Anybody can drive a car." Peru is sitting with her back against the unlocked door, feet up on the seat.

"Which makes it kind of pathetic that you can't. Will you put the seat belt on?"

"Don't be telling me what to do." Peru cranks her neck at him.

"Do you have any idea how fucking ridiculous you look when you do that?" First Maria, then this trinket rack of a child. "Sit straight, and put your seat belt on."

Peru does as he says in a slow ballet of disgust. She stares out at the blizzard while her fingers become interested in the zipper of her coat.

After a few minutes of this, Teddy says, "Why are we going to get a paycheck? I thought you ladies" — he wants to avoid the word strippers — "made all your money in tips."

"They have to pay us something on the books, too."

"Why did you quit?"

"It's too far away?"

More silence. "What exit again?" says Teddy, remembering full well that it's Marine Terminal.

The TopKat is a block-long black box near LaGuardia. It looks more like a warehouse than a nightclub. As they pull up, an airplane comes in so low overhead that an empty cardboard coffee cup rattles in the holder and a pencil walks across the dashboard. Hanging from the front of the building is a blue neon sign of a top hat, with the broken words GE TLEMAN'S CLUB.

"Give my regards to Mr. Getleman," says Teddy.

"I'll be right back," says Peru, and Teddy reflects that true wit is wasted on the young. She doesn't close the door, and he has to reach over and slam it to keep the snow from whirling in.

He leaves the car running and turns on the radio, searching for hockey or basketball, something to distract him. When was the last time a woman had slapped him? Maybe ten years ago, and he'd deserved it. On a date with one girl, he'd admired the ass of another — out loud. He'd been drunk, of course, and the ass in question had been heart-shaped and utterly remarkable, but he'd definitely had it coming. This time, though, he hadn't deserved it.

Maria had followed him outside. They'd stood in the steps to the basement, out of the wind, while Maria apologized in a flat, useless, I-can't-help-myself tone. Somehow the blame shifted from her to him. "You show up out of nowhere," she accused. "Next time, don't come over without calling." Women were masters at this guilt stuff. A guy was helpless.

"It won't happen again. Fucking believe me, it won't happen again," he said, thinking Shayn would have told him to walk away and not come back. He could have done just that, but he'd left his watch cap inside: Snow was melting on his naked pate, sluicing around his occipital bone and down his neck.

Her energy spent, Maria slumped against the cold concrete. "I know I shouldn't have hit you," she said. "Don't be mean to me. I can't take one more person being mean to me. Help me. Please." She might have cried then, but she didn't. She turned blank and empty and exhausted instead, which was worse than crying. She folded her arms, her body closed.

Teddy began to nod, saying "Okay, okay," his anger leached away. What did she want him to do?

There is a thump at the car door, and Peru flings herself back inside. "Let's go. Asshole."

"What did you say?"

"Not you. *Him.* Can we go?"

"What happened?"

"Nothing. They didn't give me the check, okay? It doesn't matter. Can we go now?"

"Uh-uh," Teddy says, turning off the ignition.

The TopKat isn't doing much business this Thursday night — the snow must be keeping people away. On a glitter-edged platform bathed in pink light, one naked girl shimmies a pole, while another butterflies her legs on the lip of the stage. Men stare into her crotch as they drink beers and shots. Some wear three-piece gabardine; others wear baggage-handler jumpsuits. The pounding music doesn't fit: It's ABBA, or some other teenage shit. A couple of muscular young bartenders man a long bar. One of them looks up, notices Peru, and scowls.

"We want to talk to —" Teddy turns to Peru, who is trying to shrink back inside her bulging parka. "Who is it?"

"Bill." To the bartender she adds, "It's okay, Shep." She nods at Teddy with a panicked grin. "He's okay. Really. Everything's fine." She pushes Teddy past the end of the bar, then yanks at his hand when he clutches a door handle. "That's the changing room," she says. As if to prove her statement, the door swings open and a big-breasted redhead wearing nothing but sparkling underpants, like a rhinestone diaper, hurries past them. Peru leads him farther down the hallway to a door marked OFFICE. Shep has followed them.

It takes Teddy's eyes a moment to adjust to the fluorescent lights. A middle-aged black woman in an orange sari sits at a desk, frowning over her computer screen as she types. Behind another desk a sandy-haired white kid in his late twenties is hunched over a Game Boy, thumbing it frantically. His dark suit is oddly conservative, like a funeral director's.

"Give me a second," he says, wrists flexing. The Game Boy blips, bleeps, and finally emits a sad spiraling melody. "Fuck," he says, then looks up and takes in Teddy. "Oh, hi, can I do something for you?"

Teddy shakes hands, embarrassed. He's not sure what he expected — maybe a fat unshaven ginzo troll with a cigar, or a brother in a long white coat and feathered Stetson.

"I'm sorry to bother you," he says, "but I have a problem with

Peru here. I think you owe her some money." He reaches back, and against her resistance pulls her next to him.

Bill's pleasant mouth puckers. "Let me ask you something, Mr. . . . ?"

"Figliolia."

"I'm just curious — what's your relationship?"

"It's kind of — I'm — I'm her father."

Bill does a double take. "Really, Mr. Figlia? I thought her last name was O'Grady." He looks at Peru. "You didn't lie on your W-4, did you?"

"Stepfather," says Teddy. "I'm her stepfather."

"You're sure? Because we try to keep that stuff straight for the tax people. Stepfather, okay." Bill nods. "Okay, you're here on behalf of your daughter. Sorry, your *step*daughter."

A prickle of heat forms at the back of Teddy's neck. "Look, I'm not . . ." He looks at Peru. "We're not . . ."

"No, no, of course not," says Bill, waving his hands in mock horror. "I believe you. *Dad.*" The woman stops typing with a snigger.

"Anyway," says Bill, "You're absolutely right. I do owe this young lady some money. How much do I owe you again?"

"A hundred and eighty-six dollars and fifty-seven cents," Peru says, after a nudge from Teddy.

"Yeah, that. In fact, Phyllis here cut a check for her, and it's sitting in my desk. But I'm not going to give it to her. You want to know why not?"

Teddy shrugs.

"Because I don't fucking feel like it," says Bill.

Teddy hears deliberately shuffled feet and turns to see a stony-faced Shep, arms folded to emphasize the biceps spilling out of his polo shirt. Teddy gives him what he hopes is an equally threatening glance. He turns back to Bill. "Do you mind elaborating on that?"

Bill shakes his head. "Sure, Dad. You see, your stepdaughter here is what you call rhythmically impaired. She couldn't dance her way out of a wet paper bag. Total waste of my time and money to put her on my stage. You think, someone's young, willing to show off her pussy, how can she fail as a stripper? It turns out she can. Fucking embarrassing, really."

"Bullshit," says Teddy. "Why did you hire her, then?"

"Oh, dearie dear," says Bill. "You sure you want to hear this, Dad? I hired her as a novelty act. Because of the hardware. You *do* know what I mean, don't you? I'm not talking about what's on her face. But it turns out, my customers think it's disgusting. One peek and they quit drinking. You can overdo anything. So, yeah, technically I owe her, but as far as I'm concerned she can bark for it."

Peru begins to cry.

"Now look what you made me do," says Bill. "This sweet young girl, your darling stepdaughter, this spastic talentless little cunt is crying. You proud of yourself, Dad?"

Teddy is half a head taller than either Shep or Bill, but they want him to do something dumb; they're hoping for it. He's tempted to accommodate them. He'd like to see Bill try his next joke with the Game Boy shoved in his teeth. Instead, Teddy says, "I'll talk to the owner."

"You're talking to him now." Bill pauses. "All right, Dad's in Florida. But you won't get him on the phone. He's sick. This is my watch. You think it's easy to run this kind of business? Someone doesn't hold up their end, it's fucking personal, as far as I'm concerned."

"You don't give a shit about the money," Teddy says. "What, she didn't do you a favor or something?"

"Now that hurts my feelings," says Bill. "Phyllis, Shep, am I like that? Peru, did I try to do anything to you? Be honest."

"No," Peru says, her voice barely audible.

"I'll tell you what. I'll give her the check if you ask nicely. How's that?"

Something in this boy's expression rings a distant bell in Teddy's mind, something to do with contempt. He thinks of Maria's face as she slapped him. Close, but not it.

"Well?" says Bill.

"Please give her the check."

"Say 'pretty please.'"

Teddy licks his lips. "Pretty please."

"With sugar on top?"

"Pretty please . . . with sugar on top."

Bill nods. "Now get down on your fucking knees and say it, you fat, bald piece of shit."

Teddy feels the four of them watching him to see what he'll do. He's pretty curious himself. He locks eyes with Bill. Fuck it, why should he get off easy? He goes down to one knee, then both.

"Pretty please," he says, "with sugar on top?"

A faint wave of sweat breaks on Bill's forehead; his blue eyes glaze over, like those of the customers in front of the stage, and his thumbs hook into his belt. For a moment Teddy is afraid Bill will undo his zipper.

Instead, Bill cracks up. Phyllis and Shep join him. The laughter is forced, but it's loud, and they laugh until they run out of breath. Bill goes around his desk, pulls open a drawer, and flips an envelope onto the floor in front of Teddy.

"Here you go, Dad. Maybe she'll buy you a rug with it."

Teddy pulls the car door shut. As soon as Peru is beside him, he hits the autolock. Unused adrenaline floods his gut, and he is momentarily overcome by nausea. He turns to Peru and hands her the envelope.

"I'm sorry you had to go through that," he says. "That guy. I should have...not that I could have...I wish..."

Words fumble through his mind, none of them the right ones. The sound of another airplane drowns out his thoughts. He starts the car and pulls out.

The snow has stopped, and the traffic on the BQE has calmed down. The long skyline of Manhattan emerges out of the clouds on the passenger side, the candy-colored dots of light smeared and refracted by water drops on the car window. The tires whoosh and spatter on the wet asphalt. The silence inside the car is unbearable. The only thing worse would be saying something.

Finally, Peru says, "That was weird?"

"Two hundred dollars — what the fuck, right?" He was supposed to help her. It was a job he'd taken on. They were stealing from a child. "Look, all that stuff in there, that never happened. We just came and went." But it did happen. He'd done that, and it wasn't going away, even if he never heard it mentioned again. "Anyway," he says, "at least you don't work at that place anymore. For that creep."

Peru pulls her feet up onto the seat and leans against the door again. He doesn't tell her not to. "I liked dancing there. They just didn't like me."

"I'll take your word for it," Teddy says, and shuts up. As hard as it is to explain this to her, it's harder to explain it to himself.

When they pull up in front of the apartment building, Teddy nods good-bye.

But Peru says, "Don't go anywhere. I'll be right back." Then, out of nowhere, she gives him a quick button kiss on the side of his head, and she's gone.

Maybe she wants a ride home and she's run inside to get her books. Maybe she wants to go put on a costume and dance for him in the snow to prove she's not a spaz. He tries to laugh at the thought, but he can't. It's not something he'd ever want to see. He only wishes he were that much of a bastard.

He settles back into his humiliation, exhausted and wide awake. He doesn't deserve this crap. It's Maria's fault for making him go, the girl's fault for dragging him into her sorry life, that stupid kid's fault for believing a suit made him a man. No. Those are excuses. This is his own shit. If nothing else, he can own up to that.

When the inside of the car steams up, Teddy draws a stegosaurus on the window, the same stegosaurus he's drawn since he was five. He likes to do the back plates very carefully, using the tip of his fingernail like a pencil. Once he gets home, he's going to take a long hot shower. A hot shower, some whiskey, and a calzone.

Now he places Bill's smirk. There had been a Sunday afternoon last fall when he convinced Shayn to take a break from his mother for a few hours. They were walking around sharing a joint when they ran into a young artist with an easel set up in the middle of the Third Street Bridge. He wore a black turtleneck and held an oval palette in one hand — the only thing missing was a red beret. Shayn nudged Teddy and they slowed down, gathering on either side of the guy and his canvas. He was painting the canal and the factories looking south.

"This is some high-class shit," Shayn said. "Where did you learn to do shit like this?"

The guy mumbled something about Pratt Institute.

"He got the letters backwards and everything," Teddy said. He pointed at the outline of the huge KENTILE FLOORS sign they were behind.

"They teach you that at Pratt," said Shayn, exhaling. "Paint letters backwards, forwards, upside down." He passed the joint to Teddy in front of the guy's face. "Look at how he's captured the way the canal looks like puke and shit at the same time. What is that, a combination of viridian green and yellow ochre?"

The painter let his brush hand slowly fall to his side. He smiled without joy and looked down at his feet, helpless, waiting for whatever came next.

Shayn was on a roll. "You've come to our neighborhood to capture — what? The ineffable fucking bleakness of it all? You know, you should most definitely put *us* in this painting. You could redeem this bleak shit with some humanity. We're going to stand right there," he said, pointing at the corner of the painting. "And you're going to paint us. Comprende?"

By the time they'd climbed down onto the landing and looked back up, the guy was gone.

"I think maybe we scared him off," said Teddy.

"Damn right. Gentrifying art school motherfucker," said Shayn, but Teddy thinks now he'd like to have that painting, with himself in it. A comforting piece of ugliness with a frame around it to prove he'd been here.

How long is he supposed to wait out here? It's been ten, fifteen minutes. He's burning gas, using up his life. It was easy to say, Don't be a dick to other people. But that never stopped anyone. That smirk had been on Shayn's face, and also, he knows, on his own.

The passenger door opens, but it isn't Peru. Maria leans in. Her hair is loosely piled up, and there is a dash of color on her lips. She reaches over the seat and lays her hand on the changing station. "Why don't you take this out and let me look at it again?"

The snow on the sidewalk hasn't yet turned to brown slush; it's still a crisp and brilliant blue white in the halogen streetlamp. The iron fence, the hydrant, even the garbage cans wear clean white coats. Teddy sets his handiwork next to the car, and Maria crouches down, balancing herself on the high heels of her boots, and gives it a good look. She takes off one glove and runs her finger along the bevel on the legs, runs it over the bumps of the egg-and-dart molding. "This is beautiful," she says. "It's just the top. The purple is wrong. That's for a queen or a pope, not a baby girl. And if it's for changing diapers, you have to be able to clean it."

"I can fix that," says Teddy.

"I'll use a towel for now."

"You want me to carry it upstairs?"

"Later. Put it back in the car. I'm freezing out here."

She climbs in the front seat, and when he joins her, she slides across and slips her arm around his. "I don't want to go back in. It's not late yet. Let's go out. I'll buy you dinner."

She fits the exact shape and size of the emptiness he's been carrying around, but his breath is tight, and there's a queasy feeling in his gut. "What did she tell you?"

Maria smoothes his forehead with her hand. Her touch is light, and Teddy turns to kiss her, trying to recapture a sense of strength, hoping to feel her lose control in his arms, but after a moment she slides her face so that they are cheek to cheek. He's feeling anything but sexy, anyway. Only part of her has returned to him. This is an effort she's making, not the real thing. This is her response to weakness and helplessness. Her body against his sets off a primal sense of relief, and yet at the same time he'd like to crawl out of his skin. It's not mere embarrassment about the changing station, or the slap, or him on his knees, or her knowing about it. It's all of it together, all of his own mess. It's being who he is, and needing someone else. He'll have to get used to it.

EMILY FREEMAN

The Loft Literary Center

THE CRITIC

Claire first saw the critic pressed up against an outside wall behind some bike racks, furiously smoking a cigarette as though the firing squad were on its way. He looked haggard, not at all how she'd expected a celebrated New York art critic to appear, and yet she recognized him immediately as the man who'd been chosen to deliver the Esther Weinberg Memorial Lecture, a lecture that she would later find out cost eight thousand dollars to book. With eight thousand dollars, Claire was quite sure she'd successfully be able to get her life in gear.

In any other place the critic would have passed as a homeless man, or maybe an older widower who lived on a small pension in a rooming house. But in this rural town five hours west of Manhattan, there were no homeless people and no rooming houses. The winter cold was enough to kill even the hardiest of souls, and none of the town's three churches stayed open all night for someone in need of shelter or prayer (if, however, some unfortunate drifter felt a fierce longing for a yoga class or a recital by a visiting Viennese pianist, he'd be in luck).

"Got a light?" Claire asked, fishing a cigarette out of her bag.

The critic looked up at her, a small smile forming under the overhang of his white moustache. He reached in his pants pocket and pulled out a matchbook.

"Thanks," said Claire.

He lit her cigarette, looking directly into her eyes as he did it, a gesture that just about made Claire weep for its quaint and outdated gentlemanly charm.

On the night before the critic came to town, Claire had spent several minutes crouched under her kitchen table, trying to make herself as small and inconspicuous as possible, while on the front porch Gregory Marx, Distinguished Professor of Ceramic Engineering, prowled around and peered through the window but never rang the bell, the engine of his car filling the street with a velvety Teutonic thrum.

Claire was mired in the confusing gray area of a postbreakup period, having recently split from her boyfriend, Paul, a graduate student in the art department with whom — or rather, for whom — she'd come to this small town in western New York state. She'd left behind a life of idleness and food-service jobs in a midsize Western city that she'd often thought of as a kind of "Never-Never Land," where everyone seemed to be engaged in a collective effort to forestall adulthood.

The breakup, which came on the heels of six months' worth of miscommunication and waning physical interest, was surprisingly amicable. It made Claire wonder what had been at stake to begin with, whether she and Paul had merely been drawn to one another out of a vague promise of mutual self-improvement, as though each had imagined there was something to be gained by their coupling. She wanted to conceive of it as some kind of animal-kingdom symbiosis, like a photo she'd once seen in a *National Geographic* of white birds that hung out in the mouths of crocodiles.

Paul moved into a spare bedroom in a friend's house, while Claire stayed behind in the apartment with their Goodwill armchair and a broken blender. Paul, nicely subsidized by a great-aunt in New Hampshire, had paid six months' worth of rent on the apartment ahead of time and seemed unconcerned that Claire was living there rent-free until she came up with a plan; so far there had been eleven of them, each of which Claire had settled on with absolute confidence and certainty, then discarded for either its elitism or unpromising pay. Currently, she was considering going back to school to become a physical therapist.

Claire felt that after suffering through a breakup on someone else's turf, she needed to do something rash and thrilling. This gesture took the form of a kiss shared with Gregory Marx, Paul's former professor, in the front seat of Gregory's car, after he'd driven her home from one of the three bars in town. Over glasses of bad Finger Lakes wine, Gregory had professed a long-standing interest in Claire, and out of politeness she'd acted surprised. He'd insisted on driving her home, and when, with one hand on the door handle, she turned to thank him for the ride, he'd planted one on her.

In this small college town, Gregory Marx was to most people either a hero or a villain. He aroused vitriol or hosannas, and those who loved him couldn't get enough of his gregariousness, his generosity, and his unmatched expertise in the area of ceramic engineering. He was one of the pillars of the school, the faculty member who brought in the most research money, and one of perhaps only two teachers on campus who attracted both graduate and undergraduate students from across the globe. There were plenty of detractors, though: disgruntled members of the administration, jealous colleagues vying for funding and notoriety, and local busybodies who didn't think it was appropriate that Gregory regularly went to the bars with students.

The Esther Weinberg Memorial Lecture was to begin at seven, and the auditorium was filling quickly when Claire arrived. She took a seat several rows behind Gregory. After his strange behavior on her porch, she wasn't sure how he would behave when he saw her, and thought it best to steer clear of his field of vision. She looked around the auditorium and saw Paul sitting with some of the other ceramics students. He spotted her and raised his hand in a friendly wave, though he didn't beckon her over.

Onstage, the critic stammered and stuttered, fussing with the microphone clipped to his shirt. Some undergraduates sitting behind Claire snickered, and she felt defensive, as if she had to stand up for this doddering old intellectual, for art itself, for New York, old men, and everything else that in that moment he represented. She spun around and glared at the students, and they were immediately silenced.

The critic spoke for exactly half an hour. The announced topic had been the future of ceramic art, but he made only cursory nods toward that subject. After concluding, the critic invited — was perhaps contractually obligated to invite — questions from the audience. These questions ran the gamut from simple inquiries about his professional life to a long-winded exploration of self that constituted a question only because the speaker remembered to add just a hint of upward inflection to his voice at the end.

The final question came from a student Claire vaguely recognized who was sitting across the auditorium near Paul.

"You write poetry," he began.

"Wrote," corrected the critic. "Wrote poetry."

A twitter rippled through the audience.

"Would you recite some for us?" the student asked.

"No," the critic said, scanning the audience for other raised hands. The students behind Claire snickered again.

Claire had questions for the critic, lots of them. They had nothing to do with ceramics, or even art in general, and everything to do with life and direction, and whether it was wrong to uproot herself once again because she'd made a mess of one relationship and seemed poised to do the same with another. She told herself she would take the critic's presence on campus as an omen, imagining for a moment that he'd been sent to help her — an oracle in no-press pants and a rumpled tweed jacket. *If you can hear me,* she thought hard in his direction, *make a sign.*

The critic lost his footing for a moment, appearing to trip on nothing, then quickly recovered. Claire sat up in her seat. *Thank you,* she thought. She looked down to the rows ahead of her and saw that Gregory had filled a legal pad with doodles: labyrinthine swirls and geometric patterns rendered with the steady, earnest hand of the hopelessly unartistic.

The dean of the art school, who must have interpreted the critic's stumble merely as a sign that it was time to end the talk, rushed up onstage. He thanked the critic heartily and invited the audience to join them in the lobby for a light reception.

Plastic cups of wine in hand, a group collected around the critic, eagerly asking questions, staring wide eyed as they listened to the responses. Claire headed over to a long table covered with food, where she saw Margaret Salsbury, a middle-aged painting teacher from Texas with whom Claire felt a certain easiness, which she partially attributed to Margaret's fondness for unapologetically comfortable shoes. Margaret made large bright paintings that reminded Claire of the pseudoscientific illustrations in commercials for toothpaste and razors. Her much-lauded *Gloaming 4,* a painting that had been exhibited in the Whitney Biennial and was now a part of the art school's permanent collection, seemed to Claire a send-up of a well-known commercial for a back-pain reliever. Margaret's work was known to be earnest to the point of solemnity, however, so Claire kept this thought to herself.

"They'll flock to anyone from Manhattan," Claire said, grabbing a plastic cup from the table where Margaret stood, topping off the pre-poured inch and a half of wine. "It's so touching."

"Oh, come on," Margaret said, scolding Claire with a furrowed brow and a slight tip of her head. "I bet you'd love to talk to him."

"Of course I'd love to talk to him," Claire said. "But not like that, not fawning all over him just because he's famous. Most of those people had probably never heard of him before he was introduced on the stage tonight."

"What would you ask him?"

"If he'd be willing to drive me back to the city and get me out of this stifling hellhole. You?"

"I don't know. Whether he thought ceramics was art or craft." Margaret snorted in mockery of what, in these parts, was a hugely important question. She took the last sip of her wine and pitched the plastic cup into a nearby trash can.

The subculture of ceramic art was one Claire had never given any thought to before meeting Paul and being whisked away to its mecca. In this town, she felt as much an outsider as if she were a guest in a hotel during a *Star Wars* convention, the lobby full of Wookiees and storm troopers as she walked to the elevators in a T-shirt and jeans.

Claire looked around for Gregory and spotted him by the large window, talking to Paul. She considered them side by side: the middle-aged academic with his paunch and thinning hair, the tall young artist with his clay-covered pants and strong hands who had at one point intrigued Claire enough to compel her to follow him to this strange place, where people spoke in a kind of ceramics patois, using words like *frit* and *slump, dunt* and *craze,* all of which sounded one letter off from things Claire wouldn't want to be called.

She looked back to where the critic stood, looking exhausted and vaguely contemptuous as he fielded questions. Claire noticed his empty glass and elbowed her way over to the table to grab him a full one.

His eyes brightened when he noticed her. "Thank you, my dear. Thank you."

The other students stared silently for a moment, dumbfounded, before launching into another onslaught of questions, like so many reporters outside of a courthouse.

The faculty, for the most part, exhibited a kind of jaded ease around the critic, as though they were comfortable — and some of them were — with people whose sphere of influence eclipsed so much of their corner of the art world. Some might have met him already; certainly all of them had read his reviews and knew who he was. Claire wondered which of the midcareer artists were still holding out hope of being discovered; which still felt as if there was time left to get a big break. This man, the critic, despite his awkward, often barely intelligible onstage ramblings, was still a very powerful man in the realm of their most sacred hopes and desires.

The next night a group gathered at Gregory's house for a small dinner party. It was the fourth in a series of parties he had hosted that semester. His inner circle and a handful of grateful graduate students were invited. Gregory was a generous host, and everyone was sure to eat and drink well. He would always grill lamb bought from farmers up the road, Mennonites whose shared worldview with academics began and ended with organic food.

Gregory had recently separated from his wife, and his daughters stayed with him on alternating weeks. His house was littered with bright plastic toys that seemed surprisingly vulgar, considering the taste he displayed in the art collection in his office. There he housed gifts from former students and admirers, pieces he'd picked up at the end-of-the-year senior art shows, as well as treasures from his overseas junkets. It was a spectacular collection, evidence of a taste that wasn't on display in his home.

Claire stood on the lawn looking up at the back of Gregory's house. It was a low-slung ranch-style with a kind of parvenu excess to the landscaping. Gregory and his wife had built the house when he'd received tenure, clearing out a section of hardwoods on a hill over-looking the university. Claire had been here before, for dinner par-ties — and for a short time she'd also been Gregory's housecleaner. She'd quickly realized that not only was she a poor cleaner, but that she was uncomfortable touching Gregory's king-size bed while wran-gling with his fitted sheets. Folding his saggy threadbare boxers was slightly off-putting as well, so after a few weeks she claimed an aller-gic reaction to cleaning products. Gregory found a local woman eager to take her place. "Hope the rash clears up," he'd teased Claire on the day she stopped by his office for her last paycheck.

Claire heard gravel crunch in the driveway and turned to see Paul's car.

Paul rolled down the window. "Hey," he said.

"Nice to see you," she said, immediately aware of the stiffness of her tone.

"I picked this up from the apartment, hope that's okay." He handed her a bottle of wine, which Claire recognized as coming from a case they'd bought the month before. Drinking had seemed, at least for a period, to calm the waters between them, so they'd arranged a series of dates to the liquor store in a last-ditch effort to shore up the relationship.

Claire reached through the window into the backseat of the car and retrieved her favorite straw hat, which looked as though it had been sat on. "Damn it," she muttered, trying to work some of the rogue stalks back into the weave.

After Paul parked the car, they walked up the hill to the house in silence. On the deck, Gregory stood up from where he'd been crouched by the grill, smoothed down his hair, and gave a confident wave of the spatula in their direction. "Evening, kids!" he called, lowering the spatula a few inches, as though framing Paul out of the picture.

Paul shook hands with Gregory and joined a group of his classmates, who were sitting in Gregory's plastic deck furniture with cans of cheap local beer in their hands. The beer had first appeared at parties accompanied by ironic comments and winks, but had quickly become a genuine, unironic fixture.

"Good evening," Gregory said to Claire, his tone of voice betraying much more than the face value of the words. Claire looked down at the bottle of wine Paul had handed her, noticing that it had a screw top. She looked back at Gregory in his faded jeans and bright baggy sweater.

"You two back at it?" he asked, gesturing with his head in the direction that Paul had gone.

Claire shook her head. "Just splitting up the belongings."

"I hear that," Gregory said with a chuckle.

The doorbell rang and Harry Marwell walked in before its three-tone chiming had ended. "Soup's on!" he called with a proprietary bellow. He laid down several canvas bags brimming with produce and began to dig through cupboards, ignoring the other guests in a mannered and unconvincing way.

Harry was a ceramic artist who made wildly colored vessels complete with gaping holes in their sides and necks so constricted as to render the pieces utterly useless for any practical purpose — his own contribution to the form versus function debate. While the party line held that one's art wasn't meant to evolve or stay put simply to keep pace with where the money was, Harry seemed to have settled on the right formula during the Buenos Aires Biennial fifteen years earlier and hadn't budged since. His work was wildly popular, appearing in innumerable private and corporate collections, galleries and museums the world over. He was a regular guest by satellite feed on *Art-Korea!*, a television program out of Seoul, and had been awarded a special Knight of Artistic Honor status from Queen Beatrix of the Netherlands. Harry spent his summers giving demonstrations at luxurious retreats in Maine and Seattle, taught one class per semester at the school, and was Gregory's best friend.

Claire had been introduced to Harry on several occasions, and still wasn't sure that he knew her name. They attended the same parties and ate at the same small restaurants, but on more than one occasion they'd averted their gazes as they passed one another in the supermarket. Harry nodded and smiled at her now, and she smiled back, until she realized that he was merely waiting for her to get out of the way of the stove.

Harry and Gregory bustled around the kitchen, as most of the guests sensibly tried to clear the area by heading out to the deck to watch the sunset. Though he always weakly invited the others to help in the food preparation, Gregory liked nothing better than to be left in his kitchen with his copper pots and his overpriced ingredients and his old friend, the two men gliding effortlessly around the stove and one another in a dance they'd perfected over the last twenty years or so of throwing these dinner parties.

Out on the deck, a couple of plates of hors d'oeuvres were being passed around. The conversation continued to feel stilted and sober as guests did their best to breach the faculty-student divide with well-meaning shoptalk. Although it was still light out, the sky above the treetops was slowly turning a bright pink.

"Tin-chrome pink," Harry said, emerging from the kitchen and gesturing at the sky with a knife. All heads turned toward the sunset. "I made a pair of vases with that glaze a few years ago. That same pink that you're looking at right now. They wound up in a museum in Omaha, of all places. It's neither here nor there, Omaha, is it?"

The students stared, not sure what the right response was, if any.

The deck chatter resumed. There was much talk of the upcoming ceramic art conference. This year it would be held in Niagara Falls, and people couldn't wait to get up there and talk slips and firing points in the rotating bar overlooking the waters.

Claire walked inside to the back bedroom, where partygoers' coats lay piled in a soft heap that in wintertime would grow as high as the windowsill above the bed. Against the far wall, stacked three deep, were boxes marked RUTH'S BOOKS. Gregory's soon-to-be ex-wife was taking her time clearing out her things from the house, and he seemed to do little more than make awkward jokes about it.

Claire looked at an earnest to-do list on a legal pad on the desk. *Clean garage. Montessori paperwork. Separation agreement to Ruth.*

Margaret appeared with a bottle of wine. "Talk to me," she said, filling up Claire's glass. "I can't stand listening to any more conversation about glazes."

"I can't *ever* stand listening to conversation about glazes," Claire replied.

"That must have made things challenging with Paul. He's out there holding forth on some wood-firing technique, and Gregory keeps correcting him in front of everyone."

"I can never figure out anything clever to add to someone's to-do list," said Claire, not looking up from the notepad.

Margaret peered over Claire's shoulder at the list.

"How about *Call for hepatitis test results,*" Claire said, scratching her head with a pen. "Is that even funny? I don't even know what's funny anymore."

Margaret motioned toward the door with the bottle of wine. "Let's go join the fray. I think they're going to start talking about porcelains soon."

Outside, a group was sharing a joint. It was twilight, and the sky was a rich blue, with a few stars just beginning to appear.

Gregory stepped outside with a plate full of raw lamb for the grill. "What have we here?" he asked, smiling conspiratorially.

Someone handed him the joint and he took a perfunctory drag off of it, making a show of holding in the smoke and then blowing it up toward the night sky. Once, in a drunken moment, he'd admitted to Claire that he liked to smoke pot at his parties to show his disregard for the administration and higher-ups. Claire had tried to impress upon him that both pot smoking and self-professed iconoclasm were qualities in men that she'd ceased to find attractive in the eleventh grade. She didn't even think Gregory enjoyed getting stoned, really. Whenever he did it at parties, he became edgy and fastidious.

Paul was sitting with his feet up on a cooler, lording over a group of grad students who seemed reluctant to bring their half of the party inside. Claire rolled her eyes at him as he took a drag. Below the deck, a couple of people were engaged in a furious competition on Gregory's daughters' swing set.

"Whoa there, guys," Gregory called out to them. "That thing's meant to support six-year-olds. You're going to pull it out of the ground."

They dutifully stopped pumping their legs, and the arcs of their swings turned shorter, the chains creaking. Beyond the swing set, a large black-and-white cat chased moths on the lawn.

Before dinner, as places were being set and dishes hauled out to the dining room table, Paul asked Gregory something about the thermal coefficient of a silky matte cone 10 glaze, and Gregory ignored him. Claire wasn't sure which one of them she was more embarrassed for and left the room before she had to draw her alliances.

In the kitchen, Margaret was standing at the counter, picking at the last of a tray of stuffed mushrooms.

"Is this a regional delicacy?" asked Claire, poking at a sodden brown bundle.

"You look so pretty tonight," Margaret said, smiling. "Can I try on your hat?"

Claire took off her straw hat and placed it on Margaret's head.

"I'll be right back," Margaret said, scampering off to the bathroom, sloshing wine on the linoleum.

From nowhere Gregory appeared with a paper towel, leaning down to wipe up the spill.

"How's it going?" he asked Claire.

"Good. Fine. I mean, you know, the same."

Standing up with a handful of soggy paper towels, he whispered, "I can't stop thinking about the other night. That kiss was white hot."

Claire's hand flew up to her mouth to halt the spray of wine. "I'm sorry," she said, laughing, as Gregory crouched down again with his paper towel.

"I'm serious, Claire," he said, sopping up the spilled wine.

"Can you please be more discreet?" Claire asked in a slightly louder-than-normal speaking voice.

A few heads turned toward her, and Gregory's nostrils flared. He shook his head and walked over to the garbage to dispose of his dripping towel.

"Dinner!" called Harry, walking out to the deck and banging two lids together with theatrical fervor.

Most of the other students declined, claiming to have eaten already, keeping their seats around the cooler of cheap beer. But Paul followed the call of the lids, high-fiving a couple of his cohorts as he left the deck.

Halfway through dinner, Harry set down his wineglass, wiped his red-stained lips with a napkin, and cleared his throat dramatically. "'I am dating,'" he began, peering around the table to be sure he had everyone's attention, "'a beautiful, though married, woman. And the worst part is not that she's married. The worst part is that we've yet to make love, despite a fondness which grows stronger with each whisper of affection on subway cars, or hand-squeeze while standing in line for fresh fish.'"

The table was silent, the other diners stunned by this pronouncement, as though someone had taken an axe to the lively din that until moments before had overwhelmed the house. "It's his poetry!" Harry proclaimed, lifting his wineglass high. "The critic's poetry, which he refused to share with us the other night — I have no idea why."

The entire party took a deep breath of relief, and laughter surged like a wave, tapering off into smiles as people reached in almost desperate fashion for their drinks.

"Where did you find it?" Gregory asked, breezing around the table refilling glasses.

"The Internet!" Harry practically shouted.

Margaret gasped. "*I* found something interesting on the Internet last night," she said, as though relieved to have suddenly remembered.

Harry scowled, never one to take limelight snatching very well.

Someone made a weak joke about pornography, which was met by a few concessionary chuckles.

The black-and-white cat suddenly appeared, buzzing up against Claire's ankles. She slipped it a piece of lamb, which it chomped down like a dog. Dishes were still being passed around the table.

"Careful of this one," Claire said, as she passed along a tray of vegetables. "It's white hot."

Gregory glared at her.

Margaret continued. "Last week the critic gave a talk at the Tate Modern. I found a little video clip of it online." She fairly drawled, her Texas accent all the more apparent now that she'd been drinking. She was still wearing Claire's hat.

"Word for word the same as ours. Every stammer, every hesitation. Even that inexplicable little fall at the end."

Claire wilted a little.

Margaret took a long pull from her glass. "Do you know what we paid for that lecture? Eight grand. For that price we should have gotten original thought."

"Or original delivery," said Gregory.

"Like he should have done it with an accent?" someone suggested.

"Or a limp," said someone else, vying for the punch line.

"Or blackface," said Claire.

There was silence for a second, and people went back to their food.

"Jesus, Claire," said Paul under his breath.

Gregory chuckled and gestured toward the chunks of lamb congealing on an enormous ceramic platter. "Plenty of food, folks, don't be shy."

"The critic fooled us," said Harry, mystified. "It was a shtick."

"No more so than anyone else's," said Claire, feeling at once woozy and invigorated.

"But no one else is getting paid for theirs," said Margaret.

"Oh, please, you can't possibly believe that," Claire said, helping herself to several more pieces of lamb. "Nice meat, by the way," she said to Gregory, who looked mortified.

"I've got one," Claire said. "I shared an unexpected kiss the other night —"

"Oh, goody, you found some of his poetry, too!" interrupted Harry, lifting his wineglass. "Recite! Recite!"

"I kissed Gregory the other night — or rather, he kissed me and I just responded appropriately because, you know, he's the boss around here."

The cat had wandered into the kitchen and was sitting softly in the corner, licking the grease off its paws.

Paul pushed his chair away from the table and walked out to the deck.

Gregory had turned quite red. All eyes, including Claire's, were on him. "Will someone get that damned cat out of here?" he said.

Claire got up and ushered the cat back out to the deck, avoiding eye contact with Paul, who had regained his seat by the cooler. From inside came the sound of dishes crashing in the sink.

Claire went back inside, grabbing the screw-top wine on her way through the kitchen. Her pronouncement seemed to have ended the meal, though several key players still sat at the table.

Gregory looked up at Claire, covering the top of his wineglass with his hand as she approached it with her bottle. With his other hand he reached for a different bottle that sat open in the center of the table. "Way to go, kid. You really know how to clear a room."

"Oh, please," she said. "You knew exactly what would happen if you got us up here and gorged us with wine and lamb until we started talking. Good one — well played, as always." She took a swig from the bottle and grimaced, then looked at the label.

A student appeared with the cat in her arms. "Your cat got outside," she said, then went wide eyed when she realized she'd stumbled into a situation.

"It's not my cat," said Gregory. "And please stop letting it in the goddamned house."

The student backed out of the room, the cat squirming.

Margaret got up from her chair, supporting herself on the edge of the table. "I'm going to go grab something from the wine cellar," she said, heading toward the basement stairs.

"Shall we go out on the deck?" someone offered.

Grateful for the suggestion, the others departed, leaving behind the unease that had landed on the table, wet and sudden like a frog.

"I guess this just leaves you and me, old man," Claire said, taking another swig from the wine and offering it to Gregory. "You really should try this. It's not half bad once you get used to it."

"Try to keep it together, Claire," he said. "This won't seem half as amusing to you in the morning."

"You could've used the doorbell the other night, when you were on my porch. Might not have looked so good if Ruth had driven by."

"I have no idea what you want from me," Gregory said, shaking his head. He stood up and left the table.

Claire, sitting alone, realized she had no idea, either, but as she watched him walk away from the table so disappointed she felt something flutter inside. Though it could've been the wine.

She took a final pull from the bottle and marched out to the deck to where Gregory was pointing, teacherlike, at the night sky.

"I don't, either," Claire barked, startling the student whose question Gregory had been answering.

Gregory stared at Claire, and she suddenly felt like the screwup daughter of a disappointed dad. Steeled by the sense that she had nothing more to lose, she grabbed Gregory's arm and yanked him down the steps toward the lawn.

"Don't be so disappointed in me, Gregory. You're not exactly exhibiting star behavior these days yourself. Hah! *Star* behavior." She pointed toward the sky.

"Claire, this isn't funny," he hissed. "Stop it right now."

"Never! To the death!" She jumped on Gregory's back and he staggered across the grass, collapsing onto all fours by the swing set. Claire held him in a choke hold while he tried to throw her off. They crawled around under the swings, wood chips collecting in Claire's hair and in the weave of Gregory's sweater.

The group on the deck began to cheer, and someone threw an empty beer can, which landed soundlessly on the lawn. A car started in the driveway, grinding into reverse and whining backward toward the street, a spray of gravel in its wake.

Claire was exhausted. She loosened her hold on Gregory and lay back in the wood chips, staring up at the night sky. One of the swings, jostled during their bout, swayed slowly in and out of her view. Claire could hear Gregory breathing heavily next to her.

"You should lose some weight," she said.

"You should get your shit together."

"Can I come to Niagara Falls with you? We could get married."

"Or go down the falls in a barrel," said Gregory, propping himself up on his elbows.

"And be dashed against the rocks," said Claire. "It would be awfully romantic."

"You got the awful part right."

"I'm a little embarrassed," she said.

Gregory shrugged. "You're not any less ridiculous or flawed than any of us, you know."

"Maybe we should try to make something work here."

"That's not what you want," he said. "It's okay, though. I wouldn't want to get in the way of physical-therapy school."

She punched him in the leg. "You could use a little yourself, you fat damaged fuck."

"Nice. What a lady."

Dish noises could be heard from inside, and laughter. Gregory sat up and looked in the direction of the house.

"Your plates will be fine," said Claire, knowing that the violent clanking of his delicate dishes in the sink was maddening to Gregory.

He sighed and lay back down.

Beyond the house, the woods were filled with the night noises of peepers and crickets. A dog barked, a sound so small and distant that it could have been coming from the next valley. The crisp, clear late-summer sky that looked down on them was filled with more stars than Claire could ever remember having seen in her life.

"I'll show you a constellation if you promise not to attack me," said Gregory.

"Deal."

"Just to the left of that long branch over there," he said, pointing.

"Where?" asked Claire, her eyes swimming in the speckled darkness.

"There."

"Oh."

"Start at the brightest light you see, and then move to the right, then straight up. That's Ophiuchus, the Serpent Wrestler."

"Like me."

"The bright star at the bottom is called a recurrent nova, and it's going to get hundreds of times brighter within the next few days."

Claire couldn't figure out where he was pointing, but was transfixed nonetheless by the vast sky overhead and the pleasantly plodding tone of his voice.

"Do you see it?" he asked.

"Yes," Claire said, her eyes now closed. "It's beautiful."

LYSLEY TENORIO

San Jose State University

SAVE THE I-HOTEL

The human barricade surrounding the International Hotel was six deep, two thousand arm-linked protestors chanting, *We won't go! Save the I-Hotel!* Inside, dozens more crammed the halls, blocking the stairwell with mattresses, desks, their own bodies. But it was past midnight now, fire engines blocked both ends of Kearny Street, and police in riot gear were closing in, armed with batons and shields.

"I hate this street," Vicente said.

"It's nothing," Fortunado said. He stood at the window watching the protest below, his fingers between the slats of blinds. "Just traffic."

"I'm telling you, it's the Chinese again. Their parade always clogging the city." He sat on the edge of his bed, folding a thin gray sweater over his lap. They were in his room on the third floor of the I-Hotel, next door to Fortunado's. "Don't worry, Nado. We'll make it through."

Fortunado closed the blinds, wiped the dust from his fingers. "We will," he said.

The threat of eviction had loomed for more than a decade, and now it was happening. The mayor of San Francisco had approved the hotel's demolition and ordered the removal of its final tenants, the elderly Filipino men who had lived in the I-Hotel for more than forty years. Earlier that day, protest organizers had gathered the tenants in the lobby to prepare them for the fight, and told them to stay in their rooms until the very end. "But pack a bag," they said, "just in case." Afterward, Fortunado hurried upstairs, woke Vicente from a nap, and, though he meant to tell him about the eviction, told him they were taking a weekend trip instead, just the two of them. He hadn't named a specific place, but Vicente was easy to persuade. These days, he barely recognized the world as it truly was: He never knew the day or time, oldest friends were strangers, and just three weeks earlier, Fortunado had found him on the corner of Kearny Street and Columbus, only a block from the entrance of the I-Hotel, asking strangers to help him find his way home. Now, in his mind, the shouting in the halls and the sirens on the street were simply the ruckus of a Chinese New Year. He knew nothing of an eviction, had no sense of the coming end.

Vicente's hands shook as he folded another sweater. Distant sirens drew closer. Fortunado thought, *This is what it means to be old.* Now he wished his youth back, and if granted, he would offer it up to Vicente, who would make better use of it. He imagined Vicente springing to his feet and running down the stairs to claim his place on the barricade, his fists raised and ready to defend their right to stay. He was, Fortunado knew, the stronger one.

It was August 4, 1977. If evicted tonight, they would have lived in the I-Hotel for forty-three years.

They never meant to stay so long.

They met on a September night in 1934. Fortunado had been in the States for five months, working fifteen-hour days in the asparagus fields just outside Stockton; this trip to San Francisco was his first chance to get away. He stepped off a Greyhound bus at the end of Market Street and wandered the grid of downtown, unable to distinguish the places that welcomed Filipinos from those that refused them. It was dark when he finally spotted a trio of Filipino men smoking cigarettes outside a barely lit doorway, and though no one said hello, they stepped aside to let him through.

He entered a long, narrow dance hall filled with mixed couples, Filipino men with white women. A gray-bearded man with a cane circled the room, calling out, "Dime a ticket, ticket a dance," and in the corner, a half-dozen women sat in metal chairs, waiting for the next customer. A banner that read WELCOME TO THE DREAMLAND SALOON sagged on the wall above them.

Fortunado bought three tickets, moved closer to the dance floor. He watched the couple closest to him. The man danced with his eyes closed, whispering into his partner's ear; the woman yawned, then rubbed a spot of lipstick from her front tooth.

Fortunado put the tickets in his pocket and took a chair by the wall. This would be a night of music to enjoy alone, nothing more, and it would be enough.

A new song began, and a man with a beer in each hand stomped across the dance floor, pestering girls for free dances. "Sorry, Vicente," a girl with a long cigarette said, "no money, no honey." She blew smoke in his face and walked off. "Your loss," Vicente shouted back. He finished one beer, drank the other. He was tall for a Filipino, lanky in his fitted blazer and trousers. He zigzagged through the crowd, bumping into couples, then suddenly tripped over the ticket man's cane. "I'm fine, everybody," Vicente shouted, gaining his balance. "I'm just fine." And to prove it he began dancing alone, swaying side to side with some imaginary partner. He was a drunk, pathetic sight, but Fortunado couldn't help but laugh.

Vicente saw him and walked over. "If I'm so funny," he said, wiping his mouth with the back of his sleeve, "then where's your girl, big shot?"

Fortunado shrugged.

"With all these fine girls around? Your head must be broken." Vicente flicked Fortunado's forehead twice, like he was checking the ripeness of a coconut. Fortunado swiped his arm away, and warm beer spilled over Fortunado's head.

"Idiot!" Fortunado got to his feet. "You want to dance so badly? Then take them." He took the tickets from his pocket and threw them to the floor, shoved Vicente aside, and walked off.

In the washroom, he ran a red cocktail napkin under warm water, wiped his head, and dabbed the beer from his shirt, the lapel of his jacket. He thought of his life in America: the hot, dusty hours in the fields, the muggy nights in the bunkhouses, all the workers who passed the time regretting the new life and lamenting the old. They were new arrivals, too, most of them Filipinos, and they never stopped telling him: *Nobody knows you here, just the work you do, just the color of your face.* They called America a mistake, and now the dream was to find a way back home, to the life you knew and the person you were. But these were the reasons Fortunado left; tonight was meant to prove that he had been right to come.

He looked in the mirror. The shoulders of his borrowed blazer were wider than his own. The sleeves fell past his knuckles. *Fool,* he thought to himself.

The door opened, and he saw Vicente in the edge of the mirror. "Never pay for dances," he said, setting the tickets on the edge of the sink. "That way, you find out which girls want your dimes and which ones really want to dance with you." He reached for Fortunado's lapel. "Messy boy. Wear mine." He removed his jacket and held it out, a peace offering.

"I'm fine with my own."

"Suit yourself." He lit a cigarette, introduced himself, then asked Fortunado his name. It was a question Fortunado hadn't heard since he'd been hired in the fields five months earlier. In his life now, weeks could pass without him hearing his own name.

So he told him.

"Fortunado." Vicente shook his head, exhaling smoke. "Too long. I'll call you Nado." He tamped out his cigarette on the wet, crumpled napkin and stepped toward the door. "This place is dead, Nado. Let's move on." He held the door open, and though Fortunado didn't move he continued to stand there, waiting. Fortunado realized that Vicente had come to the Dreamland alone, too.

Fortunado buttoned his coat, straightened it as best he could. "I'm a stranger here," he said. "You lead the way."

They exited the Dreamland. They walked up and down the streets, and Vicente named them: Kearny, Washington, Jackson, Clay. Certain blocks felt more familiar than the rest, those lined with small eateries and shops named Bataan Kitchen, the Manila Rose Cantina, the Lucky Mabuhay Pool Hall. Up and down the street, Filipino men smoked, laughed, and drank from silver flasks, hollering for each other and darting across the street, as if this city had been theirs from the beginning. And sitting on the top step of an apartment building was the oldest Filipino Fortunado had ever seen in America, gazing at the moon as if it held the face of the one he loved.

"Manilatown," Vicente said. "Our small place in San Francisco. Just like home, eh?"

Fortunado shook his head. This was better.

They continued walking, and Vicente told his story: He had come alone from Manila at the start of 1933, scrubbed toilets and floors for a miserable half year before finding better work as a bellhop at the Parkdale Hotel, a decent job with barely decent pay, but the best you could do in times like these. "It's hard out here, sometimes," he said, slowing his pace. "You get lonely, you get scared." His voice trailed off as though these were his final words for the night, the truth he finally was forced to admit. But then he stopped and turned to Fortunado. "So be tough, okay?" He reached over and punched Fortunado gently on the arm.

Hours passed, bars and restaurants closed, and they found themselves at the end of the city and walked along the Embarcadero. "Look there," Vicente said, pointing toward the water, and through the dark Fortunado saw it: the beginnings of the Bay Bridge. It would be the longest steel structure in the world, eight miles connecting San Francisco to Oakland. For now it was only a line of towers rising from the black water, half hidden in fog, and Fortunado wondered when it would be finished, if someday he might travel across it.

"I don't want to go back," he said.

"Then don't," Vicente said. "What's in Stockton, anyway?"

Nothing. Just the hard, thin mattress Fortunado slept on, the canvas bag filled with the few clothes he owned, and more days in the fields with the kind of men he dreaded becoming.

They made their way to 848 Kearny Street and entered the I-Hotel, where Vicente kept a room for six dollars a week. He offered his floor for the night and Fortunado accepted, rolled up his coat for a pillow, and used Vicente's as a blanket. It was his best night's sleep in America yet. The next day, Vicente loaned Fortunado twelve dollars for two weeks' rent, and he checked into number fourteen on the third floor, next door to Vicente's and exactly the same: a small, narrow space with a twin bed, a corner sink, a three-drawer bureau, and a single window that looked out on the 800 block of Kearny Street. Below, Fortunado could see two Filipino groceries, a barbershop, a Chinese laundry, and, on the rooftop across, an unfinished billboard with a half-painted picture of a crate of apples, the word NEW written in yellow letters beneath.

"Not much of a view," Vicente said.

Fortunado opened the window, letting in a breeze. "Good enough for now," he said.

Fortunado was twenty years old the night they met. Vicente was twenty-four.

Now Fortunado was sixty-three. Vicente, sixty-seven.

Neither of them had married. No one in the I-Hotel ever did, and when they wanted to, the law forbade them. No Filipino could bring a wife or fiancée to the States back then, and there were no Filipinas here. Marrying white women, even dating them, was illegal, and always dangerous. The same week Fortunado arrived in California, a Filipino fieldworker was beaten to death for swimming in a lake with his white girlfriend.

The law changed in 1967. "I've been alone this long," Vicente had said, "what would I do with a wife?" He was fifty-seven by then, too old and too late to bother with marriage. "She'd want a bigger place, something expensive. No thanks, I'm fine where I am." But during their Saturday afternoon walks through Chinatown, the sight of a wedding banquet always made him silent, and suddenly tired. He would want to get back to the I-Hotel, where he would pour himself a shot of Du Kang — the gold-colored Chinese liquor they drank as young men — and pace the short distance of his room as though imprisoned, then finally sit at the window with his hands on the sill, staring down at the slow-moving traffic. From below, Fortunado would watch him, knowing Vicente's regrets — the years of come-

and-go women, the time and money wasted on prostitutes, the failure to pursue a better life had he been brave enough to try. And Fortunado would think, *I'm sorry.*

Somewhere close, glass shattered. Vicente looked up from his packing, turned toward the door as if to investigate, then brushed his knuckles against his jaw. "I want to shave before we leave," he said. He went to the sink and turned on the faucet, waited for cold water to turn hot.

Fortunado went to the door, looked through the peephole: Protestors crammed more furniture into the stairwell, others hammered wood planks over windows already boarded up, and, at the end of the hallway, three men chained themselves to exposed pipes running down the wall while the rest cheered them on.

Fortunado double-checked the locks, tugged at the knob, and made sure the door would hold. "It's just the parade," he said.

Fortunado had left Stockton with no money and no plan, but in the beginning, San Francisco worked the way America should: He had a friend, a room of his own, and, soon thereafter, a bellhop position at the Parkdale Hotel.

Vicente lied to get Fortunado the job: He told his boss that a cousin with three years' experience as the houseboy of Seattle's ex-mayor had just arrived in the city, looking for work. "I told them I've known you my whole life," he explained, "so try to act like it."

The following morning, they caught the first cable car on the California line, rode to the top of Nob Hill, and stepped off at Powell and Mason. Straight ahead was the Parkdale Hotel, seven stories high, twenty windows across, and from where Fortunado stood it seemed the rest of the city had vanished behind it. Inside, a dozen marble pillars held up the lobby's mahogany ceiling, and a brass staircase spiraled upward. In the copper elevator doors, Fortunado could see his reflection: His bellhop uniform fit tightly and made him stand up straight, his pomade-slicked hair gleamed under the light, and the dozen buttons on his coat could be mistaken for gold.

Those months in the fields stooped over in the dusty heat, the brim of his hat casting an unending shadow on his face — that was someone else's anonymous life. Now, when Fortunado crossed the lobby, he would welcome guests in his best English, and they, in turn, regarded him with courteous smiles. But the best times in the day, those moments when he believed he was where he belonged, were when he passed Vicente in the hallway or on the stairs: Vicente would nod with a quick twitch of a smile, and sometimes, when no one was watching, he would reach out and punch Fortunado on the arm, just below his shoulder.

At the end of Fortunado's first month in the city, Vicente raised a bottle of Du Kang to the night sky and said, "To Nado, the finest houseboy in all of Seattle." He took a swig and passed it over. Fortunado drank, swallowing slowly to ease the burn.

They were on the third-floor fire escape of the I-Hotel, too tired to change out of their uniforms. They sat for hours, laughing as they reminisced about the night they met, as though it had happened years instead of only weeks before. But as the night grew darker and the air more chill, their faces turned serious, their voices quiet. "It's good that I found you," Vicente said. "Finally, someone I can talk to who doesn't whine about life."

"You can't listen," Fortunado said. "They'll get you down."

"But it's tough. No family. No wife. No home of my own." Vicente brought the bottle to his lips but didn't drink.

Fortunado put his hand on Vicente's shoulder. "Those things will happen. I promise."

"It's better here, yeah? We were right to come?"

Fortunado leaned in, so close he saw Vicente's eyes glisten, and said yes.

They let moments go in silence, and a solitary car drove down Kearny. "I'm drunk," Vicente said, setting the bottle of Du Kang by Fortunado's feet. "What's left is yours." He rested his head against the brick wall, blinked slowly until his eyes stayed shut. He was shivering, so Fortunado took off his jacket and draped it over Vicente's shoulders, tucked it under his chin. His hands were just below his jaw; then a finger, at the edge of his lip. He had been this close with others before — those few flirtatious men back home, who at some point became willing. But it had never been like this. Below, the street was empty and silent, every window and doorway was black, and the sliver of moon cast no light. These were signs that the world was offering up this moment, a chance to understand what it was like to kiss the one you knew, perhaps loved. *Good night,* he told himself, *that's all it means,* and he moved closer until their faces touched. He kissed Vicente, and when he meant to pull himself away he felt Vicente kissing him, too.

Then Vicente turned away. "It's late," he whispered, eyes still closed. "Time to go back." He got to his feet and climbed through the window, and Fortunado watched him walk down to the far end of the hallway, where he unlocked his door and shut it behind himself. It was almost light when Fortunado finally returned to his room. He sat on his bed, his back to the wall, and listened to Vicente on the other side, breathing and turning in his sleep.

Later, just before work, Vicente opened Fortunado's door, already dressed in his uniform. "Come on, slowpoke," he said, snapping his fingers twice. He made no mention of the night before, only that his head still buzzed from the Du Kang they had shared. Then he hurried down the stairs and Fortunado slowly got up, and when he saw his face in the mirror above the sink, he remembered how this would go — as it did back home, with silence and forgetting, the only way he knew.

All that became of their kiss was longing. Fortunado began counting off the days and weeks since it had happened, believing that enough passing time would blur the night into one that perhaps had never happened at all. But it only brightened in his mind, and when months dragged into a year and then another, it was undeniable: Once, long ago, they had kissed. On nights when Vicente caroused in bars with easy women or purchased hours in a Chinatown brothel, Fortunado would lie awake in bed, so restless that he kicked away his sheets, dressed, and walked down the empty blocks of Manilatown to the Embarcadero, where he would stand by the rail and look out at the Bay Bridge. Almost finished, it reached closer to the other side, and its progress was evidence that the world still moved forward, leaving behind a night when he was happy, and the moment he was utterly and finally known.

"I hate the bus," Vicente said, sorting through a pile of mismatched socks. "The seats hurt my back. No buses, Nado." He never wondered where they were going, only how they would get there.

"We won't take a bus," Fortunado said. He stood at the dresser, gathering their California IDs, Social Security cards, and passports, then slipped everything into a yellow envelope, along with a letter from the West Oakland Senior Center, where tenants would be temporarily housed if the eviction happened. There was no plan beyond that; some might return to another San Francisco facility, others to Daly City or San Jose.

"Amtrak is faster. We'll take Amtrak, right?"

Fortunado sealed the envelope, wrote their names across the flap. "I've got the tickets," he said. "Don't worry." He looked up at Vicente who had shaved just the right side of his face. He was careless with his grooming these days: He might remember to change his undershirt but not his underwear or socks; when he showered, he would forget to rinse the soap from his body, then go through his day with dried white streaks on his arms and neck. "You didn't finish," Fortunado said.

Vicente looked in the mirror above the sink, brushed his thumb against his cheek. Beneath the glare of the lightbulb, his stubble appeared thorny and white, as though painful to touch.

"Here," Fortunado said, "I'll do it." He filled the sink with water, took out a disposable razor and shaving cream from the shoebox beneath. He lathered the left side of Vicente's face, wiped his hand dry, then stepped behind him.

"Don't cut me," Vicente said.

Fortunado shook his head. "I won't."

The sirens were much louder now; police shouted threats of arrest through their megaphones, and in the hall the protestors whispered: *Block the front door. Check the roof. Hurry.* But if he leaned in just a little, Fortunado could hear the razor slide gently down Vicente's skin, the drops of water trickle from the faucet. Then the night was quiet again. When he was younger, he had longed for this closeness, ached for it, and now that Vicente could no longer care for himself, these were the necessary gestures of their everyday lives. And Fortunado welcomed the responsibility, secretly cherished it. Duty fulfilled desire as best it could.

Vicente flinched. There was no blood; Fortunado had barely nicked the skin. But as Vicente wiped the shaving cream from his face, Fortunado saw a spot of red, reflected in the corner of the mirror: the time on the digital clock, its numbers backward and inverted, urgent and glowing. It read 12:03 A.M. The next day already, and Fortunado realized he hadn't packed a suitcase of his own.

––––––––

1936. June. Two years in the city and nothing had changed. "What a life," Vicente said, passing a bottle of Du Kang to Fortunado. They were on the fire escape, exhausted from a double shift, and he was drunk. "Two hotels. One where I work. One where I live." Fortunado drank and passed the bottle back, but instead of drinking, Vicente turned the bottle upside down and let the rest spill through the grate. "How can you stand it?" he asked, then climbed inside as if he didn't want to know the answer.

Then, only a day later, there was a girl.

Her name was Althea. Vicente was on the seventh floor of the Parkdale, hurrying to the elevator, when a maid called out, holding a gold button between her fingers. It had fallen from his blazer, and she insisted on sewing it on for him. "Guess where she fixed it," Vicente said to Fortunado later that night. "In the Berlin Deluxe." He was bragging: The Berlin Deluxe was the hotel's grandest suite, but still under renovation two years after a fire had damaged the room. "She had a maid's key, and sometimes she goes there just to smoke a cigarette and look at the view. But we sat by the window for almost an hour. No one even saw us."

Except for the Berlin Deluxe, Fortunado had entered every guest room in the Parkdale, but just far enough to unload bags and luggage. He was never invited to look out the window, to gaze at the hotel's famous city views. "What was it like?" he asked.

Vicente looked at him and shook his head, as if what he saw was beyond Fortunado's comprehension. "You could see everything," he said.

The following Sunday, coming home after another double shift, they saw Althea on Columbus Street. She was standing in front of a Chinese mercantile, looking at the window display: a mannequin clad in black velvet, surrounded by boxes wrapped in silver paper. Behind it was a framed map of America, and Althea stared at it, as if studying all forty-eight states. "Planning a trip?" Vicente asked.

She turned toward them. Her red hair fell past her shoulders, and a lime-green scarf was tied loosely around her thin, pale neck; she was like no maid Fortunado had ever seen. "I'm just looking back at home," she said, tapping her finger on the glass. "Toward the middle, right there. Wisconsin. That's where I'm from. Mount Horeb. A tiny place."

"Do you miss it?" Vicente asked.

She shook her head. "Girls back there get married, have babies, and then they're stuck. If I'd stayed, that's what I would have become."

Vicente moved closer. "And what are you now?"

She tilted her head, smiled as though Vicente had asked a trick question. "I'm new," she said. "Like you. Like everybody here." She took a small tin box of mints from her purse, and offered one to Vicente. "What about you," she said, "do you miss home?"

Vicente took a mint. "I don't really think about it," Vicente said. Only when Fortunado said hello did Vicente finally make proper introductions.

The sun had set but the night was still warm, so Althea suggested a cold beer at a nearby tavern on Fourth Street. They walked down Kearny, crossed over to Third, and below Market the sidewalks narrowed as the crowds thickened. Fortunado fell several steps behind but could still hear them. Althea talked about living in San Francisco, about how fast everything moved — the streetcars, the people, even time. But life dragged, too: Her boardinghouse room was stuffy and dim, loud late at night, barely a comfort after long shifts at the Parkdale. "Some nights I stay awake all night, no matter how tired I am," she said.

Vicente nodded. "I stay awake, too." They walked so close their arms touched.

Fortunado stopped, and as they moved farther down the block he recognized the slight zigzag in Vicente's step. It was the way he had moved the night they met at the Dreamland, and now he recognized Althea, too. She could be any Dreamland girl, but there was a difference: When Vicente looked at her, she looked back at him.

They were half a block ahead now. Fortunado decided to leave, to return to the I-Hotel or make his way to the Embarcadero, to its darkest, emptiest spot. But then a stocky red-faced man stepped out of a bar, his sleeves rolled up and shoes untied, and stumbled toward Vicente and Althea, raving about brown men taking white women and white jobs. He grabbed Vicente's shoulder and turned him around, put a finger in his chest. Vicente stepped back, tried walking away, but the man took him by the collar and shoved him against a storefront window. He threw a punch, and Vicente fell.

Fortunado ran to Vicente, fists clenched, ready to fight. But the man was too quick, too strong, and he grabbed Fortunado by the shoulder and pushed him to the ground. He heard his name — *Nado* — and when he looked up Vicente was back on his feet, punching the man in his stomach. "I'm not scared of you," he said, "I'm not scared." With every blow he said it, until Fortunado pulled him off.

They hurried back to the I-Hotel, ran up to Vicente's room. Fortunado went to the window, checking to see if they'd been followed. "We were just walking," he heard Althea say. "That's all." But he knew the truth, and saw it reflected in the glass: Vicente and Althea on the edge of the bed, his arm around her shoulder.

The last thing left of Manilatown was the I-Hotel, and the human barricade was crumbling. Fortunado watched protestors fall to the batons of police, handcuffed and dragged away, and those still standing were not enough. A group of officers finally broke through and charged the front entrance with sledgehammers in hand. Behind him, Vicente slept atop the covers, facing the wall, wearing his coat and shoes.

In the hall someone with a megaphone told the tenants to keep their doors locked, block them with whatever they could move, so Fortunado went to the dresser and pushed it toward the door. But it was heavier than he'd expected, and he could feel his rushing heartbeat, sweat on his neck and throat. He stopped, took a breath, and just as he meant to try again he caught sight of something he had seen a thousand times before: the empty space on the floor beside Vicente's bed. Fortunado lay there once, and he remembered how well he had slept, how Vicente's coat had kept him warm. It was their only night together in the I-Hotel.

In the street, in the hall, they continued: *We won't go! Save the I-Hotel.* He had heard it all day and night. He had heard it for years, an entire life.

He had strength enough to barricade the door. To keep the police out. To trap themselves in. But he moved away from the dresser and undid the chain above, the lock beneath.

It was 2:11 A.M., and every few seconds Vicente's arm shook and his head jerked, as though he were fighting in his dreams. Fortunado went to him, placed his hand on his shoulder, and even after Vicente became still he kept it there, pressing his fingers into Vicente's arm. This was the I-Hotel's final morning, and soon police would make their way upstairs, so Fortunado allowed himself this moment and lay down beside Vicente, their bodies back to back, touching. Then he closed his eyes, but stayed awake to make the last hours feel longer than they were.

Days after the tussle on the street, Vicente would tell the story to other I-Hotel tenants. "White guy, real big," he said, "and I showed him." He punched the air as he reenacted the scene, but instead of applause and admiration all he received was a warning. *Stay away from her. It's not worth the trouble.* He called them cowards and stopped telling the story.

At the Parkdale, he began taking lunch with Althea. Fortunado would catch them by the loading docks, sitting together on over-turned crates, sharing the butter-and-olive sandwiches she packed each day. If she worked late, Vicente insisted on waiting for her, and together they would walk to their cable car stop. Their supervisor warned them about fraternizing among staff, guests stared and whis-pered, but Vicente always said, "We're not afraid."

Fortunado said nothing, swore he never would.

The heat of the summer stayed through the fall. One late Sunday night, Fortunado, Vicente, and Althea sat at a corner table in the Manila Rose Cantina beneath a slow-moving ceiling fan, trying to cool themselves with glasses of pilsner. They drank in silence, ordered more pitchers than they could finish, and when they were done For-tunado was light-headed and could see drops of sweat fall onto the paper-covered tabletop. He hadn't felt so warm since Stockton, dur-ing those noonday hours in the fields.

Althea undid her scarf, dabbed her face and neck. "Let's go to the Dive," she said, "the three of us." Parkdale policy forbade employees to be near the hotel's pool except to clean it, and it was close to mid-night now, long past its closing. But then Althea pulled a set of keys from her purse and jangled them in the air; three times a week she collected towels from the changing rooms, and she had gone for a quick, late-night swim before. "No one will see us," she said. "No one will know."

They entered like trespassers, went down the back stairs to the pool. Their footsteps echoed as they walked along its blue-tiled perimeter, and the water's surface shimmered green from the lights below.

Vicente and Althea undressed and left their clothes in a neat pile on the floor. They were naked and unashamed; they had been this way together before. Althea entered the pool and Vicente followed, and together they swam out, resurfacing in the deep end. Fortunado could hear them breathing as they stayed afloat.

Fortunado removed his clothes. He descended the three steps into the pool, the water rising slowly to his waist, his chest. He whispered Vicente's name but heard no answer, so he took a breath and held it, submerged. He moved forward, opened his eyes, and in the watery haze he finally found Vicente, swimming beneath the surface. He had seen his body before — when Vicente changed out of his uniform at the hotel, or barged into his room to borrow a shirt — but never like this, so bare and open, arms held out as if to welcome him, as if to beckon. Underwater, they were the only two, with no world above to interfere, so Fortunado moved closer, unafraid. But he mistook buoyancy for the ability to swim. Suddenly, there was no floor beneath him, and as he sank he reached and kicked, as though trying to climb water.

It took both Vicente and Althea to bring Fortunado back to the surface, to the shallow end. They held his arms but he swiped them away, then staggered out of the pool, coughing with each breath. "I'm fine," he said, and as he gathered his clothes, he watched Vicente and Althea swim away, then disappear in a depth he would never brave again.

They finished swimming, dried themselves and dressed, and hurried to the stairwell. But Vicente and Althea continued past the lobby toward the upper floors. They planned to collect unfinished bottles of wine left outside guests' doors, and drink them in the Berlin Deluxe. "I'll see you back at the hotel," Vicente said.

"When?" Fortunado asked.

"Later tonight." Vicente looked at Althea. "Maybe tomorrow."

"You're not supposed to be there."

"No one will see us," Vicente said. "And so what if they do?"

Vicente stood four steps above but he seemed much farther away, and Fortunado kept his hand tight on the rail, as if letting go meant falling. "You're not supposed to be there," he said again.

Vicente took one step down, reached for Fortunado's shoulder. "Go home," he said. Then he and Althea left, their footsteps growing fainter as they continued up the stairs.

Fortunado exited the stairwell into the empty lobby. He left the Parkdale and walked down the long hill of Powell Street toward Manilatown. It was early Monday morning. Kearny Street was deserted. Buses had ended their run, no autos drove past, and the only other person still awake at that hour was the old Filipino sitting on his top step, eyes gazing longingly at the moon.

Fortunado crossed the street and entered the I-Hotel, went up to his room. He stood by his window and stared out at the blank billboard on the rooftop across, thinking about Vicente and Althea in the Berlin Deluxe, beholders of a view he could barely imagine.

One night a week in the Berlin Deluxe became two, sometimes three, and Vicente and Althea remained undetected. They would arrive after midnight and leave before dawn, then return in uniform to the Parkdale only hours later, ready to work. But these nights left Vicente tired, which made him tardy, and Fortunado would cover for him with flimsy excuses — a stomachache one morning, a toothache the next. Weeks of this passed, and Fortunado was done. "I won't lie for you anymore," he told Vicente. They were on the seventh floor of the Parkdale, waiting for the elevator.

"Sorry, Nado." Vicente yawned, rubbing his eyes. "I'll wake up earlier next time."

"*Next time.*" Fortunado shook his head.

The elevator arrived, and they entered. "That room is good for us," Vicente said. "It's like our own place."

"You're the bellboy. She's the maid. You don't live there."

"Just leave it alone, Nado."

"There's not even a bed."

"We don't *need* a bed." Vicente winked, then gave Fortunado a quick punch to the arm.

"Don't do that," Fortunado said.

Vicente laughed, tousled his hair, hit him again. "Stop," Fortunado said, and Vicente smiled, made another fist. But now it was Fortunado who threw a punch, one so strong that Vicente stumbled backward, and Fortunado hit him again. Vicente got to his feet, pushed Fortunado against the wall, and held him there, his hands on his collar, knuckles grazing his neck. They had not been this close for years.

"We kissed," Fortunado said. He held on to Vicente's wrists, aching to tell more: how he slept close to the wall just to hear him breathing on the other side; how he kept the tickets from the Dreamland in his pocket at all times, a memento of the night they met; how home could only be wherever Vicente was. But more words felt like drowning, so he took a breath and repeated the one thing he knew to be an undisputable truth. "We kissed."

Vicente freed his hands from Fortunado's collar. "Once," he said. There was no anger in his voice or on his face, only apology.

The elevator reached the lobby. The doors opened and Vicente stepped out. Then the doors closed again.

Fortunado stayed behind. He had never struck a person before. Several times in his life he had wondered what it might be like, and now he knew: the force of who you are in one gesture at a single moment; the hope that it will be enough and the fear that it won't. No different than a kiss.

The protest was fading. Fortunado lay on his side facing the window, the room like a dream: For a moment he could believe that a final night never passed, and a life in the I-Hotel never happened. *What if,* he wondered, *that was someone else?* But then he felt the slight shift of Vicente's body against his own, and Fortunado wiped his eyes and rose from the bed, put on his coat.

He gently shook Vicente's shoulder. Vicente turned toward him and blinked until he was awake.

There was no sledgehammer, no kick to the door; it simply opened, and in the hallway two officers stood, arms at their sides and no weapons in hand. "We're under orders to evict you," one of them said. "Please come with us."

Vicente stared at them, one fist closed and ready. "I don't like police," he whispered.

"They're here to help us," Fortunado said.

"We've done nothing wrong."

"Just stand up." Fortunado helped Vicente to his feet, then picked up the suitcase and led him to the door. As they passed the dresser, he reached for the envelope marked with their names, and tucked it into Vicente's pocket.

They stepped into the hallway. Protest signs and posters were litter now, and chains dangled from the banister and exposed pipes. An officer stood by Fortunado's door, knocked twice, then opened it. "No one here," he said. "That's everyone."

They descended the stairs, moved carefully past small desks and mattresses in their path. They reached the lobby, stepped over wood planks and broken glass, and, as they crossed the fallen door of the front entrance, Fortunado took Vicente's hand. "Don't let go," he said, and he led the way out of the I-Hotel.

After the fight in the elevator, Vicente spent more nights with Althea in the Berlin Deluxe, returning to the I-Hotel only for a change of clothes. At the Parkdale, Fortunado worked the front entrance as often as he could, and whenever Vicente approached he would steer his luggage cart in another direction. After work, Fortunado would rush out to catch the next cable car back home. One night, waiting at his stop, he saw Vicente and Althea leave the Parkdale together, arms around one another as they walked down Powell Street. A light rain fell, and Vicente took off his jacket, draped it over her shoulders, and held her close. They kissed.

"Crazies," the man beside Fortunado said. He returned to his newspaper, shaking his head.

Hours later, Fortunado sat alone on the fire escape of the I-Hotel, a bottle of Du Kang by his feet. He drank and shivered, remembering the kiss he had shared with Vicente — how it had happened in darkness, in silence. And when he finished the bottle, he thought of Vicente and Althea, their kiss on the sidewalk, so reckless and unhidden, which perhaps was the point. But Fortunado understood how difficult love could be, how its possibility hinged on a delicate balance between complete anonymity and the undeniable need to be known.

He let the empty bottle of Du Kang roll off the fire escape, listened for the crash of glass and the silence after. He got to his feet and climbed inside, hurried downstairs and out of the I-Hotel. He walked to the corner and stepped into a telephone booth, and as he dialed he imagined Vicente and Althea in the window of the Berlin Deluxe, looking down at the city as though it were theirs.

The police switchboard operator answered.

Strangers where they didn't belong, he finally said. A couple — Filipino man, white woman — hiding in the Parkdale Hotel. The police could catch them. Hurry.

He hung up the receiver, stepped out of the booth. He headed toward Market, turned east toward the water, then walked along the Embarcadero, the Bay Bridge coming into view.

It was finally finished, ready for use in a matter of weeks, and all year long advertisements had announced its opening. JOINING TWO CITIES! one poster read. BRINGING THE WORLD TOGETHER! But tonight the bridge was dark and still untraveled, and the world felt more like the place it was — an endless earth in which Fortunado stood alone.

A man in a dark suit and hat approached. He stood beside Fortunado, put his hands on the rail. "Quite a bridge," he said.

Fortunado nodded.

"Nice night, too."

Fortunado looked at the fading moon. "It's almost morning."

"There's still time," the man said. Then, without asking, he took Fortunado's hand and whispered, "It's okay. I know a place."

Fortunado turned around, checking for nearby police or anyone within earshot. When he knew it was safe, they moved away from the water to a darker, unnamed place that in daylight would be impossible to find again.

The warmth he felt inside this stranger was undeniable and necessary, and each time it happened was meant to be the last. Now Fortunado feared a lifetime of this and little more, and he wondered how long such a life could be.

The next morning Fortunado waited by his window for Vicente's return. The Parkdale would have fired Vicente, that was certain, and the police might have been stern, even threatening.

But when night came and he still hadn't returned, Fortunado picked the lock of Vicente's door, went inside, and lay on his bed to wait for him. When he woke it was morning — another night without Vicente. He got up, smoothed the sheets over the mattress, and left the room as though he had never been there.

At the Parkdale, none of the bellhops mentioned an incident in the Berlin Deluxe, and when Fortunado asked his boss if he had heard from Vicente, his boss said, "Maybe he had a toothache," then closed his office door. Once, he stopped in front of the Berlin Deluxe, rattled the doorknob, and whispered Vicente's name. He listened for movement, for breath, but heard nothing. After work, he checked every store, restaurant, and bar in Manilatown. He even searched the crowd at the Dreamland Saloon, but the one person he recognized was the ticket man with the cane. "I know you," the old man said, and Fortunado left as quickly as he could.

Hours later, Fortunado made his way back home. When he reached the end of Kearny Street, he saw a light in Vicente's window.

He ran into the I-Hotel, up to the third floor. Without knocking he opened Vicente's door and found him sitting on the edge of his bed, elbows on his knees, hands clasped together. He was still in his uniform. "They found us," he said.

Fortunado stepped in, shut the door behind him. "When?"

"Two nights ago." He lowered his head and told Fortunado the rest, like a confession. He and Althea were sleeping when hotel security and two police officers forced the door open. They brought him to his feet, pushed him against the wall, shouted questions they wouldn't let him answer — *You think you belong here? Who do you think you are?* Althea stood in the corner, and Vicente told her not to be afraid, that nothing they had done was wrong. "Then one of them, the bigger one, started shouting at her. The things he called her . . ." He shook his head. "So I hit him. As hard as I could." He remembered Althea crying, then something hard on the back of his head, three times, maybe more. He remembered falling.

For a day and a half he sat in a cell with other men who looked the way he imagined criminals did, threatening and silent, always watching. "I didn't move. I didn't want to close my eyes." Vicente shook his head again. "I was scared." Before they finally let him go, an officer asked if he had learned his lesson. He promised them he had.

Fortunado crossed over to the window, closed the blinds. "Althea?"

"Gone, maybe. I don't know." From the jail he had rushed to Althea's boardinghouse, and the housemother told him Althea had taken the first bus back to Wisconsin, where she was better off, and couldn't mix with men like him.

"You'll find her," Fortunado said.

Vicente said nothing.

Fortunado saw what looked like rings around Vicente's wrists, red as a burn. "Handcuffs," Vicente said. "They kept them on the whole time." He put his hands on his lap, palm up, unable to make a fist. "It feels like they're still on."

He took off his jacket and let it fall to the floor. Fortunado picked it up, folded it, and tucked it in the bottom drawer of his dresser. "You were brave, Vicente," he said.

"I was stupid." He turned and lay on his bed and told Fortunado to turn off the light on his way out.

Fortunado returned to his room. He sat on his bed with his back against the wall, remembering what he had seen: Vicente's eye bruised purple and blue, the gash in the middle of his lower lip. And now he could hear Vicente on the other side, turning and breathing as he tried to sleep. Once, those sounds had comforted Fortunado, made him dream of them being together, holding and loving each other. But now he heard nothing more than loneliness, Vicente's and

his own. For this reason Fortunado stayed awake all through the
night, and wept for them both.

Thousands filled the street, but the human barricade was gone, replaced by squads of police who fended off protestors with batons and
shields and arrested dozens more. Fortunado squeezed Vicente's hand
as they walked farther out onto Kearny Street, moving with the
crowd. "Almost there," Fortunado shouted, as though a true destina-
tion were finally in sight. He tightened his grip, tried to move faster,
but from the side a protestor rushed by, slamming into them. Fortunado fell.

The asphalt was cold against his palms, and gravel jabbed the back
of his neck. Above, the sky was black and starless.

Two girls in Berkeley sweatshirts helped Fortunado to his feet.
"You okay?" one asked. "Do you have someone with you?" Fortunado steadied himself, and just as he told her yes, he realized that Vicente was gone.

He could hear his name — *Nado, Nado* — but everywhere Fortunado looked he saw only strangers, hundreds of them, shouting and
waving their signs. He forced his way through the crush of bodies,
searching for Vicente's voice and face, until he finally reached the
other side of the street. He staggered up the front stairs of an apartment building for a better vantage point, hoping to catch sight of Vicente. From the top step he saw the flashing headlights of a white van
at the end of Kearny Street. It was the shuttle for the West Oakland
Senior Center, and, one by one, the tenants of the I-Hotel climbed
inside. As the last man in the line boarded, Vicente approached the
van, his feet dragging. From inside the tenants beckoned to him, but
suddenly Vicente stopped and let the suitcase fall from his hand. He
was standing in the same spot where Fortunado had found him
weeks before, asking strangers where he was, if they knew the right

way home, and Fortunado remembered seeing him from afar, pacing the sidewalk corner, a man stranded on a small piece of land.

There was no pacing or panic now, just the stillness of a man taking in the view before him. Vicente looked at Kearny Street, watched police beat down and drag away protestors through the aimless mass, their signs crushed and torn underfoot. Then, as if he had finally seen enough, Vicente turned away, picked up his suitcase, and stepped into the van. Fortunado imagined him crossing the eight miles of the Bay Bridge, speeding over water as if moving from one country into the next.

The van pulled away slowly, and then it was gone.

Fortunado would make his way to the West Oakland Senior Center later; another shuttle would come. If not, then he would locate temporary shelter somewhere in the city, and find Vicente tomorrow. For now Fortunado rested on the top step, and across the street, the I-Hotel looked like a silhouette of itself, a darkness against the city. But higher up was a last square of light, and Fortunado realized he had left his bedside lamp on. His was the only window lit, and in a matter of hours, daylight would make it as dim and empty as all the others. But then night would fall and the room would glow again, until the lamp itself finally died, or until someone turned it off.

TIMOTHY SCOTT

Wisconsin Institute for Creative Writing

PLATO

Father called from the archdiocese office and said that this girl would be coming in later that day and he'd like it if I could "find a position for her." I've got nine regulars, union guys, who work year-round, and I take on another dozen or so summer workers, college boys mostly, though I've hired a few laid-off auto workers and once took on a kid with Down's syndrome, who was fine until August when he leaned against a hot carburetor on one of the Yazoos and burned his forearm so bad you could smell it. In the summer the work pretty much involves cutting grass, either up on a riding mower — the crew call them Yazoos after the company that makes them — or ground level with a Weedwacker, getting the hair around trees and grave-stones. As for the occasional burial, an old excavator we keep in the garage does most of the work. It was the Friday before Memorial Day — my ninth summer as director at Holy Sepulcher — my crew had been set for weeks, and I'd never hired a girl before.

"Well, the boys do tend to tug at their crotches a lot these days, there is only one shitter in the garage, and conversations more often than not include the word *pussy,* just so you know . . . Father."

He didn't have much of a clue what the work involved, which I suppose I should have been grateful for. He came by only once a month or so, driving through the grounds in a tan Chevette, then stopping by the office for a few minutes of uncomfortable chitchat. There was a long pause.

"Do you want *me* to have a talk with your staff, Andy?" he asked.

She came in just as I was sitting down to my lunch. I could see she was a small girl, about five foot nothing, with pockmarked cheeks and skinny arms, brown hair cut in what I call a Prince Valiant.

"I'm here regarding summer employment," she said. "I have some experience with landscaping, mainly in the residential sector. My background is in the service industry, but I enjoy the intensity of physical labor. I'm stronger than I look. My name's Julie Breaser. I —"

"Fill this out," I said. My Cup-a-Soup was getting cold.

She took a very long time filling out the application — as if things like name, address, and previous employment might be trick questions — and she handed it to me like it was something fragile.

"Philosophy?" I said, looking it over. I had added the college major question a few years back, just out of personal curiosity. I've always had good luck with history and engineering. The two worst kids I ever had were both communications, whatever the hell that is.

"That's right," she said, turning around. She'd been staring at the Jesus painting hanging on the back wall, the same one you get on a sticker if you join the Sacred Heart Auto League.

"Well, there isn't much time for contemplating the eternal verities here," I said. "We're more focused on grass."

"Oh, no," she said. "I believe in the sanctity of work." Her eyes drifted to the ceiling, as if she were reading something there. "Time is never lost that is devoted to work." She looked back at me and nodded.

I did not want to hire this girl. I looked back down at her application, buying time as I considered my options. There didn't seem to be any.

"All right then, Plato. Be here Tuesday, eight A.M."

At the end of the day, I had everyone come in to the garage a little early. The speech I gave was short and sweet and not unlike the one I gave for the Down's syndrome kid. "We've got a new hire coming in next week, someone a little different. Assholery will not be tolerated."

That night, Suze came over for supper and we grilled some burgers and listened to the Tigers lose on the radio. I'd met Suze the previous summer over at the Home Depot, where I used to spend nights and weekends back when I was building the deck we were sitting on. She was in bathroom fixtures, but she helped me twice as much as any of the knotheads over in lumber. She asked me out one Saturday while helping me get some J-bolts and galvanized screws. I hadn't been out with anyone since Lauren died, and Suze hadn't seen her last boyfriend since she testified against him at his parole hearing. We introduced each other as friends, though we'd started having sex together a few months before. Suze always left at the end of the night, and I appreciated this.

She had been pretty quiet that night, so I guessed we wouldn't be rattling the bedsprings. Our summer evenings usually ended about the time my bug zapper came on, which it had about a half hour earlier. After I yawned for the second time, she looked up from staring at the white coals and said, "What's your vacation situation like?"

"How do you mean?" I asked, though I had an idea where she might be going with this.

"I was thinking about heading up to Traverse City for a few days and thought you might want to come with." I didn't answer for a few seconds and then she quickly said, "Or maybe Sleeping Bear Dunes. Or even Chicago, if you prefer that." I could see her getting a little embarrassed then. She had meant to be nonchalant about the whole thing, and now she sounded too eager.

I had been cashing my days in for years, but I still probably had a week or two in the bank. "Let me check," I said. "Summer's our busiest time and I took on a new worker just today."

She came in ten minutes early, dressed in jeans that looked like they might still have the tag on them, the whitest T-shirt and tennis shoes I'd ever seen, and one of those shiny yellow rain slickers your mom used to put on you. I've had to send one or another of the boys home for showing up with pants falling off their asses or T-shirts with drunk frogs and shit on them — this is a cemetery after all, and as I said, Father likes to come by unannounced every now and then just to mess with us — but I'd never had anyone look too damn clean before.

I introduced her to everyone and tried not to make a big show of it, but she got all excited and shook everybody's hand, looking them in the eye and repeating their names like she'd just graduated Dale Carnegie. It was a very strange thing, especially on a dark Tuesday morning in May.

We'd had a lot of rain and strong winds over the weekend, so I put her on tree branch pickup duty out on the dump truck with Julius, a quiet old guy who'd been at Holy Sep longer than most of the dead people, and that's not an exaggeration.

On my morning rounds, I watched her and Julius haul a big branch over to the truck. She was struggling hard and she kept slipping every few feet on account of her shiny new tennis shoes.

At lunch break I took Julius aside and asked how she was doing. Normally, he said only a few words a day, usually something positive, like "New clutch works good," or "Gonna clear up by Thursday."

"Talks too goddamn much. And all nonsense."

I walked over to where she was sitting, cross-legged and by herself, on a patch of grass next to the garage. She was eating a peanut butter sandwich — I'd never seen anyone take such small bites before.

"That's smart," I said. "Bringing your lunch. Better than wasting your money on the lunch truck."

"I can be pretty ascetic when it comes to food and money."

It was warming up, and the sun had finally come out from the clouds. I generally looked forward to this time of year. The long winters and the conversations, which more often than not seemed to get around to the Super Lotto jackpot or the rising copay cost for Lipitor, could get old. The college boys did need a little more watching, and their grab-ass humor and practical jokes occasionally got on my nerves, but they brightened the place up.

The regulars and the college boys who'd been with us awhile took a certain attitude toward new hires, which basically involved treating them like shit until they proved they didn't deserve it. This sometimes took weeks, and I'd had more than one new employee decide they'd take their chances for the summer at Burger World or the country club instead.

I looked down at her — at the haircut, the bright white shoes, the rain slicker, the ninety-pound frame — and wondered what the fuck Father was thinking. I gave her until the end of the week.

I put her on Weedwacker duty for the rest of the afternoon. She had less natural aptitude for it than anyone I'd ever seen. It took her almost an hour to load the filament into the spool, fifteen pulls on the starter cord to turn the engine over. I had her practice on the side of the garage and she ended up stripping a few layers of paint off the siding. I finally had to get back to the office, so I left off telling her to be careful not to hack up any flowers planted around the gravestones, but I still got three complaints about that later in the week.

Holy Sep had been sold out for years, so we had only a dozen or so burials every summer, but we had one that afternoon. My job was just to hang out a short distance away, in case the funeral director needed anything. The plot was across from the section where I had assigned Plato to trim. She had the sense to cut off her motor when she saw the funeral party arrive, and we ended up standing next to each other as we watched everybody park and gather around the grave site. A short distance behind us, Frank and Bubba — two regulars — were hovering by the backhoe. I could tell they were anxious to get the casket in the ground so they could get over to the Honey Spot before the cover charge kicked in.

A few people were helping over an elderly woman — who looked just how you'd think a widow would look — when Plato said to me, "In some parts of India, the wife was cremated alongside the husband. Alive."

"That's devotion."

"Are you married, Andy?"

"No," I said, keeping my stare on the funeral party. *Mind your place,* I was thinking.

The priest cleared his throat and it got real quiet just as I heard Plato say too loudly, "Don't worry. You'll find somebody." A few people looked over at us, and I had a sudden urge to kick her in the ass.

A few minutes later, as the priest launched into the Lord's Prayer, I felt her sweaty little hand reach out and take mine. My face got hot and flushed, and I thought about yanking my hand away, but before I could decide what to do the prayer was halfway through, so I decided to just ride it out. When she finally let go of my hand, I glanced back at Frank and Bubba, who were chuckling their asses off.

By the time they got the casket in the ground and the funeral party had cleared out, it was after five, so while Frank drove the backhoe in, I gave Bubba and Plato a ride in the truck. Bubba and I had been chatting for a few minutes when she turned to him and said, "You clear your throat three times, every time, right before you speak. That's really interesting." It was true; Bubba did do this. He also wore gloves every day of the year no matter how hot it was and kicked each tire twice before he got into his car, I had noticed over the years.

Bubba paused a second, then turned to her and said, "You're so fucking short you can't see over that dashboard. And your face looks like my pimply ass. I think that's really interesting."

I caught up to her a few minutes later, just as she was heading to her car.

"Plato," I said, "I'm going to encourage you to apply what I call the Two-Week Rule."

She looked up at me, blinking in the late afternoon sun, her too-white T-shirt and bony arms, a little speck of dried peanut butter in the crease of her mouth.

"Your first two weeks on a new job? Just shut the fuck up."

On my rounds the next day, I saw that Father had come by in the Chevette and had stopped to talk to her, something I'd never seen him do with any of the other workers. I kept driving, and when I got back to the office he was there, leaning against my counter.

"The place looks great, Andy."

"We're getting caught up." I hung up my Windbreaker, walked around to the other side of the counter, and sat down at my desk.

"Hey, how's the new girl doing?" he asked, like it had just suddenly occurred to him.

"Lousy," I said, but he didn't seem surprised. "Why the special interest?"

He stared at the back wall for a few seconds. He seemed to be considering something. Finally, he said, "Julie's a novitiate with the IHMs over at St. Bart's."

Jesus, I thought. "She's a nun?"

"Not yet. She's living at the convent and doing her community work here."

"Always wanted to work at a boneyard, did she?"

"We had a little difficulty placing her. But we thought this might be a good, quiet place for her to reflect on her faith. Help her decide if this is something that's really right for her." His voice trailed off, and he looked down at his hairy knuckles.

I studied him for a few seconds. "They're hoping she'll talk herself out of it," I said.

"Julie had a rough time a few months back. She was in a bad car accident, Andy. She thought she was going to die."

I had opened the office windows for the first time that summer. The sounds of the mowers and the distant traffic out on 10 Mile were the only things breaking the silence.

"Made some promises to God, did she?"

"She says it changed her life."

"I'll bet."

"These types of conversions rarely last." He sighed and put his hands in his coat pockets. "Then again, they're not exactly pounding down the convent doors these days."

He turned for the door. "The place looks great, Andy. Thanks for your good work."

———

"The grass is growing so quickly and the summer crew's still getting settled in, so this isn't the best time for me to take a vacation," I told Suze. "Maybe sometime in late July or August."

She shook her head. "It'll be a madhouse by then. Don't worry about it." She left between the third and fourth innings and didn't offer to help clean up. It was still light out, and the game was tied. I decided to stay up for a while.

I'd had my own conversion many years back, but in the opposite direction. Lauren and I had been married about four years — good years, where we spent every cent we made, had sex every night, and lay around in bed planning our lives together — when she started getting up in the middle of the night, going into the living room, and smoking and pacing around. When I'd ask what was wrong, she'd just brush me off, until one night she broke down crying and asked me why I was planning to kill her. Pretty soon, she was sleeping on the couch and wouldn't eat anything I'd prepared or even touched. At her job at Woolworth's, she accused one of the other cashiers of taking money from her register. When she quit, she said it was because the floor manager was plotting to steal her organs and replace them with his. For months she stayed home and watched game shows, waiting for some special clue to appear on one of the game boards. The medication, which I could rarely get her to take, turned her into a zombie. Our lives went on like this for almost five years, until she went missing one weekend and a picnicker on Belle Isle found her body washed up onshore. Someone else had seen her walking across the bridge the night before.

During this time, people kept saying things to me like "We're praying for you" or "God has a plan for all of us" or "He doesn't give us any more than we can bear." I never figured out what kind of a plan God had for Lauren, unless it involved constant suffering. He obviously gave her more than she could bear, otherwise she wouldn't have tossed herself off a bridge. And I tried praying many nights. It didn't do shit.

I quit my job at the Chrysler plant and spent most of the next year drinking beer and eating pizza, watching the grass grow, the leaves fall, the snow melt. I finally got the strength together one afternoon to visit Lauren's grave. It was a Thursday in May, a gorgeous day, windy and blue. I cleaned up her headstone and planted some flowers. It felt so good to do things with my hands again and to feel and smell the grass and the dirt. On my way out, I stopped by the office to check on the visiting hours, but it was all locked up. One of the workers told me that the director had passed away the week before and they hadn't hired a new one yet.

Father seemed to think my background as a foreman was just what the place needed — the previous guy had apparently been a lazy old bastard who spent most of his time hiding in the office — and I was offered the job the day after my interview.

Whether this was part of God's plan or not, I couldn't say. But I can say my life slowly started to get better. The routine of work and the simple task of tidying up a large cemetery kept me occupied during the day. In the evenings I spent hours organizing and filing over a hundred years' worth of burial records. The adjustment to managing the cemetery workers came fairly easily. In all my years at Holy Sep, I'd had only two employee problems: a regular named Bill, who smoked a little too much weed over lunch hour, and a college boy named Kevin, who had a perpetual shit-eating grin and who I twice caught pissing behind gravestones. Bill left by mutual agreement and Kevin knew enough not to reapply the following summer.

Plato took my advice. For the rest of that week and the next, she barely said a word. On my rounds each day, I'd drive by and she'd wave to me, then adjust her goggles and get right back to work, whipping grass and dirt into the air around gravestones and trees. Unlike the college boys, she didn't seem to need a Walkman blasting music into her ears all day to keep her entertained. At lunch she'd sit by herself under a tree and read.

I walked over to her one day and asked, "What do you say to people when they ask you what it's like to work at a cemetery?"

She put her book down and looked at me a bit confused.

"It's a joke," I said. "You're supposed to play along."

"I don't know."

"You say, 'I've got a lot of people under me and I can walk over them and nobody complains.'"

She gave one of those fake-polite laughs — I'm not known for my sense of humor. I glanced down at her book. The title said *Spiritual Exercises*.

"Thinking about the nunnery, huh?"

"I may take my vows at the end of the summer. I think it's a worthwhile calling," she said, a little too full of herself.

"Yes, God has a plan for all of us," I said. I think she could hear my sarcasm.

"Everybody thinks I don't know what I'm doing. The vocational director. The other nuns. Father Gerard. My mother, my father. Now you, too, Andy Witkowski."

"I think you're young and you're ignorant. But that's not all your fault."

I looked out over the grounds: The grass was wet and deep green and there were flowers everywhere. The place really was looking good.

"You know I was in this car accident."

"Father told me."

"It was foggy. One of those chain-reaction things. There were four other cars. Six other people. Everybody died but me, Andy."

I looked over at where the college crew were nursing their hangovers in the sun. A few of them had their shirts off, something I had told them not to do, but apparently they needed reminding.

"Maybe it wasn't God that saved you," I said. "Maybe it was your air bag. Or your antilock brakes."

"It was God all right. I saw Him there."

"Hokay." I decided it was time to head over to bitch out the college boys. "Well, next time you see him, ask him to send me a few less fuckups for summer workers."

When I got home that night, I was surprised to see the deck all done up with balloons and streamers. Suze was sitting on the steps and came over to me and kissed me on the cheek. "Happy birthday," she said. "I've got some steaks and champagne in the cooler." I noticed she hadn't gone inside the house, even though she knew where I kept the spare key.

Neither of us were big drinkers, so we were pretty much three sheets to the wind by the time Suze brought out the birthday cake from Kroger's with my name on it and the Tigers sweatshirt she gave me for a present.

The conversation started to get a little loose, and before I knew it, Suze was telling me how she used to accidentally-on-purpose walk by the lumber aisle a lot that month I was building my deck. I told her it was okay, I used to accidentally-on-purpose check out her ass as she was walking away.

"By the way," she said, "am I your damn girlfriend?"

"Sure."

"Then start calling me that."

By the time we made our way inside, we practically had our hands down each other's pants.

———

When I woke up, the clock said 3:27 A.M. and Suze was snoring next to me. I had no recollection of how we actually got to bed. It felt very strange to have someone else in my house, in my bed. I realized I had spent every night for the past ten years alone. In a few hours there'd be someone else in my kitchen, sharing my coffee, and in my bathroom, possibly using my toothbrush.

I went to the kitchen and poured a glass of water, then walked out onto the deck. There were dirty plates all around, open bottles of champagne and steak sauce. I noticed a couple of wineglasses on the lawn and went down to pick them up. On my way back, I dropped one on the driveway and it shattered. I decided maybe I should lie down on the grass for a bit and get my bearings.

There was a slight breeze, crickets were chirping, and flashes of heat lightning lit up the clouds. I started thinking about how Suze and I had crossed a line, but I quickly realized that, halfway between drunk and hungover, I wasn't going to be able to come to a firm decision as to how I felt about this. I was almost asleep when I noticed her staring down at me.

"You were making a lot of noise out here," she said. "Is this where you plan to stay?"

I was already feeling a bit sketchy about things, and there was something in her tone that bothered me. "You were snoring," I said. "So I came out here."

She sat down next to me on the grass. She had on one of my T-shirts and I was thinking how her boobs looked a bit saggy underneath it. Maybe she read my mind, because she crossed her arms over her chest and gave a fake little shiver, though it wasn't at all cold.

"Do you want me to leave?"

"I don't know," I said. "Are you okay to drive?"

She got up slowly. "Yup, I'm okay to drive." She went inside and I could hear her gathering her clothes. The last thing I saw, when I finally lifted my head, was a glimpse of her panties as she got into her car; she hadn't even bothered to put her pants on.

By July I had Plato up on a Yazoo and she was doing okay. She was even beginning to look a little different. The sun seemed to have helped her complexion, and her arms were tanned. Her T-shirt and jeans looked a little more natural on her, not like something she had bought the day before and taken an iron to.

The crew seemed to be accepting her better, too. My nickname had stuck, and she was greeted around the garage each day with "S'up, Plato." At lunchtime the college boys and a few of the younger regulars would sometimes head over to the park across the street and drink beer—a tradition I wasn't too thrilled about, but the union had taught me not to mess with scheduled break times—and they'd invite Plato, but she'd always decline, so I found myself talking to her alone most days, sometimes about religion.

She had ideas about many things—prayer, sacrifice, the Resurrection—most of which I had long ago dismissed as horseshit. "It wouldn't be faith if it were fact, Andy. I believe it happened. Trust me on this one." She was like that—sweet, but a little terrier about her beliefs.

Some days, too, we'd just shoot the shit about the weather, baseball, flowers, and trees—I brought in some of my gardening and landscaping magazines and showed her what the azaleas and rhododendrons I had planted along my back fence would look like in a few years, and she helped me pick out a design for the pergola I had decided to build.

"You've got your own little secret garden, Andy. That's okay, everyone needs one of those."

She was an odd little bird.

————

At the end of the following week, while making my rounds, I saw one of the college boys hunched over his mower; a tree branch stuck underneath it had frozen his blades. He assured me the engine was off, but when I dislodged the branch, the blades whipped around and caught my hand before I could pull it out. I didn't know how bad it was until I looked at the exposed bone on my index finger and watched my whole hand swell up in front of my eyes. Things got woozy all of a sudden, and I started to feel cold. I lay down on the grass and tried to catch my breath, and the next thing I remember, I was in the backseat of a car and I could hear Plato's voice talking to me from the front, telling me she was taking me to the hospital.

I ended up with a splint and a half-dozen stitches, but between the lingering anesthetic and the painkillers, I actually felt pretty good.

It was a little after seven when Plato drove us back to the cemetery, and it seemed like everybody and their brother was outside doing something: teenagers in cars cruising down Middlebelt Road, Frisbees and footballs flying back and forth in the park, people coming out of party stores with beer and chips in their arms, a line outside the door at Baskin-Robbins.

Plato pulled up to the office and parked next to my truck. I happened to look out across the street and noticed that there was a Little League game going on in the park. Something about the glow of the lights and the players' movements — the pitcher winding up, the infielders rushing after the ball, the runners scooting around the bases — and the parents cheering them on made my heart leap just a little, and I couldn't take my eyes away.

"I'll follow you home," Plato said.

I thought for a while, then said, "I don't think I'm going home yet."

We sat on the top row of bleachers and picked a team and cheered them on. We ate some French fries and drank a couple of Sprites. We talked about nothing — who the best shortstop was in the majors, whether the moon that night was quarter or crescent, the qualities of the perfect French fry — and made jokes about everything. I told her how I used to pitch in high school and made second team all-Catholic in my senior year. She loved the irony of that and said, "Maybe you would have made first team if you believed a little harder in Jesus, the son of God."

"Plato," I said, "sometimes you're pretty fucking funny."

It occurred to me at one point that this park had been across the street from Holy Sep as long as I'd worked there, but I'd never set foot in it until that night. I started to get what, for me, were crazy ideas: I could come over here in the morning before work and jog; Suze and I could have a picnic over here after work some night; I could see if the league here needed umpires, or even a coach.

By the time I pulled up in my driveway and thanked and said good night to Plato, it had been one of the longest days of my life. I sat out on my deck for a while, listening to the crickets and the breeze through the oak trees, thinking about the way Lauren used to touch my neck when she kissed me, the way the lavender used to smell in my parents' backyard, the way I used to rear back on the mound and throw heat, nothing but heat.

When I woke up late the next morning, my hand was throbbing, but I swallowed some pills and headed out. I wanted to get my supplies for the pergola, but most of all, I was hoping to see Suze.

I couldn't find her anywhere. I looked down every aisle and finally asked one of the other employees, who took about a half hour to come back and tell me that Friday had been her last day. I decided to drop off the supplies at home, then head over to her place; but when I got home she was there, sitting on my front stoop. Her car, I noticed right away, was packed to the hilt: a tangle of clothes hangers, a lampshade, and a laundry basket were crammed up against the rear window. She stood up when she saw me and, of course, she looked beautiful to me then.

She said she was going down to Toledo, to stay with her mother for a while. She said it wasn't just me and that she might be back, she didn't know. But we both knew that it more or less was me and that she really wouldn't be back.

"We're in two different places with us, you and me, Andy. And that doesn't seem to be changing."

"It could," I said.

"That's what I've been telling myself for the past year."

After she left I stood there in my driveway and remembered how I would never go over to her apartment because it was so cramped and the neighbors were so noisy, how she would always kiss me first when we saw each other, how I had no idea when her birthday was.

I tried working in the yard. I marked out the lines and started to dig the postholes. But it was hot, my hand hurt like hell, and I'd taken the medication on an empty stomach — after a while I became so nauseous that I got down on my hands and knees for a few minutes. Finally, I threw up all over my nice lawn.

I spent the rest of the weekend lying on the couch, drinking down a thirty-pack of Schaefer and watching the Tigers drop a double-header. A heat wave moved in later on Saturday and — even drunk and exhausted — it was too hot to sleep. I lay awake both nights on my sweaty bedspread, the box fan blasting warm air over me, remembering all the little signs, the hints, the acts of kindness from Suze during the past year.

On Monday, at lunch break, I walked over to the garage to talk to Plato. Seeing her from a distance, sitting under her tree and reading a book, brightened my spirits a bit. She was the only one outside — the rest of the crew were all eating their lunches in the shade of the cool concrete garage. She looked up and smiled when she saw me, but just as I got to her, I heard Bubba's voice boom from inside the garage.

"See, that's God punishing Andy. He should know better. Sticking his finger in a nun's pussy!"

There was some scattered laughter and I looked at Plato, who just kind of closed her eyes and took a breath. I went past her and turned the corner into the garage. Bubba didn't see me coming until the last second, and I shoved him about as hard as I've ever shoved anyone. He stumbled backward, tripping over something — I never did figure out what — and banged his head hard against the big iron scoop on the excavator. He was out for only a few seconds, but I'd never seen so much blood in my life, and I knew right then that my days at Holy Sep were over — if the archdiocese didn't nail me for this, the union would.

When the policemen had come that morning to tell me about Lauren, I knew as soon as I heard the doorbell ring that it was them and that she was dead. That night after I pushed Bubba, as I sat out on my deck, sipping a Diet Coke and listening to the game, I knew as soon as I heard the doorbell ring that there was a tan Chevette in my driveway and a sweaty old priest at my door with a pink slip in his hand. I didn't even invite him in.

Later, lying awake in bed, I tried to think about practical matters — how much money I had in savings, what about my health insurance, how was I going to find a new job — but Plato kept coming into my thoughts and I just couldn't think straight, and again it was too hot to sleep much.

———

The next morning, I got dressed and forced myself out into the yard — I didn't know what else to do. I had just mixed the cement for the posts and was about to pour it, though, when I couldn't take it anymore and I got in my truck and headed over to Holy Sep.

I figured Father had probably come in and told the crew, for the time being, to just keep doing what they were doing the day before, so I headed out to a section way in back — a flat, open area, there was nothing but a wide marsh with tall grass and cattails beyond the fence.

When I found Plato, she was buzzing over the last swath of uncut grass, and I waited until she finished before I got out of the truck. When she saw me coming, she didn't look at all surprised. She cut off her mower and stepped down. When I got to her, we looked at each other for a few seconds but didn't say anything.

"I never asked you," I finally said. "When you saw Him, what did He look like?"

She thought about this for a while, then turned so she was looking out over the short, grassy section of what was left of the cemetery, the wide marshland past that, a few willow trees in the distance, then just the white sky.

"Look out there," she said.

I did. For a long time I stood, looking. I saw a blue jay land on top of the fence, two squirrels chase each other across the grass. I counted the links in each section of fence, estimated the distance between me and the willows. I watched the reeds and cattails bending in the wind and the clouds moving across the sky. I thought I saw a jet heading toward Metro, though it could have been a flock of geese. One of those heat bugs made its long, high-pitched sound and I felt the sun burning the back of my neck. *This is fucking stupid*, I thought. *This is not working.*

"Just wait," Plato said. "Not yet."

So I did. I waited until I couldn't stand it any longer, until I felt not only angry, but more hopeless and depressed than I had before I got there.

"Okay, now," she finally said. "Now look at me."

GREG CHANGNON

Sirenland Writers Conference

HALF SISTER

In October 1973, two months after their father died, Phoebe and Joan learned they had another sister. They were gathered together in the family's late-model Cadillac when Mother told them the news. She revved up the motor and said, "I had a daughter before you. I never told your father, but now that he's gone, I'm going to meet her at the Holiday Inn." She pumped the accelerator. The engine back-fired, belching a cannonball of smoke.

"Mother," Phoebe said, "the garage door is shut."

"Bitch," mumbled Joan.

"What's her name, Mother?" Phoebe asked. "My half sister."

"Kimberly," Mother replied. "A Miss Kimberly Bloom."

Mother poked at the button on the plastic box clipped to the visor. The garage door began to clang and fold upward. Mother jerked around and watched it go up. She looked terrified. The system was new, installed by the girls' father the week before he died. When the door was all the way up, Mother began to weep quietly.

After twenty minutes on the road, the girls knew something was wrong. Mother, recovered but still swollen around the eyes, told them it wasn't the Holiday Inn in Skokie, the next town over, but the one in Indianapolis, Indiana. That was a four-hour drive.

"We've been tricked," Joan whispered to her sister. They both sat in the back. Phoebe was fourteen and hadn't had her period. Joan, five inches taller, was twelve and had. The girls often felt as if they had gotten the short end of the stick. For one thing, they had bad hair; Joan sported fuzzy red, while Phoebe had only sad, thin strands of brown. They had been robbed of their father, their favorite parent, who died around noon but still looked alive, only sleeping, when the girls sat next to him on the couch at seven to watch *Gunsmoke*. At his funeral, a stupid affair Joan at first refused to attend, Mother had handed Joan a framed photograph to hold that, when Joan turned it over, revealed her father as a young man in his army uniform. Joan went back and forth between wanting to throw the thing at Jesus or hold it forever.

At a Texaco station south of Chicago, Joan locked herself in the ladies' room, taking the key attached to a two-by-four inside with her. Joan locked the doors to both stalls from inside and crawled under to get out.

Phoebe had to talk to Joan through a vent in the empty men's room. She tried not to look at the machine that sold stuff she didn't want to think about. "Maybe she'll be like me," Phoebe shouted, through the metal screen. "And you like me." Phoebe let her lips touch the tile on the wall below the vent. It tasted like ginger. She knew this was bad, disgusting even, but she was getting tired of hovering on the right side of decency. "You do like me, right?" Phoebe asked, her tongue skimming the porcelain.

"Only on a good day," Joan shouted back.

Phoebe tapped the wall with her finger, thinking of the bundle of freckles behind Joan's ears. She had her own set above her knee. Maybe that was how she'd recognize her half sister — by half a batch of freckles somewhere between her ear and her knee.

After five minutes Phoebe left the men's bathroom and stood guard outside the ladies' room. She watched the servicemen move from one car to another, wiping windshields and talking to customers about the weather. This made Phoebe think of her father, a plumber who had taken climatology classes through a correspondence course. He loved the weather and dreamed about a future career as a weatherman on the local TV station. Terrible, Phoebe thought, that he never got there. Now Phoebe hated the weather — its unpredictability, mostly.

Out by the car, Mother held the brim of her straw hat, the cotton daisy in the band flopping in the wind. She talked to a family that had piled out of a Winnebago — two parents, six children, and a lazy dog.

"Big family," Mother said to the father, smiling that weird half smile that made her look sad and happy at the same time.

"Big debt," the father said and disappeared around the motor home.

"How many do you have?" the wife asked, standing in bare feet and holding a stunned baby by the waist. Phoebe thought the lady looked tiny compared to Mother, as if each of her children — and now this new one — had taken a piece of her as they entered the world. Once their sister had been located, she considered, there might be less of Mother to go around.

Mother didn't answer right away. She stared at the baby, reached out to touch its nose, then turned away from the gas station, looking up into the gray, polluted skies over a line of factories to the south.

She caught a tendril of hair that blew out from under her hat. She looped it around a finger and stuffed it back inside. "Three," she finally said. "Three girls."

When Joan got thirsty, she came out. She had tried to drink out of the sink but knocked a tooth on the spigot. She wanted Mother to examine it. It wasn't painful; she only wanted Mother to feel bad. Mother took a look, kissed Joan on the cheek, and turned away.

"This is an emergency," Joan said. "I need help."

"But your half sister is expecting us," Mother said, letting her voice thin to a plea.

Trying to bribe Joan into getting into the car, Mother bought her a Coke. It didn't work. Joan just stood by the Cadillac and took slow, drawn-out sips. She put her thumb over the lip of the bottle and shook it. She felt the pressure building under her finger, the tickle of carbonation.

"Uh-oh," Phoebe said, scurrying around Joan and heading for shelter behind the Cadillac.

"You may want to move," Mother told her new friend with the baby.

Joan stopped and pointed the tip of the bottle toward both mothers. She watched the lady step back, her face tightening. The glass rim sucked on the bottom of Joan's thumb. The pop inside swirled, bubbling to a stormy hazel color. Joan was distracted. She was impressed by the power she'd set off, the anger caught in the bottle. She felt the same way about herself, as if she were about to burst inside out; as if her skin, thin as tissue, had no strength.

The other mother said, "My, she's feisty."

Joan lowered the bottle. Sometimes she thought there was a sort of weather in everyone — climates hidden beneath the bones — and her weather was bad. *Cumulonimbus, thundersqualls, mackerel skies—* words Joan had learned when her father flicked from one weather report to another, watching the men in plaid he envied, listening to reports that were never true, reports he said *he'd* never get wrong. Joan couldn't stop thinking of her father, of how he put little notes in her lunches, like "Bundle up, it's cold" or "Windy. Keep ahold of that hat." She couldn't stop thinking that if he were alive, they wouldn't be making this trip at all.

A strange feeling began to simmer in Joan's belly, something that made her think she wasn't the daughter her father had wanted her to be. What would that girl be like? Decent, maybe, like Phoebe. She lifted her finger from the bottle, slowly, so that soda drizzled over the sides.

Phoebe brought over a wad of brown towelettes. "Cram it," Joan said, shoving her guilt toward a spot deep inside, and walked straight for the Cadillac.

To liven up the driving, Mother led them through her favorite songs. Phoebe struggled to keep up with her, remembering the lyrics a second after they were sung. Joan participated only once, belting out the word *wench* in "Amazing Grace." By herself, Joan played Grocery Store, skipping letters that bored her. In the end, the list she shouted aloud, in reverse alphabetical order, included: for the letter *Z*, a zillion stolen dollars; for *S*, somebody who really loved me; and for *A*, Afros for everybody.

Nobody really noticed. Mother was somewhere else, and Phoebe was thinking about this new sister at the Holiday Inn. Phoebe pictured her with straight blond hair, maybe feathered, and a whole note-card box full of beauty tips and tampon advice.

"You ever have an Afro?" Joan asked, but Mother still wasn't listening. She was tapping a nervous finger against the steering wheel.

Phoebe squirmed in her seat, sneaking a look at her sister. Phoebe had moments when she thought Joan glowed, crackled, whistled with steam, and everybody around her took a step back. Sometimes

Phoebe imagined herself sleek and nasty, as daring as Joan. She wasn't and she knew it. She wished she could be half Joan and half herself; maybe then she would be whole.

Phoebe whispered to herself. "Phoebe...Phoebe...Kimberly and Phoebe. Kimberly and Phoebe and Joan."

Joan elbowed her. "Who are you? Miss Sentimental? Queen Corny?" Phoebe shrank into the back corner of her seat, pulling the heels of her sandals into her butt.

"Mother," Joan asked. "Did you ever love anyone else but Dad?" Phoebe waited quietly for the answer while Joan cracked her knuckles.

"I'm not certain, but it was...," Mother replied, but then her words dropped away into what, Phoebe imagined, was the same kind of sadness that had made Mother stumble in the cemetery on the day of the funeral and grab hold of Joan's and Phoebe's shoulders. "No, I didn't," Mother continued after a short while. "I thought I did, though, until your father made me see I didn't."

"Why is Kimberly a half sister?" Joan asked.

"Her father wasn't your father."

"Well, then she's the lucky sister." Joan said this, but even as she did, she thought the opposite. It was a thought she could push away, but just for kicks, she let herself touch it. This sister never knew Joan's father, never knew how he let her sip his vodka and chuckled when Joan got caught drawing her teachers in Nazi garb. Or how he smiled. Or laughed. Or never cheated at Yahtzee.

Phoebe wanted to ask about the man Mother thought she loved long ago, but she was afraid to. Phoebe's world had been twirling at top speeds ever since her father died, and she sensed her mother wasn't taking the same trip. Phoebe did not want to know something strange and new that would spin Mother, her only remaining parent, farther out of reach.

To stop thinking about these things, Phoebe forced herself to count the silos going by, letting her vision blur brown and yellow. But it didn't really work. "I wonder," Phoebe said, "what Kimberly looks like."

"She has a very pleasant phone voice," Mother said. "When she turned eighteen, she got my name and number from the adoption agency. She called a year ago, but I had absolutely no idea what to do." Joan wished Mother would stop talking. She liked to suffer in silence, but Mother was relentless. "I was shocked enough. Imagine what it would have been like for your father. So I called her back last week. The hardest phone call I ever made. It took me half an hour to dial ten numbers. She recognized my voice. Imagine that."

They passed the border from Illinois to Indiana, and Mother tooted the horn. Mother had picked up that horn habit from the girls' father. Joan remembered that he'd honked at everything: state lines, yellow lights, kids kissing on street corners, dead squirrels on the road. It just wasn't right, Mother stealing things from him like that, and so soon. Joan began to tear up the road map. Cook County, gone. Kane County, right in half. DeKalb, split down the middle. Mother's purse had slid under the driver's seat and Joan kicked at it, planning terrible things to do to it.

In the last two months Joan had tried to express some sort of good-bye to her father. She lay face-first on the couch where he died. She wandered around the house wearing his underwear. But nothing felt right. Mother caught her inside his closet, sitting far in the back, sniffing the legs of his slacks. Mother started to cry, big drops rolling down her cheeks, and Joan got up and walked out, saying, "We should burn it all."

Once into the Hoosier State, the traffic thinned and the sun dropped in the sky. Phoebe could tell by the way Mother drove that she was worried about meeting this half sister. She put on her right blinker, then moved left into the passing lane. Or she left the blinker on so it blinked endlessly. She let the Cadillac drift down to fifty, forty-five, forty, then, seeming to catch herself daydreaming, punched the gas so all three of them jerked back into their seats. She even poked her finger against the glass surface of the broken clock on the dashboard. The time in the car had been stuck on 11:43 ever since the week after her father died when Joan, running away to Las Vegas in the middle of the night, had slammed the car into the oak tree near the end of the driveway.

Mother looked in the rearview mirror at the girls and said, "Can either of you find my pocketbook?" She bent sideways, her right hand searching. She pulled away the floor mat and reached under her seat. Swerving to avoid a muffler on the road, she opened and closed the glove box.

Phoebe ducked down toward the floor, looking for the purse, thinking about Kimberly sitting at the Holiday Inn, waiting. Joan sat still, her arms folded, then spat out her gum. It missed the open window by a mere inch and landed on the glass.

Mother pulled over on the shoulder and, after the car jerked to a stop, turned around to face the back. "No pocketbook?" Phoebe shook her head.

"Joan?" Mother said. Joan stared back, then shrugged in slow motion. "Joan?" A section of hair came loose from underneath Mother's straw hat and swung into her face. It dangled like a comma in the middle of Mother's scowl. "Where's my pocketbook, honey? Do you see it?" Joan peeled her blue gum off the glass as slowly as she could and, with her eyes never leaving Mother's face, dropped it out the window, over the side of the car.

"Oh, no, you didn't!" Mother shouted. "When? When did you do it?"

"I don't know. A few minutes ago," Joan said.

"I have to find it. I have to." Mother kicked open the door and got out of the car. The wake of a truck rumbling by blew her dress to the side. The hair on her head levitated, lifting in the wind like a magic trick. She began to slog against the flow of traffic, bending into the wind. For a moment Joan suffered a terrible impulse to shout the truth to her mother: She'd thrown the pocketbook out the window twenty miles into Indiana. But she just couldn't do it. Seeing Mother walk away, furiously pumping her arms, she didn't have the courage. So she let her keep walking.

Phoebe climbed out of the car, but Mother waved her arm and told her to get back in the Cadillac. Instead, Phoebe leaned against the trunk of the car, and Joan came out, too. They watched as Mother fought her way through the brush beyond the shoulder to a small road sign bent on a diagonal into the ground. Joan read it: WELCOME TO KICKAPOO, INDIANA. For once she had nothing nasty to say.

Mother would have to walk a couple of miles to get back that purse of hers. Joan had picked it up from under Mother's seat, thinking about stealing her spare change. She searched among the tissues for contraband and came up with three purple gumballs wrapped in plastic. Not knowing how long they'd been rotting in there, she offered the first one to Phoebe, but Phoebe was busy piecing the road maps back together. Joan popped all three into her mouth, imagining they were cyanide and she was at the tail end of a fabulously secret spy mission. Now she'd join her father in the afterlife, a place she didn't believe in, though she hoped to be proved wrong. The tart, harmless flavor of blueberry spread over her tongue and she went on searching. There was Mother's brown wallet. Inside, Joan found Mother's driver's license, her library card, paper-clipped receipts from Sunset Foods, and seventeen dollars, but nothing else that seemed to matter. Nothing in there to remind Mother of her husband. Not a picture, not a slip of paper he'd written on, not even a charge card in his name. Joan plucked out the bills and put the wallet back in.

Sometimes she thought her father had only been someone she'd dreamed up rather than an actual man made of flesh and blood. For two months Joan had felt strange and out of balance, almost as if she were wearing someone else's shoes. But by the lack of evidence in Mother's purse, Joan suspected her mother didn't miss him, didn't notice the house was now full of extra chairs, too much air, and a ton of empty space. But Mother did cry at night when she thought the girls were asleep. Joan could hear her in the bathroom behind the closed door. Then again, Mother cried at everything. Commercials for long distance. Parades. She was probably crying now because Joan's father wasn't around to pay the bills. Yeah, that was it.

In a side pocket of the purse, Joan discovered a note card folded into quarters. She straightened it out and read the hidden message, words written in Mother's slanted handwriting, the lines moving upward, the letters pulled to the upper right corner as if the card had been tilted when the ink was still wet.

Kimberly Bloom, it said.

Reddish hair, brown overcoat.

And then underneath, a phone number, starting with a 317 area code.

In the back of the Cadillac, on the way to see this half sister with hair the color of Joan's and a stupid brown coat, Joan sensed the weather inside her changing, a storm system blowing in. She snapped the clasp of the pocketbook shut, leaving everything inside, including the note card with Kimberly's information. She let the storm in her body whirl until it ripped open her stomach, mangled her heart, blew off the top of her head, and sucked Mother's pocketbook up its funnel, right out the window. Mother never noticed, too stuck in the future, in what was up ahead at the Holiday Inn. Phoebe, preoccupied with fixing the map, hadn't seen anything, either. Joan turned and saw the purse bounce off the highway, spilling its Kleenex guts.

But as she lost sight of the purse and the Cadillac moved on, Joan felt the temperature cooling off inside her. Something was changing against her will, something that made it impossible for Joan to keep ignoring one simple fact: She had spoiled Mother's plans.

Now, waiting for Mother to return from her futile search, Joan couldn't help but tell Phoebe about Kimberly and her out-of-state phone number.

"Do you remember what it was?" Phoebe asked. "The number, Joan? What was it?" Phoebe wished she were psychic, like the woman her father hired for Phoebe's thirteenth birthday party, the one who told Joan she was going to marry a preacher and predicted Phoebe would one day be a showgirl at the Moulin Rouge.

"Slap me," Joan said.

"Huh?"

"Slap me. I deserve it."

"No."

"Yes. Do it."

"I won't."

A car blew past. Joan turned to Phoebe and said, "Chicken."

Forty minutes later, Mother came back down the highway empty-handed. Strands of her hair were plastered across her nose and mouth. Her eyes were wet — whether from the wind or from woe, Phoebe couldn't tell.

"Okay," Mother growled, her words fluttering into the gust. "I have had it."

"What do you mean by 'it'?" Joan asked.

"I mean it all!" Mother shouted. "I mean my fifty-dollar purse. I mean all these years of the sass and the lip. I mean the crank calls you two made to Immaculate Heart of Mary. And Joan, the blindness you faked the winter you were seven. I mean all that stuff." Joan knew Mother hadn't even gotten to the bad things yet. This would take all day.

"And you, young lady," Mother said, turning to Phoebe. "What about you? I know it probably wasn't your idea, but couldn't you, at the very least, have done something?"

Phoebe gulped, regretting the last hour, regretting her whole life. The way Mother looked, all tossed around, shaking her arms and fists, as frantic as a one-man band, broke her heart. Should she tell Mother she saw Joan with that pocketbook but pretended to be busy with the torn road map? Phoebe couldn't take the empty feeling she had, the absence of anything good. But being decent wouldn't help now. Joan had ruined everything and Phoebe had watched.

"You two are fiends. You know that?" Mother gathered her own hair with her hands. She throttled it and pulled it over her shoulder. "My lipstick. My driver's license. My lipstick. I'll be arrested." She spun Phoebe around and pushed her toward the back door. Joan tried to look bored and unimpressed, but Mother grabbed her bare arm just below the sleeve and pulled her along. Joan resisted, digging her heels into the gravel. A semi chugged by close to the shoulder and honked enthusiastically.

Joan had never seen Mother like this, not even after her botched escape to Las Vegas, not ever. It shocked her, and Joan was a girl not easily jolted. Mother's fingers dug into her arm, and she could feel the blood pulsing around the dent in her skin. The socket in her shoulder burned, and Mother grunted once, twice. Joan expected to take cruel pleasure in Mother's anger, but instead she found herself wanting to hug her mother. It was a strange feeling, and Joan tried to figure out where in her body it came from.

A vein bulged under Mother's left eye, her two front teeth buried in her lower lip. She began to hiss, softly, like a raft losing air. Joan knew that something strong, something scary, was crossing over to her through her mother's grip. When Mother let go, Joan could still feel fury in the air, like the moment right after a thunderbolt. Her arm still hurt, but that pain was nothing compared to the shame pinching her insides.

Phoebe reached out the back and pulled at Joan's shirt. Once Joan was inside, Mother slammed the door shut and then got into the driver's seat. She turned around and said in a terrible whisper, "Buckle up. Right now."

Later, after they were on the road, Joan and Phoebe were afraid to talk. The girls rarely wore seat belts, preferring to be bounced around the car like loose marbles. Phoebe felt tied up, as if she were riding in the back of a paddy wagon. She stared at Mother's head, wondering who this woman was.

Mother's shoulders began to shudder. She was weeping again. Joan thought this might be the moment she could finally do the right thing. She reached her hand forward over the driver's seat but stopped five inches from her mother's back. Was this how you did it?

Before she could touch the fabric of Mother's dress, Phoebe slapped Joan's hand away and shook her head.

Forty-five silent minutes later, Mother pulled off the highway, fist over fist on the steering wheel. She circled around on the access road, and the low afternoon sun slid into the frame of the windshield. Phoebe and Joan shaded their eyes, peeking out between their fingers. The light beyond Mother shimmered along the outline of her head, making her look electrified, gigantic, as hot as the sun. From out of the glare, the Holiday Inn sign emerged. Phoebe reached for Joan's hand, but couldn't find it in the space between them.

Mother bumped into a parking spot. "Here I am," she said, "fabulously late." She reached for her purse, then snatched her hand back. She wrenched the rearview mirror to capture her entire face, and Phoebe turned away. "And I look something awful." Mother faced the back and stared at Phoebe, stared at Joan. "For the love of any god you choose, do not move."

The girls obeyed, staring after their mother as she ran down the sidewalk and disappeared into the coffee shop. They had weary looks on their faces, stupefied gazes that could have landed them roles in *The Poseidon Adventure,* the last movie they'd seen with their father.

Joan rested her forehead against the side window, thinking of ways she and Phoebe, like mad scientists, could reverse the day, making time tick backward, so that they could get Mother to this Holiday Inn on time. A maid pushed a cleaning cart piled high with dirty towels along the sidewalk in front of the car, making a sharp turn toward a concrete block of hotel rooms. Maybe there was a maid with red hair they could dress up like Kimberly, give her a twenty to talk to Mother and point out that she already had a pair of daughters. But Joan only had seventeen bucks. And besides, Mother wouldn't believe it.

Joan tapped Phoebe and pointed to the red splotch on her arm where Mother had grabbed her. The mark was fresh and hot, its edges clear. Joan blew on it, hoping it would turn blue or purple or green. The girls watched it as if it were a Polaroid picture, waiting for shapes and faces to appear.

"It's a beetle," Phoebe whispered. "A Japanese one."

"It's a beauty mark," Joan said, in a voice that barely came. "It runs in the family, and Kimberly doesn't have one."

"It's a television screen. We can watch shows wherever we go."

"It's a brand," Joan said. "From a hot poker." Phoebe wanted to touch it, but Joan wouldn't let her. "She owns me now. Look at it. I'm from Circle Mother ranch." She stuck a finger in the middle and felt a dull ache run up her arm and fill her body. She did it again, enjoying the twinge, reminding herself of the crazy look in Mother's eyes, the bite in her grip.

"Relax, Joan," Phoebe said. "It's just the start of a bruise."

In the window of a room directly in front of the Cadillac, a little girl in an orange dress stood behind glass, clutching a half-naked doll to her chest, patting its back, burping her. Phoebe couldn't help thinking of herself at that age. Maybe she could take that child and give it to Mother.

They were still buckled up in their seat belts, just sitting there as if waiting for an awful carnival ride to start. Mother wasn't coming back. Neither girl wanted to consider what this meant.

"Come on," Phoebe said, letting herself free and kicking open the door. "I can't just sit here."

"Wait." Joan followed her out and grabbed her hand, right as Phoebe was about to scale the curb. "Where are you going?"

"Don't you want to see what we're up against?" Phoebe stared at her sister.

Joan dropped to the curb and rested her head on her knees, trying to slow down her breathing. Things were happening so fast for her, she could hardly keep up. But never before had Joan been able to take such deep clean breaths. It almost made her dizzy, as if she were balancing on a high dive, teetering on the edge of the board, hoping to swan dive into the bluest water she'd ever seen. This new feeling scared Joan, so she reached back for her old self. There were her fingernails bitten down to the bloody quick. There in her pocket were the seventeen bucks she'd stolen from her mother. And there, on the top of her left foot, right above the strap of her sandals, was the spot where she had tattooed her skin with a skull and crossbones three days ago. She'd used a felt-tip marker, a permanent one.

"I can't take this anymore," Phoebe said and started walking to the coffee shop. It took only a moment for Joan to rise from the curb and rush to her side. They grabbed hands, blood pulsing through their grip. They stood with their backs to the wall just inches from the door of the coffee shop. The girls turned and leaned to look through the glass door, Joan on top, Phoebe on the bottom. Mother was in a booth in the corner, fiddling with her hair. She straightened her silverware, then moved the spoon and fork apart, brought them together again.

And across from her, in a red sweater, was somebody else. A brown coat was draped over the back of the vinyl seat. This woman sipped from a coffee cup, wiped her lips with her napkin, laughed. Joan wished she would turn around. Joan was dying to see her face.

Mother took a cigarette from a pack in the middle of the table. She'd never smoked before, not that the girls knew of. It was strange the way she brought the thing to her lips, her cheeks already puffed out as if she were about to blow up a balloon. The other woman struck a match with ease and lit the thing. As Mother blew out, she disappeared bit by bit in a thick haze of gray smoke. It seemed to Phoebe as if this were the first cigarette of a stranger's life.

The girls had the nervous suspicion that they'd gotten the short end of the stick again. The woman they saw before them was a more interesting mother. Joan suspected that this mother held weather inside of her, too, weather that was full of fronts and systems and a thousand different types of clouds, weather as unpredictable as her own.

They remained at the window, palms up on the glass, noses almost touching the pane. As they spied on their mother and their new sister, Mother's attention drifted up and she saw them. Mother raised her hand to wave, then pointed them out. Kimberly began to turn her head.

TED THOMPSON

The Bread Loaf Writers' Conference

SOME THINGS I'VE BEEN
MEANING TO ASK YOU

Cuppo squinted under his permanent-markered eyebrows, nodding at the girl who was feeding coins into the ice-cream machine. "That's the one." Her cottony sweater hung like a robe from her narrow feminine shoulders, and draped down her back until it hit the substantial shelf of her rear. She turned around and unwrapped her Fudgsicle.

"Look at that," said Bobby Sausage. The entire brown top disappeared into her mouth. "Those are some skills."

"Practically bovine," added Cuppo, then he turned to me and raised his eyebrows. "You gonna hit it?"

"I don't even know her," I said. She wore layered yellow tank tops and had a pageboy haircut that flipped out under her ears. Backlit by the glow of the Good Humor machine, she looked for a moment like a squash someone had adorned with a cape.

"What do you need to know?" Bobby said. "She craves your

dong." Word had come down from Cuppo's sister, who sat next to her in chorus, that she was interested.

"She's from Oregon," Cuppo said, as we watched her cross the cafeteria to a lone table by the window. He nodded slowly. "West Coast."

"What does that even mean?"

He rolled his eyes. "West Coast women are the easiest in the country. It's proven. I can give you a study on it. They're downright filthy." Sausage stifled a laugh with his palm. He hadn't grown anything but body hair since the sixth grade, and the back of his little hand was covered in it.

"You guys are assholes."

"Hit it and quit it, Myles," said Sausage. "No shame in that."

Look at us, Dad. Can you see us lounging on the benches at the far end of the cafeteria, our hair shaggy and terrible, in tattered sweatshirts and markered Airwalks and worn T-shirts from Phish tours we were too young to have ever attended? Can you see the way we look over our shoulders and divert our eyes and bury our hands in our hoodie pockets? Can you tell we secretly loved fantasy books and video games and that this was the first girl to pierce our male adolescent force fields? Why? Because she noticed us. Why else? Because we were remarkably late to this game, because it had been played around us since the fifth grade and we'd watched it like foreigners staring through the chain link at a green and distant land. Without even knowing it, she'd opened the border.

"Go say something," said Cuppo, pushing the back of my shoulder. "Ask her if you can have a lick." With that, Sausage finally burst, roaring and slapping his leg and making a scene, and I could see her look up from her table by the window, alone, and notice us. It seemed mean, and it was, so I walked over to her, hearing Sausage's laughter dissolve behind me, and sat down.

"Can you do me a favor?" I said. She had a cold chunk in her mouth and she took a moment for it to melt.

"What."

"I want you to talk to me for a minute, just like this, like we're having a good time, and then I want you to slap me in the face."

She waited for the joke. "What?"

"I want you to smack me hard on the cheek and then walk away. It'd be a big help."

She scanned my face, then looked over to the gawking boys in the corner. "No." She crossed her arms and leaned back, looking out the window at the blazing midday parking lot. Her Fudgsicle sat warming on its wrapper. There was no right answer, I realized, for her in this.

"I'm sorry," I said, reaching a hand across the table. "I'm Myles."

"Agatha," she said, and shook it. The guys hooted and whistled behind me.

"Don't listen to them," I said, and she smacked me hard across the face. It was loud and painful, and as she walked away I sat there alone in a plastic cafeteria chair. Cuppo and Sausage were silent. From across the room I saw her leaning against the wall, beaming back at me. Her teeth were so finely orthodontiaed that they looked, top and bottom, like single strips of ivory.

This was before you were gone, believe it or not, nearly a year before, and I'm starting here so that you get a clear idea of where I was all that time. I wonder if the lives of teenagers are ever as inscrutable to their parents as we assume they are. There's a chance that you knew all of this, that you watched it carefully from afar, as unfazed by it as by those years of diaper changing that you apparently endured without complaint. But you couldn't have known everything, since the facts only show the very tip of things, and, like learning later the make and model of the convertible that ran you over, or the name of the woman who was driving—or even that she has dyed red hair and wears sunglasses in the vegetable aisle at Grand Union and lives alone on Salt Pond Road in a house that should sleep thirty—there's so much more, always, left to understand.

I looked for Agatha later that week in school, and when I finally found her it was in the parking lot after the buses had left with the mobs, and the only people there were the sporty kids, counting off their stretches like sad little militias on the green patchwork of lawns. Her bags, three of them, were full of SAT-prep books, about as heavy and interesting as the Yellow Pages, so I offered to help her carry them to her car.

There we talked about the pros and cons of early decision, about how Cuppo's father, the onetime head of an international corporation, had left his family and moved to Vermont for a man, but if she told anyone I swore I'd kill her. We talked until our cars were the only two left in the parking lot; until my feet hurt from standing; until my left shoulder ached from my backpack, then my right; until the sky overhead turned an autumn gold, then red, then navy.

In that parking lot, under a sky like black ice, with my hands shoved stiffly in my sweatshirt pockets, I could see Agatha was waiting for it. My last and only kiss had been in the seventh grade, when I had ghostly wisps in my pits and a chest as pink as the day I was born. She came toward me with her eyelids down, smiling. She didn't open her mouth when she touched it to mine, all electric and buzzing. I could feel the blood throbbing in my throat. My balls were heavy as lead.

When I was young, no more than seven, you took me out to run errands for Mom. Do you remember this? It was the first time I could remember being alone with you outside of the house. We were doing what Mom and I would normally do, but it was with you and therefore it was different. We went through the grocery aisles backward, we bought lunch instead of making it, we stopped at a hardware store that smelled sharply of sawdust. You bought caulk and I loved its dispenser because it was shaped like a gun.

Because I was good, we went to the beach and you took me out on the sailboat. Do you remember this? It must've been October — the sky was opaque and gray, the water like cement churning — but we sailed anyway. First you caulked the hull, and then, because I was good, we sailed through the thickening gray into evening.

Here's the truth: After Agatha Berger and I kissed I lied about it to Cuppo, and to Sausage, and to anyone else who may've asked. Something changed. I noticed her pear shape, the smooth excess skin that gathered beneath her chin like a gel cushion when she laughed. I was embarrassed. I don't know why. The day after we kissed she came up behind me while I was eating with Sausage and put her hands over my eyes.

"Who is it?" I asked.

There was nothing. I could tell by Sausage's silence that he wasn't amused.

She pulled her hands away and leaned over me, grinning. Her cheeks were flushed as she pulled up a chair.

"So," she said, looking in my eyes. "What's for lunch?"

I showed her the gooey edge of my sandwich. "Egg and cheese."

"Can I have a bite?" I held it out for her and she took one. Sausage disappeared into his bologna on rye.

"Delicious," she said. "I'll be right back." She ran her hand playfully along my shoulders.

Sausage squinted at me. "What was that?"

"What?"

"Can I have a *bite*?"

"I don't..." I shook my head. "Nothing. Generosity."

He cocked his head and pointed his thumb toward Agatha. "Is she your girlfriend?"

"No," I said, shaking my head, as if I'd never thought of it.

"She ate from your sandwich."

"I guess," I said, swiping the bitten edge through a blob of ketchup. "I mean, she's in some of my classes. She's nice."

Sausage shook his head. "That girl wants your junk."

"I don't know. I don't see it."

He looked over at her, waiting in line at the grill. "It's a little weird," he said.

"Weird?" I looked up at him.

"Yeah," he said. "Like pathetic."

And so it continued. Every time Agatha approached there were looks, and when she left there were denials, and soon Cuppo and Sausage had created a series of Agatha jokes. "How many Agathas does it take to screw in a lightbulb?" Cuppo would say. "A hundred. One to deal with the bulb and ninety-nine to stare at Myles's dinger while her back is turned."

"And to diddle her vajiddle," Sausage would add. "What? We're talking about Berger, not about you."

Here's also the truth: I was Agatha's only friend. And after school, what Cuppo and Sausage didn't know — or chose not to know — was that I spent hours with her. Her family had a pool house that was built for guests, fully furnished with a bedroom loft and a kitchen and a television with premium cable. Her father, like you and so many other men in this town, did something inscrutable with stocks, and her mother was at work somewhere, and so for hours we would roll around half clothed on that bed, dry-humping and sucking face and rubbing our paws over each other's zippered crotches, until one day she opened my fly and pulled out my dick and squeezed it in her fist as if trying to strangle a goose. I wasn't sure she knew what to do with it, so I helped her and she helped me with the labyrinth of buttons on her baggy pantaloons and then the sliding off of her polka-dot panties and then we were fumbling on each other, naked, writhing around, embarrassed and happy, as though we'd freed each other from the unfathomable burden of adolescent secrets. *Here,* we said. *Look, this just happened beneath my clothes, I couldn't share it with anyone. Here,* we said. *See? See me? This is what I've become.*

"My friends in Oregon want to meet you," she said one evening in the empty silence as we lay atop the sheets, recovering.

"Are they coming here?"

"No, probably not." She sat up, her breasts wobbling like goat-skin canteens. "But we could go there."

"How?"

"Drive. You and me, this summer."

"That's a long trip," I said, rolling onto my side.

"Or fly. We could fly."

I climbed out of bed and slipped my boxers on, then searched for my T-shirt in the heap of clothes. I liked to dress immediately after. It felt cleaner. I would pretend to pee so I could scrub my hands, and I would flush the condom so there'd be no trace.

"You don't have to meet them if you don't want," she said when I came out of the bathroom. She had the sheet up to her shoulders like a dress. "It was just an idea."

"No, I'd love to meet them someday. I really would," I said, looking for my balled socks in the leg of my corduroys.

"Your friends aren't very nice to me," she said.

"What? Where did that come from?"

"I'm pretty sure they think I'm a skank. I think they think I'm stupid."

"Ridiculous," I said. I kissed her dry lips, then pulled my corduroys on.

"Do they even know about us?" she said, but I could tell she intuitively knew the answer.

"It's none of their business."

She began to cry. It was an awful sight, Dad. She was trying to cover her paleness with a thin musty sheet.

"Of course they know," I said, lifting her quaking chin, and staring as earnestly as I could into her unprotected face. "Of course they know. Listen, I love you."

I hid from her in the halls. I took the long way to class to avoid her. I memorized her schedule and spent my day flanked by others — even people I didn't know well — so that if I did run into her, intimacy of any kind wasn't an option. I ate lunch at the French table, I ate lunch in the faculty section, I skipped lunch altogether. I came late to Physics and sat by the door, I came early to AP Mod and sat with the laptop dorks at the front table. And then at three thirty I drove straight to her pool house and let myself in and slid off my shoes and waited for her on the sofa while watching *People's Court*.

All of which meant I was never home, and when I was it was after you and Mom had gone to bed, and I would find a dinner plate Saran Wrapped on the kitchen counter and eat alone with a single light on, the broccoli cold, the couscous lumpy. Soon even Cuppo had stopped calling. He and Sausage had jokes I didn't understand.

"Here," he said, handing me the Phish tapes he'd borrowed. We were in the parking lot, outside his rusty Grand Caravan, whose upholstery still carried the distinct smell of children and car seat. It had been his mother's van when Cuppo had been a figure skater as a child, where she'd fed him countless McDonald's dinners as she drove him around the Tri-State area to compete. It was a life he didn't mention much anymore.

"Any of the old sparkly costumes in there?" I said, peering over his shoulder.

He made an obnoxious laugh.

"How about tights?"

"Take your fucking tapes."

When Cuppo had shown up in the sixth grade, he was six inches shorter and delicate, exempt from gym because of "outside physical demands." Everyone knew him then as Pierre, but he hung up the skates when he thickened with puberty. His hair curled into a wiry nest. His dad was gone. But his lunch, which was still packed by his mother, always contained the trademark "Cup O' Vanilla" pudding. The change of name seemed only appropriate.

Cuppo fiddled with his new cell phone, a hand-me-down from his mom. He liked to pull it out whenever he could, just to look important, while the rest of us bummed quarters for the pay phone.

"What're you, a fucking banker?"

"Just seeing if anyone called."

"Mom. Mom. Mom. Mom," I mimed, clicking through the call list on my phantom phone.

"So when are you getting married?" he said.

"That's not really funny."

"Your mom says you're never home. Where are you all the time?"

"Different places. Nowhere special."

"Your mom says you missed most of Christmas."

"Why don't you and my mom get married?"

"When she's single, call me."

Cuppo teased me about being a father, about getting married at eighteen like Macaulay Culkin and being just as screwed up.

"I hope it's worth it," he said.

"How's your father doing?"

He shook his head, squinting at the long lot of hand-me-down cars. "She's weird, dude," he said and lifted his hood around his giant triangle of hair. "Forget her. And call me back sometime." He turned toward the school building, stepping on his ratty cuffs with the cork heels of his Birkenstocks.

I know you were up alone in the mornings while we slept, unwrapping your laundered shirts and cinching your neck with a Windsor knot, and in the evenings, after the train dumped you back on our granite doorstep, you had all of an hour left in you to chat over marinated chicken breasts and sautéed spinach, before you would sink into the sofa, your eyelids heavy, and be gone.

It couldn't have been much past six when you opened my door, the blue morning light outside like a fluorescent bulb just beginning to brighten. You were only a shadow in your spring trench, your briefcase like a plumb weight on the end of your slack arm. I couldn't remember the last time you had entered my room. The mattress gave at my feet with your weight. Your hand smelled soapy and clean as you put it to my hot cheek.

"I have something for you," you said and clicked open the tabs on your briefcase as if starting a meeting. The box was shiny and medicinal as you placed it on the covered lump of my chest. The condoms sat there, perched like a toy locomotive at the crest of a hill.

"Dad."

"Use them" was your advice.

"I don't need them."

You sighed and looked down at me. The softened flesh of your throat, where it had just been shaved and soothed with lotion, gathered above your stiff collar. "It's okay," you said and patted my leg. "Just let me know when you need more."

I understand now, nearly three years later, that it was a fatherly duty, like ball throwing and knot tying and stick-shift driving, and perhaps the last on the paternal checklist. And the funny thing is that, try as I might, when I think back on it these days, driving through town in the winter with the windows open and the stereo thumping and my elbow turning pink and raw in the vacant window frame, it is the last private interaction between us I can remember. I know there were more — a dinner or two, a bear hug after gradua- tion, others — but I remember little outside the thickening fog of my own self-interest and those condoms, in their glossy and embarrass- ing package, like a UNICEF collection box, rising and falling with each breath.

Do-overs don't really exist, so I try not to dwell on these things, but I do get a lot of thinking done these days, driving around town late into the night with the music crawling from my open windows. I've been delivering booze for Downtown Spirits, cases of wine, mostly to your friends, and since everyone's long gone — Agatha to Bryn Mawr, Sausage to Skidmore, Cuppo to Puget Sound — the whole town sometimes feels like it's mine.

But did I tell you that Mom and I ran into the lady with the con- vertible? We were in the produce aisle when that Raggedy Ann hair, a ridiculous red, stopped us both. She was squeezing an onion. She held it in front of her face like a softball pitcher starting her windup, looking so closely it was nearly touching her sunglasses. Sunglasses! In the white light of the supermarket! Maybe she was hungover. Maybe she'd come from a funeral. I wanted to watch some more, to see what else we'd find, but that's all I got before Mom was gone. She was already out the automatic door, and then I was going after her, and when I looked back from the parking lot all I could see was our cart, abandoned with our food still in it.

By April I was ready to be done with it all, and so was Agatha, as I learned one teary night when she ambushed me in her car about why I hadn't asked her to prom.

"You're just mean to me," she said, wiping her eyes with her palms. "You don't acknowledge me. It's like you're two different people completely. Why? I don't get it."

When I shrugged, she kicked me out of her car, which I assumed I was supposed to resist, but instead I walked home in the warm spring air, kicking a pebble in front of me and feeling somewhat pleasantly off the hook. I spent prom night taking bong rips in my rented tuxedo before passing out in Sausage's basement. I saw her occasionally from a distance in the hallways, and in the sea of cheap nylon robes at graduation, but she never seemed to notice me.

I could tell you about how it all felt right, that I felt like a kid again, spending all my time with my doofus buddies and our arsenal of inside jokes, enjoying plastic pouches of fruit snacks and unafraid to recite aloud with the video our favorite scenes from *Total Recall*. I could tell you about the adamant decisions that passed unanimously in the House and Senate of my mind. I could tell you that although she had done nothing wrong, Agatha Berger had begun to represent everything I hated about myself. I could tell you these things, but they wouldn't make sense with the rest of the story.

It was in the invincible joy of early June, at a pool party, no less, that I saw her again. She looked happy, splashing around in the deep end with a quartet of guys I didn't know—buzzed, I assumed, on something. It was dark and the light from the pool was the only one on in the yard, casting its wavy radioactive glow on the heavy maple limbs above. She wore a plaid bikini that tied around her neck like the uniform of a waitress at a lewd Dutch Pantry. She had lost weight, and yet her breasts looked bigger somehow. When she pushed herself out of the water I could see she was wearing some other guy's lacrosse shorts.

"Look who's here," said Cuppo, reaching for my nipple with his vicious pincers.

We found each other by the creaky lawn furniture on the shadowy edge of the yard, where I'd been trying unsuccessfully to light a corn-cob pipe (it was a phase). She'd pulled a loose tank top over her bikini and was, it seemed, looking for a place to pee. The party was late, anonymous, strewn with cups and bottles, as if the very act of littering was part of the thrill of cutting loose.

"Latrine's over there," I said, pointing at the house.

She looked up at me and squinted. "Is that a *pipe*?"

"Maybe," I said, cupping the flame against the wind again and nearly burning a lighter smiley into my thumb.

"Let me see it." She snatched it from my hands, clenched it in her teeth, and with a single flick had it lit. She placed it back in my mouth as if feeding me a carrot. "My dad smokes one."

"I'm still trying it out," I said, surprised by the ashy taste filling my mouth. It always smelled so sweet clamped in the jaws of old men, filling an entire block with its aroma. I'd assumed it'd taste something like a Werther's Original.

"Your hair's gotten longer," she said, pulling on the straggly bits behind my ear.

"So has yours." She now had a full ponytail, which she wrapped on the top of her head with an elastic, and, in the shadow, it looked like a big stringy squid had made its home there. Her hand combed through my dangling hair, then around to the back of my skull.

"I've missed you," she said.

I nodded and she led me by the hand into the soft, twiggy woods, where we stumbled together in our sandals until there was no light from the party at all and we could feel more than we could see, and there I pulled down those damp lacrosse shorts and yanked free her swaying tits and we pushed each other onto the prickly ground. She tasted of the stale chlorinated air at the Y. We screwed until my aching knees had sunk into the earth with last year's leaves.

The whole thing took all of three panting minutes. "That was nice," she said when it was over, pulling up her shorts, readjusting her top. There were twigs pressed into both of her knees, and as I heard her brush them off, then retie her hair, I felt, suddenly, like sobbing. "What?" she said. I was still sitting on the ground, cross-legged, my boxers around my ankles.

"Are you going back to the party?"

"Why?" she asked. "You want to cuddle in the dirt?" She pulled the tank top back over her head. As my eyes adjusted, I saw her sniff casually at her pits.

"I just thought... I don't know... what the hell did we just do?"

"We fucked, Myles. We had a quickie."

"I know that, I just..." I didn't actually want to talk, Dad; what I really wanted was for her to touch my forehead, or say something nice, like she used to, about my scrawny ribs. *Look at those birdcage ribs. That's a home for a cockatiel; that's a home for a whole canary family.* She would tickle me, and I would leap from the mattress in a wiggling naked squirm.

"Fine then — I'm pregnant," she said. She crossed her arms and looked down on me with the glassy eyes of a teddy bear.

"What do you mean?"

"I mean I have a baby inside me, or a zygote, or something. I'm fertilized."

"What?" I said, rising and pulling up my shorts, messing with the tinkling belt.

"Why does everyone have that reaction? It's not that big of a deal."

"Of course — of course it is."

"Don't worry about it. It's not your problem." She pulled the elastic from her hair, which fell again in damp clumps around her shoulders.

"Wait a second. There's a possibility it is, isn't it? I mean, we did a lot of stuff. I mean, how do you know for sure?"

She shrugged. "Laws of probability."

It would be a lie to say I didn't hold a private vigil of relief. It would also be a lie to say my throat wasn't knotted tightly in disappointment. All I could do was try to remember the right chapter from the good-guy handbook, its many onionskin pages, its footnoted, endless code of conduct. Chapter 10: Pregnancy — support, support, support. "Congratulations," I said.

She glared at me. "Don't be an asshole."

I pulled her wet head firmly against my shoulder, let its cold spot seep through my T-shirt. She left it there, and I could feel her shoulders relax for a moment, before she gave me a little shove and walked back through the woods to the party. I looked up at the clouds cruising through the night sky, just above the bushy tops of the trees, and sat back down for a moment to catch my breath. The party was tinny and distant, as if dubbed too many times on an old tape, and as I listened to its sad babble, I looked down at my splayed legs, which were finally covered in ugly, dark hair.

I looked for Cuppo in the keg line and up on the deck, but he wasn't anywhere, so I went back out to the pool, which was full of people in their clothes, floating in the water with their shirts billowing around them like jellyfish. He wasn't there, either, but Agatha was, bent over a foam noodle with a beer in her hand. "Ready — one, two, three," I heard someone bark poolside, and before I could see who it was, she flipped on her back and began to chug.

———

On the ocean like churning cement we sailed without care or worry. I held the jib sheet and kept it taut — taut! — and you sat back with the rudder, unaffected entirely by the early winter breeze. On the shore, the sand on the beaches was darker, the snack bar abandoned and boarded up. We cruised along at a slight angle, the hull slicing the water, which made a quiet hissing sound like a newly opened can of Coke. You wore a baseball cap only on the boat and you had it pulled down so your eyeballs disappeared under the bill. You seemed to steer us effortlessly. You seemed to steer us even though you were blind.

Cuppo has a weakness for crazy ideas. He not only comes up with them, but he can actually follow through. He's my go-to guy. That's how we ended up running naked down Main Street in March and replacing all the chairs in the faculty lounge with toilets (did you know that was me?). And that's how I ended up skipping out of summer school — that bullshit gym credit they were making me repeat — and filling the back of Cuppo's caravan with all of the essentials: fifty-three boxes of Kraft Easy Mac, a dozen cartons of Cap'n Crunch with Crunch Berries, a garbage bag of T-shirts and boxers, and Sausage's life-size cardboard cutout of George Burns, which we all agreed would look splendid in the passenger seat.

"You sure you don't want to make any calls?" Cuppo's Groucho Marx eyebrows were obscuring his eyes.

"Yeah, let's go."

"Not even a message for the folks?"

"Or the missus?" said Sausage, looking around for a laugh. I flipped him the bird and pushed it all the way against his flat ugly nose.

"I left the Phish newsletter on my bedside table. It has all the dates. Just drive."

"You hear that, George?" said Cuppo, looking at his passenger. "He left clues."

The tour started in Kansas and ended in Indiana, via Atlanta and New Jersey. We would go to twenty-three shows total, through thir-teen states and two countries, sleep in the car, eat only what we brought, and return a month and a half later with exactly one week to spare before shipping off to college. We had no tickets yet, but we had five hundred dollars in cash between us, Mom's Mobil card, Sausage's George Foreman grill, and Cuppo's dad's Diners Club card. I-95, shimmering and distorted, gave way to I-80, which was pristine and hummed a low little theme song: *ba-bum ba-bum, ba-bum ba-bum.* In the front seat George, cigar in hand, was waving.

We left without warning. Otherwise, it wouldn't have worked. I left you and Mom and Agatha without an explanation or a hint.

There are some things I've been meaning to ask you. We spoke deeply about so few things that now I find myself only wanting to ask you questions. Like, have I asked you why you were on a benefit ride for MS, of all things? Did you actually know someone who had it, or was it just a random act of generosity? Or have I asked you why you were riding a bike when I've never seen you ride one in my life? Have I asked you these things? Have I asked you why a car was on the road when it was supposed to be closed? Have I asked you if she was speeding? Or why you were riding so close to the yellow line or why, if you were in a pack of riders, only you fell, and why no one stopped to help you? Have I told you I was in Indiana? That Cuppo told me he had his cell phone just in case something went wrong, but when we got to Pittsburgh and we were going to call you, he smiled a stupid smile and laughed in a loud, uncomfortable burst and said he must have left the charger on his bed at home? Have I told you I left Mom that cell-phone number on my bed? Have I told you

Cuppo's a goddamn idiot? Have I told you I heard all of Mom's messages on Cuppo's phone, about the bike, about the funeral, about how it was a beautiful service, a real tribute, about who showed up and what they brought, about how she told them I was on the Appalachian Trail and that's why I was unreachable and absent — the fucking Appalachian Trail? Have I told you she spoke to Cuppo's voice mail as if it were me? That she called Cuppo's phone a few times a day? That she thought maybe I was ignoring her calls? Have I told you that I still have no idea what I'm doing? That at times I wish that baby had been mine, that it may have been pear-shaped and ugly, but payback nonetheless, payback? Can you see that I am sorry, I am sorry, I am sorry, I am sorry? Can you see that? Have I told you that babies are the currency of the universe, the severance package of the grieving? Can you see that I've paid my dues, that I was offered redemption and I turned it down, that there is a balance to things that is only apparent in hindsight? Have I told you that I would've traded all that time with Agatha Berger to have been with you, all of that lost time? Have I told you that I would've actually spoken to you, would've asked you how to navigate the awful fact of growing up, would have asked you to do the impossible and stop it, to pause it all right there, and allow fathers to be just fathers and children to be just children, so that for once we could all stay together, so that for once no one would die?

DAVID LOMBARDI

University of Houston

FLIGHT

Chuck Silversmith stood knee-deep in rushing water and watched the birds. They were tiny purple-colored birds with short tapered wings like sharpened blades. He couldn't say how many there were, but they were a swarm. And they were fast, too. He couldn't believe how fast they were. They flitted and danced; they streaked, soared, and skimmed over the streambed. On agile, widespread wings they carved the air.

He didn't know what to call them. He didn't know what they were called. Martins, he thought, purple-backed martins. On another night he might look at them and see grace and beauty; he might, in fact, feel humbled to live in a world such as this, with birds such as these. But tonight they left him feeling only confused. It was as if each bird carried a strand of thread in its beak, but these aerial weavers were not, as in some fairy tale, sewing a magical dress, but were instead spooling a massive ball of knots. Standing in the current, holding his fishing rod, Chuck watched them build it.

The martins seemed to have materialized out of thin air. In the last five minutes a grayness had settled over the water, and with the grayness a swarm of bugs, and with those bugs, these birds. Conditions were bound to improve, but Chuck was of two minds. He didn't know if he wanted to keep fishing; but if he didn't want to keep fishing, he didn't know what he'd do. It was getting late and the muscles in his calves were tired. Truthfully, his whole body was tired. He was seventy-two, but felt older. Over the last two months he felt he'd aged years. He couldn't say how many, but years.

He didn't look old. He was still handsome. He had always been handsome. He had good skin and thick white hair, pale eyes, and long-fingered, meticulous hands. If he left the river now, he thought, where would he go? He wasn't sure. He'd go somewhere, someplace else. There had to be somewhere he could go. He could go anywhere, really, anywhere but home.

Tall firs lined this slow-curving bend of the Snoqualmie, and an hour earlier, in the slanting sunlight, their sap-soaked, orange-barked trunks had all been ablaze, but now, minute by minute, the darkening air stole their color. The trees cut a deep and narrow chasm to the water, and in the dying light their gray trunks seemed to blur together like cliffs of sheer stone. Chuck stood at the bottom of this chasm and looked above their points to an acetylene-blue sky. Shielding his eyes, he squinted against the overly bright light. The long summer sun had not yet fallen behind the mountains. Still, he knew it was coming — dusk, nightfall; it had already settled in all around him.

On the far riverbank Chuck spied a deep eddying pool. Trout were beginning to rise. Their mouths sipped at bugs floating on the water. In the air, martins continued to swirl. They had forked tail feathers and amber-colored breasts. Watching the sheer improvisation of their flight, the way their bodies banked, dipped, and dove, he was surprised they never collided.

Chuck looked up at the sky again. If he left the river now he still had no idea where he'd go. Instead of leaving, he decided to try his luck and make a few casts. He had come to the water first for peace, then fish, but so far, on this night, had found neither.

From a pocket in his fishing vest he removed a plastic case and selected a fly. He was a surgeon, and with a surgeon's precision he tied a size-18 Blue-Winged Olive onto his leader. In this part of the river the fishing was all catch and release, all barbless, and Chuck put the hook between his teeth and bit down on the sharp spur of metal, smoothing it.

Through deepening water he trudged toward the pool. He leaned into the current, and its heaviness pressed against his waist and thighs. His boot soles were lined with felt, but the rocks still seemed slippery as globes of wet glass. He thought about Anne. What would happen, he wondered, if he just let go? If he lay down and let the river swallow him? The current would be his processional, and the trees his mourners. Everyone has their own path, she had said. And maybe she was right, and maybe Chuck would make this his.

The one thing he knew he wanted most in this life was the one thing no one could ever give him. He could never have her back. She was *gone*. Even the word had a terrible finality about it. Saying it was like giving voice to a black hole. But that didn't stop him from wanting her back. It was a foolish and impossible desire. But what if it wasn't? What if it wasn't foolish? What if it wasn't impossible? What? If? He knew this was a dangerous way to think, a dangerous path to trod, but every day, and more and more often, he found himself going down it, and each time he stepped onto this path he followed it a little deeper.

Standing in the middle of the river, close enough to make the cast, Chuck waved his fly rod back and forth. He sashayed line with economy and it unfurled behind him with calligraphic rhythm. Measuring the distance with his eyes, he made one more false cast, adding length to the line, then snapped his wrist toward the glassy water. He fired a tight-hooked curl, but as soon as he cast the line he knew he'd sent too much, and to keep the line from tangling in the riverbank's bunchgrass he jerked the rod's corked handle. Like a whip, the leader snapped and he felt a tiny snag. There was a small splash in the water, and at first he thought he'd lucked into a rising trout, but then the line came straight back at him. Hoping to avoid it, he ducked, but the line changed direction. In a slow bending arc like an asymptote nearing an axis, the fly line began to rise. It was almost vertical when he saw the wings. Still, it took a moment for him to process it, and even then he couldn't believe it. He'd caught a bird! He'd snared one of the martins. One of the martins was on the end of his hook and its wild flapping wings carried the line higher and higher.

Chuck tried to save the bird. High-stepping through deep water and ripping line from the reel, he followed its path. He was hoping to give the bird enough slack to free itself, but like a kite in the wind it only continued to climb. Soon, though, the weight of the fly line became too great. The bird couldn't carry it any higher and stalled in midair. For an instant it hung in the dazzling blue sky like a dark five-pointed star. It hung, then fell, and as it tumbled Chuck Silversmith made a wish.

The bird landed upstream, and Chuck quickly anchored the rod between his ankles and started pulling in line hand over hand. The bird floated with the current, and when Chuck saw it he dipped both hands into the water and scooped it into his palms.

He couldn't believe how small it was. It looked even smaller now with its wings folded in on its body. Beads of water rolled off its feathers. He hoped the bird was only stunned, only temporarily shocked. Holding it in one hand, he turned it over and found the hook. It had speared the bird square in the breast, and beneath the hook he saw a tiny carmine pinprick. With the light, steady-handed precision that had made him an exceptional surgeon, he unhooked the metal. He let the bird lie in his palm and waited for it to move. When it didn't, he quickly raised his hand, hoping the bird would take flight, but it only landed back in Chuck's opened palm.

The bird had a purple widow's peak and black lines like racing stripes over its eyes. Its beak was a stubby black triangle; with his fingernail Chuck touched the tiny seam of its mouth. He opened the bird's beak, and when he removed his nail it closed as if on a hinge. Then he unfanned a wing and at the base of every feather found a small white dot. The perfection and intricacy were stunning, and his first thought was to give the bird back to the air, to throw it high into the sky, but that seemed both careless and cruel. He knew it would only land back in the water. Then the river's current would carry it and deposit it on the bank for some fire ants to find. Instead, he decided to keep it, as if it were a charm. He reached his hand beneath his fishing vest and tucked the bird into the breast pocket of his shirt.

I'm ready, she had said.

What do you mean, you're ready?

I'm just telling you so you won't be afraid.

Afraid of what? Chuck asked.

Of me.

Why would I be afraid of you?

Of finding me.

But I'll be with you. I'll be right here.

But if you're not.

But I will be.

But if you're not, Anne said. If you're not, don't be afraid. That's all I'm saying.

The air had a disorienting, Martian haze about it. Walking the worn path back through the forest, Chuck felt as if he could reach out and grab some of its gray-blue phosphorescence. The trees, the trail, the sky—everything was bathed in gloaming. Even his car seemed to have an otherworldly glow. When he stepped back onto the road and saw it tucked under the trees on the far shoulder, he thought it resembled a smooth-molded sphere. It was a gunmetal-gray Porsche Carrera with a 3.6-liter twin turbo flat six. It had a four-point safety harness and a speedometer that topped out at 220 miles per hour. He loved driving it, and more than anything he loved driving it fast.

Chuck stood by the side of the Porsche and shed his waders and fishing vest. He opened the hood and set his things in the trunk. The car's interior was hand-stitched black leather, and when he turned the key there were so many glowing circles and dials he felt as if he were in the cockpit of a one-person jet. He revved the engine, checked the rearview, and pulled out onto the road.

As he drove, he thought about his life. It was not loneliness he struggled with. He still enjoyed the company of his friends. He still enjoyed his work. He was not sentimental. He did not sentimentalize. His children lived far away and, while he loved them, they didn't need him anymore. When he went back to the house where, for so many years, they had made a home, he did not go to the bookshelves and hold framed photographs in his hand. He did not cry. He was not nostalgic. He did not shed tears. The one thing he *had* done was keep her bed. It was in the family room near the windows. It wasn't even her bed, though he had come to think of it as hers. It was the hospice agency's bed. They kept calling him. They wanted to know when they could pick it up, but he never called them back. The sheets were crumpled and strewn. He'd never remade it. He had intended to, but sometimes, if he looked long enough, he felt he could still see the outline of her body.

When it happened, when she passed, it was just as she'd predicted; he wasn't there. Anne had asked him to do something for her. She had a taste for something and if it wasn't too much trouble...?

Of course it's not, he said. What do you want?

It's silly, she said.

What is it? he asked. I'll get whatever you need.

I'd like some cider, she said.

Some cider?

I told you it was silly.

He stood beside the twin bed. Now he was having second thoughts.

That means I'll have to leave, he said.

Anne nodded.

If you really want it, he said, I'll go.

I'd appreciate it, she said, and squeezed his hand.

Be back in ten minutes, he said.

When he returned from the store and opened the front door, he knew; he knew she was gone. He knew he should never have left. Her neck was at a weird angle and her mouth was unhinged.

For days he was angry with himself. Friends tried to console him. Don't beat yourself up, they said. Maybe that's the way she wanted it, they told him, maybe she knew. His friends and family were kind, generous, and full of sorrow. They had the best intentions. They sent cards and flowers. They attended the rituals; they grieved, they told stories about her, and with handshakes or hugs they offered him their condolences. And he appreciated their thoughtfulness, their sincerity, and believed in it. But then, for them, it was over. She was gone, forgotten, and they returned to their lives. But not Chuck. Chuck was adrift; he was unmoored. She had been his tether. Day after day, he didn't know what to do. He went to work. He played tennis at the club. He tried to find a routine. It was difficult to explain. He was a doctor, a surgeon. He was supposed to know how to deal with death. And he did. For the most part he did. But not with hers, not with Anne's. He'd never been very good with words, but this was the thing. This was the thing people didn't seem to understand. This was the thing that, on a daily basis, Chuck could not wrap his mind around. He was not lonely; he was alone.

Very quickly the world began to change for him. The world in which Chuck lived was not the world he wanted to occupy anymore. Every morning, without fail, the first thought that entered his mind when he opened his eyes was, *When? When would it happen to him? When could he join her?* There was no way to know. It could be today. It could be tomorrow. It could be twenty years from tomorrow. But he didn't want to wait that long. He couldn't. He didn't think he could. Who said he had to go on, anyway? It was a decision he could make or not make. It was all up to him, wasn't it?

But he had also promised himself that whatever he chose — if he, in fact, ever made a choice about this, about going on or not going on — he would not choose out of fear. No fear, he had said. And hadn't Anne pretty much said the same thing? So little can be done through force, she had told him.

Like an Indy car, the Porsche had paddle shifters beneath the wheel, and Chuck kept the tips of his fingers on the paddles, ready to tap into higher or lower gears. But there was no reason to be aggressive. He had settled into the curving rhythms of the country road and was feeling relaxed in a pensive sort of way. A couple weeks ago he woke up and there was a new question. Instead of asking himself *when* he started asking himself *how*. And he began to investigate things. He pulled knives from kitchen drawers and studied their silver glinting blades. He turned on the gas stove and stared at the blue ring of flame. Objects became implements. Even the leather belt he threaded through his trousers every morning gave him pause.

At first this line of thinking frightened him. It went against everything he'd ever believed in, every oath he'd ever taken. But he found he couldn't stop asking the questions. After *how* it became *where* and he considered the clichés — the bathtub, the bedroom, the garage. And he realized the clichés were the clichés because they were accessible and easy.

It almost seemed like a game to him, asking these questions. It was like a crossword or brainteaser; it was something to kill time, something he could do when he didn't feel like doing anything else. The questions helped him make it through the day and, weirdly, they seemed to give his life purpose again; if not purpose exactly, then at least some semblance of direction. And because one question always seemed to summon another, Chuck had decided they were leading him somewhere like a trail of breadcrumbs, and he had chosen to follow.

He kept a light, comfortable grip on the wheel. He had trained himself to be relaxed. Over a lifetime of surgeries he had trained his hands to be calm, to be as delicate and precise as the blade of his scalpel. And he had trained his eyes, too. He had trained them to look, and not to look. His eyes were not to look at the patient; his eyes were to look at the body. He was not to consider the stakes. He had always attempted to remove all emotion from his eyes. It was a skill that could not be taught. But if possessed, it could be practiced, honed, and, over time, perfected. And he had perfected it. The incision was only an opening, the organs were only circuitry, and his eyes were only instruments of vision. When he stood at the operating table, his eyes were as bright and clinical as the orb of light suspended over his shoulder. The only problem was that now, for Chuck, it seemed that there was no distinction between his work and his life. His eyes felt like that all the time.

Wrapped in its sheer purple cloak, dusk had finally come. The Porsche banked around a long S curve and in the middle of the road, not fifty feet away, was a deer. Chuck saw it in plenty of time. Neither he nor the animal was in any danger. The deer's head swiveled toward the oncoming high beams, its flank tensed, and before it bounded away Chuck saw a paired flash of holographic green. And with his own eyes he began to sense something, too. It was a thought, distant, but quickly coming into focus. It was another question, and before he could say what it was, before he could find the words to say it, he could feel it. He felt it in his hands. They were tingling. *Did he have the guts?* That was the question. It was the only one left, and the only one he didn't know how to answer.

He had been sitting on the edge of her bed, looking at his hands. He paused, then lifted his eyes. She smiled at him. There was a tube of oxygen beneath her nose.

I've been thinking, he said.

Thinking about what?

Lots of things. You, mostly.

Good things, I hope.

Both good things and bad.

Why bad? she asked.

Nothing bad about you. Not that. Just bad thoughts.

Bad how?

Bad because I'm thinking about what I'm going to do.

What you're going to do when?

Afterward. Later. When you're gone, he thought, but didn't say it. He couldn't. He touched his forehead.

I never thought it would happen this way, he said. I never thought I would have to face this.

You'll be fine, she said.

I'm not so sure. You've always been stronger than I am, Anne.

She raised her right arm, a mock flex. It made him laugh.

I'm sorry I brought this up.

No, she said, this is important. We *should* talk about this.

I feel selfish, he said.

Answer the question for me.

What question?

What is it you're going to do?

That's the problem. I don't know.

What else can you do, she said, but go on.

But why? he asked, and shrugged his shoulders. Why should I?

Because, she said.

He felt like a child.

Because why?

Because of the beauty.

What beauty? he asked.

This beauty.

Where?

She lifted her arms and spread out her hands.

Here, she said. Everywhere.

On the side of the road in a small clearing, Chuck saw beneath a streetlamp a table with a white awning over it. He slowed down. A handwritten sign said CHERRIES. It was the season. In fact, the season had almost passed and he hadn't eaten any yet. He pulled over and stepped out of the car.

A man and woman, both Hispanic, were sitting in lawn chairs near an old Chevy truck. The truck was green with a wide white stripe down the center of the body. The tires sagged a little, but there were no rust spots. The truck looked as if it had traveled many miles, and the wide, sturdy chassis seemed to promise the strength and durability for many more. On top of the truck, perched over the truck bed, they had mounted one of those unwieldy-looking sleeper cabs.

As Chuck approached the table, the man rose. The cherries were separated into individual bowls, and each bowl was mounded with fruit. The fruit was a plump, deep burgundy. Nine bowls were scattered around the table, and with his thumb and knuckle the man tucked them together until he'd made three rows of three.

Bing cherries, the man said. Sweet. Very ripe.

Just picked? Chuck asked.

The man nodded.

Chuck raised his fingers.

Two, he said.

You choose, said the man.

Chuck pointed at the bowls he wanted, and as the man dumped the fruit into a plastic bag, Chuck looked at the man's wife. Hands resting in her lap, she met his gaze and nodded.

He paid for the fruit and got back into the car. He tossed a cherry into his mouth and started to drive. Holding the cherry between his teeth, he bit down to the pit, then halved the fruit and tucked both pieces into his cheek. It didn't seem to have any flavor. With the tip of his tongue he removed the seed, then pressed a button and rolled down the window. As he turned to spit he felt something in his chest and it scared him so much he swallowed the pit. He didn't know what it was, and then it happened again — a wild fluttering. He angled the car to the side of the road. Was he having a heart attack? Was he dying? He touched his chest and felt something in his pocket. Then he remembered. It was the bird. Had it come back to life? Had it never been dead? Is that what he'd felt? He removed the martin from his pocket and held it in his hand. He touched it, but nothing happened. Its eyes were still closed, but the mark on its chest, the prick of blood, was gone. Chuck put his hand over his heart. Nothing. He put the bird back into his pocket. He had made a wish upon it, and holding on to the bird was a way of holding on to that wish. Instead of going home, he decided he needed a drink. He drove to a bar he knew in Cle Elum, and as he drove he found himself thinking: *I wish it had been my heart. I wish it had.*

He sat on a stool and rested his elbows on the wooden bar and looked around. Some men were in a booth drinking and playing cards. The bartender was watching the Mariners on a flat screen mounted on the wall. Chuck's face felt hot. He looked in the mirror behind the bar. Bright pink. Sunburned, he thought. He touched his cheekbone, then lifted his finger away. If she had still been here she would have reminded him. Don't forget your sunscreen, she would have said. It was only a small thing, but somehow it seemed bigger now. She'd always tried to protect him in any way she could.

Chuck ordered a double Grouse, neat, and the bartender set a small beveled glass on the counter and poured a caramel-colored stream. Chuck took a sip of the whisky. As he sat on the barstool he thought of the Hispanic couple selling cherries on the side of the road. He thought about them in their truck, inside the sleeper cab. Surely, after a long day, they would be sleeping by now. Surely, by now, they would be asleep. He thought about their bodies in that cramped space. Every night it was getting colder and colder, and he thought about how warm they would be, how cozy they must feel.

What's going to happen? he had asked her.

It was one of their last conversations. She was sleeping a lot. The doctor had given her a handful of days.

I didn't know if we were going to talk like this, she said.

He made himself smile, and with bright eyes she smiled back.

I've enjoyed it, she said.

And we'll keep doing it. We'll keep talking this way.

Of course we will, she said, but he knew she didn't believe that. He knew she'd only said it for his benefit, and that angered him. But he didn't know if he was angry with himself for his denial or with her for her false optimism.

Did you ask me something? she said.

He nodded.

What was it? I've forgotten.

He didn't know if he could say it, and then he did.

Are you afraid? he asked.

She didn't have to think about it.

Yes, she answered, I am.

I thought you said you were ready?

I am. I am ready. But I'm still afraid.

What's going to happen? he asked.

Nothing.

I meant afterward.

I know you did.

And that's your answer?

Yes, she said. Time without consciousness.

That's it?

That's it.

What about the soul? he asked.

I don't believe in the soul.

He looked at her. He was beside himself. How was it he'd never known that?

She was wrong. She had to be wrong. Chuck was on the service road heading toward the expressway, and he would prove it. He would prove how wrong she had been. It had been bothering him this whole time, ever since he'd found her. How could she believe that? That afterward there was only emptiness? He would see her again. He would be with her again. He had to be.

At the last stoplight in Cle Elum, he buckled both shoulder straps and suddenly the seat felt as if it had been built around him, as if it had been built *for* him. He felt clasped to it. The light went green. He stepped on the gas and glanced in the rearview mirror and saw the headlights of cars that had been stopped with him at the light. They were so far back it looked as though they hadn't even moved. He drove five hundred feet, banked right, and when his wheels were back in line he floored it. The on-ramp was a long rising chute and, tapping through the gears, he took it like a straightaway, still accelerating. The Porsche sunk low with speed and for a few seconds, bending across his chest like some kind of invisible body armor, Chuck felt the press of gravity.

He was traveling on I-90 heading west toward the Snoqualmie Pass. It was a six-lane superhighway, and with his hands measured across the wheel, his elbows loose, he saw his speed on the speedometer. He also saw it in the distance between his car and the cars in front of him, and how quickly that distance was eclipsed. He closed hard on their red taillights and, barely turning the wheel, wove past them. Then his eyes were up the road again, looking for other cars to pass.

It would be like this, he thought. It would be exactly like this. Like waking up. Like waking up and never having to go to sleep again. And never wanting to. He would wake up and she would be there. She would be there waiting for him. She was waiting there right now, and soon he would join her. Soon he would open his eyes and she would reach out to him and he would grab hold of her hand and never let go. And looking into her eyes, seeing her again, would be like looking into old photo albums, but instead of looking at old pictures and saying, *We were so young. Look at how young we were,* they would *be* young. Their eyes and their bodies, too.

Chuck hoped there were no cops. Then he hoped no one would call them. The road climbed into the foothills of the Cascades, and the more it climbed the twistier it got. He remembered a driving lesson he'd taken in Arizona at Bondurant's. She'd given him the lesson for a birthday present. Brake in a straight line, they'd taught him. Brake going into turns, but accelerate through the apex. In advance of a tight left turn he scanned his mirrors and, finding no other cars and disregarding all laws and prudence, he steered the Carrera wide, cutting across the two outside lanes. Then he touched the brake once, hard; his head jerked forward, but the slats of the harness kept his shoulders tight to the seat. Applying pressure to the gas pedal, he veered left toward the concrete embankment. But he'd chosen the wrong line, too steep, and coming out of the turn and barreling in on the steel guardrail, he smoked the tires and the back end went sliding away from him. With a tight grip Chuck held the wheel. He prepared for impact, but didn't hit anything. At the last moment the Porsche had found its balance. He was within a few meters of the rail. His headlights were bright against the metal, but instead of breathing a sigh of relief, he simply hit the gas again, drove back onto the road, and looked ahead to the next turn.

Something was happening to him. He didn't know what it was, but he could sense it, he could feel it. Maybe it was the wish he'd made earlier in the day. Maybe it was coming true. He wasn't sure yet. But as he climbed toward the summit, he had a feeling he hadn't had since his youth. As if he were indestructible. As if time didn't matter. It was almost as if he were outside of time, as if he were already dead. The night was pitch-black. There was no moon, no stars. Only his headlights illuminated the darkness, and they cut a swath, a path, a stream of light, but he felt that what he needed to see, what he needed to know, lay just beyond their reach.

At the top of the pass the road leveled, and Chuck removed his foot from the pedal and let the car coast. There was no engine and no sound. For thirty seconds there was perfect stillness, and he felt as if he were floating, as if he were flying through space. Then the road began to slant again, to tilt downward, and he began his descent.

There were no other cars around. None. It was as if he were in a race and he'd left everyone else behind. He felt comfortable at the wheel and with driving so fast, and he didn't make any more mistakes. He cut high into every turn, then dove in toward the embankments, shaving away angles and maintaining as much speed as possible while keeping his line as straight as possible. He knew these roads like he knew the touch of her skin. He knew them like he knew the story of their lives, and the faster he drove the more relaxed he became. In two miles, near the base of the mountain, the eastbound and westbound lanes would split and divide. He knew there was a long straightaway followed by a slow-bending right curve. The long right curve would take him into Issaquah, and beyond that was Bellevue, and in Bellevue was the home he was not returning to. He repeated her words aloud. Everyone has their own path, he said, and as in so many other things, she was right, and he was thankful because he'd finally found his.

As he approached the straightaway, he felt as if a question was being asked of him, and then he knew it was being asked. The question was, *Did he have the guts?* And as he entered the straightaway, Chuck Silversmith — doctor, surgeon, husband, father, and widower now for exactly sixty-six days — knew the answer.

He pressed the gas pedal to the floorboard and didn't lift his foot. The car was a bead of mercury, a speeding blur of light, and as the needle leaned into the far side of the dash he began to unbuckle his seat belt. He removed the straps from his shoulders, then reached toward the panel and turned off the headlights. He was not frightened by darkness, nor was he frightened by the speed at which he was moving through it. He was not frightened at all, and to prove to himself that he was not frightened he lifted his hands from the wheel and crossed them over his chest. But when he touched his chest with his right hand there was a fluttering again, stronger and even wilder than before, and this time he was sure he was having a heart attack. But then the bird flushed from his pocket and its beating wings and feathers were flapping in his face and Chuck was scared. He was scared because he didn't know what was happening. He didn't know what had happened. By instinct he grabbed the wheel and stepped on the brake. But when he stepped on the brake the wheels went cockeyed and the Porsche spun. It spun three times counterclockwise and, still carrying speed, the left front tire found a seam in the road. The far wheels rose up off the ground, and the entire car began to turn in midair. It rose and turned with a stunning grace, and as it turned, as it floated through the air, the contours of the car resembled bodies entwined in silver sheets. Then the car struck the asphalt and everything went fast again. The gunmetal-gray Porsche landed hood down, and that's when it began to roll.

In a glaring haze of white fluorescence, Chuck Silversmith woke. He felt groggy. His head hurt. He felt as if he were living inside a light-bulb. That's how bright it was. It blinded him. In fact, he didn't even know if he could see. He couldn't see what he was looking at. What he was looking *for* was her, was Anne.

I'm here, he thought. I've finally arrived.

There were voices, but he couldn't hear them. They seemed a great distance away. He didn't know what they were saying. He wondered if they were angels.

I'm here, he said.

He didn't know if he was actually saying it. He didn't think he could move his mouth. He didn't think he could move anything. He tried. He wiggled his toes. He felt them moving. He wiggled them some more.

I'm here, he thought. I'm here, but where are you?

A man was there, hovering over him. It looked like a man. He had a mask over his mouth. He was wearing glasses. The man was look-ing down at Chuck. He was looking down at Chuck's body. His body was lying on something. There were other people looking down at him, too. He could see them now. He could see the light. He had been right about the light. It was as bright as the sun.

He heard someone say something, and the man with the glasses who was wearing a mask and looking down at Chuck's body lifted his eyes from what he was doing and looked at Chuck's face. He looked into Chuck's eyes, and Chuck looked into his. Then the man looked away again. But Chuck saw something there, in the man's eyes. He saw he was young. He could tell that from the quickest glance. And he could tell he was young because he could tell he hadn't been practicing that long. And he could tell he hadn't been practicing that long because he hadn't learned to hide his emotions. Chuck saw he was nervous. He was probably the only one at the table who could tell the man was nervous. But beneath his nervousness, Chuck sensed a confidence, too. He had not been startled by Chuck's eyes. The surgeon had looked, nodded, then gone back to work.

Chuck was starting to feel drowsy again. He wanted to sleep. He needed to sleep, and he knew his body needed it, too. He looked at the people working on his body and felt himself falling away from them. He felt as if he were floating. Had they given him more drugs? Was he dying? He didn't know. He felt himself slowly sinking, as if hands were lowering him onto a soft, comfortable mattress. And as he fell back into its warmth and comfort and safety, he told himself he had to remember something. Before he left this light there was something he needed to do, there was something he needed to say. The light was evaporating, the light was getting farther and farther away, and as he fell back into the darkness his voice reached out toward it. Good-bye, he said. Good-bye, good-bye, good-bye.

LESLIE BARNARD

University of Oregon

HERO

Dan woke to light cutting his eyes, his father standing in the doorway, expectant, smiling.

"You ready?" his father asked.

Dan knew his dad had been awake since before dawn. By now
he'd made two ham sandwiches, one with mayonnaise, one without.
He'd sharpened the auger blades and packed the gear in the truck. He'd
filled a thermos with black coffee and probably rigged Dan's line so he
could be the first one in.

Dan also knew his father wouldn't let him drive to Hill City,
though he was old enough and always begging for the chance. His
dad would make up some excuse. "Better to learn when it's nice out,"
he'd say. But this was winter. It hadn't been nice out for three months
now, since mid-October, when Dan's mother left.

"I ain't going," Dan said, rolling onto his stomach.

Dan's dad pulled his covers off. Chilled, the skin on the back of

Dan's legs tightened. "Come on, now," his dad said. "Rise and shine."

Dan glared through puffy lids. "Don't you get it?" he snapped. "I ain't interested." As he turned to yank the covers back over his body, he caught a glimpse of his father's chubby face, slack as a dog's. Facing the wall again, he could feel his dad standing there a long moment before turning the lights off and shutting the door.

Dan caught a ride to Parmelee with Liz Waldner's cousin, Ira. Ira was a big man, and the steering wheel smushed against his stomach, kneading it, every time he made a turn. Most of the time, Dan couldn't tell what Ira was saying, but he'd smile and nod and Ira'd keep going, mumbling through his wide-spaced yellow teeth.

With a little salute, Ira dropped Dan at the first entry, where the Thunder Shields' white pony stood tied to their trailer, a rope looped once around its speckled muzzle and another time around its neck. Dan noticed the pony's gray eyes, leaking like overripe fruit, and wondered if it was too much for it, this cold. There was a deeply grooved crater of muddy sludge under the pony's feet, but beyond that spot, the ground was blanketed in day-old yellow-white snow. Churned to slush the day before, the snow on the roads had refrozen overnight into solid ice.

Dan walked to the corner where some boys from school were standing, hands stuffed in their pockets. Rodney Black Bull noticed Dan first and raised his chin slightly, not smiling. Rodney wore a navy do-rag knotted around his head, and his two older brothers stood on either side of him, both smoking, eyelids heavy, heads shorn to the scalp. The Wounded Face twins were there, too, and a kid Dan didn't know, wearing a black sweatshirt with the hood cinched tight around his hard, angular face.

Rodney told Dan he had to go first because he was white. Dan's stomach turned. A warm, salty taste rose into his mouth. He knew it had nothing to do with his mother leaving. On another day, he wouldn't have been white enough. But he thought of her anyway. He thought of her long hairless brown arms, her nose like his nose. He thought of her green winter coat, hanging on the rack by the door. Dan had pulled it down once, in front of his father, just to see if he could stand it. Dan's father had said nothing. He had picked up the newspaper, hid his face in its seam.

There was no use making something of it, so Dan stood, waiting, thinking of his dad bundled up so only his nose and eyes showed, hunched in his lawn chair out on the ice. Deerfield Lake, Dan's dad insisted, was a place where records had been broken, a place where success was practically guaranteed. Alone, his dad would need to pull the corn from the bag himself. He'd toss a handful down the hole and lean forward to watch the little golden kernels shrink to specks and disappear. Then he'd put his gloves on again and imagine that beneath him, something was happening — packets of complex sugars exploding, silver tails flashing in the dark. Dan could already predict what his father would say at supper. "An off day, sky clear as a mirror," or "You know how it is when the water's too cold. Fish too tired, too numb to feed." Dan would make a point of not answering, not looking up.

Devorah Cutt's old minivan, with wood paneling on only one side, clunked up to the intersection and paused to let a car pass. Dan couldn't see if it was Devo driving or her ugly younger sister — the one with big, low-slung breasts and pockmarked cheeks — but he moved quickly, heart pounding. He lay down on his back and hooked his hands under the rear bumper. He recalled a story his dad had told, about a pair of kids whose hands had frozen to somebody's bumper. They died like that, according to Dan's father, dragged to death on the highway. Just then, something that felt like a sack of

rocks pounded into Dan's side, knocking him loose. He heard the
van accelerate, and when he looked up he saw the kid in the black
sweatshirt flying along behind it, faceup, eyes wide. His skinny body
zigzagged over the ice, ass and shoulder blades bouncing hard, heels
cutting lines in the snow. As the minivan sped around the corner, the
kid held tight, screaming and laughing and cussing in a voice that
was low — deep, even — but, Dan realized, distinctly female.

Justice Clairmont had told Dan never to meet her at her place. Her
grandma got pissed, she said. Justice lived out past Mission, anyway.
So she'd come holler at Dan's window or throw things — "Too hard,"
his dad said. "Why can't she just knock?" — and Dan would try not
to sprint down the stairs. If he forgot and raced out to meet her, she'd
say something like "You really ain't got much going on, do you, white
boy?" Or she'd stare while he caught his breath and ask if he had
asthma, too, like his dad. Dan told her he didn't. Only his dad was
sick, he said.

Sometimes Justice and Dan would walk across He Dog Lake, then
follow the creek back through the valley. Dan's dad never fished the
lake anymore because it was full of fertilizer, maybe, or manure.
Whatever it was, the fish had gotten smaller and didn't fight the way
they used to. The last time they went, two summers ago, Dan's dad
didn't even realize he had one until he reeled in to change his bait and
found a little smallmouth bass dangling off his hook, listless as a
hunk of weeds.

One day in January, Dan and Justice went out after a storm. There
was snow on the lake, drifts thick in places. Justice pushed Dan into
one and he called her a cow and threw snow in her face.

Justice was wearing the same black sweatshirt she'd had on when
they met and a pair of boy's jeans so baggy the crotch hung near her
knees. Her cuffs and canvas tennis shoes were soaked through, but

they always were and she never mentioned it. Dan wore snow boots and a wool cap, but his father had suggested he bring gloves so he hadn't, and his hands burned in the cold.

Justice bolted ahead, the ice crackling and groaning under her like something dead, waking. Dan followed, stepping into her footprints. Near the opposite shore she stopped, waving him over.

When Dan caught up, he saw that beyond the ledge where Justice stood, only a skin of transparent ice covered the gray water. A few small bubbles pressed against the surface.

"Think I can make it?" she asked.

"Make what?"

"Make it across, you dumbass." She backed up and pulled her sleeves over her hands, wadding the ends in her fists.

"You kidding me?" Dan said. "Let's just cross somewhere else, farther down." It was at least eight feet to the shore. When Dan was a kid, he and his dad would come to this spot in the summer. The bottom dropped off almost immediately at the shoreline, so Dan and his father would count to three, then dive in, reaching for the shifting muddy bottom with their fingertips. Dan rarely touched it, but his dad would come to the surface with his hands full of earth, brown streams running down his arms. Back then, Dan's dad's arms were taut and muscular. They looked like the glistening, bulging bodies of snakes that have swallowed too much. Now his body was padded with fat, and his arms' pale, fleshy undersides sagged.

Dan's mother never swam with them, but sometimes she'd sit in a lawn chair on the shore, watching through dark sunglasses, her face tightening whenever water sprayed her knees. She'd cheer them on and tell Dan how brave he was to dive so deep. When she was there, Dan would go deeper. He'd do somersaults and show her how long he could hold his breath underwater. So they wouldn't be chilly on the drive home, she always brought Dan and his dad a change of clothes. She brought sandwiches for them, too, but once, when Dan complained that his had mayonnaise, she tore the sandwich from his hands and threw it in the dirt. Afterward, on the drive home, she breathed in choked bursts like she might be crying, but Dan couldn't be sure because she still had her sunglasses on. "Your mother's just tired," Dan's dad had said, patting Dan's knee. Dan could still remember the relief he'd felt, how he'd leaned back in his seat, let his eyes fall shut.

"You can cross wherever you want," Justice said, white breath puffing from her mouth. "I'll see you around." Then she backed up a little farther and started sprinting toward the dark gap.

Without thinking, Dan threw his arms around her waist, pulling her down hard. They both tumbled backward, slamming their asses on the ice. Their legs overlapping and their faces close, Dan felt her warm breath wetting his mouth. She was smiling, lightly flushed. Dan realized there were things he hadn't noticed. Her high cheekbones; her dark, deep-set eyes. Then her face changed suddenly. Her lips peeled back, showing bright teeth. She burst out laughing. "You think you saved me!" she screeched. "You think you're a fucking hero!" She jumped up and ran ahead, down the shoreline. Dan followed, breathing hard.

Justice had recently transferred to He Dog from Crazy Horse School in Wanblee. But she rarely showed, and when she did, she usually convinced Dan to leave early and walk to the Red Owls' barn to smoke. She taught Dan how to smoke without looking like a fool. She told him it didn't count if it didn't hurt a little, if it didn't grab hold of his lungs and squeeze. She taught him to bring an extra shirt and chew mint gum and peel an orange before he went home, so his dad wouldn't know.

In the beginning, Dan followed every procedure meticulously —

the shirt, the gum, the orange — as if he were casting a spell. Then he'd creak the door open and walk in, half expecting to see his mother sitting at the table, letting the steam from her tea rise into her face. Instead, Dan would find his father asleep in his chair, still wearing his dirty work clothes, hands black with grease. Even the insides of his ears wound with black spirals of oil. He'd sleep all night like that, the phone in his lap. Some nights Liz Waldner would be there, too, cleaning the kitchen or patching the knees or the crotch of Dan's father's pants. She'd usually offer Dan a snack, but as she handed him a plate or a napkin she'd gesture toward his dad and say, "He was waiting for you," as if waiting could have killed him. Sometimes, while Dan filled a glass with water, Liz would walk over to Dan's dad and pull a blanket to his chin, or remove his shoes, and every time, Dan would notice how chubby she was, how flat and sloppy her ass looked, like a sheet of the green Jell-O they always served at wakes. Eventually, Dan stopped chewing mint gum just so he could breathe his smoker's breath into Liz's face on his way upstairs.

Justice always brought plenty for both of them and never asked Dan for money or anything in return. He didn't offer, either. They'd sit on the rotting front steps of the old barn and stare down at the blank white valley. The few trees along the creek were skinny and bare, scarred black to the knees by a brush fire that had come through years ago. Dan could remember watching the sky darken in the distance during dinner, his mother serving lasagna a church lady had brought by with a note that read *Get Well!*, and his father, sounding proud and encyclopedic, saying fires actually help maintain the health of certain ecosystems. She'd nodded, staring past him at the rising plumes of smoke.

Once, Justice showed Dan how she could hold her lips in an O, then push her jaw forward and puff out a perfect white ring.

"Cool," Dan said.

"Try it."

"I ain't trying it."

"Pussy."

Dan aimed as if he was going to put his cigarette out on her arm and she laughed.

She puffed out again and they watched the white halos dilate and disappear. "My brother taught me."

"Never met him."

"You couldn't have," she snapped, glaring. "He's in the Gulf. Been there and back twice already."

"Damn. Sorry," Dan said. "I mean, sorry, I didn't know."

"He's a fucking wild man," she said. She had forgotten the cigarette she was holding, and as she spoke, its ashen tip grew heavy and fell. "I mean, can you imagine it? Thinking *This is it, I'm dead, I'm dead,* every fucking day?"

"Man, that'd be something, all right." Dan's father's asthma had kept him off the ground in Vietnam. He had been a nurse instead, but he'd never told Dan about it, except to say that afterward he quit medicine and started taking cars apart.

"Yeah." She paused to suck on her cigarette. "You know, he's been injured a lot, my brother. But he always comes back, like that," she said, snapping her fingers so close to Dan's face his eyelids fluttered.

Dan thought of his father. It was pathetic, the way he slept now, slimy with sweat, dirty, the phone curled in his hand. She hadn't called once. And if she ever did, what would his father do? Hand the phone to Dan? Or have Liz speak for him, let *her* beg Dan's mother to come back?

Dan noticed Justice looking at him, her head slightly tilted, and it occurred to him how he must appear — pale, bony, a child. "Has he killed people?" Dan asked. "Your brother, I mean."

"Oh, yeah. But he's usually far off, so it's easy." She pointed an imaginary rifle at the valley and cocked it. "He never sees their faces."

"Oh."

"One time, though . . ." She paused, turning the imaginary gun to Dan's chest.

"Yeah? Come on."

"One time there was a foreign guy," she began, leaning back, "some traitor who was supposed to be on our side but had turned around and killed a bunch of our guys. He was a faggot, too, always looking at my brother and everybody else. And my brother was assigned to execute him, you know, just bring him out, stand him against a wall, and shoot him in the back of the head. One bullet." She laughed through her nose.

"Shit. What'd he do?"

"I can't tell you," she said languidly, drawing attention to the movement of her lips.

"Come on." Dan had a sudden urge to touch her, put his hand down the front of her pants.

"Only if you promise me something." She was looking straight at him now. "Only if you promise never to tell anybody about my brother. The stuff he does over there is secret, you know? People shouldn't even know he exists."

"Okay, okay. I won't tell."

"You swear?" She spit on her palm and reached for his hand.

"I do," he said. She raised her eyebrows.

He said, "I swear," and shook her hand.

"So my brother puts this motherfucker up against the wall and he's about to shoot when this fucking idiot, this fucking ass-fucker turns around, faces my brother, his whole body shaking, you know, his hands, his lips — shaking. And there's this moment — not even a

second — where they look in each other's eyes. They see each other."
She leaned back, smiled, indulged in a long pause.

"Yeah? Then what?"

"So then my brother shoots this guy, this faggot, but not once like
he's supposed to. He shoots him twenty-six times. Starting with his
dick, then his hands, his ankles, and here —" She slapped her palms
against her thighs. "So he'd die slowly, you know? So he'd have time
to realize what a disgusting piece of shit he was."

"Damn," Dan said. "Shit." He imagined Justice's brother, big
shouldered and dark skinned, with a mouth steady as hers, never
flinching, walking away from the splattered mess in crisp, clean
fatigues.

"So, do I have a brother?" Justice asked.

"What?" Dan said. She frowned and he understood. "Not that I
ever heard of," he said.

"Good man," she said, and Dan smiled without meaning to.

"You know, I'm going, too, someday." She finished her cigarette
and crushed the butt under her shoe. "Soon as I'm old enough."

"If there's still a war, you mean?"

"Shit," she said, barely looking at him. "You really are a dumbass."
Then she pulled the cigarette he was smoking out of his mouth and
put it to her lips. She breathed in deeply, and Dan could almost see
the smoke grabbing hold.

Dan was walking to school when Justice came up behind him, out of
nowhere, and shoved a folder full of papers into his hands. "Turn this
in for me, will you?" she said quietly. She was looking around, not at
Dan.

"Why?" Dan asked, staring at her bare neck, noticing the way her
thin T-shirt clung to her flat chest, the fabric so worn the fibers were

splitting apart, becoming see-through. He realized he'd never seen her without her sweatshirt on before.

"What do you mean, why? Just do it. It's everything, you know, for the term." She turned to go.

"Ain't it too late, anyway?" Dan called out. "Ain't it past due?"

She looked back at him. "Don't worry about it, man. I got it all worked out with Mizz J."

"Where you going?" Dan called.

"Nowhere, just — you know — out with some people. Don't read it, all right? Just turn it in. Okay?" Her eyes looked tired. "You know I'd do it for you, bro," she said. Then she ran off, her long black hair twisting in the wind.

Ms. Jenny, as she told them to call her, waited longer than usual — a full ten minutes — then scanned the room, squinting, marking the attendance sheet. Dan noticed several kids were absent, including Rodney. Dan pulled Justice's folder from his backpack and put it inside his desk. He propped a book in front of his face but was too distracted to pay attention to the story.

Ms. Jenny came by once to ask if he needed help. She got low and looked into his face like there was something wrong with him. She was new this year, fresh out of school, and you could see it in everything she did, even in the clothes she wore — little fuzzy sweaters that shed when she crossed her arms, and pointy cream-colored heels she'd change into after hiking over in boots lined with rabbit fur. Dan told her he didn't need help, he was fine. He knew she'd probably heard what a good student he used to be — hardworking, dependable, kind. She probably wondered what she'd done wrong. Dan got up to deposit Justice's work in the turn-in tray, but instead swiped the crumpled bathroom pass off the door and walked down the hallway with her folder spread open in his arms.

He picked out an essay. It was a full seven pages, written in blocky, childlike script. As Dan flipped through it, he noticed the paper was rough and ground thin in spots, like Justice had erased and rewritten some parts more than once. Dan recalled the assignment. They were supposed to write about *A Tale of Two Cities,* which Justice had told Dan she hadn't read, because why would she? Who fucking cared? They'd both agreed it was shit. It was all shit. Dan hadn't read it either because of her, because of what they'd decided, together. As Dan skimmed the essay, he felt his palms and armpits growing damp, his breath becoming short like his father's.

Justice started out talking about the book, blabbing about how Dickens creates two worlds, two men that are really one man, whatever that meant. By the end, though, she was going on about how humans are evil by nature, how we are drawn to violence — destined, she said, to seek it out. Dan couldn't stand it, the words she used. *Destined.* Who was she trying to kid?

And where was she, anyway? What was so important that she had to run off and put this on him — and dressed like that, without a coat? Dan could feel his cheeks redden as he imagined it: Justice meeting the Black Bulls over at her place, then sneaking out with them to huff off somebody's propane tank, getting so high she couldn't walk straight and leaning on the two oldest brothers' broad shoulders, laughing about how once, at the lake, Dan Wilcox thought he'd saved her life.

Dan crumpled the essay, shoved it in his pocket. Then he stood over the garbage can and let the rest of Justice's folder fall from his hands. He figured most of the work couldn't be hers, anyway. It was probably stolen or copied off somebody, some rancher's kid from one of the country schools, maybe someone she'd cornered after a ball game and threatened with the old bicycle chain she kept coiled in her back pocket, just in case.

———

Justice didn't come to school for a week. Dan kept expecting the at-
tendance-enforcement officer to walk in with his hairy hand locked
on her shoulder, but he never showed and neither did she. Dan
started sitting at Rodney's table during lunch, not in the middle —
where Rodney sat, surrounded on all sides — but on the end, connected to the inner circle only by the ketchup bottle that was passed
up and down the table. Justice finally reappeared Wednesday, in the
middle of Ms. Jenny's English class. Dan didn't look at her, and at
lunch he didn't join her at their usual spot. Instead, he sat at the far
end of Rodney's table, where the guys had started to leave him a
place.

Justice caught up to Dan on his way home. He saw her, but kept
walking.

"You pissed or something?" she said. She was wearing the same
sweatshirt, looking the way she always had. Dan didn't answer. He
walked faster. He could feel the rims under his eyes getting hot and
couldn't explain it. "You know," she said, blocking him, "I meant to
thank you for getting my stuff in." She grabbed his arm, hard. He
stopped trying to dodge her. "I mean," she said, "I been meaning to
thank you."

They went to the Red Owls' like usual, but this time she drove
them in her grandma's old pickup, its floor so rusted out Dan could
see dirty slush and grass racing by under his feet. He thought of asking Justice to let him try driving, but didn't. He'd tried only once before, with his mother. A few days after Dan's dad took him to get his
permit, his mother drove him to the Rosebud clinic in a station
wagon she'd borrowed from a church friend of hers. She dropped
Dan off on time, but an hour after they pulled his dead tooth, leaving a tender socket in the back of his mouth, she still hadn't returned.
Dan thought about asking the lady at the front desk if he could use
the clinic's phone, but couldn't think what he'd say if she asked why,

so he walked all the way out to the highway, then hitched a ride home with Devo's younger sister, whose beat-up lowrider smelled like beer and piss and had a plastic Indian doll with bright red skin swinging from the rearview mirror.

When Dan came through the door and his mother realized her mistake, she started pacing and pushing her hair off her face and asked him what she could do to make it right. Dan told her he wanted to practice driving, and she handed him the keys to the station wagon. When she didn't make a move to put her shoes on, Dan said, "With you."

At first things went well. She showed him how to step on the clutch, shift into neutral, then turn the key and give it gas. But when they got out on the road, she stopped paying attention. She rolled down the window and stuck her hand outside. "You feel that?" she kept saying. And Dan said, "Yeah," even though he had no idea what she meant. Then she stood and leaned her whole body out, so Dan could see only her shoes on the seat and her long legs disappearing out the window. He could imagine how beautiful she looked, though, her sunglasses reflecting the landscape, her hair rushing back from her face, and her silky pink blouse thrashing, writhing, struggling to pull loose and fly. Dan's dad had passed them then, on his way home from work.

Justice drove leaning back, one hand draped slack on the wheel, like she'd been doing it forever and wasn't excited about it anymore. When they got to the barn, she pulled out some smokes and they sat together on the steps. The valley below was a patchwork of snow and yellow half-dead grass. Spade-shaped He Dog Lake had grown increasingly dark around the edges, but its center was still solid white. That, Dan thought, would be the last thing to thaw.

As they sat in silence, the sky dimmed and Dan could feel the temperature dropping, the breeze cutting through his clothes. Justice scooted closer, leaning a skinny shoulder into him. "Want to do something with me?" she said.

"Like what?" Dan asked, putting his half-smoked cigarette out in the dirt.

"Why're you doing that?" she snapped, slapping his hand.

"Don't want no more."

She pulled the cigarette from his hand, but it was bent like an elbow and she threw it back in the dirt. "It's a waste," she said, standing and unbuttoning her jeans. Dan stood and started walking toward the woods.

"What the hell?" she said, making a face at him. "You don't want to?"

"I thought you was taking a piss."

She scooted her pants down over her hips, then knelt to untie her shoes. Her thighs were skinny but soft looking, with dimples in the sides like someone's fingers had pressed there. She stepped from her pants and gestured with her chin for Dan to come over. He did, and she told him to take her underwear off. Dan felt cold looking at her and asked if they should go inside. She said it didn't matter either way to her.

They went inside the barn and Dan swung the door closed. The only light was a thin blue band glowing under the door where the wood had rotted away.

She took off her sweatshirt and Dan put his hands on her chest. She had no real breasts, but through her shirt he could feel the outline of her nipples, puffy and swollen, like two lovely wounds. He had dreamed their color, dark pink, almost purple. He was aroused now, remembering that first time on the lake when he'd felt her breath on his face. Remembering, too, how she'd taunted him, how she'd made him a fool.

"You do it," she said, so he started to pull her underwear down.

He could smell her then, and even in the darkness he could see her hair down there — a thin, fuzzy layer, like lines sketched in pencil. It was nothing like you see in movies, nothing like the full brown mound of curls he remembered his mother having, the one time he'd caught her coming out of the shower. He felt the wispy hairs under his hand and almost pulled away.

Then Justice lay down and motioned for him to get on top. He slipped off his pants and laid on her. As he did she gasped, like the weight of him was making it hard for her to breathe. Not meaning to, he kissed her cheek, the side of her mouth.

She mumbled.

"What?" he asked.

"You're something," she said, and Dan was glad he couldn't see her face, because her voice was high and quivering.

That was when Dan started to lose it. Justice tried to get him hard again, but it made things worse — feeling her hand there, feeling her trying to fix him.

"Sorry," Dan said, standing up and shifting his boxers into place. "I — I got to go."

Inside the dark barn, Justice's face was a featureless outline. For a long time she didn't move or say anything. Then, finally, she stood and turned from him, zipping her jeans. She shoved her underwear in her pocket. "Better catch your own ride then," she said, her voice flat, familiar.

Dan pulled his clothes on and pushed open the barn door. The sun had set and there was no moon, just a black sky pricked with stars. Dan looked for the road but couldn't make it out. Even the lake was swallowed in shadow.

The night before his mother left, Dan had come home and found her at the kitchen table, sipping tea. She'd smiled, skin glowing, and asked him to sit with her. He sat, and she put her hand on his shoulder. Told him he was a good boy. Dan noticed then, at that moment, how clean the house was. The tabletop smelled of lemons. The floor sparkled. When he went up to his bedroom, he found his bed made, all the clothes that had been on his floor washed and put away. Later they would find the food she'd made, the cartons of frozen soup in the freezer, the chicken potpies, the stacked trays of tuna casserole.

The next morning, from his window, Dan had watched his father follow his mother out the door. He'd watched as halfway down their long dirt drive and only a few paces behind her, his father had stopped, folded in half, hands on his knees. The stranger parked at the end of the drive wore a white cowboy hat cocked too far back, so his whole long greasy forehead showed. He smiled and gave Dan a little wave, like it was all a private joke between them. Dan didn't wave back. He ran downstairs in his underwear and stood in the doorway watching, waiting for his father to get in his pickup and chase after them, kill the man if he had to, maybe shake Dan's mother, throw her down, even hit her in the mouth; something, anything, to make it stop. But Dan's dad only called to him to get his inhaler. Then he stood sucking on it while the truck sped toward the highway, dipped downhill, and disappeared. Afterward, Dan's father had held him and apologized, his voice breaking, thinning to a whisper. Dan had ducked out of his arms, disgusted.

"Sorry," Dan said again, still turned, not looking at Justice.

"Your loss," she said, and he heard her lighter click twice, then spark.

Dan slipped and fell crossing the lake. Cussing, he stood and kept going. When he got home, he didn't go in the front door. He went through the garage and into the kitchen, where he knew his dad's coat would be hanging. He wrapped his hand around the keys in his dad's coat pocket so they wouldn't jingle as he pulled them out.

Dan started the engine, shifted into drive, and hit the gas. There was a chance his dad wouldn't even notice he was gone. His dad might be gone, too, might be out somewhere with Liz.

Dan had a little trouble at first. He kept braking late, and once he accidentally ran a stop sign on his way through Parmelee. When his wheels hit the smooth black pavement of the 18, though, he relaxed a little, let his shoulders drop. On the unlit highway, all he could see was the fringe of quivering grasses that flashed white as he passed and the painted yellow line that dropped off completely just beyond the scope of his lights.

He wondered if his mother had felt this way as she'd sped off, leaving everything behind; if she'd felt this relief, this beautiful black lonely peace. He imagined her and the cowboy laughing, maybe passing a beer between them, while Dan's father sat at home, eating nothing, jumping every time the phone rang. Dan tried to guess where they might have gone, imagined finding them, seeing his mother's body bent over the cigarette counter in a small-town grocery store in Nebraska. Dan would walk up behind her and say only, "Hello." She would turn around and tip her sunglasses below her eyes and see him, really see him, for the first time. But in Dan's mind, when his mother turned, it was Justice's face he saw, Justice's dark eyes staring, waiting for an answer.

The way it unfolded in slow motion, Dan had time to consider the fact that he might die. His tires slid on a patch of ice, and when he braked, the truck spun. It kept skidding backward, swinging from side to side, the headlights swinging, too, drawing dizzy yellow streaks across the black road and sky.

First the noise of the tires screeching. Then a quiet, lifting feeling, followed by a jolt, an explosion of sound — groaning metal, splattering glass. Darkness. Shards of something biting his cheeks. The incredible thinness of the air. Wanting a taste. Then nothing.

Dan hadn't seen Justice since the afternoon at the Red Owls'. At school, a new kid — a white kid with an earring — took a center spot at the lunch table, so Dan had to sit farther down, near the edge. Dan heard someone toward the middle say Justice's name. Willie Bordeaux was telling people she hadn't passed, so she'd have to repeat. Tyler Wounded Face asked where she'd been so long and Rodney said she was at home wiping her retarded brother's ass because her grandma was too drunk to get off the couch.

"He's older, you know, twenty or something, but he's got Down's," Montana Kilgore said, crossing his eyes. "Poor retarded fuck." He slapped a curled hand against his chest and moaned.

A couple guys laughed. "Damn," said Tyler, raising an eyebrow. "I wonder if she ... you know. I mean — a man's got needs." They laughed, punched Tyler's shoulder, called him a perv.

Dan said, "You don't know shit about her brother, Kilgore."

"What?" said Rodney, leaning in to look down the line of faces.

"I've been over there," Dan said. "I met her brother."

"No way, man," said Rodney, grinning, glancing at his buddies. "Nobody's been, but everybody knows he's a —"

"I wouldn't talk about him," Dan said, and it was easier to say with stitches curving from his ear to his lip and a cheek still stained yellow-blue. "He's the type of guy who wouldn't stand for that kinda shit."

Dan hadn't been, but he would go. His dad would let him drive. Dan's dad and Liz had found Dan the night of the accident. Dan's dad had laid him across the backseat of Liz's van, elevated his legs, splinted his left arm with a rolled-up magazine, and stopped his split-open shin from bleeding by pressing two fingers against the back of his knee while they drove an hour to the nearest hospital. Weeks later, when Dan was feeling better, his dad had come into his room holding the keys to Liz's van. He'd said, "Ready to give it another try?"

"Is it nice out?" Dan had asked, pulling the blinds open. It wasn't. There was still snow on the ground and the winds were high, making the trees bow and the grass lie flat. But they went anyway. They practiced on the country roads a long time before going out on the highway. Dan could see the beads of sweat gathering above his father's lip, so he drove slowly and asked lots of questions about where people had been catching trout lately and with what.

Dan and his father would go together soon. On the way they'd pass He Dog Lake, glistening now, its surface a dark blue mirror. They'd drive down a long rutted road, turned to mud by the melted snow. The tires would spin and Dan's dad would coach him out of it, tell him to reverse and then power straight through without stopping. It would be as Dan had imagined it, way out in the country, a gray double-wide caving in on itself, one window patched with plastic garbage bags, a three-legged dog asleep on a pile of trash under the porch. Inside, Justice would be reading a book to her brother, a children's book she'd stolen from school or been given by Ms. Jenny, and her brother would be laughing, clapping his hands. Dan would walk up the porch steps, Justice's essay folded in his pocket, and even if she didn't answer, even if she locked him out, maybe for a second — or not even a second — they'd glimpse each other through the glass.

ANDREW BRININSTOOL

University of Houston

PORTRAIT OF A BACKUP

Mornings

His wife moves toward the honeysuckle vine with a pair of enormous shears. She has been in the garden since daybreak, left him oatmeal on the stove. He watches her from the bay windows; in the six weeks since they left Miami, she has spent every morning planting tropical shrubs: brunfelsia and tree ferns and lancepods and orange blossoms. Last week the man at the nursery told her: *Those plants won't grow here in Dallas.* She drove home and dug deep holes for sabal palms.

At Training Camp

He walks with the Kid to practice, cleats clacking on pavement, sun centered in a sky so blue it's violet. Fans press against the chain-link fence, screaming for autographs. They hold limited-edition playing cards above their heads. Ball caps and miniature footballs.

The Kid — only twenty-four, only a handful of months out of USC — acts as if this is routine. He smiles. He signs. He kisses a leukemia survivor.

The Backup tries to remember his first training camp, whether he had that swagger. But five concussions have left only a faded snapshot, a partial memory imprinted with the bad hair and music of 1989.

He signs a Shoney's napkin for a two-year-old: *Best wishes in your future endeavors — The Backup.*

At Bob's Steakhouse

His daughter slouches in boredom, mouth hanging open. The table closest to them is shared by a group of Perot execs who've emptied eight bottles of Cain Five, and the girl half listens to a story one of them tells about a hooker he knows in Little Rock named the Cave.

His wife orders a martini. She looks tired and speaks slowly of the repairs needed for the house, complains of the homeowners' association, the erratic weather, how the women in Dallas put on mascara just to run errands.

She says, I ran into Rebecca Wells at the gas station. She had her hair done and was wearing a tennis bracelet and Bob Mackie perfume. I could smell it over the gasoline. So naturally, I asked her where she was going. And do you know what she told me? Nowhere. *Nowhere.* She was just out, filling the Volvo. Can you believe it?

The Backup grunts, eyes his daughter. She is seventeen now, with a soft face, her mother's face. But she is nearly six foot two, with a body as broad as a refrigerator. Seventeen now. Smells like sex. He noticed this first in March — the musky residue of a thin-ankled boy. The kid is something of a wannabe rock star with too much hair. His mane would never fit into a Schutt helmet. They met, if he remembers correctly, in orchestra class, and at first the Backup believed the boy was helping her with the French horn.

You'd never see that in Florida, his wife continues. Everyone there has melanoma, sure. But they're *normal*.

She stares at her husband for a moment, sucks on an olive. When the waitress comes, she orders another. The Backup orders a seven-ounce steak and an extra baked potato. Tomorrow is the season opener. He won't play — the Kid has been given the go-ahead — but the Backup is hardened to the dietary ritual: red meat the night before and as many carbohydrates as possible; half a peanut butter sandwich four hours before kickoff; then water, water, five salt tablets, water, Gatorade, water.

And they're all married to pilots! his wife says, as if she has been mulling it over. She gives an incredulous laugh. She's drunk now. She says, Have you ever noticed that, honey? All of our neighbors wear aviators.

No, I haven't.

He hasn't taken his eyes off his daughter. Sometimes the smell on her is so overpowering, he blushes; she seems not to know, or care. Anyway, she has, for the most part, quit talking to him. He chalks it up to her age, to angst. But if he were honest — and there's no easy way to say this, but if he came clean about it — the Backup would have to admit that he has quit trying to reach out to her, too. His daughter moves through the house like a specter from some past life: Tuscaloosa of the eighties, when his senior year put him in the running for the Heisman, and he and his wife shared a duplex and the postcoital routine of watching *Jim Vandergaarten's Sports Roundup*, tracking win/loss records of pro teams to guess where they'd end up:

If I'm drafted by Detroit, we're going to have to buy new parkas and chains for the tires. If it's Oakland, we could live in that condo your mother owns for a while.

There's a picture of him and the girl as an infant, taken the spring before they left for Cleveland. He sits on a tree stump near the Black Warrior River wearing tight Wranglers and Reeboks and holding the little girl close to his chest — he smiling, she still burgundy from the womb.

What has happened since then? An ACL tear. The blur of travel — stops in those rust-belt towns where football replaced good food and lovemaking.

The Backup's wife breaks the silence. She says to the girl, Why don't you tell us about your upcoming performance?

The girl shrugs. What's there to tell?

Are you nervous? Excited?

I guess.

The Backup tells her, You'll do fine. Better than fine. When is it again?

A long time from now.

The middle of October.

I'm not even thinking about it.

Are you practicing? You've got to practice.

I'm practicing.

Your father will be there, honey.

The Backup nods, grins. He says, I sure will. That's no problem. I'll be there, darling; I wouldn't miss it for the world.

He takes a sip of water and clears his throat and sits up in his chair and proclaims loudly, In fact, I'll be around a lot more. I'll be able to spend time with both of you, just like I've always wanted.

His wife gives him a small smile and pats his hand. His daughter is leaning on the table, eyes on the ceiling. One of the men at the

bar shouts, SO SHE SAYS, BLOW JOB? WHO SAID ANY-
THING ABOUT A BLOW JOB? and the family is once again
drowned in laughter.

It takes him a moment to consider what he has said. Around. Retired. How will that day be, the one in January when he announces
he won't be returning for an eighteenth season? The greats hold press
conferences, start off with jokes before breaking down, weeping into
their Armani ties. Some can't even make out the word. But for him?
A blurb in the Sports section. Quick mention on ESPN. They'll flash
a list of ten or so players calling it quits, and somewhere in that mix
he'll see his own name followed by career stats, numbers pegging his
life to a mathematical truth: 2711 Comp; 4242 Att; 63.9 Pct; 29004
Yds; 150 TDs; 134 INTs. Overall Rating: 82.9.

Week One

Final minutes of a game that has gone wrong. The Kid has shown his
age, his lack of experience. Nervous before kickoff, he drank too
much water and vomited on a sound speaker.

He has settled down since, pulled Dallas to within a field goal.

Not much time left. Commercial break. Two-minute warning.
When the cameras zip across the guy-wire above the field and focus
on the stands, fans jump to their feet and cheer and wave to people
at home.

The Backup chews gum with a ball cap twisted backward on his
head. He listens to the uproar, fans filled with beer and eight-dollar
nachos and dread of tomorrow's commute. The Kid takes the field
with the ball at Dallas's thirteen-yard line. He has his work laid out.
He's smiling, though — has been since the end of the third quarter.
It's taken him only three-fourths of a game to figure out what some

players never do: This is the same game you have been playing since Pop Warner — since you were six and your helmet weighed so much you couldn't hold your head straight.

The offensive coordinator paces, shouts at wide receivers; he holds his headset in his hands. But the Backup knows the game belongs to the Kid: the way he held himself during commercial break — hands kneading the towel hanging from his waist, eyes on the scoreboard, standing alone at the four-yard dash while his teammates shifted weight, their hands on their hips, short of breath from excitement. Body language. The game is body language. Or maybe it's like playing bass behind a jazz legend. Or maybe it's more of an improvised dance. Keep with the tempo, go where the game goes; don't think; don't think; feel the rhythm and follow it without pause or deliberation, without reflection; it's just an uncontrolled pulse, despite steps learned and strategies studied. The game has its own intentions, and once you feel it and fall into the syncopation all there is to do is do, is move. Action only; only action — the body moving, every vein and organ and strand of hair unified: gall bladder, toenail, uvula. You reach this point and the secret schemes devised in meetings come into full view: blitz packages, signals from the bench, headset tête-à-têtes transmitted from above the field, the calls by middle line-backers — *Tango, tango; Oskie oh-one, stay on him.* All of this surfaces all at once, as clear as the click of the play clock. In black and white. In *X* and *O*. The Backup knows this kid knows.

He hits a slant for eight yards. Picks up seven more with a shovel pass. Pump fakes to the left, comes back the other way, then sees a seam in the cover two. Ball to midfield. Time-out. The whistle bleats and the stadium is deafening, the hot Texas night falling down through that giant hole in the dome *so God can watch His favorite team, America's Team — blue star on silver helmet, yes, sir: That's the team the Most High puts money on, and when He gambles don't you know He don't ever lose.* The Kid jogs to the sidelines. His face gleams with sweat. Short of breath. Grinning. He is there, in the dance. All procedure now. No way to break the pulse.

The Backup smells antiperspirant rising from beneath his shoulder pads.

They're going to bring a weak-side rush, the coordinator says.

What do you think, bud? the Kid asks the Backup.

Look for the out route. Let the receiver get to the sideline to kill the clock. If they blitz or no one is open, toss the ball through the back of the end zone. Don't take a sack. Don't throw into coverage. Play for the tie if you have to.

The Kid nods, winks. The commercial break ends and the crowd rises like a sheet caught by a breeze.

It took the Backup four years to find the rhythm. He fell in and out of it in Cleveland, in a matter of six plays. Similar situation as tonight. Light snow, though. Winds north/northeast at ten to twelve miles per hour. He completed four in a row before a nose tackle rolled into his leg. Helmet against ligament. When he tried to get up, one of the Backup's teammates shoved him back to the ground, told him to relax, to stay down, man, it don't look too good. Stay down, brother; you're all right, baby.

He learned later it was his right guard who held him down. In the training room the guard said: Your knee went off as loud as a gunshot. Welcome aboard the SS *Crippled.* The man tapped on his own knee brace.

The ACL tear put him up for the rest of off-season and left him with a taste for Lorcet and a six-month trial separation from his wife.

The defense shows blitz.

Blitz! the Backup shouts from the sideline. Blitz!

He should check off. He should call an audible, shout, *Easy, Easy!*

Check red eight-one! Red eighty-one!, a safe play holding the tight end to block.

Instead, he drops back. The Backup pushes his head through between the coordinator and the punter. He watches a defensive end wrap an arm around the Kid, watches the Kid break free, dodge another tackle, and spring toward the line. He rifles a pass into the end zone to the tight end. The pass looks high, but the Backup can't see the outcome. He doesn't have to. The stadium erupts. His teammates leap past him onto the field. The coordinator tosses his laminated game plan, trots out with his hands raised. The Backup spits out his gum.

Postgame

He is drunk by midnight. He sits in the living room with his knee up on a sofa pillow and a heat pack beneath it. Force of habit; there is no pain tonight. The television flashes highlights from the game. The Backup twists a tumbler in his hand, watches the Kid squirm out of danger, fire the ball into the end zone. Smiles and laughter during the press conference. Questions about the future of the team. The Kid says, We can only take it one week at a time.

His wife is in their bedroom. A former neighbor called, a friend of hers, one of the women she used to play cards with. Often he hears his wife's laughter, though most of what she says is muted by the loud thud of music coming from the room above him, his daughter's bedroom, into which the girl has disappeared with her boyfriend.

It is late. It is time for the boy to go home. The Backup has been waiting for his wife to do it, for his wife to go upstairs. He imagines the boy again — the nest of hair, the tight jeans, the shitty, oxidizing car parked catawampus outside the house. The boyfriend never looks him in the eye, has never introduced himself or shaken the Backup's hand. He's never complimented the Backup, never told the man the kinds of things (sure, it'd be bullshit, but what's wrong with bullshit?) he always imagined a boyfriend would say: *Nice to meet you, sir. Yes, sir, I like football. I LOVE football. Gosh, it's such an honor to meet you. I remember that game...* Instead, he hides beneath his bangs, stands a half foot behind the girl, and waits, as if in painful desire, to disappear upstairs.

He hears his wife say, Everything you'd imagine it to be.

The Backup finishes his drink and pulls away from the couch with a grunt and the cracking of joints. He walks upstairs, the bass of hip-hop thudding down the hallway. He stands outside the girl's bedroom, almost knocks but drops his hand and, instead, presses an ear against the door. He waits. He listens.

In the Garden

His wife has had the Saint Augustine torn out. Today it has been replaced with carpet grass. The project is completed.

The Backup stands on the porch and watches his wife amble across the new lawn. With hands on hips and a wide smile, she turns to him and says, Do you know what's missing? A swimming pool. We had one in Miami and used it all the time.

I wish you'd said something before it was resodded.

She ignores him. Joining her in the yard, the man has the strange sensation of being in two places at once; she has created an exact replica of their yard in Florida. He wants to say more; he wants to remind her that this is not Miami, not even with a pool. A pool will be useless half the year, and the orchids and ferns she had shipped from the coast will freeze, will wilt soon, will be dead by Thanksgiving. But his wife lets out a long, pleased sigh, and for the first time, standing in the rich green grass, she looks like she's at home.

With a Neighbor

He meets Martin Wells at the edge of the pond. Martin's house abuts the water directly across from the Backup's property line. Each Monday the two men take to the jogging trails that run between their houses and through the hills of the neighborhood, past the tennis courts and public pools, and finally, jut away from the streets and cul-de-sacs to disappear into a thick copse of sumac and briar and rabbit grass.

The knee brace clicks every time the Backup's sole hits asphalt. Three miles in and tendonitis flares.

How do you like the neighborhood? Martin asks.

Click. Click. Click.

I like it. It's taking my wife longer to adjust. She thought we were staying in Miami for good. She thought last season was the end of the road. We lived in a neighborhood where all the mailboxes looked like tiny houses. We knew the mailman by his first name. The women played bunko every Thursday night, and even our dogs were all friends. She cried when I told her I'd been traded.

Why didn't you just retire?

The Backup shrugs, says, The money was good. Plus, I thought I'd have a shot at starting here.

The answer is the best he can think of, though he knows immediately it isn't true. He could tell Martin he thought the trade would do him good. He could say he is worried the game is his iron lung, the only thing keeping him alive, or that on some nights he gets out of bed and sits in the living room unable to sleep, terrified of his own home, worried that once the constant travel has ended he will be left with a kind of reverse motion sickness — the calm proving his bearings are shot to hell.

Click. Click. Click.

Wells says, I hear that. Continental wanted to move us to Chicago. Rebecca had a fit, said she couldn't stand to leave. I ended up taking a worse contract. But we're happy. We are where we want to be.

The Backup slows.

Click. Click. Click.

The muscles in his thigh constrict. Can we take a breather? The Backup puts his hands above his head. Low sooty clouds move in quickly from the north, and the sun disappears.

Aw, shit. Getting old sucks.

Martin chuckles, wipes his brow. He is a short man, bald, with rings of silver curly hair around a steeple of pink flesh. The Backup suddenly realizes his neighbor is older than he is, perhaps by as much as a decade.

You know, Wells says, we're hosting a neighborhood party in two weeks. Anyway, if your wife is having a hard time with the change — if she wants to make friends — the two of you are more than welcome.

The Backup nods, spits again. His breath returns, but the pain in his knee comes in currents; the spot where face mask met joint aches in the cooling air. Okay. Yeah. Count us in.

Week Nine; Or, In Kansas City

Third quarter. The Chiefs rush seven and the Kid's thumb catches between two helmets and splinters at the middle knuckle. He doesn't tell the trainers, doesn't come out of the game. Dallas loses, and by the time the players have made it to the locker room, the thumb is swollen and discolored. It looks like a giant slug. The coaches tell the Backup to prepare for Washington.

Preparation

He skips his daughter's performance. He tells her he has to study the playbook. He says, Washington runs a complicated defense. Blitz packages called off at the last second, zones, sometimes no down linemen.

She nods, says, Okay, Daddy. Says it without emotion, as if he'd just told her he was running to Home Depot. He waits a moment in the doorway, and when she says nothing else, he raps his knuckles against the jamb and leaves.

The Backup sits in his media room, watching film from the prior week. He looks for patterns, for pantomiming signals coming from the safety. He looks for body language. The pond between his house and Martin's shimmers black through the windows. Stars reflect on the smooth plane of the water. Martin's house is dark and the Backup's is quiet and the only noise is a slight breeze running through the tops of the trees.

Studying for a game was something he used to do with his wife. Their duplex was not far from Bryant-Denny Stadium, and he would walk home after games and find her sitting cross-legged on the carpet, drinking cheap beer and rifling through a worn composition notebook she used to track his statistics. Every completion, every down, every snap. She was his best critic. They fell in love dissecting SEC defenses on shag carpeting.

The Backup hears her Saab pull into the driveway. The engine turns off. He listens to domestic noises: cabinets banging, kitchen chairs grating against wooden floors. Later, footsteps thud up and down the stairs. Bedroom doors slam. Showers run. Televisions blare.

Then, quiet.

It's one thirty in the morning.

He slips out into the backyard. The jagged shadows of the tropical plants reach toward him. He walks down to the edge of the pond and puts his hands in his pockets.

They are 15.2 miles north of the airport. Sometimes the 747s fly so low he swears he can smell jet fuel in the air.

At 35,500 Feet

When the clouds thin, he sees the twinkling lights of some American city — someplace, God knows, he has been before.

At RFK Stadium

He takes his time suiting up: jockstrap, undershirt, knee brace, pants with thigh and knee pads, ankle braces, socks, cleats, cleat tape, rib vest, shoulder harness, back plate, shoulder pads, elbow brace, wrist coach, wrist tape, wedding-band tape, eye black, helmet, chinstrap, mouth guard. It's a chore to walk through the bowels of the stadium.

Twenty degrees colder in D.C. The crowd is already riled. Cowboys and Indians. The Backup stands in the tunnel next to police officers, shifting his weight from one leg to the other. He listens to the noise of the fifty-five thousand crammed into the stadium. When his name is called, he jogs out onto the field, feeling as if he has just stepped inside a giant hornet's nest.

Washington gets the ball first and makes a good drive out of it. They settle for a field goal and go up by three.

Commercial break.

The Backup tries to keep warm, tosses the ball on the sidelines. A cameraman zeroes in on him, waits for his cue. The Washington fans near the sideline call him motherfucker and old-ass man. He's heard it before. The taunting doesn't faze him, though he's never been able to block it out completely. These are other grown men, strangers — CPAs and foremen and chiropractors and paralegals — praying for his bodily injury.

He takes the field beneath a harmony of boos. He turns to the head referee, says, Hey, Bruce, let me know when we're back from commercial.

The man looks down at his watch and says, Forty seconds. I'll blow the whistle when we mark the ball.

The Backup nods, cups his hands and blows into them. The referee takes a final look at his watch and sets the ball. Then, just before he places the whistle in his mouth, he puts a palm on the Backup's rear end and mumbles, Good luck to you, bud. I've always liked watching you at work.

On only the second play, Dallas's running back breaks through and goes thirty-eight yards, finally tackled at the eighteen. The crowd quiets and the Backup high-fives the offensive line.

They break the huddle and come to the ball in an offset-I, and the Backup reads coverage, calls a hot route, raises his palm against the center's groin. The ball jolts into his hands. He fakes a handoff and rolls a little to the right, side-arms a pass to the slot receiver. The ball rattles against the receiver's chest before he pulls it in, breaks a tackle, and crosses the goal line. The Backup pumps his fist and jogs to the sidelines. He takes off his helmet and grins for the camera.

His second drive is equally effective, though an offsides penalty forces the team to settle for a field goal. By the end of the quarter, they lead ten to three.

It doesn't last. Washington is quick to score a touchdown, and whatever rhythm the Backup has found quickly dissolves after he misreads a zone blitz and is blindsided by a linebacker. The ball pops out of his hand. Washington recovers. The linebacker says, Stay down, cutie pie. Brother, it's going to be a long night for you.

He watches the mistake on the JumboTron. He walks off the field and throws his helmet at the placekicker's net. Halftime approaches. Washington scores again. Someone in the crowd throws a beer at him.

He knows it's his body. His mind is working all right; he can see who is where, what's coming. But his arm follows a fraction of a second later.

Swarmed by a half-dozen trainers, the Kid disappears into the tunnel and emerges ten minutes later without the metal stint. Instead, his fingers and wrist are heavily taped. They've given him a cortisone shot.

The Backup notices the coordinator speaking quietly to a trainer. The Kid's knitted cap has been replaced with a helmet. Snow flurries spin in front of the gigawatt bulbs. The Backup is told he did just fine; he's told to keep loose, that they might need him again.

He spends the rest of the game on the sidelines, trying to keep warm. Same fans heckling him.

Dallas loses, though the broken finger plays no role.

The Kid tells a reporter after the game, We just have to prepare better for next week and hope the outcome is different.

At Dallas Love Field

His wife stands near baggage claim. She has her keys dangling from her hand, arms crossed. He waves and grabs his suitcase and meets her with a kiss. They leave DFW in silence and cut across lanes of traffic for their exit home. She doesn't mention the game. She tells him the orange blossoms have fallen from the tree and some of the palm leaves are browning. She says she met with a pool company and they'll be back next week with an estimate. She tells him about the orchestra performance. She says, Your daughter stole the show.

Was she upset?

His wife doesn't respond.

I'll apologize.

The jaundiced blaze of streetlights whips across her face. She says: I went to Neiman Marcus today and bought you a new jacket. It's more autumnal than anything you own. For the party at the Wells's.

Shit. I forgot about that.

The Backup leans into the leather seat and yawns. Only played one half and he can feel his muscles as tight as coils, ready to spring.

He is sore by the time they reach the house. He decides to change into his pajamas and robe before visiting his daughter. He sits down to unlace his shoes.

The Backup falls asleep sitting upright at the edge of his bed.

At the Party

He wears the new blazer — burgundy houndstooth — with dark slacks and boat shoes. No socks. He and his wife walk along the pond and to the party. Rebecca Wells meets them with hugs and guides them to the kitchen, where ice chests of beer stand open on the floor.

The Backup grabs a bottle and moves into the backyard. Men sit on patio furniture, chuckling and rocking in deck chairs.

Martin Wells shakes his hand and introduces him to the rest. His wife was right: All of them are pilots. Jimmy Slocum flies for Northwest, and Chuck Brennan is with Delta. Erik Montgomery and Junior Wright are both with American. Lee Henrietta pilots a private jet for a real estate mogul.

Wells says, We're glad to have a nonpilot on the block. Finally, we can talk about something besides wind shear and holding patterns.

The Backup sits on a chaise lounge. Nobody speaks. The men stare at him, skeptical that he's the same man they saw on Fox last Sunday.

Chuck Brennan breaks the silence: So, what's it really like to play pro ball? I mean, what does it feel like when you've got a heavy rush coming at you?

The Backup drinks half of his beer in one long swig. He tells them, It probably feels like getting an airplane up to full throttle and then tossing the yoke out the window.

They laugh. Jimmy Slocum says, We saw that hit you took in Washington.

Martin whistles and shakes his head.

Junior Wright asks, Did that hurt?

Lee Henrietta says, *Did that hurt?* What kind of a question is that?

Erik Montgomery says, The guy wasn't going in for a hug.

Brennan says, And he's a pro-bowler. Won the Nagurski Trophy in college.

Actually, the Backup says, it doesn't hurt, not until the next morning. When you're out there, you don't feel much of anything. But a hit like that, coming from a player like that. Well, the next morning, it's a bitch just to take a leak.

The men laugh, then Lee says, Tough loss.

You did what you could, Martin Wells says.

Oh, sure, Brennan says. The outcome was about what we expected. Don't take that the wrong way, he says. I mean, we were all cheering for you, hoping for the best.

The Backup glares at him. Lee Henrietta says, At least it wasn't like in Cleveland. At least he didn't go low on you. Lee has a red face, a drunk's leathery skin. His bloated stomach is tufted into a polo shirt. He holds a thin, unlit cigar and a tumbler filled to the rim with bourbon. He says, It's all right! All you've got to do now is pray to the sweet Lord that the Kid doesn't get injured again.

Chuck Brennan says, Lay off, Lee.

Montgomery says, Lee's had one too many. When he has one too many, he likes to give people a hard time. He thinks it's funny to give people shit.

Martin says, It's the reason he doesn't have many friends.

Lee says, Except these assholes! They're pansy enough to put up with my mouth. No, but they're right. That's true about me. Anyway, I'm sure you're used to it. I mean, my God, that team you had in Miami. What a disaster. Lee chuckles, says, That wasn't your fault. You had a bunch of morons for teammates. Still, for a million in signing bonuses, I think even I could score every now and then. Lee lets out another guttural laugh.

The Backup smiles. He says, I don't see how it's any different than flying a plane. I mean, what do you guys *do,* anyway? Press a few buttons and try not to hit the side of a mountain?

The pilots rock in their chairs. They finish their drinks quickly. Lee seems to be the only one smiling. He says, Okay. I can take it. I'll take that and dish it right back out. Even with this gout, even with this gout here in my left leg, I could've picked you off eighteen times the other night.

The Backup says, You want to give it a try?

The men glance at each other. The Backup stands and takes off his sports coat and drapes it over the back of a lounge chair.

Give it a try?

Marty, you've got a football around here somewhere, right?

In the garage, Marty says, baffled.

Get it. And pump it up, too. Don't give me a fucking loofah to toss around.

The men follow him into the front yard and stand beneath the street-lamp. Martin comes out of the garage with the ball. The Backup puts his hands up, whistles, and Martin lobs a wimpy, crooked pass.

The Backup says, Here's how it works: I want Erik and Martin and Junior. Jimmy and Chuck are on defense. Lee, you are, too.

The pilots are motionless. He eyes them. He slaps the ball. He says, Well? Are we going to play or are we going to look at each other and pick our asses?

It's a game of two-below. The Backup huddles his offense and gives them directions: a hook and lateral; a pump-n-go; a play-action fake. Against Martin's soft Bermuda grass, the men relive their younger years, replay what they've seen on television. They sprint, catch, move with the game; their breath holds in the chilly air and the ball floats through the soft light. It hits them in the back of the head. In the chest. Mumbles of *shit* and *my bad, man.* They lose penny loafers and wallets. They keep going, keep reaching toward fantasy pylons and first-down chains. The Backup scores five touch-downs before the women come out onto the sidewalk. They shout, What on earth is this? What are y'all doing? They laugh at the mistakes, at these bloated strangers doing impressions of the young men they married twenty years ago. They sip wine and watch the men gallop in a meaningless game, a bad decision, a choice that'll leave them with nothing but stiff muscles and doctor's appointments. Cries for

Icy Hot and Bayer. The Backup's wife stands in the middle with her arms crossed. She gives him a long ugly glare.

He feels the game. The air comes in through his nostrils and stings his lungs, and the ball feels natural in his hand as he huddles his team. He smells the liquor-tainted breath of his neighbors, stares over them to where their opponents stand holding the places that already ache. Only the women are watching. But he feels as if it is more than that.

Let's burn these sons of bitches, he says, using his calloused palm to draw routes. They break the huddle and the Backup hikes the ball and drops back. Erik Montgomery lopes along the rosebushes, but it's Martin Wells he zeroes in on. Martin is open. The Backup plants, fires a spiral into the end zone. The ball hits Wells in the hands with a loud thud. Ricochets. Floats above his head and into the arms of Lee Henrietta.

Lee pauses in disbelief. He looks down at the ball as if it dropped from another planet directly into his hands. Then he grins and struts past the women, his voice shrill and pocked with laughter. I picked him off! Did you see it, Helen? I picked him off!

Henrietta's plump figure saunters through the light, ball raised in front of him. For a short moment the Backup's eyes lock with his wife's. Then he focuses on Henrietta. Everyone else has sat down — exhausted, drained.

There's a group of holly bushes behind Lee, and already the Backup sees himself knocking the man into them. He sprints toward Henrietta. Henrietta turns and sees him — all six feet five inches, all 234 pounds, charging. Lee's face sinks. He stops, tightens his body, closes his eyes. The Backup squares his shoulders. A few feet away, though, he feels his ankle turn in the soft grass, followed by a quick tingle in his leg. Then a loud click — a noise similar to one his brace would make if he were wearing it.

Lee walks into the driveway and drops the ball, looking as if he just narrowly avoided being hit head-on by a Greyhound bus. The Backup grabs his knee and bites his lip. He knows something has gone wrong, though he says nothing.

Lee's wife, Helen, says, Are we done, boys? I mean, can we go back inside?

The men congratulate each other and move toward the foyer of the house. The Backup thinks surely someone must've realized what has happened. But Chuck Brennan only slaps him on the shoulder. Good game, man. Don't worry about that last throw. Wells should've had it.

The Backup takes a step and grimaces. He tugs his shirt away from his sticky chest. He acts like he's catching his breath, calming down. He waits. He doesn't move again, not until everyone has disappeared inside.

In the Garden

Behind him the bright lights of Wells's house make the woods look ablaze. He limps through them, each step tougher than the last, leaning on tree trunks for support.

The back door is locked. He moves the length of the house with his hands against the brick. Halfway along, the toe of his loafer catches on a stake one of the sabal palms is tethered to and his knee gives. The Backup shouts and falls forward onto an air-conditioning unit. He sits there for a long while, cupping the throbbing joint between his hands. He can feel the swelling already.

It is quiet now. It is as quiet as it has been in a long while. The Backup leans against the side of his house and slowly closes his eyes.

He is jolted awake by a noise he first mistakes as a gunshot. The

Backup struggles to his feet and limps toward the side of the house, leans again against the wall. From there he can see the boy's battered car. It pangs and ticks and lets out a belch and dies. Then the passenger door opens, and his daughter's long figure steps out into the cold. She stands alone for a while, arms wrapped tightly around her chest. For a second the Backup thinks the girl has spotted him, and he moves back into the shadows.

When he peeks out again, he sees that the boy has joined her; he moves his arms around her waist. They kiss. The Backup expects himself to get angry. But the kiss is not crude, he thinks. Just a quick moment shared by two people who are young, who believe they are onto something no one else has ever been lucky enough to know.

He hears a sound from behind him and turns and sees his wife carrying the burgundy jacket. She stops in the middle of the yard, looking for him. But the Backup says nothing; he leans all of his weight against the house and peeks out toward the street. He hears the couple talking.

Honey? his wife says. Honey, are you out here?

The Backup doesn't respond. He wants to hear what the boy is saying to his daughter. He tries to hobble closer, close enough to make out the words. And though the pain is tremendous and the stress on the joint is causing the injury to worsen, he knows this is something he cannot miss. He forces himself to the edge of the house and cranes his neck as far as possible. And just as he hears his daughter laugh and begin to tell the boy something, a jet cuts above them, flies directly over the house, the pond, the lawn — low enough to drown out any sound down here on earth.

ANDREW MALAN MILWARD

University of Iowa

The Burning of Lawrence

I have not enjoyed myself much or felt very happy since I left home, for happiness depends on contentment, and that has not fell to my lot, and it seems to me never will.... merry little birds make one wish he were as happy as all around him; but that cannot be; as this earth is not a heaven for man; for we at the happiest day feel a burden of sorrow which we cannot throw off here.

—William Clarke Quantrill,
letter to sister, February 8, 1860

(1) Photograph

In the photograph from 1912, taken forty-nine years after the raid, the remaining men kneel, sit, and stand in wide rows three deep. As

I count it, there are nearly fifty men in all. The photographer had to move the camera so far back that their expressions are only the ghosts of expressions. You can tell they are hardened, though — gaunt and weathered; these are faces for breaking firewood over. Some look as though they might be smiling, others grimacing. By virtue of their posture and the positioning of their heads, one gives off an air of pride while his neighbor communicates shame. By this time they were old men in suits with canes and prickly gray beards. Before the raid they had all been farmers and had survived the bitter fighting of the Civil War as well as the onset of industrialization. They were on the cusp of World War I and likely unable to fathom the ways fighting had changed, how massive numbers of people could be slaughtered in an instant. These men survived the raid, but they weren't survivors of the raid. They were what was left of Quantrill's band of 450 that rode through Lawrence, Kansas, in August of 1863 and murdered most of the men and boys in town. So I return to the photo: How long had it been since they'd seen each other? Whose idea was it to have this strange reunion? How had their memories of the past changed? Did they speak of the raid? What on earth did they talk about?

(2) *The Secret Bride*

On the eve of the raid, Quantrill is sullen, stalking, brooding — in love. He has left his men at the camp, hidden in the covering brush and mouthlike gorges of Sni-A-Bar, and snuck away to see his young mystery bride. The men whisper about her; there are rumors, but few have ever actually seen her. He can't explain the need to keep secret his marriage to a thirteen-year-old other than that he is a gentleman and, well. . . . Tonight, he and Kate walk through the spinney of oak trees near her parents' home — fingers laced, intertwined — and he builds a fire along the banks of the creek. She pronounces his name "Quantrelle" after a misspelling in the newspaper, and he hasn't had the heart to correct her, thinking the sound sweet and exotic. For a time she lets his hand inch up her naked thigh, beneath the thinning gray dress she's worn all summer, and he knows he should take her right there and make love to her, but he can't. His mind's awash, away, thinking about tomorrow, the ride into Lawrence. He knows he very well might not return, knows the chances of not returning are quite good, in fact, but this is a war after all, even if he and his men are uncommissioned, unofficered, and unacknowledged by Southern leadership. A few nights ago, prior to taking the vote, he announced his intentions by yelling, "We're gonna burn that bitch to the ground," and his men thundered their approval, stamping their boots and rifle butts in the dirt, then passing the vote unanimously. But as he worked to finalize the plans over the next few days, he walked through camp and heard mumblings of *suicide, impossible, tyrannical.*

"I'm going to Lawrence tomorrow," he says now, and Kate smiles, taking his hand. She wants to say, *Take me with you,* or to ask why he's going there, but she thinks better of it, not wanting to appear maudlin, knowing well enough the answer is simply that he must go. Like every other time he's left her, she fears he won't return, that she'll never see him again. She wants to seize his hand quickly and say something — *Don't go* or *Put yourself on me and give me a baby* — but can't bring herself to speak, her young body fit to explode in a burst of light and heat, sounding something like *sssshhhhhhoooooom,* or maybe a whispered *I love you.* For some time they sit, silent, letting the stars wink and flames tongue all around them, until she grabs his hand and says coyly, "How many men have you killed?" This is a joke they have, a game, something she asks often in jest, though in truth the thought excites her. He is, after all, famous. He is Wanted — and by none more than her. And Quantrill, being a gentleman and a liar, responds, "None, my dear. I've never harmed a soul." He leans forward and, as her father does every night, kisses her forehead before leaving. She *is* only thirteen years old, and sometimes when they kiss he thinks of his own sister he's not seen in years.

(3) Book, Monument

Written during the Depression, *The WPA Guide to 1930s Kansas* describes a Lawrence with three hotels, twenty-five-cent movie houses, and a population of 13,726. It tells the origin of the University of Kansas and of the institute of higher learning that would become Haskell Indian Junior College, where "smartly clad Indian coeds and white-collared braves seek to adjust themselves to a new culture, replacing lacrosse and old war cries with football and 'Rah! Rah!'" There is mention of the town's historical importance to the abolitionist movement, noting John Brown and other Jayhawkers who fought to keep Kansas a free state after the Kansas-Nebraska Act of 1854 allowed the citizens of the territory to decide for themselves. Northerners, many from Massachusetts, flooded into the territory, armed to the teeth, as did pro-slavery Missourians, and what followed were years of bloody atrocities. In the history section of the guide there is a quick reference to Quantrill: "At daybreak on August 21, 1863, Lawrence citizens were aroused by the sound of firing and the shouts of guerilla raiders who swept down on the town from the east, led by the notorious irregular, William Clarke Quantrill. . . . After four hours they withdrew, leaving 150 dead and the major portion of the town in ruins. So futile was the resistance offered by the surprised and terror-stricken citizens that the Quantrill band retired with the loss of only one man."

By the time I enrolled at KU in the mid-nineties, the town's population had swelled to nearly a hundred thousand, and the movie tickets were seven dollars. Haskell had grown to become one of the largest Native American universities in the country, and needless to say there were many more hotels by that point. Having grown up in Lawrence, I'd learned about the raid as a young girl, probably in school, and promptly forgotten about it. Without ever really understanding what it meant, however, the name *Quantrill* floated in my unconscious, something — like so many occupants of that dream space — at once intensely familiar and strangely foreign. It wasn't until my sophomore year of college, when I went on a dark walk with a boy, that Quantrill returned to me permanently.

This boy and I shared a row in the huge auditorium that held our American history survey class. Lost in a sea of people who looked exactly like us, our eyes had met, and afterward he told me he thought the band on my T-shirt was all right. He liked music, too — he played, he said, asking if I wanted to hear some songs he'd written. This was years before he'd given up on supporting himself as a musician and shipped off to fight in the war, to die so far away. That night he walked me — guitar over his shoulder, bottle of red wine in hand — to a cemetery. I followed, curious. I expected something dramatic. I expected recitations of Baudelaire and running naked past gravestones, but we just drank wine while he played a few songs. I made a joke about him trying to seduce me and he laughed and then got serious, asking what I thought of his songs. I said they were beautiful and he smiled. But later, when we had finished the bottle of wine, I moved closer to him, setting my hand on his knee, and he shook his leg so that my hand fell from him; as if nothing had happened, as if I'd only just asked him a question, he said earnestly that these songs were about trying to connect, that they were written for his girlfriend. I felt embarrassed and walked away from him as he bent over the body of the guitar, picking at the strings. Then, with those notes traveling in the air between us, I came upon the large granite monument and, aided by the soft light from the moon and stars, made out the engraved tribute to the victims of the raid.

(4) The Calming

The second in command, George Todd, handsomely dressed and devilishly sharp with a pistol, makes one final stop before meeting up with Quantrill. Thinking it better to travel in smaller numbers, Quantrill sent him to the Northland for a few days, dispatching a rider to give word of his plan to attack Lawrence. Never one to back away from a fight, Todd is excited, but he has some unfinished business to attend to before joining the others. There is a man, supposedly sympathetic to the abolitionist cause, living in _____; and for Todd his presence is a personal affront. This is Missouri, after all, not Kansas, and there's really no place for that sort of thing here. So he and his crew of twenty men pay a visit to _____. When they arrive, Todd has fifteen of his men circle the perimeter of the house, rifles loaded, pistols cocked, and with four others he dismounts and stalks to the front door, calmly knocking on the smooth oak as if he is a neighbor wanting to draw from their well. Todd can hear footsteps inside and then the blood coursing through his body. When an older woman answers the door, she avoids staring at the bulging growth below his midsection by admiring his blue eyes, the way he stands out — with his short, well-kept brown hair and fancy attire — from the others beside him, shaggy, slouched, stinking. First, playing nice, he inquires, "Is Mr. _____ home?" But when she says he's in Kansas City and not to return for another three days yet, he pushes the door open. "Where is he?" he says, all rotten teeth and sneer now, as she backs away. But she's telling the truth, she swears, and so he and the men begin tearing the place apart, looking for her husband. A bit of the dandy in him, Todd opens the lid of a large wooden chest in the bedroom, thinking at least he might find some nice clothing, but these people are farmers; holding up a pair of plain brown trousers with holes in the knees, he grows angry and overturns the chest, sending clothes flying through the air.

After thoroughly searching the house, Todd is satisfied with her answer but not satisfied. No, he wants to prove a point — that there will be no quarter for abolitionists in Missouri — and this woman has stolen his thunder, kind of like how Quantrill does when Todd, so popular among the men, oversteps his bounds. His blood has cooled, settling inside his limbs like the thick lip on curdled milk. He looks around the room, his men's eyes expectant as puppies', waiting for the order to torch the place. But what Todd spies by the window, overlooking the stretch of poorly tended wheat fields starved with drought, is an organ. He moves over to the bench and lets a mischievous pinky ease down a key. The sound is loud, booming, elephantlike. The woman startles. Now he lays both hands on the keyboard, the old lessons coming back. His fingers move with a long-hidden familiarity, and the sound is calming. He looks at the others in the room as he plays — outside, the horses shudder and twitch to the arresting sound, his men wondering what the hell is going on in there — and what he wants to say is, *I'm trying to tell you all something. This is how I feel.*

(5) Song

There exist words for a song about Quantrill, though the date is undetermined. There are only two verses and a chorus, so perhaps it was never finished. The words are:

Quantrill was a man
Who came upon the land
From Missouri with his band
With a Colt in every hand

Hey, can you hear the cries from Lawrence?
The end is upon us
Hey, can you hear those cries?
Everybody's gonna die

He put his gun in every eye
That ever tried to smile
To burn the town he did try
While the babies all asked, Why?

Senior year, working on my thesis, I went to the historical archives at KU to seek a field recording of the song, something in the Alan Lomax vein, but there was none. One night I took the words to that friend who played guitar. We still hung out quite often. By this point he'd withdrawn from school and was tending bar downtown, trying to finish songs for his album. His girlfriend smiled at me when she opened the door and said she was running out for cigarettes but would be right back. I returned her smile, then looked down as I walked inside. He was sitting on the couch and I sat across from him in a chair, and the two of us talked for a while. He lit a joint and took a few drags while I told him about the raid. Born out of state, he'd never heard of it. "It happened right here in Lawrence," I said, exasperated.

He nodded, unimpressed, his eyes bloodshot, and passed me the joint. "Why don't we remember this kind of shit?"

I asked him if he could put music to the lyrics, and he took the paper from my hands and looked at it a minute. He sipped his whiskey, picked up his acoustic guitar, and strummed a couple chords, humming a little. Then he put the guitar down and said, "Is this political? I don't do political stuff." I told him it was historical, and he dropped his pick and reached for the joint. "I write love songs, girl."

(6) Pelathe

Pelathe is the hero you never hear about in all of this, the Indian Sisyphus. When Quantrill's men storm into Kansas unscathed, blowing right past a number of Union Army checkpoints that line the entire border, it's clear to the Union leadership in Kansas City that the raiders, now in the neighborhood of 450 strong, are heading for Lawrence. They know they must get word to the people of Lawrence of the hellfire headed their way, but Lawrence is fifty miles away from the city yet, and who could beat Quantrill's men on their superior horses?

Pelathe, a Shawnee Indian scout, happens to be accompanying one of the Union leaders when the news comes about Quantrill, and he pleads to be allowed to go, to try to beat the raiders to Lawrence. Lacking a better plan, they saddle up Pelathe with their best horse and tell him to fly. Sometimes known among other scouts as the Eagle, Pelathe does feel like a bird as he burns a trail for Lawrence through the brambled scrub. He rides full speed for one hour, and then two, through the night until the horse begins to fail, coming to a dead halt in the pitch-black early morning, no water in sight. There are still miles to go. He considers the beautiful animal a minute, running a slow hand through her mane, then imagines all the people in Lawrence, and so he pats her head, whispering a few final words in her ear, before unsheathing his bowie knife and stabbing it into her sides. The horse cries out as Pelathe rubs gunpowder into the wounds, and be-

fore he can restirrup, the sorrel mare takes off again. Through this sacrifice he's able to get a few more miles out of her before she expires,
collapsing, Pelathe flying forward over her. He must keep going
though, he tells himself, so he begins to run on foot until his legs give
out at a Delaware Indian tribe's camp near the outskirts of Lawrence.
He tells them what is happening, of the urgency, that they must get to
Lawrence to warn the townspeople, and with fresh horses they head
out, thundering through the purple of early morning. But when they
get to the ferry landing on the Kaw River they see it is too late, that
the horror has already begun; Quantrill has beaten them to town.

(7) Seeds

A few points of interest:

- A previous raid of Lawrence occurred on May 21, 1856, nearly
  five years before Kansas became the thirty-fourth star on the
  flag and seven years before Quantrill's raid. Led by former
  president pro tempore of the Senate David Atchison, a large
  group of Missourians stormed into town and shelled the
  Free State Hotel and the printing press and looted most of
  the stores.
- Following Atchison's raid, Senator Charles Sumner of
  Massachusetts delivered an impassioned speech on the Senate
  floor, lasting two entire days, called "The Crime Against
  Kansas." A few days later, upset by the rhetoric of the speech
  and the blame assigned to Southern states, Congressman
  Preston Brooks of South Carolina calmly walked up to
  Sumner and began clubbing him with his golden-knobbed
  cane for several uninterrupted minutes until the cane broke,

upon which time he attempted to stab Sumner with the splintered end, giving the senator a beating from which he would not recover for three years.

- When news of the caning reached Kansas, John Brown, a radicalized preacher and leader of the abolitionist cause, demanded retribution. With his company of Free State Volunteers, he set out for Pottawatomie Creek, calling for the lives of five pro-slavery men. This, he said, was what God demanded. First he directed the group to the Doyle family's cabin and led Mr. Doyle's sons outside, where they were stabbed, dismembered, and pierced in their sides in front of their father and mother. Afterward, Brown removed a pistol and shot Mr. Doyle in the head. After two more stops of a similar fashion, Brown had his five.

- And so it went, back and forth like this for the next several years, raids perpetrated by both sides with the innocent often paying the price, such as the women who were rounded up in Missouri by federals and taken to Kansas City and placed in a dilapidated jail cell on suspicion of aiding the rebel bushwhackers. Some of these women were in fact the wives, mothers, and sisters of Quantrill's men, so when the jail collapsed and killed a number of women, one knew there would be consequences. Eight days later, Quantrill was leading 450 men back into the center of the abolitionist movement.

(8) Forever the South

The first to go are the young boys from the Fourteenth Kansas Regiment, camped on the edge of town, training to join up with the Union Army. Quantrill's men cut right through them, picking the thirteen- and fourteen-year-olds off as they sleep, or as they wander out of their tents, scratching their heads and balls, rubbing eyes, wondering what the hell all this racket is — *We're trying to get some gol'darn sleep* — then boom, they're dead. They are unarmed and defenseless thanks to a recent city ordinance forwarded by Mayor Collamore that decreed all weapons in Lawrence must be kept locked up inside the armory as a safety measure (including all the powerfully accurate Sharps rifles sent by train to Lawrence from eastern abolitionists in boxes labeled BIBLES to avoid discovery).

Two blocks away, the Second Colored Regiment, a camp of black troops, reach for pistols that aren't on their hips, rifles that aren't slung over their shoulders, and must make a tough decision. Twenty or so stay long enough to be slaughtered while others flee for the river, away from Quantrill's men, wading across, silently cursing their lack of weapons, then themselves for their cowardice, their unwillingness to be martyred.

At five thirty in the morning, Massachusetts Street is bedlam, horses thundering every which way, raiders firing potshots at scurrying store owners — targets as easy as lone whiskey bottles atop fence posts. Quantrill watches with an unsettled, pensive look: Things are going too well; any minute, surely, the Union Army will sweep through and send his men hightailing back toward the border; he is supposed to die today. But the army never comes, and soon his stony look gives way to amusement as cries of his name, audible over pistol shots and whinnies, sound all around him: *Long live Quantrill! Long live Jefferson Davis! Forever the South!* Sure that this raid will win him the respect and recognition of the Confederate Army, he is already savoring the sweet assonance: *General Quantrill.*

He visits the Free State Hotel, setting up in the lobby after his men have cleared the rooms and rounded up the guests. "How about some breakfast," Quantrill says to the proprietor, who's straight backed with fear. The man hurries to the kitchen to prepare the food himself. Up-stairs, Quantrill's men loot the rooms, stuffing into their pockets watches, jewelry, and women's silken undergarments of absinthe blue, rouge, and Nile green. Downstairs, the collected guests wonder if they are about to be executed, and are silently saying prayers, smatterings of whispered mercies, as they watch the back of the man who will issue the order, if it is to be. Quantrill sits down at a table by the win-dow, waiting for his biscuits and eggs, listening to the anxious shifting of bodies behind him; yet his mind is elsewhere, thinking of Kate, humming a ballad: "I don't know when I'll see you again, my dear." He closes his eyes and sees her face, beautiful, but then it starts to fade, her mouth asking why he's left her and gone to Lawrence.

"What do you want to do?" George Todd asks. "Leave 'em or kill 'em?"

Quantrill thinks a moment, as one of the ladies moves her weight to the other foot, nudging a chair that squeaks, before deciding to spare them. He tells Todd to take them over to city hall as prisoners of war. As Todd is about to lead the prisoners out into the street, he notices one of them is wearing a Union uniform: Captain Banks, provost marshal of Kansas. He inspects the man's clothing, examin-ing the pretty blue coloring and careful stitching. He moves over to Banks, hand on his gun, leans close to the terrified man's face, and says, "Gimme yer clothes," making the captain undress right there in front of him.

(9) Film

In Ang Lee's 1999 film *Ride with the Devil,* Tobey Maguire plays a Dutch emigrant, now living in Missouri, who takes up the Southern cause, joining the irregulars waging guerrilla warfare on the Kansas-

Missouri border. It's a fictionalized account, based on a novel called *Woe to Live On,* though, interestingly, the movie's title is stolen from an earlier biography of Quantrill. It's mostly a buddy movie and a love story, but Quantrill does make an appearance, a kind of historical cameo almost no one would recognize. Lee halfheartedly attempts to re-create the raid on Lawrence, but the results are rather tame. He devotes roughly ten minutes to it, and many of the sequences are about as compelling as the Wild Wild West reenactments in Dodge City. The best part of the movie is before the raid, when Quantrill and his men gather on a hilltop, looking down at the sleeping, unsuspecting town. Quantrill, played by John Ales, passes out death lists bearing the names, ranked by importance, of the men to kill. He offers a few words, something like, *Boys, you know what we need to do. You know what we must do. No quarter for them federal sons a bitches!,* which elicits a booming cacophony of threats and swears. A hodgepodge of syllables belonging to words like *abolitionistfuckerswhoresniggersfreesoilers* flies through the air, and with the raise of their hats and scarves they head down the mountain in a thunderous swirl of dust, hoofprints, and rebel yells.

The movie came out soon after I graduated. I was working odd jobs around Lawrence, thanks to my history degree, and I saw it seven times before it left Liberty Hall. Sometimes I went in the middle of the day and sat alone in the dark theater. Once, I took the guitar player with me and spent most of the movie leaning over to explain the historical references and occasional inaccuracies. He listened politely, eyes moving between the screen and me. When it was over he said he was glad I had brought him and we both smiled at one another. It seemed like something might happen. But when I told him that just once I wished I could see the movie the way he had, without any background knowledge, he grew distant and said it seemed like I enjoyed it pretty well anyway.

This was around the time he was starting to get local gigs, playing that night at the Bottleneck, a big deal. He was stuck on some new girl, he said, and was writing great songs about the one who had just left. I told him I wouldn't be able to come, but showed up later, halfway through his set, and stood in the back of the bar nursing a beer, watching him sing songs about girls he'd left and been left by.

(10) Three Ghosts

A. GETTA DIX

Proprietor of a boardinghouse for local workers, Getta draws a hand to her chest when she realizes what's happening. Her husband, her love, is over at the Johnson House with his brother. She leaves her children with a nurse and rushes into the street, knowing the raiders won't harm her. When she reaches the house she sees her brother-in-law stumble down the back steps, falling to the ground before her. She cups his head in her hands. He looks at her with the eyes of one who has seen God — with unflinching terror, burbling blood, an inability to speak — and then his lids slide closed. She tries to remove her hands, but part of his brain has fallen out the back of his head and now rests in her palms. What she yells then, looking down at her hands, is not his name but her husband's, and she drops the bits of jellied brain into the dust and scrambles up the steps of the house, where she finds a trio of bushwhackers, three sheets to the wind, holding several local men at gunpoint. Her husband is among them and she hurries over to his side, pleading for his life, screaming, spitting. She's convincing, too, very nearly talking two of them out of killing her husband, but the third, the leader, is too soused to abide any talk of mercy and pushes all seven men outside to the street, unloading several rounds into their chests. Getta watches her husband's body fall; it happens so quickly — *crack, thump* — that it's not until he's on the ground that everything slows down. Her soul is fleeing her by way of small, rapid exhalations, and all that's left is the absence of feeling, of care. She sits on the bottom step of a storefront near the body and watches the world pass before her, the horror it has so quickly become. A straw hat belonging to one of the dead blows along the street like tumbleweed, and her hand reaches for it, placing it over her husband's placid face. She walks away slowly, desultorily, between the bustle of canting horses, the giggle and snarl of drunks, the mangle of the quiet, lonesome dead.

B. KASPER KASPAR

Son of wealthy German immigrants — the owner of the *Lawrence Tribune* and his epileptic and nostalgic wife — seventeen-year-old burgeoning newspaperman Kasper Kaspar is at the press early on the morning of the raid. He doesn't know it yet, but his father is already dead, killed while asleep in bed, and his mother is in shock, still shaking the body, expecting it to wake at any moment. What brings young Kasper to the office so early, however, has nothing to do with newspapering. He's locked in an embrace with the office printer, an older man affectionately known as Rooster. It is as Kasper finally works up the nerve to take the tip of Rooster's penis in his mouth that he first feels the heat closing in, a warmth more than their own bodies' doing. The raiders have set fire to the building, which goes up almost instantly, like tinder, because of the printing chemicals. There's a moment as the two men huddle naked amid the flames, watching smoke funnel under and over closed doors, when they have a decision to make. A future as outcasts awaits them if they run out into the street as they are, naked, shivering, womanly: a life of hiding in attics, of food pushed under locked doors. Their decision is communicated through look and gesture as they embrace, kiss, and then whisper in the other's ear as the fire overtakes them. Barely audible over the hiss of burning wood and the sizzle of steaming printer blocks are their oaths and cries: *Hold me. Did you hear me? Hold me tighter. I'll see you on the other side.*

The flames then consume them, the heat so intense that their bodies dissolve, scatter in the wind, and disappear. For this reason Kasper's mother will, for the rest of her life, believe he is still alive, setting a place for him every night at the dinner table.

c. Mayor Collamore

Mayor George Washington Collamore, he of the infamous and untimely gun seizure that leaves his town unarmed, wakes to find his house surrounded by raiders. With his hired hand, Patrick, he dashes out of the kitchen, through swaths of wheat, and into his well house. Patrick lowers the mayor down the shaft first before joining the anxious and fearful old man at the bottom of the stone well. There, the close proximity of quarters forces them to huddle, looking up at the circle of light above them, waiting for either the mayor's wife to tell them it is okay to come out or for a man in a slouch hat to fire his Colt blindly into their hiding spot.

It turns out, though, that neither happens. The raiders grill the mayor's wife for a while but she won't, on pain of death, give up her husband. Frustrated and drunk, the bushwhackers loot the place of all its valuables and then set it on fire. They wait out front, figuring that if the mayor was hiding in the house somewhere he would come running. But really, the beauty of the fire is what transfixes them. They've been lighting them all morning, have been doing so for months, in fact, yet none like this one. Something inside — perhaps the canisters of furniture wax and shoe polish — feeds the blaze, a tongue of fire shooting dragonlike out the chimney top. The smells

of burning linens and flowers from the garden bloom from the con-
flagration until the walls come crashing down and the house collapses. Only then does this audience finally disperse.

As the mayor's wife rushes to the well house, she doesn't realize
that smoke from the fire has funneled all oxygen out of the shaft like
a whirring gust of wind on the open prairie, leaving the mayor and
Patrick to a much slower and more horrifying death than if a gun
had just been put to their heads and unloaded into their brains. In-
herent in those last moments, in the groping push and pull of their
hands as they slowly run out of air, is nothing amorous, but a simple
prayer of human touch, an instinctive hope: *You can get me out of
here, can't you?*

(11) Correspondence

Date: 08/21/2003
From: Janice_Stallings@missouri.edu
To: jayhawkergirl@hotmail.com
Subject: re: Inquiries?

Thank you for your interest in the State Historical Society here
at MU. Excuse the formality, but I'll answer your questions in
kind:

    1) Yes, we have a good deal of material on Quantrill, specifi-
cally, and rooms full of general Civil War–era Kansas/Missouri
material: letters, newspapers, books, pictures, paintings, etc.
You should come visit—Columbia's only a three-hour drive
from Lawrence.

    2) There is certainly a small but avid group of enthusiasts in-

terested in—some would say obsessed with—that border war period. There are a number of Civil War battle reenactments across Missouri that attract good-size crowds. More than the reenactments, however, there is a culture that goes along with it, some of it truly bizarre. I've heard of small-town bars where patrons dress as Confederate soldiers or bushwhackers. I once even came across a "woman seeking man" ad in the *Weekly* in which a woman was looking to marry anyone who could prove a family connection to Quantrill.

3) I don't know if I can offer a definitive answer on how people here today look back on those times or how they feel about men like Quantrill, George Todd, and Bloody Bill. I think a lot of people in Missouri feel that even though we now consider what these men were trying to preserve—the institution of slavery—as abhorrent, they were not simply bloodthirsty monsters. I think some people feel, as the historian Donald Gilmore writes, ". . . the Missouri guerillas were legitimate partisan warriors who fought bravely for their cause against insurmountable odds." When you're on the wrong moral side of history and constantly reminded of it, you get defensive. I'm not saying that's how I feel. It's complicated.

4) I mean, can anyone ever understand the horrors of the past? There have been countless books written about awful events like the raid on Lawrence, but they're at best approximations, in my opinion. We'll never understand. That's the thing about history, right: It's not graven—it's points of view.

Thank you for your interest and please don't hesitate to contact me again. I hope you do decide to come visit, even if you are a KU alum . . . just kidding.

Best,
Janice Stallings

(12) Poor Kansas, Poor Bleeding Kansas

As the raid wears on, the bushwhackers anticipate the out-the-back-door-and-into-the-potato-vines escape, and now they simply set the fields aflame and wait for the men to stream out. The raiders make sport of it, this killing of the fleeing men, a sort of target practice.

But as the hours pass, the guerrillas also get sloppy. Drinking and looting take priority, and this truancy affords a few hard-won victories for the people of Lawrence. There is the incident in which an elderly man quickly shaves and dresses as a sickly old woman. When the raiders arrive, they carry him out of the house on a bed, Cleopatra-style, before torching the place. Some townsfolk, emboldened by the rush of their own imminent deaths, begin fighting back. Lacking guns, a few men challenge the bushwhackers with pitchforks and knives. Surprisingly, many of Quantrill's men simply leave when confronted in this manner, either because they respect the suicidal gumption of the defenseless or simply because they are cowards.

When the raiders open fire on a crowd of local men gathered on Massachusetts Street, Josiah Simeon falls to the ground, feigning death, and then pulls the bodies of the dead atop him. The blood trickles down on him, the pleas for help worm through the pile to his ear, through crevices and openings between skin, until all is still, dead. Sometime later he hears a noise, footsteps nearby, bodies being turned over, rummaged through. When the body above him is removed, he can't stop from opening his eyes, expecting to be staring straight into the barrel of a Colt. But what he sees instead are the vacant, soul-deadened eyes of a woman trying to find her husband and son among the heaps of dead and dying. And at last, here, she has found her son, whose body has thus far saved Josiah's life. Josiah looks at her, into those eyes, and says, "Leave him be — it's my only chance," pulling the woman's son out of her hands, back atop him.

(13) Painting, Drawing, Newspaper

Lauretta Louise Fox Fisk depicts nearly all of Lawrence aflame in her painting *The Lawrence Massacre.* You likely wouldn't recognize the subject on an initial viewing, however, which is one of the painting's interesting effects. In the foreground, raiders ride their horses down the main thoroughfare, Massachusetts Street. Their guns are drawn, but their numbers are not great, nor are they particularly menacing. The tone of the scene is oddly calming. In the background, the burning town is easily mistakable for a tawny sunrise to the casual eye. This contrasts greatly with the pencil drawing that ran a month after the raid in *Harper's Weekly,* titled *The Ruins of Lawrence,* which looks anachronistically more like a postwar bombed-out Berlin than a torched Wild West prairie town.

A curious thing about the burning of Lawrence is the lack of an absolute death count. Most references cite "nearly one hundred fifty," while other estimates range from one hundred thirty-two to one hundred eighty-six. The August 23, 1863, edition of the *New York Times* reported "about one hundred eighty murdered" under the heading THE INVASION OF KANSAS. The granite monument in the cemetery abides the general estimate of one hundred fifty victims, but the surrounding gravestones all etched with the same date make estimates inadequate.

His grave is in another cemetery, far from the monument but very present to me here. He enlisted for the money, he said, for the experiences that would give him new material to write about so he could stop singing stupid love songs.

(14) The Living and the Dead

After four hours Quantrill's men leave town, and the people of Lawrence abandon their hiding spots to survey the destruction and roll over bodies, searching for husbands and fathers, sons and lovers, and more often than not finding sadness and horror. All over town, long wailing cries, like those of animals caterwauling while rutting, populate the air. A makeshift hospital is raised in the only church that survived the onslaught, but the remaining doctors are little more than morticians and bartenders, dispensing whiskey to the newly amputated or slowly dying.

Massachusetts Street is completely devastated. People uselessly hurry pails of water from nearby wells and the Kaw River to the burning buildings, persevering through that first morning, mostly in silence now, mostly in vain, in an effort to salvage what they can of Lawrence. And that sound passing among them — the sharp and single cries amid the vast stretches of oppressive silence — is the echo of loss.

(15) Confession

Shortly before he shipped out, we were walking up and down Massachusetts Street, stopping at our favorite haunts — listening to records at Love Garden and combing the stacks at the Dusty Bookshelf — strolling in the early fall with a beautiful ennui. I suggested we drop by the city's history museum. He'd never been. I told him of the most abject statue of Langston Hughes on display in a hall honoring famous Lawrencians.

A volunteer near the entranceway, an old woman revealing bits of corn chip in her teeth when she smiled, informed us we were the only ones there. We walked through the building, so dark and dusty, lit solely by shafts of sun penetrating the high windows. They had added something new since I'd last been: a multimedia program of significant moments in the state's history. We skipped around the timeline, stopping on Quantrill's raid. I wanted to tell him how I felt, to unburden myself, to ask him not to leave. But I knew he didn't feel the same way about me, never had. How impossible it seemed then that two people ever connected. He controlled the mouse, advancing to the next screen, saying, "Man, that must have been crazy. Can you imagine things like that ever happened here?" I murmured agreement and asked if he'd miss playing guitar while he was over there, but he didn't answer, just clicked the Stop button.

(16) The Journey of the Body

By the time Quantrill's raiders leave Lawrence, the Union leaders in Kansas City have finally mobilized forces that head to intercept the guerrillas before they cross into Missouri, where they'll disappear into the brush and thicket, gully and wood — into the very soil — and become ghosts, their story spreading, growing mythic. The Union forces stage two dramatic attempts to stop the rebels, but ultimately they fail.

Now it is almost twenty-four hours after the ambush began, and with a clutch of Union troops shrinking behind him in the distance, Quantrill feels as though he could sleep for a year, maybe two. He is weary. He knows they'll be safe if they can just make it to Missouri, and he's oppressed by the desire to ride straight to Kate's home and see her face again, that face slipping from his mind's grasp. Amid all the death has been her memory, the longing to touch her again. Despite this pull, he will take his men to Texas to hide out and let things settle, and there his men will gradually betray him one by one. But he doesn't know this now, as they race together for the border. There is so much, in fact, that Quantrill doesn't know.

He doesn't know that he'll never receive the recognition he so covets from the Confederate Army — no legitimization of him and his men, no General Quantrill; he doesn't know that months from now his men will abandon him, taking up with either Bloody Bill or George Todd, or so racked with guilt over their hand in the burning of Lawrence that they can no longer fight, returning to their families and farms; he doesn't know that only a handful of them will follow him to Kentucky, where he'll continue to fight in vain; he doesn't know that there he'll be shot and will die farther away from Kate than ever, buried in a simple idler's grave in Louisville; he doesn't know that his skull will be stolen and his eye sockets destined to garage the limp pricks of awkward freshman pledges in a generational fraternity ritual; he doesn't know that it'll be more than a hundred years before his body is exhumed and returned to the loam of Missouri, the people there split on whether to celebrate the occasion or to riot. What he knows now is only a word containing a desire, a wish of coming home, really: *Kate.*

It is morning once again, and the last twenty-four hours have taken on the coloring of whole calendars of time. There in the distance, as he crosses into Missouri, the sun appears in the sky, purple shading into blue shading into red, forming slowly up over the far-off hills like a blister, a blemish, a birthmark.

BAIRD HARPER

The School of the Art Institute of Chicago

INTERMODAL

The thing I wasn't allowed to tell anyone, especially my mother, was that my father lived in a portable freight unit with the Velvet Jim Morrison. He called it his river house, as if it were a place to spend a long weekend. I never spent a whole weekend there, but Dad and I had our Friday nights together, so I got to see it then. On Friday afternoons he'd pick me up and we'd drive around in the Dodge Diplomat for a while before making our way down through the abandoned factory district and into the shipping depot where he lived. I was fourteen years old and under permanent orders to tell my mother that we only ever went to SlugFest to hit the batting cages. It seemed a strange way to deceive her, but I decided to get over it when my father said I wasn't going to be a man until I got comfortable lying to the women in my life. But besides Mom, there were no women. "And *that*," he said, "is exactly what I'm trying to tell you."

After she kicked him out of the house, my father lived for a while at the Big Shoulders Motel. But he got sick of paying for rip-off Coke machines and a hot tub that wouldn't bubble, so he moved into a portable freight container in a massive shipping depot. The container was one of those oblong steel boxes covered in foreign graffiti with a garage door at one end. They came and went on train cars and flatbed trucks, and sometimes by the dozen on barges that trudged in from across the lake and parked on the river that bisected the shipping yard.

My father's container was right along the river. The metal was painted Chicago Bears colors, which he said he picked out so I'd be comfortable visiting him there. It had the words LU KANG INC stamped on the side, and one end was tagged with a spray-painted picture of a single bare breast with a dagger through it. When he took me to see the place for the first time, he explained that my mother wasn't to know he was in storage.

I told him it was getting hard for me to remember all the right things to say.

"You'll do fine," he said. "Besides, it won't be for long."

I watched one of the cranes loading other containers onto flatbed semitrucks. Dad scrambled my hair like he always did and said, "Oh, I get it." He picked up a chalky piece of gravel and wrote *Do Not Ship* on the door of his unit, and then below that, for the overseer's sake, he wrote, *Nein Shippen zis Craten!*

To stay at the shipping yard, my father paid off the overseer, a German self-mutilator whose Kraut guts we hated. Just talking about how much we hated him took up a good deal of our time together. Every day of his life the German wore a soccer jersey with the name of some Nazi town across the chest — Linz, Salzburg, Innsbruck — and a first-aid fanny pack around his waist for easy upkeep of his self-inflicted injuries. He was always covered in gauze pads and Ace bandages, as if for him each day were a break from the front of some nearby war no one else was fighting. The girls like that at school were called cutters. Mr. Bisoulis, the health teacher, had described it as a tragic and unpopular thing, but really it lent an air of mystery to the actress who starred in the movie they showed us, *You're Cutting Yourself to Pieces.* The German was no cutter. He was, according to my father, just pathetic and weird and probably dying for some attention.

"Tough guys don't draw attention to their wounds," said my father. "They go on like the injuries aren't even there. Tough guys just walk it off." In the seventies, he walked off a deadly snake bite. The story changed frequently. One time it was a blood viper in the redwood forest, and another time it was a dagger boa near Tijuana. Neither of those are actual snakes, but that didn't matter. He was trying to toughen me up from too much time spent with my mother, who'd already sissified me almost beyond his help.

The German allowed him to use the port-o-johns and to siphon electricity and water from the overseer's hut into his container, but the place still needed what my father called "bach-pad essentials," so we had work to do. One Friday evening the Diplomat pulled up in the alley behind the house, its engine roaring like a jumbo jet. As I came out of the house, I said, "Can't wait to hit the cages!" loud enough so he'd think Mom might hear.

"Just get in the car already." He was wearing his favorite hat, a white foam-bill cap with a Jiffy Lube logo on the front that had been scratched out with black marker. He craned his head, trying to find her face in the windows, and popped the trunk so I could ditch my backpack. I found what looked like a pipe bomb lying inside. It was a large metal thing, bulbous in the middle, with cut lengths of steel tubing coming out its top and bottom. Black fluid leaked into the wool trunk liner in a skull-shaped puddle.

My father drove with an ear turned upward, listening to the howl of the motor, and whenever we hit potholes he scanned the rearview, as though he feared parts might be falling off. In the console between us there was a syrupy amber liquid in a glass juice bottle. On the bottle's label someone had written JUST IN CASE.

I asked if there was something wrong with the car, but he acted as though he hadn't heard me. After I'd given up waiting for him to respond, and joined him at watching his hands on the wheel, he cleared his throat and said, casually, "Diplomat's running a tad loud today."

The velvet portrait of Jim Morrison, which he'd had cleaned and put into a new frame, rode upright in the backseat, buckled in. They'd been together — my father and the Velvet Jim — since the great high school days in California, and because I was the newer addition to Dad's life, I sometimes thought the Velvet Jim was jealous of me.

"What does your mother say about me coming back?" Dad asked as we thundered through a stale yellow light. "I'm interested in how this intermodal experiment goes, but everyone knows I really belong at home."

"What's an intermodal?"

"The big storage thingy," he said. "It's called an intermodal."

"Oh, cool. What does *Lu Kang* mean?"

"Jesus, I don't know." He slapped the sun visor up against the ceiling. "Forget that. Has she said when?"

"Not really."

"What *has* she said about me?"

"She hasn't said anything."

He gave me his famous sideways glance, as though I were guilty of buying into some grand scheme of hers. "She's sending me messages, son, and *you're* the messenger. So pay attention, or this little game she and I are playing is going to get all confused."

I screwed the top off the juice bottle and took a whiff of the amber liquid for no good reason. The vapors sizzled the insides of my nostrils.

"Jesus Christ, that's motor oil." He waited until I'd recapped it and put it back into the cup holder before smacking my hand away.

Part of me wondered if he was planning on drinking the stuff. I knew that you could drink rubbing alcohol, and I knew that meth was basically just Drano and cold medicine, so I figured you could probably get high off anything powerful. And if the stories his friends told were true, my father was the kind of man who would drink almost anything on a dare. Sometimes my mother asked whether he drank much while we hung out on Fridays, and I'd remind her that they didn't serve booze at SlugFest. "Oh, right, of course," she'd say, already dropping the subject. "I forgot. The *batting cages.*"

When I asked him if he was planning on drinking the oil, he erupted into a wild seizure-laugh and swerved the car as though the question were stupid enough to have almost killed us. "What? No," he said. "That shit'll kill you." I wondered if he meant this literally, or if it was just too strong for people less manly than him. "Besides," he added, "I'm sober now." Hearing himself say this, he nodded, agreeing with the idea.

We crossed the tracks and angled onto the street where all the pawnshops were. Boulevard Swap was stolen electronics. Ukrainian mobsters smoked unfiltereds in the gangway while waiting for trucks to show up. Goose's Secondhand was clothing: cracked leather jackets and polyester suits people had died in. The back room had shelves and shelves of old *Playboy*s fatigued with dog-ears and heavy with the oil off people's hands. Chi-Pawn was lethal exotics: cases full of Nazi bayonets and tooth necklaces, throwing stars, and a giant wall of broadswords. Once in a while, my father would take me in there just to look. "I'll get you a sword," he'd announce as though he were daring me to hold him to it. Mel's Seconds was housewares, and that's where we were headed, because Dad needed a lamp and a hot plate for the river house.

"I guess I'm nesting," he said. As the engine died it made a sound like a dog does when it's trying to cough up its stomach. He popped the trunk and lifted the pipe bomb gingerly into his arms as if it were a drooling robot baby.

Inside the shop we browsed, trailing drip spots behind us. We found a hot plate with a corner where the white plastic had turned the color of toasted marshmallow, a miniature space heater with screws missing, a power strip a dog had gotten at, and one of those classy bronze desk lamps with the green glass dome like you see in the pictures of Harvard's library.

"These things are all damaged," said Dad, parking the bomb on Mel's glass-top counter. "I'll expect a serious discount."

"What the hell is that?" said Mel. A scar the shape of a lightning bolt zigzagged from the bridge of his nose to the corner of his mouth.

"Catalytic converter," said my father, tapping the metal housing. "There's a hundred bucks' worth of platinum in there. All you gotta do is take it to a salvage yard."

"Platinum?"

"Sure, it's a catalytic *converter*," he said, his voice growing exasperated. "The gangbangers cut them off the bottoms of cars all the time. For the money."

"A hundred bucks?"

"Maybe more, maybe a hundred and fifty," said my father. "Eighty, at least."

Mel dragged glazed eyes across the things in my arms. Spiderwebs and dead bug parts clogged the empty bulb socket of the Harvard lamp.

"A hundred bucks my ass," Mel said. But then, casting a hateful look at the catalytic converter, he shrugged and said, "What the hell."

"How do you like that?" said Dad. "We're bartering now."

While I loaded the things into the trunk, Dad unscrewed the bulb from the electric lantern above Mel's door, giving off a little yelp each time he touched it. I was sure that Mel was going to see him doing it and come out and kill us, but Dad didn't quit until the bulb dropped into his hat.

The Diplomat screamed back to life. It sounded as if different parts of the engine were battling each other, and there was a large puddle of fresh oil where we'd been parked, but Dad didn't seem to notice any of it. As we sped away, he hung a satisfied look on his face, turning toward me occasionally so I could see he'd planned things just the way they were going.

"What's a catalytic converter?"

"It isn't anything," he said. "It's a scam is what it is."

"Is that why the car's dripping?"

The satisfied look drained off his face. "I might've nicked the oil pan with the Sawzall. No big worry." He made a long, phlegmy throat clear to recapture the conversation. "A catalytic converter isn't shit, you see. It's just a thing to make you pay a higher sticker."

I had my doubts about this, but if there were any areas in which my father could claim expertise, cars might have been one of them. He knew about smelt fishing — that was for sure — and he knew all the kinds of clouds, but also I think he knew how cars worked. I'd seen him change tires and buff out a scratch on a door, and once, before going missing for an April some years earlier, he'd had a job interview at Jiffy Lube.

The engine began surging wildly. It could have been a motorcycle gang revving behind us, except that there was no one else waiting for the light to turn.

"What should we eat?" he yelled above the noise.

I'd had Indian food on my mind ever since my mom had brought home leftovers from a place on Devon, but my father's jaw was clenching each time the RPM needle spiked, so I decided to keep it to myself and said, "The Saber, of course."

The Saber was a diner like all those kinds of diners are, except instead of a condom dispenser in the bathroom, there was an iron box that spat out baseball card–size photos of naked chicks riding horses through mountain meadows. Back when I first started collecting them, I used to think there was a ranch somewhere out West where the models and their horses hung out, and that all they probably did all day was wash their hair and eat carrots while waiting for the most ideal summer weather to go out and do a photo shoot. It was a place that had entered my dreams, and I believed for a long time that someday I'd go try and find it.

Since our last visit, the dispenser had been dented horribly. There were black rubber streaks all over it, as though someone had been shooting a hockey puck at it, and the whole thing slumped away from its mount in the drywall. I already had the entire series of cards — twenty-four in all — but I put a quarter in just to see if the machinery still worked. The thumb dial wouldn't turn at first, and then with some force it swallowed my quarter, but no card dropped down. I'd been hoping for the tan girl with the Indian braids and the gleaming hatchet on her belt, which was the only thing she wore, if you didn't count the saddle horn and the windblown mane of the gray colt, which obscured certain parts of her in an exciting way. I already had two of her back home with all the others, but for some reason I really wanted to see her right then, right at that moment. I gave the iron box a shake, felt the wicked dents beneath my fingers, and backed off.

"I ordered you a burger." My father was working some dirt out from under his fingernails with the tine of a fork. "What took you so long in there?"

"Nothing." I could still feel the dispenser's metal on my fingers.

After dinner we got to the shipping yard just as the German was beginning his evening rounds. He'd done something awful to the back of his hand, and as he strolled about he kept the wound elevated by holding the cuff of his sleeve in his teeth. A roll of gauze was wrapped around the hand, but even from a distance we could see the dark red flower coming through the bandaging.

"Look at this idiot," said Dad.

We pulled past the German and parked beside a deconstructed tugboat hull. The car gave off two loud pops, and then the engine died almost before my father could turn it off.

The German balanced his wounded hand across the top of his head, waving at us with his good hand. "Remember!" he shouted across the gravel. "Monthly!"

My father didn't wave back. "Don't even acknowledge that," he whispered. "We had a deal I'd pay by the week, and now that Kraut wants a whole month at a time. Like I'm some sort of renter."

He looked at my face and I knew what he wanted me to say, but I couldn't say it.

"Like he thinks he's my goddamn *landlord* or something." My father leaned into the backseat to unbuckle the Velvet Jim. "I'd put down a month's worth and the next day your mother would call and beg me to come back." He looked at me again, a straight-on stabbing look. "Trust me," he said, pulling his eyes back out of me, "that's always how it goes."

The intermodal had improved since I'd seen it the week before. He'd gotten a mini-fridge and a fraying wicker love seat. The mattress had been pushed to the far end, and an old faux-wood radio perched on a milk crate beside the bed. He put the Harvard lamp on the crate and said, "There. Something to read by."

I looked around for anything with words on it. The bottom of the frame on the Velvet Jim read: MR. MOJO RISIN. I suppose I hated the Velvet Jim as much as it hated me. The day my mother had had enough of my father, he came into my bedroom with an empty duffel bag and that portrait tucked under his arm. He said, "Well, son, we're taking off for a while." I thought that "we" meant him and me, and that I was perhaps going into that duffel bag. But he shook his head and laughed. "I'm already in enough trouble with your mother as it is." A few minutes later, the screen door clacked. My father put the Velvet Jim in the shotgun seat, and the two of them peeled away together.

Now he pulled the little brass chain on the Harvard lamp and the intermodal filled with a soft green light. He tested out each of his new appliances, and when they'd all proved themselves, he flicked on the radio to the classic rock station. He got a Coke from the fridge for me and, without hesitation, a beer for himself. We pulled beach chairs to the open end of the intermodal so we could watch the orange evening sky fade beyond the river. Wisps of cirrus clouds glowed above the city like warm coals.

"Just the men tonight," he said. "Who needs anybody else?"

We talked fishing for a while, agreeing that if we ever trolled the bottom of that river, there'd be heavy fighting carp down there, giant poisoned catfish. Nothing you could eat, but if we could get one up on land, he said, we could have a hell of a time beating it to death.

"What's she doing tonight, anyway?" He snapped back the ring on a new beer.

I wondered if there were enough cans left in the fridge to put my drive home in any kind of jeopardy. "I think she went out for Indian food."

"*In*dian food," he said, forcing breaths through his teeth to make the sound of laughter. "I believe *that*. Who eats *Indian* food?"

"Yeah, she doesn't even like it."

The lights of half a dozen planes hovered in a perfect dotted line connecting down toward O'Hare. I was sure we were both seeing this, but turning to him, I could tell his thoughts were somewhere else. His brow was furrowed over his eyes as if he were performing long division in his head.

"Then why would she eat it?" he finally asked.

I closed one eye, held my arm out, touching each sparkling blip in the sky.

"If she doesn't even like it," he said, "then what? Someone's making her eat it?"

"Mr. Gupta," I said.

"Who's Mr. Gupta?"

I didn't know, really, except that he was the man who taught the entrepreneurs' course my mother had been taking on Wednesday nights. When I told Dad this, he did another moment's worth of math in his head. He threw the beer can against his mouth and I could hear his teeth scraping the aluminum as he chugged it.

"Entrepreneurs' class?" He stood up, letting the empty can teeter and fall off the arm of his chair. "We should join them for dinner."

"I think they're just friends," I assured him.

He looked startled by what my words assumed. "Oh, yes, I'm sure of *that*. She and Mr. Goober are *just friends*."

Right then, the reek of the river hit me — the smell of rust and mushy tires, toxic fish skeletons. A sip of warm Coke stalled like syrup on my tongue, and when I stood up in search of a fresh pocket of air, Dad took my sleeve and we charged off toward the car, pacing along the green belt of lamplight. Inside the Diplomat it was dark, fully night, and I could see nothing except the silver edges of my father's face and the glints off his class ring.

"But I don't even know what the restaurant is called."

"How many Indian places can there be in this city?" He turned the key, but the car wouldn't start. It wouldn't even try. There was only a clicking sound and the static tinkling of electricity filling up wires. And then the crunch of footsteps coming at us across the gravel. Dad kicked his door open and spun back out of the car. The battery continued emptying its charge into the engine block, and I was sure that if I touched the metal door handle it would electrocute me.

In the mirror on my side of the car, the German came mincing out of the darkness. Half his face lit up as he stepped into the stream of light stretching from the open end of the intermodal. "Excuse me," he called out, waving his big gauze-wrapped hand. "I don't think you heard me before, so I —"

My father's body streaked into view, his arm and fist turning a quick arc through the air, and when he'd passed across the mirror, the German was gone.

I grabbed the door handle and it popped open, innocently. The German lay behind the rear bumper, facedown, his arms clearing angel wings in the gravel. Finally, he got ahold of the ground and pushed himself up into a kneeling position. His palms came together on either side of his nose, like he was going to start praying, and the first lines of blood spread down its bridge. He dropped his hands away, digging into his fanny pack. The blood tracked into the creases framing his mouth. Eels of pink snot darted in and out of his nostrils with every wheeze.

My father stood back, watching the German from a space just beyond the light. He turned the class ring, opened and closed his fist. "You wanna be hurt?" He lunged forward, seized the German's injured hand, jammed a thumb into the red spot on the gauze. "Next time you wanna hurt yourself, come over and I'll do it for you." He kicked some gravel as though it, too, were testing his patience, then stalked back to the car.

The German curled downward, pushing his face toward his knees, blowing his nosebleed into the bandaging. As I knelt beside him to see how bad the cut was, I could hear my father twisting the key in the steering column, pumping the accelerator. The underside of the car dribbled oil, and when the starter suddenly cranked and the engine lit up, black fluid gushed out. I got back in.

We hauled down the dock flats toward the western hazmat exit. The planes over O'Hare were crazy now, like lightning bugs circling the dark, blind to everything but each other.

"Why does he do that to himself?" Dad yelled into the center of the steering wheel. "It's like he's been begging me to kick the shit out of him."

"Are we still going to the restaurant?" I asked.

The engine's scream choked off, leaving only a hollow revolving sound like a quarter fluttering against a tabletop. The steering locked up, and Dad jammed the brakes to keep us from careening into the river. He took his hands off the wheel and dropped them into his lap. The glow coming off the dashboard instruments made the streaks of blood on his knuckles look black.

"Do you have any idea," he said, "how many Indian restaurants there probably are in this city?"

I had no idea. I figured dozens by the tone of his question, but there was definitely at least that one. And Mom was there, probably ordering another basket of naan and chatting with some guy neither of us knew. I could see them in my head — all those great suffocating Indian food smells curling around them, Mr. Gupta telling entrepreneur stories, and Mom listening hard, knowing there were probably lies inside his words, but also maybe some truth.

I could hear the battery still offering charge, but the engine wasn't going to start this time, and we both knew it. My father pushed back against the headrest, trying to pull deep breaths into his chest. His hand had little strings of knuckle blood down to where he wiped them off against his pant leg. Then he turned on the radio. It was one of the songs he knew all the words to, but he wasn't singing along.

"We could get out," I suggested, "and look under the hood." I wondered if the bottle full of oil was the answer, wondered if I should tell him how bad the leak was under the car.

He caught me staring at the bottle, snatched the thing from the cup holder, and carried it out onto the slim band of concrete between the car and the ledge. When I got out on my side, he'd disappeared. But then I found him sitting against the front tire with his legs dangling over the edge.

"What a lousy night," he said, twisting the bottle's cap off and on.

"It hasn't been lousy," I protested. "I'm having fun."

The radio faded into a Doors song, but it didn't seem to register with my father, so I went to turn up the volume. When I came back around the trunk, I could see the German, football fields away, stumbling toward us along the flats.

"I can always tell when you're bullshitting me." My father had the cap all the way off the oil bottle now. "But I suppose it's okay to be a lousy bullshitter. I bet some people even like you for it." Dad hadn't spotted the German yet, but the German had seen us, and he was getting closer. He tugged himself through the darkness with a severe limp, and as he drew near I could almost hear the snot buzzing in his nostrils.

My father stared into the bottle. It was the way he looked at a beer before chugging it, as if it were going to tell him the truth about everything. "I'm sorry," he called out, loud enough to stop the German in his tracks.

"What?" I asked.

"I'm not talking to you, son, I'm talking to Adolph there." He looked up and squinted out at the figure standing off in the darkness. The German had covered the cut on his nose with a butterfly bandage and wrapped his hand in a fresh mile of gauze. "Is that what you want to hear? That I'm sorry?"

The German shifted his torso from one hip to the other. "I could throw you out of here."

"Why the hell do you cut yourself up like that?"

"You're wrong about me." The German scratched his cheek near the new bandage. "I'm not even German. I am Austrian. And my name is not Adolph."

They kept talking like that, like people who couldn't even hear each other. And I stood there, feeling the night settling into the Diplomat's steel shell, listening to the river carry their words away like so much useless sludge.

The next Friday, my father called the house to tell my mother he wasn't going to be around to have me over. Some weeks after that, a postcard arrived with my name on it. The front had a picture of a sea otter floating on its back, with the words LOVELY MONTEREY BAY written in big orange lettering. *They shipped me away after all!* read his note on the back of the card, and then it continued on with a brief description of how salty the seawater was. More postcards came every few weeks after that — a black bear at "Majestic Yosemite," an old photograph of the Birdman of Alcatraz — each offering minor details of his life, and each stamped by the Illinois post office from which they'd been sent.

Around Thanksgiving, after I got a postcard with a whale on it from some place called Big Sur, I rode my bike down to the shipping depot. It was almost too cold to ride, but I wanted some answers before winter descended on the city. The shipping yard hadn't changed much, but it had changed a little. The intermodals were organized into neater rows than before, stacked five and six high like apartment buildings, and the corridors between them were quiet gravel streets. I could imagine someone living in every single unit, a town of movable river houses, everybody's father waiting for the call to come home.

His intermodal was still there, but badly damaged. One side of it wore huge indentations I could almost sit in, and at the far end were several pairs of holes looking like the stabs of forklift tusks. I hunkered down behind a pile of scrap metal and staked out the overseer's hut. I wasn't sure what I was doing there exactly, but in my coat pocket I held a rusty railroad spike.

An hour into my stakeout, my ears began to ache from the cold. I'd been sharpening the rail spike against a broken truck axle to keep my blood warm, but the afternoon sky had gone dark gray and I wasn't sure how much longer I could wait. Then a figure flashed behind the venetian blinds and the German came out of his hut. But it wasn't the German — it was an old man with silver hair and a warm-smelling pipe he lit up as he began his rounds. I followed this man down a long gravel corridor into a field of old ship anchors and truck tires, until I finally lost sight of him behind a city block of freight.

When I got home, I went up to my room to get another look at the postcards. I kept them hidden behind a Jimi Hendrix poster, in a hole I'd punched in the drywall. They were there with the naked chicks on horseback and some money I was saving. "The intermodal has been shipped again!" he'd written on the top of the Big Sur postcard. Mom knocked, and I tossed the nudes into my desk drawer. She came in and touched the cold away from the edges of my ears, reading over my shoulder. She asked me what an intermodal was, and even though it didn't matter anymore, I managed not to tell her.

CONTRIBUTORS

Born in the Seattle area, LESLIE BARNARD is currently an MFA student at the University of Oregon in Eugene. She is working on a collection of short stories.

ANDREW BRININSTOOL's work has received the 2007 Sherwood Anderson Foundation Fiction Award from *Mid-American Review,* runner-up notation from the *Playboy* College Fiction Contest, and the Editors' Prize from *New Ohio Review,* and has appeared in numerous journals. A recent graduate of the University of Houston's MFA program, he is currently at work on a novel.

GREG CHANGNON received his MFA from San Francisco State University. His work has appeared in the *North American Review,* the *Atlanta Journal-Constitution, Paste Magazine,* and elsewhere. His story "How the Nurse Feels," which appeared in *Scribner's Best of the Fiction Workshops 1998,* was adapted into a musical that was presented in 2008 at the 13th Annual ASCAP Foundation/Disney Musical Theatre Workshop. He teaches junior high in Atlanta, Georgia, and is currently at work on a memoir titled *Better With Strangers.*

EMILY FREEMAN grew up in the suburbs of New York City and currently lives in Minneapolis. She received an MFA from the University of Minnesota, and participated in the Mentor Series in Poetry and Creative Prose at the Loft Literary Center, where she also teaches. Emily is working on a novel and a memoir.

BAIRD HARPER wrote "Intermodal" as a student at the School of the Art Institute of Chicago. His fiction has appeared in *Best New American Voices 2009, Tin House, CutBank, Mid-American Review,* and *Cairn.* He lives in Chicago with his wife, Anastasia.

DAVID LOMBARDI was born in Michigan. He is a graduate of Miami University and received his MFA in fiction from Eastern Washington University. Currently, he is a Ph.D. candidate at the University of Houston and is working on a novel called *The Revelator.* He lives in Houston with his wife and their beautiful daughter, Josephine.

ANDREW MALAN MILWARD is a graduate of the Iowa Writers' Workshop and is currently the James C. McCreight Fiction Fellow at the University of Wisconsin. His stories have appeared in *Zoetrope, The Southern Review, Columbia, Conjunctions, Arts & Letters, The Literary Review, Crazyhorse, Failbetter, Fugue, Confrontation* magazine, and *Nimrod.* Having just finished his first novel, he is at work on a book about the radical social and political history of his home state of Kansas, to which "The Burning of Lawrence" will belong. He lives in Madison.

CHRISTIAN MOODY is a Ph.D. student in English (fiction dissertation) at the University of Cincinnati. His work has appeared in *Best American Fantasy 2008, The Cincinnati Review, Faultline, Indiana Review,* and elsewhere. He received an MFA in creative writing from Syracuse University and a grant from the Constance Saltonstall Foundation for the Arts. He's currently finishing the second draft of a novel about a secret museum of voyeurism, the Underground Railroad, strange methods of blackmail, a themed housing development, and the disappearance of a spouse.

Since earning a BA in English from Yale in 2002, CLAIRE O'CONNOR has taught in Morocco, in Massachusetts, in the woods of New Jersey, in California, and at the University of Idaho, where she earned her MFA in creative writing. In between teaching gigs, she has worked, among other jobs, as a bartender, a dog walker, a tour guide, a retail sales associate, and a freelance music reviewer. She grew up in Fallbrook, California, and currently lives in New York. "Cape Town" is her first published story.

BOOMER PINCHES's work has appeared in *The Massachusetts Review* and *Global Widespread Panic.* He has lived in Boston, London, Istanbul, and Australia but considers New York his home. He received a fellowship to attend the MFA Program for Poets and Writers at the University of Massachusetts, where he received the Deborah Slosberg Memorial Award for Poetry. He has just completed a collection of stories and is currently at work on a novel and a book of poetry.

DAVID JAMES POISSANT's stories have appeared in *Playboy,* the *Chicago Tribune, Willow Springs,* the *Chattahoochee Review, Redivider,* and the anthology *New Stories from the South 2008.* He has won the *Playboy* College Fiction Contest, the AWP Quickie Contest, the George Garrett Fiction Award, second prize in the *Atlantic Monthly* Student Writing Contest, and he was runner-up for the 2006 Nelson Algren Award. His stories have been nominated for the AWP Intro Journals Award and the Pushcart Prize. He is currently a Ph.D. candidate at the University of Cincinnati. This is his second appearance in Best New American Voices.

EDWARD PORTER is a recent graduate of the Warren Wilson MFA program. He was a creative writing fellow at the University of Wisconsin–Madison for 2007–2008, and his fiction has appeared in *Colorado Review* and *Inch Magazine.*

TIMOTHY SCOTT is a graduate of the MFA program at NYU and was recently the Carl Djerassi Fiction Fellow at the Wisconsin Institute for Creative Writing. His fiction has appeared in *The Massachusetts Review, New Orleans Review,* and *Colorado Review;* two of his stories have received Pushcart Prize nominations.

LYSLEY TENORIO was a 2007–2008 John Steinbeck Fellow at San Jose State University. His stories have appeared in *Atlantic Monthly, Ploughshares, MANOA,* the *Chicago Tribune,* and *The Pushcart Prize.* A former Wallace Stegner Fellow at Stanford University, he has also received fellowships from the University of Wisconsin, Yaddo, The MacDowell Colony, and the National Endowment for the Arts. In 2008, he received a Whiting Writers Award. He has completed a collection of stories and is currently working on a novel. He teaches at Saint Mary's College in Moraga, California.

TED THOMPSON grew up in Connecticut. He is a recent graduate of the Iowa Writers' Workshop, where he was given a Truman Capote Fellowship. He has also been a Work-Study Scholar at the Bread Loaf Writers' Conference. He is currently completing a collection of short stories and working on a novel.

LAURA VAN DEN BERG received her MFA from Emerson College. Her fiction has appeared in *The Literary Review, Boston Review, American Short Fiction, One Story,* and *The Best American Nonrequired Reading 2008,* among others. "Up High in the Air" is from her debut story collection, *What the World Will Look Like When All the Water Leaves Us,* which will be published by Dzanc Books in November 2009.

PARTICIPANTS

Backspace Writers Conference
P.O. Box 454
Washington, MI 48094
732/267-6449

Binghamton University
Binghamton Center for Writers
P.O. Box 6000
Binghamton, NY 13902-6000
607/777-2713

Boise State University
MFA Program in Writing
1910 University Drive
Boise, ID 83725-1525
208/426-2413

Boston University
Graduate Creative Writing Program
236 Bay State Road
Boston, MA 02215
617/353-2510

Bowling Green State University
Creative Writing Program
Department of English
Bowling Green, OH 43403-0215
419/372-8370

The Bread Loaf Writers' Conference
Middlebury College — P&W
Middlebury, VT 05753
802/443-5286

Brown University
Literary Arts Program
Box 1923
Providence, RI 02912
401/863-3260

California State University, Sacramento
English Department
6000 J Street
Sacramento, CA 95919-6075
916/278-6586

The City College of New York
English Department
6/219 North Academic Building
160 Convent Avenue
New York, NY 10031
212/650-5407

Colorado State University
MFA Creative Writing Program
English Department
1773 Eddy Hall
Fort Collins, CO 80523-1773
970/491-6428

Columbia University
Writing Division, School of the Arts
415 Dodge Hall
2960 Broadway
New York, NY 10027
212/854-4391

Cornell University
Department of English
Goldwin Smith Hall
Ithaca, NY 14851
607/255-6800

Eastern Washington University
Creative Writing Program
705 West First Avenue
Spokane, WA 99201-3900
509/623-4221

Emerson College
Department of Writing, Literature,
and Publishing
120 Boylston Street
Boston, MA 02116
617/824-8500

Fairleigh Dickinson University
MFA in Creative Writing
M-MS3-01
Madison, NJ 07940
973/443-8632

Fine Arts Work Center
in Provincetown
24 Pearl Street
Provincetown, MA 02657
508/487-9960

Florida International University
English Department
Biscayne Bay Campus
3000 NE 151st Street
North Miami, FL 33181
305/919-5857

Florida State University
Creative Writing Program
English Department
Tallahassee, FL 32306-1580
850/644-4230

George Mason University
Creative Writing Program
English Department
4400 University Drive, MS 3E4
Fairfax, VA 22030
703/993-1180

Georgia State University
Creative Writing Program
Department of English
38 Peachtree Center Avenue, Suite 923
Atlanta, GA 30303-3083
404/413-2000

Grub Street
160 Boylston Street, 4th Floor
Boston, MA 02116
617/695-0075

Hamline University
MFA in Writing Program
Graduate School of Liberal Studies
1536 Hewitt Avenue
St. Paul, MN 55104-1284
651/523-2047

Humber College
The Humber School for Writers
3199 Lakeshore Boulevard West
Toronto, Ontario M8V 1K8
416/675-6622

Hunter College
MFA in Creative Writing
Department of English
695 Park Avenue
New York, NY 10021
212/772-5164

Indiana University
Creative Writing Program
English Department
442 Ballantine Hall
1020 East Kirkwood Avenue
Bloomington, IN 47405-7103
812/855-9539

Johns Hopkins University
The Writing Seminars
3400 North Charles Street
Baltimore, MD 21218
410/516-6286

Johns Hopkins Writing
Program — Washington
1717 Massachusetts Avenue, NW,
Suite 101
Washington, DC 20036
202/452-1123

Kansas State University
Department of English
108 English/Counseling
Services Building
Manhattan, KS 66506-6501
785/532-6716

Lesley University
MFA Program in Creative Writing
29 Everett Street
Cambridge, MA 02138
617/349-8369

The Loft Literary Center
Mentor Series Program
Suite 200, Open Brook
1011 Washington Avenue South
Minneapolis, MN 55415
612/215-2575

Louisiana State University
MFA in Creative Writing
English Department
Baton Rouge, LA 70803
225/578-5922

Manhattanville College
MA in Writing Program
School of Graduate & Professional
Studies
2900 Purchase Street
Purchase, NY 10577
914/323-5239

The Manhattanville Summer
Writers' Week
Manhattanville College
2900 Purchase Street
Purchase, NY 10577
914/323-5300

McNeese State University
Department of Languages
P.O. Box 92655
Lake Charles, LA 70609-2665
337/475-5197

Miami University
Creative Writing Program
Department of English
356 Bachelor Hall
Oxford, OH 45056
513/529-5221

The Michener Center for Writers
University of Texas, Austin
702 East Dean Keeton Street
Austin, TX 78705
512/471-1601

Mills College
Creative Writing Program
5000 MacArthur Boulevard
Oakland, CA 94613
510/430-3130

Minnesota State University, Mankato
MFA in Creative Writing
Department of English
230 Armstrong Hall
Mankato, MN 56001
507/389-2117

Mississippi State University
Department of English
P.O. Box E
Mississippi State, MS 39762
662/325-3644

Napa Valley Writers' Conference
Napa Valley College
1088 College Avenue
St. Helena, CA 94574
707/967-2900

Naropa University
Program in Writing and Poetics
2130 Arapahoe Avenue
Boulder, CO 80302
303/546-3508

New Mexico State University
Department of English
Box 30001, MSC 3E
Las Cruces, NM 88003
505/646-3931

New York University
Creative Writing Program
Lillian Vernon Creative Writers House
58 West 10th Street
New York, NY 10011
212/998-8816

Northwestern University
Master of Arts in Creative Writing
School of Continuing Studies
405 Church Street
Evanston, IL 60208-4220
847/491-5612

Ohio State University
MFA in Creative Writing
Department of English
451 Denney Hall
164 West 17th Avenue
Columbus, OH 43210-1370
614/292-2242

Oklahoma State University
Creative Writing Program
English Department
205 Morrill Hall
Stillwater, OK 74078
405/744-9474

Pennsylvania State University
MFA Program in Creative Writing
117 Burrowes Building
University Park, PA 16802
814/863-0258

Purdue University
Creative Writing Program
Department of English
West Lafayette, IN 47907-2038
765/494-3740

Roosevelt University, Chicago Campus
School of Liberal Arts
430 South Michigan Avenue
Chicago, IL 60605-1394
312/341-3710

Rosemont College
MFA in Creative Writing
1400 Montgomery Avenue
Rosemont, PA 19010
610/527-0200, ext. 2994

Rutgers–Newark
MFA Program in Creative Writing
Department of English
622 Hill Hall
350 Martin Luther King Jr. Boulevard
Newark, NJ 07102
973/353-5729

Saint Mary's College of California
MFA Program in Creative Writing
P.O. Box 4686
Moraga, CA 94575-4686
925/631-4762

San Francisco State University
Creative Writing Department
1600 Holloway Avenue
San Francisco, CA 94132-4162
415/338-1891

San Jose State University
Steinbeck Fellows Program
Department of English and
Comparative Literature
San Jose, CA 95192-0202
408/924-4432

Sarah Lawrence College
Graduate Writing Program
1 Mead Way
Bronxville, NY 10708-5999
914/337-0700

The School of the Art Institute
of Chicago
MFA in Writing Program
37 South Wabash Avenue
Chicago, IL 60603-3103
312/899-5094

Sewanee Writers' Conference
119 Gailor Hall
735 University Avenue
Sewanee, TN 37383-1000
931/598-1141

Sirenland Writers Conference
P.O. Box 248
Bethlehem, CT 06751
www.sirenland.net

Spalding University
MFA in Writing
851 South Fourth Street
Louisville, KY 40203
502/585-9911

Stanford University
Creative Writing Program
Department of English
Stanford, CA 94305-2087
650/725-1208

Syracuse University
MFA in Creative Writing
420 Hall of Languages
Syracuse, NY 13244-1170
315/443-2174

Taos Summer Writers' Conference
Department of English Language
and Literature
MSC 03 2170 1
University of New Mexico
Albuquerque, NM 87131-0001
505/277-5572

Texas A&M University
Creative Writing Program
English Department
College Station, TX 77843-4227
979/845-3452

Texas State University–San Marcos
MFA Program in Creative Writing
Department of English
601 University Drive
San Marcos, TX 78666-4616
512/245-2111

University of Alabama
Program in Creative Writing
Department of English
103 Morgan Hall
P.O. Box 870244
Tuscaloosa, AL 35487-0244
205/348-5065

University of Alaska Fairbanks
MFA Program in Creative Writing
Department of English
P.O. Box 755720
Fairbanks, AK 99775-5720
907/474-7193

University of Arizona
Creative Writing MFA Program
445 Modern Languages Building
P.O. Box 210067
Tucson, AZ 85721-0067
520/621-3880

University of Arkansas
Program in Creative Writing
Department of English
333 Kimpel Hall
Fayetteville, AR 72701
479/575-4301

University of Baltimore
MFA in Creative Writing and
Publishing Arts
Office of Graduate Admissions
1420 North Charles Street
Baltimore, MD 21201
410/837-6022

University of British Columbia
Creative Writing Program
Buchanan E462—1866 Main Mall
Vancouver, BC V6T 1Z1
604/822-0699

University of Calgary
Department of English
1152 Social Sciences Building
2500 University Drive NW
Calgary, Alberta T2N 1N4
403/220-5470

University of California, Davis
MA in Creative Writing
Department of English
One Shields Avenue
Davis, CA 95616
530/752-2281

University of Central Florida
MFA Program in Creative Writing
Department of English
P.O. Box 161346
Orlando, FL 32816-1346
407/823-5254

University of Central Oklahoma
Department of Creative Studies
Department of English
Edmond, OK 73034-0184
405/974-5667

University of Cincinnati
Creative Writing Program
Department of English and
Comparative Literature
ML 69
Cincinnati, OH 45221-0069
513/556-5924

University of Colorado at Boulder
MFA in Creative Writing
Department of English
Campus Box 226
Boulder, CO 80309-0226
303/492-1853

University of Denver
Creative Writing Program
Department of English
Sturm Hall
Denver, CO 80208
303/871-2266

University of Florida
MFA Program
Department of English
P.O. Box 117310
Gainesville, FL 32611-7310
352/392-6650, ext. 225

University of Houston
Creative Writing Program
Department of English
229 Roy Cullen
Houston, TX 77004-3015
713/743-3015

University of Idaho
Creative Writing Program
Department of English
P.O. Box 441102
Moscow, ID 83844-1102
208/885-6156

University of Illinois at Chicago
Program for Writers
Department of English
M/C 162
601 South Morgan Street
Chicago, IL 60607-7120
312/413-2200

University of Illinois at
Urbana–Champaign
MFA in Creative Writing
210 English Building
608 South Wright Street
Urbana, IL 61801
217/333-2391

University of Iowa
Creative Writing Program
102 Dey House
507 North Clinton Street
Iowa City, IA 52242
319/335-0416

University of Louisville
Creative Writing Program
Department of English
315 Bingham Humanities
Louisville, KY 40292
502/852-6801

University of Massachusetts, Amherst
MFA Program for Poets and Writers
Department of English
130 Hicks Way
Amherst, MA 01003-9269
413/545-0643

University of Miami
Creative Writing Program
Department of English
P.O. Box 248145
Coral Gables, FL 33124
305/284-2182

University of Michigan
MFA in Creative Writing Program
Department of English
3187 Angell Hall
Ann Arbor, MI 48109-1003
734/936-2274

University of Minnesota
Creative Writing Program
222 Lind Hall
207 Church Street, SE
Minneapolis, MN 55455-0134
612/625-6366

University of Mississippi
MFA in Creative Writing
Department of English
Bondurant Hall C128
Oxford, MS 38677-1848
662/915-7439

University of Missouri–Columbia
Creative Writing Program
Department of English
107 Tate Hall
Columbia, MO 65211-1500
573/884-7773

University of Missouri–St. Louis
MFA in Creative Writing
Department of English
One University Boulevard
St. Louis, MO 63121-4400
314/516-6845

University of Montana–Missoula
Creative Writing Program
Department of English
Missoula, MT 59812-1013
406/243-5231

University of Nebraska–Lincoln
Creative Writing Program
Department of English
202 Andrews Hall
Lincoln, NE 68588-0333
402/472-3191

University of Nebraska–Omaha
MFA in Writing
6001 Dodge Street/WFAB 310
Omaha, NE 68182-0324
402/554-3020

University of Nevada, Las Vegas
MFA in Creative Writing International
and Schaeffer Ph.D. in Creative Writing
English Department
4505 Maryland Parkway
Las Vegas, NV 89154-5011
702/895-3533

University of New Hampshire
MFA in Writing Program
Department of English
Hamilton Smith Hall
95 Main Street
Durham, NH 03824-3574
603/862-1313

University of New Mexico
Creative Writing Program
Department of English Language
and Literature
Humanities Bldg., 2nd Floor
Albuquerque, NM 87131
505/277-6347

University of New Orleans
Creative Writing Workshop
Department of English
LA 279
New Orleans, LA 70148
504/280-7454

University of North Carolina
at Greensboro
MFA Writing Program
P.O. Box 26170
Greensboro, NC 27402
336/334-5459

University of North Dakota
Creative Writing Program
Department of English
P.O. Box 7209
Grand Forks, ND 58202
701/777-3321

University of North Texas
Creative Writing Division
Department of English
P.O. Box 311307
Denton, TX 76203
940/565-2050

University of Notre Dame
Creative Writing Program
Department of English
356 O'Shaughnessy Hall
Notre Dame, IN 46556-5639
574/631-7526

University of Oregon
Creative Writing Program
144 Columbia Hall
P.O. Box 5243
Eugene, OR 97403-5243
541/346-3944

University of Pittsburgh
MFA in Writing
English Department
526 Cathedral of Learning
4200 Fifth Avenue
Pittsburgh, PA 15260-0001
412/624-6506

University of San Francisco
MFA in Writing Program
2130 Fulton Street, KA 302
San Francisco, CA 94117-1080
415/422-6066

University of South Carolina
MFA in Creative Writing Program
Department of English
Columbia, SC 29208
803/777-4203

University of Tennessee
Creative Writing Program
Department of English
301 McClung Tower
Knoxville, TN 37996
865/974-5401

University of Texas, Austin
Creative Writing Program
Department of English
1 University Station B5000
Austin, TX 78712-0195
512/471-5132

University of Utah
Creative Writing Program
255 South Central Campus Drive,
Room 3500
Salt Lake City, UT 84112-0494
801/585-6168

University of Virginia
Creative Writing Program
219 Bryan Hall
P.O. Box 400121
Charlottesville, VA 22904-4121
434/924-6675

University of Washington
Creative Writing Program
Box 354330
Seattle, WA 98195-4330
206/543-9865

University of Windsor
MA in English: Literature and
Creative Writing
Department of English Language,
Literature, and Creative Writing
401 Sunset Avenue
Windsor, Ontario N9B 3P4
519/253-3000, ext. 2288

University of Wisconsin–Madison
Program in Creative Writing
Department of English
6195 Helen C. White Hall
600 North Park Street
Madison, WI 53706
608/263-3374

University of Wisconsin–Milwaukee
Creative Writing Program
Department of English
P.O. Box 413
Milwaukee, WI 53201
414/229-6991

University of Wyoming
MFA in Creative Writing
Department of English
P.O. Box 3353
Laramie, WY 82071
307/766-2867

Vermont College of Fine Arts
MFA in Writing
36 College Street
Montpelier, VT 05602
802/828-8840

Virginia Commonwealth University
MFA in Creative Writing
Department of English
P.O. Box 842005
Richmond, VA 23284-2005
804/828-1331

Virginia Tech
MFA in Creative Writing
Department of English
323 Shanks Hall
Blacksburg, VA 24061-0112
540/231-6501

Washington University in St. Louis
The Writing Program
Campus Box 1122
One Brookings Drive
St. Louis, MO 63130-4899
314/935-5190

Wesleyan Writers Conference
Wesleyan University
294 High Street, Room 207
Middletown, CT 06459
860/685-3604

Wesleyan Writing Programs
Wesleyan University
294 High Street, Room 207
Middletown, CT 06459
860/685-3604

West Virginia University
Creative Writing Program
Department of English
P.O. Box 6269
Morgantown, WV 26506-6269
304/293-3107

Western Illinois University
Department of English and Journalism
1 University Circle
Macomb, IL 61455-1390
309/298-1103

Western Michigan University
MFA and Ph.D. Programs in
Creative Writing
Department of English
Kalamazoo, MI 49008
269/387-2584

Wichita State University
MFA in Creative Writing
Department of English
1845 Fairmount
Wichita, KS 67260-0014
316/978-3456

Wisconsin Institute for
Creative Writing
University of Wisconsin–Madison
Department of English
Helen C. White Hall
600 North Park Street
Madison, WI 53706
608/263-3374